The
Broken
&
Beautiful
Life
Of
Camry
Hughes

a novel

by Emmie Brown

Table of Contents

Chapter 1

Cursing the fact that I'm wearing stilettos today, I sprint up the subway stairs. My eyes dart to the large clock in the nearby public square: 7:57am. "No, no, no, no, no!"

I dash down the sidewalk, tossing apologies to all the people I bump into and rush past. Before me, the TMC tower looms large in the Manhattan skyline, and I push myself faster toward its heavy glass doors, silently whispering prayers that I'll make it to work on time. Unseasonably warm weather for October has sweat trickling down my back, my bangs sticking to my forehead.

Luck must be on my side because the 'walk' signal lights up as I approach the crosswalk and I dash into the street, skirting around the car that tries to run the light. Waving my arm behind me at the obscenities shouted my way, I race into the building. The lobby, with its sky-high ceilings and walls of glass is bright in the morning sunlight. The atmosphere's usual buzzing of comings and goings is almost electric as waves of employees rush to get to work on time. Across the lobby, past security, the elevators open and shut quickly with each passing round of people. The TMC Tower is home to many businesses, but the top floors are dedicated to the Travers-Moreau Corporation, the massive Parisian-based marketing firm for which I work, and the namesake of this glittering structure.

One elevator, stuffed to the max with people, prepares to close its doors and begin its ascent. I bolt forward, flash my badge over the security buzzer and wave frantically at Michael, the security guard who knows me - and my frequently rushed mornings. With one last burst of speed, I squeeze my hips into the cramped space between workers and the elevator doors slide closed as the last lock of my hair whisks in behind me.

My eyes flit to my watch and see the time: 7:59am. "Whew! Just made it!" Rolling my shoulders, the tension relaxes from my body. I awkwardly shift around in my tiny bit of elevator real estate, attempting to tidy up my disheveled appearance.

The elevator lurches to life, and I lose my balance. A small squeak escapes my lips as I rocket forward, comically ping-ponging around those closest to me until I find my footing.

After receiving an annoyed look or two, I murmur apologetically to the people on either side. "Oh, sorry. I'm sorry."

From behind me comes a cough, suspiciously reminiscent of a stifled laugh. I stiffen and stand up taller, nonchalantly trying to turn my head and see who it might have come from but all I can make out behind me is a cell phone held in a large hand and a hint of red hair over it, hiding the person's face from view.

I turn back around and once I am assured that the people nearest to me are focused solely on themselves, I attempt to covertly straighten out my blouse and skirt, rearranging some wayward strands of hair that have escaped from my bun. Shifting my head, disheveled bangs fall in my face, and I hastily

3

puff my breath upwards in a few failed attempts to blow them to the side.

This time, the soft chuckle that hits my ears is not disguised and I twist fully around to see that the cell phone and red hair from earlier belong to none other than the executive director of our New York branch, Laurence Mercier.

Caught off guard at his presence, I stammer out a greeting. "G-good morning, Mr. Mercier."

"Good morning, Miss Hughes." He replies politely, his light French accent reinforcing an aristocratic air, though he does little to disguise the humor in his voice. "In a hurry today?"

Alarmed at the fact that he knows my name and that I've made a fool of myself, I blurt out the first thing that enters my mind. "I can't be that late; you're here too."

All too briefly his eyes widen slightly... a split second later and that same gentle smile is on his face again.

"Indeed." He says nothing more.

Realizing my faux pas, my hand snaps up to cover my mouth in horror. "Oh god, I'm so sorry!"

The corners of his pale, almost silver eyes wrinkle as his smile deepens. "Do not worry, Miss Hughes. As you said yourself, I have no room to speak to tardiness today, do I?" He shrugs his shoulders as if to admit his guilt with little remorse.

I stand there gaping, causing Mr. Mercier to incline his head questioningly at me. Finally I snap out of it, turning back around to face forwards, silently cursing myself.

Before I can spend any more time considering our awkward interaction, the elevator dings and arrives on my floor. I shuffle out with a few other employees and make to leave for my desk. I'm three steps out when I hear his calm voice over my shoulder.

"I look forward to our working together. Good day to you, Miss Hughes."

Baffled by his words, I turn around and my gaze rests upon the man, now glancing at his phone again as if he had never spoken. He looks up, our eyes meet, and the doors slide closed.

I stare blankly at the elevator doors for a moment, shaking my head to clear my mind of the bizarre encounter. I turn on my heel in order to move to my desk, but as I take my first step I run smackdab into someone.

"Ow..." Rubbing my forehead, I look up and there, gently holding onto my shoulders is my coworker and friend Alex. We share a cubicle and he is standing there with an exasperated look on his face.

"Seriously, Camry, you are the clumsiest person I know." He rolls his eyes and gives my shoulders a firm squeeze before stepping aside. "Late again?"

"I'll have you know I was in the elevator at 7:59 today!" I shoot him my best dirty look but I know he sees right through my feigned aggravation. Our proximity at work has made Alex irritatingly aware of my various personality quirks and lack of punctuality. I grab his arm and drag him off toward our desks.

"Wait just one second, Camry! I was going to get a coffee."

"Fine. Bring me one too!" I let go of his sleeve and stalk off towards our cubicle. I can hear his laughter echoing in the halls the whole walk over.

I slump into my chair and open my bag. Peering at Alex's desk I can see that he has already been doing work for quite some time. I guiltily turn on my computer and boot it up.

By the time my email is open, Alex is back with the coffee.

"Oh, you're a lifesaver." I accept the cup graciously, inhaling the rich aroma.

Alex eyes me intensely, taking in my appearance. A teasing smirk appears on his lips.
"Late night last night?"

"No, not that it's any of your business. The gallery I volunteer at closed an exhibition last night and I was there until nearly two in the morning. I barely had time to wake up, walk Shakespeare, and get showered this morning before I had to catch my train." The last half of my sentence is suffocated in a yawn.

He snorts out a laugh. "That drooling, wide mouth look is a good one on you. Who was the artist?"

"Absolutely brilliant, that's who; a young woman whose art told the story of her upbringing in East Harlem. Her cubist paintings are in vivid colors, and she played lively music in the gallery to emphasize the frenetic energy of her childhood. It was a captivating exhibit, and the music alone seemed to pull passersby in off the street."

Alex looks at me with a kind smile. "There you go again."

"What?" I lift my eyebrows in question.

"You always get this incredible look on your face when you talk about art. I'm almost jealous of how much it means to you."

"I guess..." Deciding that a change of topic is the best way to avoid this uncomfortable line of conversation, I bring up his sister. "How's Jess doing?"

Predictably, Alex takes the bait, his eyes lighting up as he talks about his favorite person in the whole world.

"Good. Really good. She's got the lead in the next play and her professors all say she's got a ton of talent. She called me on my way in today to tell me, all bright eyes and giggles." He looks at me, smirking. "She's definitely a morning person, unlike someone I know."

I shoot Alex a playful glare over the rim of my coffee cup before taking a glorious first sip. "Mmm, that's good." I lift my cup again, drinking deeply, unable to keep a sound of pleasure from escaping my lips.

Alex's smirk widens and a mischievous glint I know too well settles into his eyes. "God, Camry, watch those noises. We're in the office!"

Shock and the urge to laugh force coffee both out of my mouth and up my nose. I cough violently, snorting and wheezing and grab a napkin off of Alex's desk, slapping it over my mouth. I can feel the hot beverage soaking my clothes, a light stinging sensation on my skin from the heat. When I have swallowed what's left of my sip of coffee and settled the fire in my nostrils, I hiss at him. "What the hell?!"

Looking down, I can't help the frustrated groan that escapes from my lips. My cup lies empty on the floor and as I suspected, my light pink blouse is soaked in coffee, baring to the world my red satin bra.

"Um..." Alex looks away awkwardly. "Go to the bathroom. I'll cover for you if anyone comes by."

"You'd better!" I snap.

I snatch a folder off my desk, clutch it to my chest for cover, and bolt to the hallway for the bathroom.

When I make it inside I quickly strip off my shirt and soak it in cold water, hoping to prevent the stain from setting. I'm grateful that bathrooms are often deserted at the start of the day. I'm not sure I want to be caught shirtless at work, in the restroom or not. Once

I have rubbed it clear as much as I think I can manage, I hold it under the hand dryer for a few seconds.

But before I can make any progress, my phone vibrates on the counter with an incoming text from Alex. *Jones is looking for you. Says it's urgent. I'm so sorry!*

I groan audibly, then rub the fabric together a few more times under the hand dryer and quickly toss my shirt on again. I check my appearance in the mirror; it's still totally soaked through! Gritting my teeth in frustration, I try and formulate a plan. If I keep my folder in front of me while I'm walking I should be okay... and if I'm at my cubicle turned to my computer no one will see anything, right?

I sigh for what feels like the millionth time this morning and clutch the folder tightly to my chest. I give my shoulders a little shake and exit the restroom.

I barely make it ten feet before I hear my manager's booming voice. "Camry! There you are!"

Stopping dead in my tracks, I plaster on my most enthusiastic smile. "Mr. Jones! How can I help you?"

"Yes, yes, you are just the girl I need right now, my dear. I have some amazing news to share with you." My department manager, Jameson Jones, is every bit the high powered executive playboy from the movies. He flashes his megawatt smile and puts his arm around my shoulders while steering me into his office. I hunch awkwardly trying to keep my precious folder barrier in place.

Once through the door, my legs nearly give out from shock. Sitting in one of the chairs in Jones' office, flipping casually through pages in a file is none other than Mr. Mercier himself. His long legs are crossed elegantly, and his lean frame and impeccable posture give an air of regality. He looks up, making eye contact, and my heart stops. Of all the people to see me in this state...

He smiles at me as he stands, greeting me formally as if meeting me for the first time today. "Good morning, Miss Hughes. My name is Laurence Mercier, and I am the Executive Director here in New York. I trust you had a relaxing weekend?"

I blink a few times but quickly find myself. "Yes, I did, thank you."

"Wonderful, wonderful." He holds out his hand and I accept it, giving his warm hand a firm shake. I have no idea what is going on but I'll be damned if I act foolish in front of him now! Once today was more than enough.

Clapping his hands together, Jones breaks the awkward silence. "Let's get right down to it! Please, have a seat." Jones motions us to the chairs and we all sit down, with me still clutching my folder to my chest. Jones looks at me and he begins to speak.

"A few weeks ago, Mr. Mercier asked for my assistance in an important matter. It is once again time to plan for the Legacy of Health gala: The Metropolitan Hospital system's big annual fundraiser in February. We here at Travers-Moreau Co. are, as always, the main host and sponsor. This year, the gala wants to focus on art as a means for healing, recognizing the positive effects art can have upon the human body as part of a holistic approach to medicine. Ideally, the gala tries to keep its focus local, so this year the emphasis will be placed on artists living in greater New York and exhibit their work. Mr. Mercier is, as always, in charge of this project."

Mr. Mercier nods his head in deference. "I have presided over this event for the past few years but in this case, I find I am facing a multitude of problems. To begin with, my assistant is the one who has handled the day-to-day management of this event each year in the past. I was recently informed that she has decided not to return from her maternity leave so now that position is vacant. I would step in and oversee things myself until the gala is over, but I am occupied at the moment with an international deal that was supposed to have been completed. We have had delays and the date has been moved and this change in timing is inconvenient." His professional tone remains but I can pick up the slightest hint of weariness in his voice as he speaks.

"In addition, we received word only this morning that the venue we had booked has cancelled its contract with us, which puts us at a serious disadvantage." He presses a finger to his temple, closing his eyes for the briefest of seconds. "That will take a mountain of red-tape and legal action that I simply don't have the time for, and we will of course need to select a new venue." He crosses his legs, leaning back slightly.

"Lastly, if I may embarrass myself, Miss Hughes, this year's theme is far beyond my comfort zone. I know very little about modern art that is trending these days. I much prefer the classics."

Jones quickly picks up the conversation. "Mr. Mercier asked me to find him a suitable partner to help him plan and organize the event. He sought one with impeccable organization skills, communication excellence, and art expertise, but also most specifically, someone who could be instrumental in choosing which artists to present. And that, Camry, is why you are here. I believe you know why I have picked you?"

The blood drains out of my face. The only thing that makes any sense is that Jones has seen the small and quite unremarkable blog I keep on art. I can't imagine how he has access to it, or how he knows that I write it.

My utter astonishment betrays me and my tone is anything but professional. "Sir, surely you don't think I am the right choice for this. This project is far beyond the scope of anything I have done so far at Travers-Moreau, and I am in no way an expert on up and coming local artists!"

"Nonsense! I've done my research and you wouldn't doubt your boss's intelligence, now would you?" Jones winks at me. "Not only was your work on the advertising for the New York Mets anniversary campaign excellent, but you show unique understanding on the art scene today."

Mr. Mercier leans forward in his chair. "If I may, Mr. Jones showed me your blog. I was rather impressed with your knowledge and interpretation of the artists you showcased, and your commentary was both insightful yet playful in its style. That ability to walk between entertainment and information is precisely what I'm looking for."

"Excellent. That settles it then!" Jones claps his hands together. "Camry, you'll be relocating to an office on Mercier's floor for the next six months. I must admit that I'll miss your presence here but I'm positive that you'll produce nothing but a job very well done."

The two men stand and I just sit there, dumbfounded. "But, how did you... where did.... I just don't understand!" I finally get a few words out. "How do you even know about my blog? It's not even written under my name!"

Jones chuckles. "Ah, well, let's just say that when a certain member of my team heard I was searching for someone to take this position, this person clued me in to that particular hobby of yours." The hint in his voice leaves no doubt. Alex. There are only two people in this entire company who know, and he's the only one who could have shown Jones about my blog and spoken about my passion for art.

"Now, Miss Hughes, if there is nothing left to discuss...?" Jones' voice takes on a slightly more cutting edge than his normal casual banter, and he shoots me a significant look. I realize I am the only one still seated while the two men are standing.

"Oh!" I exclaim as I realize my faux pas, and I jump up out of my chair, still so shocked that I forget about my current clothing situation... and my folder falls to the floor.

Both men freeze for a second before I catch myself. I can't stop the startled sound that escapes my lips as I fall to my knees and begin to urgently grab at the folder's spilled contents. Papers are everywhere and my cheeks are on fire.

Suddenly a hand comes into view. I raise my head to see Mr. Mercier crouched before me, holding out a stack of papers with a forced smile. I slowly reach out and collect the pages, stuffing them back into the folder before standing and once again clutching it to my chest. Mr. Mercier stands as well and speaks calmly, "Miss Hughes, please come to my office when your lunch break is finished. Take the morning to pack up your desk and finalize any open projects. We will get you situated this afternoon."

He nods once at me and once at Jones before striding past me and exiting the room.

"Oh my god..." I breathe out slowly. A low whistle from Jones and I look up at him with mortification plain on my face. "I am so, SO sorry!"

He suddenly bursts out laughing, loudly filling the office with his amusement. "You are one hell of a woman, Camry. Go get to work."

I spin as fast as I can and rush back to my desk, flying into my chair and putting my head down on my desk.

"Oh my god. Oh my god. Oh my GOD!"

Alex's bewildered expression carries a hint of concern. "Cam, what happened?"

My head snaps up and I muster the worst glare I can for him. "YOU!"

His face morphs to shock and confusion. "Me? What did I do?"

"I've been assigned to work with Mr. Mercier on the hospital gala and do you know why? Because *you* ran your mouth at Jones about my blog! And then I was pushed into that meeting like *this* -" I rip the folder away from my chest and sit up straight, daring him to stare - "and I totally made a fool of myself! This is ALL your fault!"

At least Alex has the grace to give me a sheepishly guilty look, rubbing the back of his neck. "Look, Camry, you're the right person for the job. You love art and I couldn't have stayed quiet if I wanted to. There's nobody better at this than you and I wasn't going to let you get passed over for a dream assignment just because nobody else knew about that."

His eyes are kind while he smiles at me and I find I can't stay mad at my friend. "Ugh. Fine. You know what this means though, don't you? They're moving me for six months."

His eyes widen. "What?"

"Yes, they're sending me to work with Mr. Mercier! I have to pack up my desk this morning and I'm transferring after lunch."

"No way! I object! Never mind you helping, this is terrible!"

I begin to laugh. Alex chuckles too, and reaches under his desk, pulling out a t-shirt. "Here, put this on until your blouse dries. I always keep a spare in my gym bag."

I gratefully tug the much-too-large shirt over my head and tie it off in a knot on the bottom. Alex eyes me with a few brief nods before breaking out into a grin. "You look ridiculous."

"Yes, well, it's better than the alternative! And may I remind you that this is all your fault?" I snap back playfully and he ruffles my hair.

"Hey!"

He laughs again before turning back to his computer. I do the same.

Finally able to focus on my emails, I read over what is there, send off a few to people I think will need to know about my departmental change, and then send an email to my oldest friend Hayden. She was hired into the print media department here at TMC straight out of college, and after I left my last position at a small marketing firm Uptown, she helped me to find work here. She and Alex have been friends since they started around the same time. My fingers quickly punch out an email, nerves of excitement and anxiety vibrating up and down my spine. "Lunch today? So much to tell you!"

A few minutes later and I have a reply. "Yes! Our usual?"

I reply positively and then begin to pull things out of my desk. Jones walks over with a box and raises his eyebrows at my new attire, smirking as he hands it to me and stifling laughter returning to his office. I hand files to Alex that we have been working on, gathering my personal belongings into the box, and slowly my desk returns to its original state. Five months of work may not seem like a long time, but you can really accumulate a lot of stuff in that span!

Alex and I casually go over the status of each file, tabbing them with sticky notes to mark our current progress, and before we know it, it's lunchtime. Spinning on my chair, I stretch widely to the ceiling. "I'm going to lunch with Hayden. Want to come?"

"Nah, I brought mine."

"Suit yourself." I take a deep breath and stand up.

"Meet me after, though. I'll walk you up to your new domain."

I smile fondly, then subtly peek inside the oversized t-shirt. My blouse seems mostly dry and the translucence has faded to an appropriate level, so I pull Alex's t-shirt off and hand it back to him.

"Here you go. Thank you so much."

"You bet!" He takes the shirt and smells it. "Mmm...
eau de Camry! Maybe I'll keep this in my desk when
I'm missing you for the next few months."

"Ew, Alex. Don't be gross."

His face softens, typical teasing expression falling
away. "Not trying to be. I really am going to miss you.
But you'll do great."

He smiles again and grabs his lunch before winking
and walking off towards the elevator.

****

Hayden and I meet for lunch at our favorite cafe. It's
quiet, small, and just one block further than most
TMC employees like to venture during lunch so we
find we can gossip as much as we want with little
chance of being overheard.

She listens to me with rapt attention, her overly
expressive face a rapidly shifting range of emotions.
When I finish my tale, she settles on a cheery smile.

"Geez! What a day, and it's only lunchtime!"

I offer a self-deprecating smile, still somewhat caught
up in the events of this morning.

She leans back in her seat and sighs. "That Alex. He
certainly does know how to work things, doesn't he?
Still, I think it's great that you're being offered this

position! Maybe it will morph into something long term, with opportunities for advancement."

"Maybe..." I answer noncommittally. "They didn't say anything about that, though. To me it's clear this is a temporary gig to bail Mr. Mercier out of a jam." I shrug, and she nods in understanding.

"You're still feeling stuck?"

A slight grimace graces my lips. "Yes, I am. The job you got me here is great. I won't lie. I like the work and it's a lot better than the tiny marketing firm I was working at Uptown. But I still can't shake the feeling that I'm supposed to be doing something else. I'm not exactly young anymore, and women still face age discrimination in the workplace. What if I end up just wasting away in a cubicle, staring at a computer screen writing copy for the rest of my life?"

"Would that be so bad?" Hayden frowns, her small frame straightening up. "Your work doesn't always have to be what drives you. Your art blog is brilliant - enough that it landed you this opportunity! That could be where you spend time with your passion. You might never make it as an art dealer or a professional critic, but you can do a job you're good at, and enjoy art on the side. Don't put so much pressure on yourself all the time! You've still got a long career ahead of you."

She grins, satisfied with her speech and when I roll my eyes and nod in defeat, her smile shifts, eyes gleaming with mischief. "Anyway, I can't believe Mr. Jones and Mr. Mercier saw your bra!" She cackles loudly, drawing attention from other guests.

"Don't remind me! It was mortifying! I was afraid I would get fired right there on the spot for being so unprofessional."

Hayden smirks. "I'm sure Mr. Jones didn't mind... he's always been a lady killer at the office and you're one of the few who has escaped him." She wiggles her fingers teasingly at me.

"And gladly, too!" I huff at her comment.

"I bet Mr. Mercier freaked out on the inside but kept a pretty composed face. He always comes across as such a quiet, demure gentleman." She trails off, tapping her finger against her lips, then smirks. "Or maybe he liked it. Maybe that genteel front is just hiding his secretly perverted nature."

My fork slips from my fingers, clattering noisily on my plate. "Hayden! I have to work with him! How am I supposed to look at him now?"

She flashes a cheeky grin. "You'll tell me if you ever find out, right?"

I roll my eyes and slump backwardly, leaning against the booth. "Hayden, he's my BOSS. He's YOUR boss. He runs everything here! You can't talk about him like that!"

She laughs. "Ah, sure I can! Besides, he's young, rich, powerful, and hot as hell. What more could you want?"

"Plenty. That is not exactly my list of 'ideal boyfriend' characteristics."

I give her a look of pure frustration and she laughs out loud, a mirthful smile on her lips. "Regardless, I am so happy for you and this new job! Just, do your best, okay? Nobody really knows what he's like, so you're walking into the unknown."

I grimace. "Yes, I am well aware."

We sit quietly together for a moment before she speaks up again. "Well, it's right up your alley; Alex was right about that, and I think you'll really enjoy it. It's super exciting! I think you'll do great!"

"Thanks, Hayden. I hope so." I twist my fingers closely together, and Hayden reaches over and gives them a squeeze.

"You'll be fine. Don't be nervous. You could run circles around anyone when it comes to this. Just show them what you've got and you'll be set."

I smile at her, and the rest of our lunch passes amicably. We sip our drinks and eat, chattering away about all sorts of things until lunchtime is over.

When we get up to leave, Hayden gives me a big hug. She reaches up and throws her arms around my neck, embracing me fiercely. "I'm just so excited! Call me tonight and tell me all about your first afternoon!"

I laugh as I return her hug. "Sure thing, Hays."

We may be different in more ways than we are similar, but thanks to her reassurance and authenticity, my nerves settle. We exit the cafe together, walking back with arms linked and giggling to each other in excitement.

Chapter 2

Thirty minutes later, I suck in a deep breath and let it out slowly. The elevator begins to move upwards but this time my knees are locked so tightly that I don't stumble. Alex stands next to me, carrying my box of belongings under one arm. I can feel his eyes on me. I look up at him with a nervous expression and he smiles sweetly.

"Don't worry. You'll do great."

I try to return his smile but it comes out as more of a grimace. He chuckles and reaches over with one finger, poking my face. He gently smooths his touch across the wrinkle on my forehead, then squeezes my shoulder. I close my eyes, focusing on the rhythmic in-and-out of my breathing.

The elevator ride is far too short and before I know it, we've come to a stop and the doors open. A receptionist is sitting at a desk, with large gleaming silver letters behind her.

"TRAVERS - MOREAU CO. - EXECUTIVE SUITES".

She looks up and smiles politely. "May I help you?"

My voice shakes a bit as I introduce myself. "I'm Camry Hughes. I'm here to see Mr. Mercier."

She looks at me as though expecting me but then turns her eyes to Alex. "And you are?"

He grins, shifts my box to under his other arm, and extends his open hand. "I'm Alex. It's very nice to make your acquaintance.... Ashley." He checks out the nameplate on her desk and calls her by name. I know that smile of his and I bite my lip to keep from laughing. Unfazed by Alex's attempt at flirting, she asks why he's here, ignoring his outstretched hand.

"Ah, I'm here as moral support for my dear friend here."

"Very well." When the receptionist's head is down dialing into her phone, he winks at me. "Mr. Mercier? Miss Hughes and a friend are here."

Alex grins. The receptionist hangs up and smiles unenthusiastically at us, ever the picture of professionalism.

"Mr. Mercier will be out shortly. May I offer either of you a coffee or water?"

"What fancy service!" Alex elbows me playfully.

"No, thank you," I say, ignoring him completely.

"Of course." She returns her eyes to her work and after a brief moment, Alex turns to me.

"You look terrible." He peers into my eyes with a mixture of concern and teasing admonition.

At that instant, a door opens at the end of the corridor and Mr. Mercier strides out, his gentle air from this morning replaced by the aura of a man in charge. Confidence and intelligence seem to melt off of him in waves. His long legs carry him down the hallway and he wears a stiff smile as he approaches Alex and me.

"Ah, Miss Hughes and... Mr. Epworth. Thank you for assisting Miss Hughes with her belongings."

Mr. Mercier abruptly takes the box from Alex's hands, ignoring the look of mild irritation that crosses Alex's features.

"Now, Miss Hughes. If you would please follow me?"

I frown a bit at this dismissive encounter, but Mr. Mercier is already off at a brisk pace moving down the hallway from where he had emerged and I look over my shoulder at Alex with an apologetic glance, mouthing 'thank you', as I quickly attempt to catch up.

Mr. Mercier stops at a small door, a name plate shining brightly upon it. I gasp to see my name already engraved upon it. "Um, when did you know I'd be working here?"

He smiles and pushes open the door. "Last week is when I approved your transfer. Now, welcome to your office."

I step across the threshold and intake my breath sharply in surprise and delight. I move in what feels like slow motion as I take in the room. A large desk sits off to the left with three sleek chairs positioned in front of it. Glossy white built-ins fill the wall behind the desk. The other half of the posh yet comfortable space contains a rose colored tufted sofa, a glass coffee table and two beige armchairs creating a cozy meeting space. Feminine yet contemporary decor is set around and a large mirrored vase of fresh peonies sits on the coffee table in the center of the office. The room has a calming atmosphere and is far more sophisticated than I could have imagined. As I look around I notice that there is a large area vacant of any furnishings in one corner of the massive room. This entire space seems far too luxurious for a simple employee like me.

Mr. Mercier, apparently satisfied with my reaction, enters the room and sets my box down upon my desk. His eyebrows draw together, and he reaches into his pocket, pulling out his phone. I watch him carefully, awaiting his direction, unsure of what to do. He frowns a bit, types something out, and reads intently. His lips purse slightly and he releases a soft sigh before tapping more out onto his phone screen. His ginger bangs shift and fall loosely across his brow, and his lean frame seems so elegant and poised in this moment I can't help but stare. He's a gorgeous picture to behold, commanding of presence and yet with a decidedly gentle air.

Finally, he seems to catch on to me and he looks up, eyes wide with embarrassment as if he has been caught with his hand in the cookie jar.

"Forgive me, Miss Hughes. I seem to have forgotten myself." His graceful fingers brush his hair away from his eyes and he slips his phone into his pocket.

"No, it's nothing! I'm sure you're a very busy man." I quickly avert my eyes, knowing full well I was staring.

He smiles noncommittally and casts his gaze around the room.

"I hope it is to your liking."

"Oh my goodness, yes!" I exclaim. A genuine smile spreads on my face. "It's so big though! Surely this space could be put to better use? I feel like it is wasted on me."

Mr. Mercier gestures around the room with his hands. "No, this is perfect. You will need to keep lots of resources here, entertain clients, and this open space will be perfect for artists who need to meet with you. If they have anything to bring, display, or store here in advance of the gala, this will work quite suitably."

I know that Mr. Mercier must be at the top of his game in order to be so young and in such a high position in a company like Travers-Moreau, yet even so I am struck by his attention to detail. His foresight makes me feel small and inadequate, and for the hundredth time today, I question my place here. "You really did think of everything, didn't you?" I whisper, half to myself.

"What was that?" Mr. Mercier looks at me questioningly.

"Oh, sorry, I was just thinking out loud for a moment. It was nothing."

I trail off and return my gaze to the room. Finally I see what I had failed to notice before. Large windows stretch across the wall opposite and the panorama before me is absolutely stunning.

"Oh my god! This is gorgeous!"

I can't help my lapse in professionalism as I race over to the window and peer out. "I hadn't even considered the view from up here. This is simply amazing!"

"I'm very glad you like it. Now, Miss Hughes, I hate to be so rude, but if you'll excuse me, I must step away for a meeting. I will return later this afternoon. Please take this time to get acquainted with your surroundings and unpack your belongings. If you need anything at all, please feel free to speak with Miss Davis at reception."

"Thank you, Mr. Mercier. You've been very helpful."

He turns to leave but stops at the last minute. "Oh, Miss Hughes, do you enjoy coffee?"

Perplexed by his question, I tilt my head as I answer. Then I blush wildly, recalling this morning's meeting. "I don't make a habit of spilling it on my clothes or anything!"

"Oh, is that what happened this morning? I had wondered." He laughs softly. "But aside from unfortunate accidents, you do enjoy it?"

"Very much so."

"Excellent. I thought so. Ah, someone will be by in..." he pauses and looks at his watch, "... thirty minutes or so to set up a few things in your office. I hope you are comfortable."

And with that he closes my door and disappears down the hall.

I let out a deep breath and relax my shoulders. I feel like I'm in a dream. This is all so new to me and I don't have any idea what to expect.

As I stare out at the city before me, I feel like I'm standing on a precipice - of what, I don't know. I close my eyes for a brief second. Alex and Hayden are right - this IS a good opportunity, and one I will enjoy. Whether it's about making connections in the art community or expanding my professional skills, I want to prove myself; to be able to do this well. I can't predict the future, but I know I'm going to give this my all.

I turn and walk over to my desk. I run my fingers along the wood, tracing the smooth lines of the grain. The stark contrast of my cubicle with its gray particleboard and carpet tile flooring to this luxurious space overwhelm me for a minute.

I take a few more calming breaths and then set my shoulders. "Alright, time to unpack!"

I move to the box that Mr. Mercier had put on my desk and begin to sort through my belongings. A picture frame with a photograph of my brother and me, my favorite scented candle, a bud vase with a vivid pink daisy, and a small antique china dish that my grandmother gave me. I lay them around my desk, and the shelves behind me, then begin to take out a few other items; pens, notepads, hand lotion, and other office supplies. I place the pens in a beautiful glass cylinder on my desk, and then sort the rest of the items into my drawers. For the next few minutes I wander around the unfamiliar surroundings. I plop into the arm chairs, breathe in the sweet scent of the peonies, open a few empty cupboard doors, and do a few twirls in the open space, laughing to myself, before finally I slump into the couch. Not much to do yet. I stare up at the ceiling and imagine hosting local artists here. I visualize all sorts of fabulous art in this space, and serving tea and coffee to museum curators. My imagination is running wild.

A smart knock sounds loudly from my office door, bringing me out of my reverie. Sitting up straight, I realize that I'm so unsure of the etiquette in this situation! Do I call to them to enter? Do I open the door myself? Oh, I am so unprepared for this!

The knock comes again - I shake my head and rush over, opening it to see two men dressed in maintenance uniforms with a large cart full of boxes, and another man behind them, dressed in a short sleeved button-up shirt and tie.

"Hello, Miss Hughes. We are here to set up your office."

"Oh, of course! Please come in." I step aside and let them in.

The two maintenance workers get right to work. They begin to unpack boxes and unload items. The first items out of boxes are a massive computer monitor and CPU, which they set up. When the computer is assembled, the third man sits at my desk and begins to work on the computer.

I peer cautiously over his shoulder and steal a glance at him. "Are you from IT?"

"Oh, yeah. Hi. I'm Sam."

"Hello," I reply.

Sam, however, seems to be focused intently on the computer and doesn't respond or even give an indication that he has heard me.

I turn and look at the other men. They are unloading boxes at lightning speed. One pulls boxes of files out and sorts them into my desk drawers while adding other books to the shelves behind me.

The second is working on setting up some sort of large contraption in the corner of the counter along my built-ins. It's only when I get closer that I notice that it is an elaborate espresso machine that looks like it could brew any sort of coffee beverage I could imagine in a fancy cafe.

I watch curiously and after a few minutes the man stands up. "Here you go, Miss. This is the manual. I'd read it!"

He laughs and I take it from him. Eyes wide, I see that this thing is over 50 pages long! I flip through it seeing the names of all sorts of espresso beverages and other terminology I am completely unaware of.

"Um, excuse me! How do I make a simple cup of coffee?"

"Ah! Here you go. Just pour the beans in here, and fill this with water, and press this button. Make sure you have a cup here, of course, and if you want to make enough to entertain, you can use this part over here." He gestures to each piece and part as he talks, walking me through the design, but he goes so quickly my head is swimming and I'm unable to follow along precisely.

"You have a mini fridge here," he says, opening the cabinet below to reveal a small refrigerator filled with cream, milk, and water. "Your syrups and coffee will be up here." He opens a cabinet and puts four bottles of different coffee syrups and quite a few canisters of coffee and espresso beans. They are neatly labeled with various blends, aromas, and regions of beans. "Mr. Mercier sent over these, but if you want any other kinds of coffee or need your fridge restocked, call Miss Davis at the reception desk and she'll have it sent over."

He points to the other end of the lower cabinets. "There's another mini fridge over there - it's got your standard soda, water bottles, and other cold beverages for yourself and clients."

I follow his gaze and ask a question. "Um, is there space in there for my lunch?"

He laughs and looks at me with a mix of understanding and pity. "You really are quite green, aren't you? You won't be needing to bring your lunch."

"I... won't?"

He simply laughs again. "Miss, you're working on the executive floor now. Miss Davis will be by each morning to take your lunch order."

He grabs a clipboard and peruses the details. "Alright then. I just have a few more things for you. Do you have any special requests for your office?"

"What do you mean?"

"Plants, artwork, knick-knacks, furniture... is there anything else you'd like in your office?"

"Oh! Can I really say?"

"That's what I'm here for." His casual way of speaking to me is helping me feel more relaxed and I find a confidence to voice my opinion.

"Um, I really love this office, but could I have something to make it feel a little less... stuffy? Maybe something alive? Like, a plant or two. And maybe a rug?"

"Yeah, sure." He taps his pen against his lips, gazing at the office. "How about a fig tree here in this corner and a peace lily over there?" He points around the room, already aware of what he wants to bring. "And I can bring a rug up; I know just the thing. White faux fur; soft yet a bit daring."

"That sounds lovely!"

He makes a few quick scribbles on his notepad. "Anything else?"

"Um, well.... No."

He eyes me, clearly not believing my words. "What else?"

"If I had a painting I really wanted here, but I already have it, could I please bring it and have someone hang it for me?"

"Is that all? Absolutely. Do you need help getting it here?"

"Oh, no not at all! I can bring it myself. Thank you!"

He nods and packs away his clipboard. "Not a problem. Alright, I think we are done. Sam, you finished yet?"

"Just about," Sam replies, the look of slightly bored concentration never leaving his face. "Write your employee ID on this for me, please." Sam hands me a notepad and pen and I quickly scribble it down. He takes it and turns back to the screen, entering information.

The kind maintenance man turns to me again. "Alright, we'll get things cleaned up here then." The men begin to break down boxes, collect packaging, and move things out into the hall.

Sam stands up, stretching a bit. "You're all set, and your personal profile is logged in. You've got considerably more security now, but you won't notice it, so don't worry about it. Any questions, dial my extension." He hands me a business card and I thank him. He leaves the office without any more to say.

Gently smiling at the other two men, I clasp my hands together. "I really do appreciate all your help, gentlemen."

"Just doing our job. Have a great day." They exit the room, and with the sound of the door closing, I am alone again.

What to do first? After the day I have had, making a cup of coffee is most tempting but I need to look over all the documents and files that were just given to me. I'm sure educating myself is the right way to start out.

I decide to open the file drawers and begin my investigation. As I sift through the materials given to me, I see information on past galas, files on TMCs philanthropic endeavors, and even the winners of various art competitions in New York over the past five years.

"Mr. Mercier, you really are incredible, aren't you?" I mutter to myself, in awe over his attention to detail and the preparation he has given me. There is a wealth of information here and I'm amazed.

Once I take mental note of the detailed information in front of me, I lean back in my chair and relax a moment, allowing my mind to wander to the person for whom I am now working. My new boss is a bit of a mystery. I begin to believe that the reputation he carries is at least partially misguided. Guarded and formal, he feels somewhat distant most of the time. But then there are those little moments when he issues a witty retort or speaks with a smirk on his face and I have to wonder... what he is like when he's not at work? I picture Mr. Mercier golfing or sipping tea from fine china; two activities I am sure fit his polished demeanor, and I snort loudly to myself. Abandoning this train of thought, I refocus on the information in front of me.

I decide to pull out the files on recent local art award winners - starting here, I can get the best idea of the current direction of art in the city. After I get the files on my desk, I wander over to the coffee maker.

I frown at it, still overwhelmed by the mechanism, until I find the parts I am looking for. I have no idea which beans to choose, but I grab the darkest ones I can find and open the canister, inhaling deeply.

"Oh, that is amazing!" I carefully pour some beans into the reservoir and find a pitcher of cold water in the mini fridge below. I pour in the water, place one of the elegant coffee cups under the drip, and I press the button.

The machine beeps and flashes a little light, but nothing happens.

I frown and hit the button again. More beeping, more flashing... no coffee.

This is not the time to deal with this, so I march out of the office and into the corridor, approaching the desk of the receptionist.

"Excuse me, Miss Davis," I say softly. She looks up at me expectantly. "I'm sorry to bother you, but may I please have a cup of coffee?"

She silently stands and walks across the waiting area to the coffee machine, and in just a few minutes she hands me a steaming cup. "Here you are. Will you be needing anything else?"

"Nope! This is perfect, thank you." I gratefully accept it and gingerly walk back down to my office. I blink again, seeing my name on the door, and something in my stomach flip flops at the sight of it.

Setting my coffee on the corner of my desk, I sit and begin to look over the paperwork in front of me. I decide to start with the Chelsea International Art Competition and before I know it I am totally engrossed in the information and images before me.

I am so thoroughly caught up in my work that I don't realize the change of the sun's position in the sky, nor that my nearly empty coffee has now gone cold. It takes some time before I hear a soft voice calling my name.

"Miss Hughes?" Mr. Mercier stands in front of my desk, peering down at me.

"Oh! I'm so sorry!" I leap to my feet and almost knock my cup over, but Mr. Mercier quickly reaches out and picks it up before it can fall.

"Not to worry. I'll assume you were thoroughly engrossed in your work."

"Yes, I suppose so." I carefully reach forward to take my coffee back from him. "Um, thank you for that."

He looks at the Styrofoam cup, and then at the espresso machine with the empty mug, waiting to be filled. "Could you not understand how to use it?"

"I tried, but I didn't want to take the time away from my work to learn it so I just went and asked Miss Davis for some. I hope that was okay."

"It's fine. But it is here, so let's have you learn how to use it. After, you can share with me your impressions on the project and what you have looked over so far."

He moves over in front of the machine and I follow, narrowing my eyes in concentration.

"What would you like to drink?"

His proximity does not go unnoticed, and I detect a soft fragrance, woodsy and warm, floating gently past me every time he moves. The aroma of his cologne and the way his arms brush against mine have my stomach doing flips, so I step back and look at him, trying to calm myself.

"Sorry, can you repeat the question?"

He asks a second time.

"Just a cup of plain old black coffee, I'm afraid. I never really grew into a taste of those fancy drinks."

His gentle chuckle lands softly near my ear. "I believe that most people never grow into plain black coffee, but I take it you're not 'most people' are you?"

"Does that make me weird?" I feel a bit called out and ask the odd question that pops into my mind.

"Not at all." He gets to work, slowly explaining all the steps to me, gesturing and patiently walking me through it. "Now, you give it a try. Learn best by doing, *oui*?"

I nod, then face the machine again. I mimic the steps he showed me and my mind drifts. As the machine warms beneath my touch, the bitter and comforting aroma of coffee overwhelms me, calling forth memories of my mother. She always smelled of coffee and lavender soap. Perhaps my penchant for drinking coffee is due to my mother, her well-loved purple mug never far from her side and always full of the steaming dark liquid. Subconsciously, I begin to hum a little as I watch the coffee drip slowly.

Mr. Mercier's voice takes me from my memories. "What are you singing?"

"I'm sorry! I didn't realize I was singing out loud. It's a song called 'I see the moon'. My mother used to sing this as a lullaby. I was just reminded of her because she always smelled like coffee and lavender."

"No need to apologize. You have a beautiful singing voice, and the memory with your mother sounds lovely. Did she sing to you often?"

I frown in thought, conjuring a mental image of her; she's laughing in my vision. "She did sing quite a bit. Music was a great love of hers and she loved to dance more than anything in the world. But what I remember the most are her cheerful expressions. It's hard not to picture her without a smile on her face. She had the best sense of humor, and everyone loved her."

He smiles warmly. "She sounds absolutely wonderful."

"Yeah, she was..." I trail off lost in my thoughts.

"Was?" he looks at me cautiously.

"She died a few months ago." I look down at the ground, rubbing circles on the floor with the tip of my shoe.

He clears his throat. "My apologies. I am sorry for your loss."

"No, it's nothing for you to be sorry for." I force a small smile, not meeting his eyes, until a gentle hand reaches out and places a steaming hot cup between my fingers. Our fingers brush together and the warmth of the mug and the touch of his hand calms me with gentle assurance.

"I hope this is to your liking."

"Thank you." I inhale the aroma and take a tentative sip. "That's really good! It might even be the best cup I've ever had. I bet my mother would have loved this too."

A smile lights up Mr. Mercier's face. "I'm glad. Well, then. Let's talk business, shall we?"

Chapter 3

Mr. Mercier's fingers sift through the files laying on my desk. "What were you working on?"

I show him the files I was sorting through. "I was starting with the past award winners. Thank you, by the way, for all of this information! It's so helpful and thorough and I'm really sensing some trends and direction in this material. It appears that the prevalent themes in the past years have focused largely on issues of social justice. I've found art reflecting immigration, feminism, racism, the LGBTQ community, and more. There's also been winners who drew art inspiration from hardships related to divisive and politically charged arguments and environments." I look up at him, feeling my passion come through my words. "Art's always been a vehicle for social commentary and change, obviously, but I'm really amazed at the formal recognition in here, where the focus of the WHY behind the piece is being taken into account far more than in the past, like there would be no art without the experience. It seems like there is a more in-depth review based on the artist and the experiences they want to convey, not just the art itself. It's a fascinating movement and one I think we will need to really be attentive to in our selections this year."

Mr. Mercier seems to let out a deep breath. "Yes, indeed. This is a fine reflection and understanding."

He relaxes his shoulders and making eye contact, speaks directly to me. "What do you think about this year's theme, using art as a vehicle for healing and growth?"

I chew my lips, my brow settling into a frown of deep thought. "I think it's too broad, and we should narrow it down. From personal experience, my mother did much better when listening to music she loved, or traveling, and I think art is similar. It's healing, very much so. I bet I could find a study somewhere about patients doing better in facilities with artwork than in facilities without." I pause and drum my fingers on my desk. "That being said, not just any art will do. Art that tells a story along these lines might well be best, so that we can include perspectives both from medical patients and artists, and the best is a combination of the two. We also should be sure to include both physical and mental illnesses. I guess the next step is to come up with a list of what we really are looking for in the artists we will present, and then we can get the word out to the local art community. If we have a specific ask for artists that fit our parameters, we might get some response."

I know who would be perfect for this, but would he be available tomorrow? Would he even meet with me? It's been so long and I've been avoiding him. "I know of someone we might be able to start with. I'll have to make a phone call or two and it will be difficult but I wonder..."

I take a seat on the sofa, tapping my pen against my lower lip, trying to decide whether I should call him and ask to meet. But I suppose no one gets anywhere by holding back, and I decide to find out. I turn to Mr. Mercier. "Is your morning busy tomorrow?"

Mr. Mercier looks momentarily confused. "Miss Hughes, I'm afraid I am always busy, but what did you have in mind?"

"There is an artist I think we should talk to. I'm honestly not even sure he'll be willing to see us, but he's the kind of person who doesn't plan ahead or wait around. I want to see him tomorrow. This could be a personal project for him if he agrees and he could be the right starting point for us, so the sooner we can meet with him the better. I'd like to call and ask if we could visit him in the morning."

Mr. Mercier frowns a bit in thought. "I'm not sure that would be possible with my schedule. Can we look at a website or online gallery of his work? If I give the go ahead, I'm sure you could speak to him yourself and convince him to be a part of the project."
He sends me a look that makes me think I won't convince him otherwise. But something stirs within me and my answer is out before I can stop myself.

"No."

"No?" He looks momentarily caught off guard, and I can see his eyes flash. *Shit,* I think. *Way to piss off the boss on the first day.*

Mr. Mercier silently walks over and sits down next to me. "Explain it to me." He sits straight, as if at attention. I don't feel any anger or hostility from him. Instead I feel like he is willing to listen... he seems like a logical man. I know I'm right, so I can't back down now, but I need to be able to argue my case succinctly and effectively. If I don't, I imagine he won't appreciate his time being wasted.

I take a steadying breath and look up at meet his gaze. I begin to speak, pacing myself and choosing my words with precision.

"Forgive me for my blunt reply, but I stand by what I said. First of all, as a self-proclaimed aficionado of art from some of the more historically prolific eras, you surely will understand that viewing art through a screen or second hand vehicle is in many ways, ineffective. Art is meant to be lived, breathed, and witnessed in person. Anyone can see a beautiful painting in a book or on a computer screen, and be moved, but viewed in person it comes to life, inhabiting the very space in which you yourself exist.

"It is in my very humble opinion that art should never be accessed via shortcuts unless absolutely necessary. I realize that there are exceptions, of course, and there are circumstances where viewing art in person is impossible, so an image of it must suffice. But can one truly pass judgment on a piece of art without viewing it in person? You could say that the Mona Lisa appears to be a well-executed but otherwise unremarkable painting of a woman when viewed in a textbook, but your assessment would be overridden upon seeing it in person. The beauty, the detail, the way the light changes... it's all magical. If not in person, you will never truly appreciate the piece enough to formulate a genuine criticism."

Mr. Mercier watches me carefully. He doesn't respond in any way to my impassioned plea, but speaks softly. "And secondly?"

"I'm sorry?" I'm caught off guard by his comment.

"You said, 'first of all,' so I assume you have a subsequent argument?"

"Oh! Well, yes. I..." I trail off and I furrow my brow. The thing I wish to say next is a rather dangerous subject to broach with a higher-up as I don't want to seem too critical or superior.

"Go on, Miss Hughes." His voice now carries the slightest hint of warning. I realize my delay is making him impatient. I'm more nervous than ever, but I've come this far. I need to speak my mind.

"You see, sir, you are the person in charge of this event, are you not? In that case, I believe that your personal touch on the organization of this gala is necessary. If I were to be the one to approach the artists directly, be their liaison and direct communicator, while you, the chief organizer, are not a part of the negotiations and conversations, my message will appear thin and shallow. We know that art itself is something that speaks many things to many people, but we need to be careful not to come across as using the artists for our own personal gain. Art is, in many ways, symbiotic - the creator receives healing, or catharsis, or renewal via their work. The community that has access to the art then receives something in turn - that could be any number of things; sometimes it is a challenge or discomfort. Often though, it is beauty, inspiration, or direction. The community then supports the artists with appreciation, recognition, support, and income, and with those assets, the cycle can begin again. If I, some relative nobody who happens to have a passion for art, act as the bridge between groups, it may come across as Travers-Moreau using me to do the talking, but with little to no interest in truly forming these relationships and listening to what the artists are trying to speak through their work. It would look as if I was a convenient buffer, here for the project, so that you could get what you needed from them, making the event successful while keeping the artists at a distance. It would be like we were using them for our own benefit and no more. And that will foster nothing but negative and hurtful feelings within the art community as a whole. If you took the time to be a part of this as well, it might go a long way to show the artists we approach that we value them as partners, as collaborators, and not some vehicle for achieving our own means."

I finish my piece and hold my breath. I silently whisper, please, oh please, let him understand!

Mr. Mercier stares at me. He doesn't move, other than slowly twisting his cufflinks around with his agile fingers. He sits in silence, and I start to wonder if I have signed my own pink-slip.

When he speaks, it is one word. "Alright."

I blink. "Alright?"

"Yes. Alright. You've convinced me."

I almost choke on my own disbelief. "I... have?"

He nods slightly. "Make the call. I will rearrange my schedule if it works out."

"Thank you!" I'm sure I must look like an idiot, but I cannot wipe the ridiculous smile off of my face. I'm so thoroughly excited.

After an awkward pause, he points to the phone on my desk. "Go on, then, call your artist friend."

"Right now?"

"Right now," he replies calmly.

"Yes, sir!" I leap up and run over to my desk. I lift the receiver and then realize there is no dial tone. "Um... how do I...?"

He shoots me an exasperated look. "You need to select a line. The buttons on the right."

"Thanks." I punch a line and then dial the number.

I hold my breath as it rings once, twice, three times. Finally, the line connects. "Hello?"

"Marcus? It's Camry."

"Camry?" Too much time passes and I begin to get nervous. I hear him take in a deep breath, before he speaks again. "It's been a while, *mijita*."

"I'm sorry it's taken me so long to get in touch. I've been... dealing with things."

"Uh huh." His reply is understanding, though he doesn't add more. I grip the phone tighter and continue.

"I really am sorry."

"Don't worry about it. It's good to hear from you. Are you doing okay?"

"I guess I am. I just got promoted, actually. Today."

"Oh yeah? Good for you." His voice much lighter now; the familiar tone makes me smile.

"So is that why you called? To tell me about your promotion?" Feeling somewhat guilty, I know he won't like the reason I'm calling, especially not when I haven't called for so long.

"If I'm being honest, I'm calling for this new job. I'm wondering if you could meet with me and my supervisor tomorrow morning at your studio. I want to show him your current work and ask you a question."

There's no response. "Marcus?" I timidly say his name.

A deep sigh meets my ear through the handset. "Why?"

"I think what you're doing right now has the right message, and I believe it could help a lot of people."

"A lot of people? You know this project isn't public. This is meant for ME - not for anyone else."

"I know. I do. But please, just let us come talk to you. You have every right to say no once you hear me out."

"I don't know, Camry." He sounds tired, but I think I hear a hint of resignation in his voice.

"Please? Think of it as a favor for an old friend."

A long pause, and then, consent. "Fine. 9 a.m. Don't be late."

"Thank you! I'll see you tomorrow. You won't regret it!" I enthusiastically flash a thumbs-up at Mr. Mercier to let him know we have permission.

"Yeah, yeah. We'll see. Tomorrow, *querida*." And with that, he hangs up.

I gently lay down the phone. "That was hard. But we're in. Tomorrow at nine in the morning. His studio is in Jackson Heights so it will take us some time to get there." I bite my lip, trying to figure out the travel time.

"Very well. I will pick you up tomorrow morning."

"That's very kind of you, but I don't know if I should come into work tomorrow or simply meet you there. The travel time might make it prohibitive."

He stares down at me for a few seconds. "I meant I would pick you up at your home."

"What?" I blink stupidly, unsure.

"Do you not live in Brooklyn? I believe I read a Brooklyn address when I reviewed your employee file. If so, it would be far faster for me to come and pick you up tomorrow morning than for you to travel here before heading back to Queens."

"Oh, uh... yes." I swallow awkwardly.

"Very well. Please be ready by eight o'clock. I will contact you when I am at your building. Now, if you'll excuse me, I need to go reschedule quite a few prior engagements. Please continue to do the appropriate research today, Miss Hughes. I will see you tomorrow morning."

"Of course! Thank you!" I follow him to the door. "Goodbye."

"Goodbye." He nods curtly, and then walks down the hall.

****

A yawn stretches my mouth wide and I quickly follow it with a large gulp of coffee. I stare at my French press sitting on my kitchen counter and give it a significant look, remembering yesterday's morning. My dog Shakespeare pushes his nose between my fingers, begging for a good scratch and my hand mindlessly rubs his pointy ears while trying to calm my quickly growing nerves. I haven't seen Marcus since my mother's funeral and I feel awful about it, but for a long time just thinking about him was too painful.

I'm musing over the events of the day when my phone chimes with an incoming text. "Downstairs."

I quickly type out a reply and grab my bag and a sweater. "Alright, buddy. I have to go. Be a good boy for me, will you?" I lean to nuzzle his face and give his head a few quick pats, before he runs over and plops down on his bed, gnawing on his favorite toy. I pour my coffee into a travel mug and pick up the folder of papers I need. With one final look around my apartment, I make my way downstairs.

I've seen fancy cars before, but when I exit the door I see a sleek and stunning sedan parked at the curb and I subconsciously let out a low whistle. The passenger window slides down and Mr. Mercier calls to me from the driver's seat.

"Good morning, Miss Hughes."

I walk over and open the passenger door. I slide into the smooth seat and pull the door shut.

"Thank you for coming to get me."

"It's not a problem. Where is the address to which we are headed?"

He presses a button which opens a hidden screen. I tell him where we are going and his elegant fingers deftly input the address. Before long, we are slowly moving along through the busy streets of the morning's rush hour traffic.

I peer curiously at his face. His eyes are focused forward, but there is something more relaxed and comfortable about him while he drives. A far cry from the almost robotic way in which he carries himself at the office, here his posture is more languid, less exact. He leans back, long legs extended, casually resting one arm on the car door.

Feeling that I've spent a few seconds too long observing my boss, I take a sip of my coffee. I look for a cup holder, but then I notice two cups from an incredibly popular local cafe.

"Oh, um, those coffees..."

Mr. Mercier clears his throat awkwardly. "Yes, I brought us some drinks for the morning."

"That's so nice of you! I'm really sorry, I didn't think. I just brought along my own."

"It's quite alright. I didn't tell you I was bringing anything. It was more of a moment of weakness on my part. I was passing by the cafe and simply had to have some."

"Oh, okay."

"That, and..." he trails off.

"What?"

He laughs, a sound that seems wistful and somewhat awkward. "Once I had purchased them, I realized that coffee seems to be a running thread to you and I, no? It seems much of our time together as of yet has revolved around it." He grins at me teasingly, his ginger bangs shifting across his forehead.

I am torn between laughing and becoming defensive. A nervous chuckle escapes my lips and I grin. "I will have you know that I am not usually that much of a klutz! I mean, well, kind of. It was just a very overwhelming day for me and I had no idea how to use that machine. And yesterday morning Alex made me spill coffee all over myself. I was just heading back from the restroom after washing my shirt when Jones dragged me into his office. I had no idea you would be waiting for me."

"Alexander Epworth, yes?"

"Yeah. He's been my partner since I started at TMC five months ago."

"You two seem to get along quite well."

"He's a great friend, absolutely. And we work well together."

"He's not your boyfriend?" Mr. Mercier glances at me out of the corner of his eye.

"God no! I could never, and I mean NEVER, date Alex."

The laughter out of Mr. Mercier is hearty and sincere. "That was quite the outburst."

"Well, it's not the first time someone thought that, but if you've ever hung out with Alex you'll know that he's got a doctorate in flirting and he uses it indiscriminately on any living person he finds even remotely attractive."

"Understood. Now I'll know for the future that he isn't serious about me, but just having some fun."

His face is dead serious but there's a hint of humor in his voice.

"Mr. Mercier, did you just... make a joke?"

He looks slightly abashed for a moment. "And what if I did? What sort of man do you imagine me to be?"

"Well... if I'm looking simply at the last twenty four hours, you always seem focused and driven at work. And while I know for a fact that you are kind and, um, tolerant of my consistently awkward behavior, I never quite got the impression that you were much of a jokester."

He lets out a breath at my assessment of him, rubbing his chin as he thinks. "I admit that I am often focused or in 'work' mode at the office, yes. I suppose it is natural for you to find me a serious person."

I take another sip of my coffee and ask a question to steer the conversation in another direction. "So what kind of coffee did you get?"

"I purchased one dark roast and one light. I wasn't sure which one you preferred."

"Why don't we give one to Marcus when we arrive at his studio? You can drink the other, and I'll drink from my mug."

"Alright, that sounds fine. What coffee are you drinking?"

"I love a good dark roast in my French press."

"Ah, a woman with simple yet refined tastes."

I'm somewhat stunned. Did Mr. Mercier compliment me? I have always seen him as the refined one, so I'm blushing to hear the comparison.

The conversation ends there and we drive for a while in silence. There is no music playing, and the only sounds are the noises from the city outside our windows and the quiet, robotic directions from the GPS. Stealing a glance at Mr. Mercier, I see he seems totally at peace and comfortable, while my own anxiety is making this feel awkward. To break the silence, I ask, "Um, did you find my apartment okay?"

"I did, yes. The building looks quite charming from the street. Do you like living there?"

"I do. It gets a little loud sometimes from the bar underneath, but I really love my apartment and my neighbor downstairs is great. No complaints."

He smiles a bit but says nothing more.

"What about you?" I venture.

"What about me?"

I look over at him. "Do you like living in your home?"

I think I see the smallest flash of emotion on his face, and I quickly apologize for the question. He waves me off, his usual schooled expression in place once again.

"I suppose I do. Though, I am not often there. I don't get much time to relax and enjoy myself at home."

"Oh. Too busy?"

He looks on, unimpassioned. "In truth, yes."

Eventually the car slows and we pull up in front of Marcus's loft. We find a place to park around the corner. Mr. Mercier gets out of the car and picks up the two coffees, cradling them in one palm. I push open the door and begin to try to stand up, but the awkward angle of being so low to the ground makes it more difficult than I had imagined. My left hand gripping the door frame, my right holding my precious travel mug, I attempt to hoist myself out. Mr. Mercier stands before me with a bemused look on his face. "Need a hand?"

"Sure, thanks." He grips my hand tightly, helping me stand.

"Are you ready?" His hand slips from mine and I smile awkwardly, the lingering warmth of his fingers replaced by a cool breeze.

"Yep! It's this way." I begin to walk off towards the studio.

When we arrive at the door, I reach out and ring the buzzer. A few moments later the intercom clicks. "Marcus! It's me!"

"Come on up." The line cuts off and the door beeps as the lock disengages.

I pull open the door to reveal the small entryway. I step forward and push the button on the elevator and we wait while its mechanical thrum fills the air. "After you, sir." I gesture to Mr. Mercier as the doors open and he steps inside.

"Thank you, but you don't need to call me sir." He gives me a pointed look, leaning past me to push the button for the upper floor.

I frown, tilting my head to look at him. "It feels weird though. We're here to meet a client and you are my boss. I don't think I can just casually refer to you."

He nods. "If you must."

The doors open and I smile happily as we step out into the studio. The nostalgia hits me immediately, feeling like a brick landing on my chest, and my smile vanishes. The incredibly high ceilings, massive windows and comfortable furnishings remind me of all the days I spent here in my youth, curled up on the couch reading a book while my brother Ciaran raced cars around the slick floors, my mother and Marcus laughing or singing together while they worked. Everywhere I look I see glimpses of her, and my chest constricts painfully and it becomes hard to breathe.

I press a hand to my chest and try to calm myself, and then a gruff voice snaps me back to the present. "*Mijita*, you look well." Marcus is there waiting, arms outstretched. A monstrosity of a man, his frame looms at somewhere near seven feet, and the red Henley he wears emphasizes his burly frame. Ever the gentle giant, a wide smile slowly stretches across his face.

Suddenly the oppressive feeling leaves me, replaced by one of peace and being at home. I fly towards him, burying my face into his chest. He envelops me into a large bear hug, lifting me off the ground and slapping my back. I return his embrace tightly, inhaling his familiar, comforting scent. I step back and look at him fondly. "I've missed you, Marcus." His grin is infectious, mimicking my joy at seeing him again. "Oh! Ciaran tells me that you got new gear! Let me see!"

He sends me a glare that I know is feigned malice, but he reaches down to his ankles and pulls up his pant legs a few inches, revealing some of the titanium and carbon fiber appendages. The brick-red and sleek silver coloring catches the light and I can tell the technology is superb. "Whoa! These are awesome!"

He drops his pant legs and straightens up, rapping his knuckles on my skull. "You haven't changed, I see."

I stick my tongue out at him but then remember that we have company. "Oh!" I whirl around and see Mr. Mercier standing there politely. "Marcus, this is my supervisor that I spoke to you about. This is Mr. Laurence Mercier, the director of the New York branch of my company."

"It's a pleasure." Mr. Mercier reaches across to shake Marcus' hand. "I apologize; I am afraid I don't know your surname. How would you like me to refer to you?"

Marcus eyes him somewhat suspiciously before returning the handshake. "Just Marcus is fine, but my last name is Carrera."

"Thank you then, Marcus." Mr. Mercier offers him a coffee. "Would you care for a coffee? I brought two from Cloud Coffee."

Marcus reaches out and takes the nearest cup. "Thanks." He slogs down a large gulp and then looks expectantly at us. "So, what's with the visit?"

"Well..." I look between the two men. "Do you mind if we go sit for a bit and talk?"

Marcus bobs his head and leads us over to a few dark velvet couches and we sit. I look at Mr. Mercier and he nods slightly to me.

"Mr. Mercier, before we begin... Marcus was a dear friend of my mother's. I spent many days here in my youth. I've known Marcus my whole life! She was actually his mentor as he grew up and they stayed close all through his adolescence and into his adulthood. To me, he's somewhere between a brother, uncle, dad, and friend?" I laugh, looking at Marcus. "Anyway, Marcus spent a lot of time in the US Army. I didn't see him much until he came home in 2003."

I pause, taking a breath and looking at Marcus. "May I?"

He shrugs. "You went this far."

"Marcus came home after losing both his lower legs in Afghanistan. Since then, he's dedicated his life to art. The current project he's working on is not one he's planned to share with the public. But I think it fits exactly with what we are looking for."

Mr. Mercier has been sitting, patiently listening to my words with little reaction. Eventually he looks to Marcus. "Thank you for your service. Truly."

Marcus inclines his head to him. "Yeah, thanks." He tips his coffee in Mr. Mercier's direction, then looks at me. "So what's this project, then, that makes you think you are going to use my work?"

His gruff tone is there for a reason. I know he loves me, and I know he trusts me, but I also know that this is very personal... a long time coming to finally grapple with the loss of his legs, fifteen years after the fact.

I explain to him the details of our project, of art as healing, as a part of medicine, as part of the human experience of pain, growth, and renewal. He listens intently, only the smallest facial movements any indication of his thoughts on the subject.

When I finish, no one says anything and the silence descends around us like a heavy fog. I'm nervous. I know what I'm asking him. Finally he runs his hands up and down his thighs, sighing loudly.

"Come on."

He stands up and we follow as he walks over to the part of his home that he uses as his studio. He pushes back the large curtain and what I see is so beautiful that it takes my breath away.

Chapter 4

The forms in front of me are superb. Copper wire sculptures of multiple people stand life-size in form and realistic in shape. It is quite simple to recognize the jumbled groupings of wire as humans, from the molding and crafting into shapes easy to see. The wires held together give the impression of life - of sinew and bone, active and yet passive at the same time. But what really grabs my attention is that inside each, near where the heart would be, is a glass orb of some sort, vividly colored in variations of gold. The orb catches and scatters droplets of light around the room. I walk slowly through the statues, in awe of their shape, their form.

Then I see it. Each statue is missing something: an arm here, a leg there, part of the torso missing from a third. Each statue is posed as if in motion, from the simple act of reaching for something to a fully running stance.

"Remarkable." I hear the single word fall softly from Mr. Mercier's lips as he stands staring at the collection.

"I agree. Marcus, this is simply amazing!" I look at him, and see a myriad of emotions written on his face. Embarrassment, irritation, grief, and pride. I walk over to him and clutch his arm. "They're beautiful. It's like I can feel them."

Mr. Mercier turns to look at Marcus, all business. "What will it take for me to convince you?"

Marcus stares straight at Mr. Mercier, his lips pursing. "I'm honestly not sure if you can."

My fingers tighten around Marcus' arm. "You know that I wouldn't be here if I didn't think this was right. I knew what you were working on, I just didn't know... gosh, Marcus, I can't even express it. Don't you see? It's stunning but not only that, it speaks. It speaks so loudly. It is just here screaming at me that what's missing doesn't matter because you're still whole; that parts don't make a person, but the soul. I feel so many things looking at this, and I've never experienced anything like what you have." I take a few deep breaths. "Marcus, please. Don't you think this will help other people, too?"

Marcus runs his fingers through his hair, blowing out air. "Can I tell you tomorrow, Camry?"

I grin. "Of course. I just, I want you to know, I really love it."

He smiles at me, with all the warmth and love I have come to know from him. *"Gracias, mijita."* The corners of his eyes wrinkle in affection. "You know, you should call me more often. I'm wounded that you rang only for this and not for some company or some Muna tea, okay?"

I sigh, looking at him. "I know. I'm sorry. Forgive me? I promise I'll come by soon." I laugh a bit and poke his arm. "Although, if you agree to work with us, you'll see a lot of me over the next few months!"

He groans in exaggerated style, sliding downwards before straightening up again. Then he laughs jovially and we hug again.

"I really have missed you." I step up on my tiptoes and plant a kiss on his cheek.

"Alright, alright. Let me tell you tomorrow."

"Okay!"

Mr. Mercier is still standing, gazing at the forms. He suddenly turns and approaches Marcus and me. "Marcus, truly, I am impressed. Miss Hughes had not given any descriptions about what we would be looking at today, nor what your art was about. In fact," he laughs and smiles wryly at us, "she did not speak to me about anything at all except that she knew someone whose art she was interested in viewing. I must say, your work has blown any expectations I had out of the water and far beyond. Thank you for allowing us into this sacred space of yours. I can imagine that this work is both cathartic and difficult and I am honored to have viewed it. If you do decide to work with us, I promise that I will listen to your concerns. I will treat you as a partner, not as a pawn."

Marcus and I stand there, slightly stunned, at this speech.

Mr. Mercier clears his throat awkwardly, perhaps becoming self-aware of his impassioned plea. "Miss Hughes, we should be getting to the office now. Thank you again, Marcus. It was a pleasure."

He extends a hand and Marcus reaches to him. Mr. Mercier is tall, but even he needs to look up to meet the eyes of the artist. Marcus smiles and squeezes his hand. "Take care of my girl, yes? Her head's not on quite straight all the time, but she's got a good heart."

I groan loudly, slinking out of Marcus' arm. "I'm not a child! I'm twenty eight years old and can take care of myself!"

The two men laugh at my outburst as they follow me to the elevator.

"We'll talk tomorrow, okay? I'm holding you to that!" I pull Marcus into another hug. "Thank you," I whisper into his ear.

His embrace is genuine and I'm grateful for our visit, brief and official though it has been.

Mr. Mercier and I board the elevator and I wave as the doors slide closed.

I can barely suppress the grin on my face, and as soon as we begin our descent and I'm sure he can't hear us anymore, I burst out. "He'll do it."

Mr. Mercier looks at me, surprise written on his face. "How can you be so sure of that?"

"I know him, and I know the look on his face. He never lets his guard down around people he doesn't know and after a while there he was just being himself. He thinks he's a tough guy but inside he's some big softy and I know he'll call tomorrow with good news."

"Let's hope you are right."

The rest of the elevator ride is quiet and I reflect on the time spent with Marcus and his sculptures. Conjuring the images of the sculptures in my mind, I close my eyes. I remember the look on his face and can see all those emotions in the work itself. I can imagine how crafting them must have been so raw and emotional. I sigh, opening my eyes slowly. The doors open and I walk to the car in silence, still deep in thought.

When we arrive at the car, Mr. Mercier opens the car door for me. "Oh, thank you," I mumble, slipping inside.

He gently closes the door and walks around. When he gets in and starts the car, he looks over at me. "Are you alright? I don't think I've yet seen you this quiet."

"Huh?" I look over at him, momentarily embarrassed by my disconnection. "Oh, yeah. I was thinking about what he must have been going through making those. He's never really dealt with the loss of his legs. I mean, when he got back from Afghanistan, we went to visit him and he just seemed empty, like he wasn't really here anymore. But he got better, he started in a wheelchair, moved to some basic prosthetics, and over the years he's advanced to walking upright. I think now that he's been walking tall for a while, he's feeling more like himself and he is able to really face this head on. He turned to art to express himself but he never really let himself heal the one thing that he needed to heal. He had never properly grieved the loss of his limbs nor the change in his life, nor his loss of purpose in having his career in the military taken away. Outwardly, he handled it fine, but I don't think he ever got to the point where he really loved himself again until now. All this time I think he has been processing this. I knew he was doing sculptures of people who had lost limbs but... I wasn't expecting this."

I take a deep breath. "That and..."

Mr. Mercier's eyes find me. They are kind, kinder than I've ever seen, and he dips his head, encouraging me to go on. "And?"

"And I haven't seen him or been to his place since my mother's funeral. He makes me think of her and it's only been a few months. It hurt too much. It hurt today."

I take a deep breath. "It was hard being there today without seeing her. It felt wrong. I've been avoiding him because it always felt like my mother and he went hand in hand. It doesn't seem right to have him without her."

Mr. Mercier reaches into his pocket and pulls out a handkerchief. He hands it to me and I take it, unsure, before realizing that there are tears trickling down my cheeks. "Oh." I quietly dab at my tears, erasing the warm tracks from my face. When I'm finished dabbing at my eyes, I clutch it tightly. "Thank you. I'll bring it back tomorrow. I'll give it a wash tonight."

Mr. Mercier slides the car out of the parking space, glancing at me out of the corner of his eye. "That's entirely unnecessary."

"No, I insist. I'm sorry I was crying. I shouldn't be getting this emotional at work."

"It's alright. Besides, we aren't at work at this moment, are we?" He gives me a sympathetic look. I send him a grateful smile, tucking the handkerchief into my bag. The car glides along the streets of the city as we return to work, the rest of the drive spent in a comfortable silence.

****

When we step into my office I toss my bag and sweater down on the couch and flop down next to them.

"What's next?"

Mr. Mercier stands in the doorway for a few seconds before crossing the room to sit in one of the chairs across from me. "I suppose we need to make some decisions about the next steps. I am hopeful that your initial hunch will pan out, but let's keep moving forward. Do you have any thoughts on the direction or schedule you want to run with?"

I look at him thoughtfully, and sit up straighter. "I have a few ideas on the artistic side of things but before we talk about those, can you tell me a little about the gala in general? I apologize but I didn't get to the files on past galas yesterday. What kind of people attend? What is the vibe? Things like that. I want to know what sort of direction we are heading in. I think it won't be going too far out on a limb to guess that it's pretty formal."

"It is indeed a black tie affair, yes. Individual tickets begin at $1,000 and sponsorships go up to $50,000."

My eyes snap open. "What?!"

"Believe me, that is rather typical when it comes to high society fundraisers. We are here to fund something important and in this case, it requires catering to a specific population. We need the income to cover the expenses and support the hospital with a substantial donation, but at the same time, we also need to be able to provide guests with the sort of evening and entertainment that warrants the price tag. The gala is a complicated affair."

"I guess I knew those things, but hadn't really thought much about that. You're very right." I purse my lips in thought, furrowing my brow. "I don't know anything about high society. I grew up pretty poor, to be honest. Single mother who was a free spirit in New York City. I can't even imagine what it must be like to live in that world. I'm fairly certain my most expensive dress cost like thirty dollars."

Mr. Mercier looks pensive but his face relaxes quickly. "Do not worry about that part. I will help you in that regard. We are working on this together, are we not? You are here in part to advise me on the artists and exhibitions for the gala, so I can clearly answer any questions and help make decisions on the other topics."

"Thank you, Mr. Mercier." I let out a breath of relief.

"That being said, if we really are to be acting as partners in planning this event, please feel free to be less formal with me. You are welcome to call me Laurence."

I blanch at his words, taken aback and unsure of what to do. I stammer out a few awkward syllables. "I don't know about that! I couldn't possibly call you L-Laurence."

"While it is true that I prefer to keep a certain professional distance from most of the employees here, in this case, we are working closely together. I would like you to consider me an equal as we work on this project, and I don't want you holding back your thoughts or opinions for the sake of respect or formality. I promise to no longer call you Miss Hughes only if you will allow it, but I prefer that you speak to me now as Laurence." He looks at me with imploring eyes, and I shift in my seat.

"Well, okay then, Laurence. You can call me Camry, as well."

"All right. Now, what other questions can I answer for you?" He leans back and crosses his legs, one arm casually resting on the armrest of his chair, his chin propped by the other.

"How many people have come to the gala in the past few years?" I pull a notebook out of my bag and poise my pen above, ready to take notes.

Laurence rises and walks to my desk. I go to meet him and he takes out some of the files from my drawer. "That information should be in the files I had sent over. Let's take a look here." He flips through the file labels until he finds what he is looking for. Lifting a few, he lays them on the desk and sifts through the pages, gazing at facts and figures, spreadsheets and data, until he has a few pages laid out in front of me. "Here's the information on attendance, ticket sales, sponsorships and vendors for the past five years."

I lean over and pick up the pages, examining them carefully. "You had over three hundred and fifty people at last year's gala? That's at least $350,000!" I quickly sift through the pages, looking for financials. "Last year you raised over 1.1 million dollars. Oh my god."

I glance up and meet Laurence's eyes. "Are you absolutely sure you want me on this project? I have never in my life even imagined working on a project of this scale!"

Laurence nods, looking at me directly. "Do not lose your confidence now that you have seen the scale of this. I hired you, and based on your critiques yesterday and the thought of choosing Marcus to be the featured artist, I am completely committed to you being in this role. You can do this. Just work *with* me, and this will be an amazing event. I'm sure of it."

I slowly agree, a concerned smile pressing my lips together tightly. "I'll trust you only because I'm afraid I can't trust myself."

"That's all I can ask for now." He stands up straight and looks at his watch. "I have quite a few items to attend to yet today. Take some time to look at the photographs of past galas - get an idea of the theme, colors, decor, floral arrangements, lighting, etc. We will need to settle on the mood of the event before we do much more. Send me your top three proposals for that by the end of the day. I will choose one of your three as the final that we will go with. Then tomorrow, I would like you to begin to research venues and entertainment options that fit the aesthetic and mood of the theme you have chosen. Booking those quickly is imperative, and must be done before anything else. Finding a suitable venue this late in the game will be difficult, but I trust it can be done. This is New York, after all. Conduct research to find out how large of a space you will need for a full seated dinner, dancing, silent auction, and cocktail hour. Entertainment-wise we need a band, DJ with full sound system for an Emcee, and of course, all the art we need will have to have a space to be displayed. Decor, lighting, floral arrangements, caterers. This will all be settled on eventually, but first we need the theme and venue. Focus on that. It's Tuesday now. Can you have those things settled by Friday?"

I sit there dumbfounded. "Um... can I write all that down?"

He patiently recounts everything he said to me before and I take notes. As my scribbling comes to an end, he taps his fingers on the notebook. "I know that we said this is all new to you. Do not worry; I will help. Email, text, call: any questions you have I will answer. I have no intention of throwing you to the wolves. I know you don't understand this yet."

"Okay, thanks. That makes me feel better." I slowly let out a deep breath and relax my shoulders. "I'll work really hard."

He considers me for a moment before slowly nodding, and I feel a gentle warmth in his expression. "Yes, I do believe you will. Miss Davis will be here shortly to take your lunch order. I'll be back by the end of the day to go over the theme proposals."

"Alright."

He begins to walk away but before I know what I am doing, I reach out and grab his wrist as he goes. He stiffens in surprise and I drop my hand quickly. "Um!"

"Yes?" He stands expectantly, waiting for my reply.

"Thank you for guiding me. I'd be lost right now, and I really appreciate your help."

"There is no need to thank me, Miss Hughes. I am merely doing what is right, as I too would like to see the gala be successful. The reputations of both the Metro Hospital System and Travers-Moreau are in play, and we must put together an event worthy of our names."

A crushing weight settles on my heart. Why had I assumed he was there to support and help me? Of course he is only offering help to ensure I don't make a complete mockery of the company by putting together a failed event. I force a smile on my face and see him to the door.

Once he is gone, I release a deep breath and sit at my desk, pushing away my anxieties and embarrassment, ready to move forward with my day.

****

It takes two hours longer than I anticipate, but we finally settle on a theme for the event. Laurence patiently listens to my ideas, and provides constructive criticism while we finalize our work. In my mind, we work well together. He understands my descriptions and rough sketches, and I am encouraged by his flushing out of the details, making ideas and suggestions more robust and meaningful. Finally settling on "The Timeless Art of Healing", we have a vision of something classic yet modern, navy and gold with hints of silver, warm lights and faintly flickering candles, while art pieces are displayed to catch the eye of the guests, immersed in the audience for an intimate and fluid experience. I feel more confident moving forward, but as I am preparing to leave work I realize how much energy this has taken out of me already. Feeling depleted emotionally and physically, I can't help the embarrassingly wide yawn that escapes my lips. Laurence cocks an eyebrow in my direction, then looks at the clock on the wall.

"It's near 7pm. I can finish here for the day and you look positively exhausted. I'll take you home."

"Oh, I couldn't possibly take you up on that offer! Please, it's fine, really. I'm okay taking the subway."

"It's quite alright. I'm meeting someone in Park Slope later this evening as it is, so it's really no trouble."

"Oh, well, thank you then."

He nods, thinking briefly. "Give me ten minutes to gather my things and close up a few small tasks."

"Sure." I watch as he leaves, and yawn again, secretly grateful for a ride home in his comfortable car and not on the brightly lit subway train.

****

As we arrive at my apartment, I smile and thank him and begin to exit the car when suddenly the image of my painting pops into my mind. "Oh!"

His expression falters for a moment, caught off guard. "Yes?"

"Do you think you could do me a favor? It's... sort of an odd request."

"I generally do not make a habit out of agreeing to something before I've heard what I am agreeing to, but I will listen to your request."

I try to roll my eyes at him but can't help but grin. "When I moved into the new office, I was told I was allowed to bring a painting from home to hang on the wall. I didn't bring it in this morning because I was worried about it getting damaged on the train. Do you think I could put it in your car and you could help me get it to work tomorrow? I figure since you're here..." I trail off, wondering if this is indeed too bizarre of a request.

Laurence blinks a few times, clearly not expecting that to be the question. "Alright..."

"Is this weird? I don't mean for it to be weird."

He still looks slightly stricken and awkward, but he shakes his head. "I can help you with your painting."

Trying to ignore the potential awkwardness, I speak too loudly. "Great! There's a secret little parking spot here in the alley. The bar owner downstairs lets me use it when my brother comes to visit. Just pull in there and then come up. I'll go see if I can dig out the painting."

Internally, I'm mentally assessing the state in which I left my apartment this morning. I think everything is clean...

I jump from the car and fling open the door, racing up the stairs to my third floor walkup.

When I step inside, Shakespeare bounds up to greet me excitedly. His curled tail frantically waves back and forth, and he chases after me as I dash around the apartment, tossing the stray dirty laundry into my hamper and putting this morning's dishes in my sink. I check the bathroom and make sure everything looks clean and straighten out the disheveled sheets on my bed.

"Shakespeare, we have a guest coming up! Be on your best behavior, okay?" Shakespeare lets out his typical husky-chatter in confirmation, and lays down at my feet.

Then I text Laurence. "Apartment #302... Sorry no elevator. I have a dog!"

I roll my shoulders. Maybe this was a bad idea. What was I thinking, inviting him into my apartment? I am pacing the floor, Shakespeare frolicking at my feet in play, when I jump from the knock on the door. I look at my dog and in a firm voice I command him to sit still. "Sit, boy. Stay."

I open the door and step back awkwardly. "Come in!" My voice squeaks a bit and inwardly I scold myself for losing so much of my cool. No big deal, Camry... He's just here to help.

Shakespeare stays sitting on the ground but begins to whine seeing the newcomer and I quickly walk over to him and put my hand on his collar. "Laurence, this is Shakespeare. He's a little too friendly, but I hope you won't mind him."

Laurence kneels down on one knee and pats the other. "*Viens, viens!*" My dog leaps up and bounds over to him, nose flying in every direction, tail whipping around so fast I'm worried for the safety of my nearby trinkets and potted plants. Laurence rubs his hands around Shakespeare's face, laughing and giving as well as he is getting. A few moments later, he pats Shakespeare on the side and stands up, looking particularly at home and happy. It strikes me as odd how much I enjoy seeing this man here in this space, and my chest tightens a bit at the scene in front of me.

Shaking my head to clear my thoughts, I step closer and gesture around. "So, this is the place. My place." Laurence's eyes do a quick once over... My small apartment doesn't take long so he quickly turns to me.

"Where is the painting?"

I walk over to my bedroom and push open the door. "It's under my bed. I didn't have anywhere else to store it." I crouch down and pull the tightly wrapped bundle out. The size of the painting is large, almost half the size of my five foot nine inch frame. "It's a little heavy; would you mind helping me get it to the living room?"

Laurence bends over and gently picks up the painting, being careful not to put pressure on the bindings. His firm but delicate grip secured, he lifts it up and walks it over to the living room and props it up on the back of the couch, carefully making sure the canvas is protected.

Staring at the fabric and bubble wrap, he gently taps the frame. "What painting is this?"

"Have you ever heard of Ivan Rusiecki?"

"I can't say that I have." Laurence tugs on his chin in thought.

"He does mostly oils and palate knife work and I've never seen a painting of his that I haven't loved. They're all so alive."

I sigh a little in wistfulness, filled with memories and emotion. "My mother was a huge fan of his work. He was little more than an unknown at the time, but from the unusual circles she ran in, she knew of him and fell in love with his art. One day she met him at a cafe in Brighton Beach and they got to talking. She told him about how his art had helped her get through tough times, deal with how she was always sick those days... she had so much to say." I shuffle a bit. "I suppose I get my talkative-ness from her."

Laurence smiles at me kindly, letting me continue. "They became friends after that. He left New York but they wrote letters and emails. And one day, ten years ago or so, this painting arrived addressed to her. He knew she was going through a tough time and sent her this."

I frown, looking at it. "It's really the only thing of value my family had, possession-wise. My mother took us traveling whenever we could afford it, but we lived in a crappy beat up apartment and the places we stayed weren't that nice either. But she was such a happy soul that it never bothered us - we always caught her infectious spirit and life was really wonderful."

I bite my lip, trying to hold back the emotions that threaten to spill over.

"I haven't done anything with this since she died. At first I shoved it under my bed because it hurt too much to look at it. Then I couldn't figure out where to hang it. Or at least that's what I told myself. I think I'm still afraid, somewhat."

Laurence's eyes again scan the room, taking in all the artwork I have up. "I see. And now?"

I smile up at him. "Now I feel like I have something to be proud of, something to show her. I want to hang this in my office so I can see it every day and work hard for her."

"I am sorry you lost your mother. I remember the tumult of emotions I felt when my father died. But as I was glad that I had him, even if it meant a sad farewell, I am also very glad you had her, and I am happy she was who she was. It sounds like you knew you were loved."

"I was."

"Do you want me to take it down to my car now?"

"Yes, please."

He smiles at me, before saying, "Help me with the doors."

I step ahead, remembering to grab my keys off the counter, and together we make our way onto the landing, down the stairs, and out the door to the parking space in the alleyway.

Laurence slides the painting gently into the backseat. "'I'll take good care of it," he promises.

"Thank you. I'll see you tomorrow."

"Indeed. Goodnight, Camry."

"Goodnight."

I shyly smile and watch as he drives away into the night.

Chapter 5

Back in my apartment, I realize that the exchange with Laurence has keyed me up, and I'm not so tired anymore. I text Hayden, asking if she can meet for a late dinner, and she quickly responds that she's happy to.

Twenty minutes later, I'm sitting in a quiet booth in the corner of my local diner when Hayden bounces through the door, a flurry of energy and the look of someone on the hunt. "Camry!" she squeaks, flouncing into the booth opposite me. "What happened?"

The urgency in her voice makes me think that something is wrong, but the massive grin on her face tells me otherwise and I wrinkle my face at her. Not wanting to encourage her overactive imagination, I calmly ask, "What do you mean?"

"Your day today! I mean, we talked a little last night, but I want to know. What happened with Marcus? How was the rest of work? What did you do?"

"Okay, okay, calm down. Let's order first and then we'll talk." After we place our orders, I turn to her and begin to speak.

"This was the longest working day of my life. To start with, Marcus is doing well. It's been so long since I've seen him that I hadn't realized how much I missed him until I got there. It was a good visit, even though it was too short. But Hayden, oh my god. His art... It was perfection. I wish you could see it right now. It would blow you away."

Hayden smiles, beginning to dump sugar packets into her cup of coffee. "I'm glad you were able to see him again. I'm sure he missed you too."

"Yeah, that was nice. I think, well, I'm ninety-nine percent sure that he'll say yes and join the project."

"Oh really? That's great!" She glances up at me happily, and after the fifth packet of sugar is upended into her mug, I snatch her hand.

"Down, girl." I release her hand only to grab for the cup of sugar packets on the table and tuck it beside me, safely out of her reach.

Hayden huffs and sits back on the bench, pouting at me and I laugh at her obvious annoyance. We meet eyes and she purses her lips. "It just tastes gross unless you do that! Honestly I don't know how you drink it the way you do."

"Well, don't tell them this," I tilt my head in the direction of the counter, leaning closer and lowering my voice, "but the coffee here is pretty terrible." I smirk and sit back, laughing softly to myself. "Let me make you a cup again. I promise you'll like it."

Hayden wrinkles her nose and seems to take a large breath before sipping from her mug. Once she has swallowed and made a satisfied sound, she sets down the mug and looks at me intently.

"What do you think you'll do if Marcus says no?"

I think it over, knowing all too well that I'm not entirely sure. "I can't say that I know that yet. When I first got the information yesterday and began reading about the project, it's like he was all I could see. People being healed by art, you know? He's the freaking poster boy for that. Plus..." I trail off, a little uncomfortably.

"What?" Hayden asks innocently.

"I'm pretty sure I'm going to hell for saying this, and if Marcus knew I thought like this he'd never speak to me again."

Hayden props her head up on her wrist, observing me quietly.

"He's good optics." I shrug and shake my head a little before continuing. "He's a Peruvian immigrant, a decorated war vet, and an exceptional artist. He would look great standing on a stage, or describing his methods, et cetera."

Hayden breathes deeply. "Oooh I see."

"Yeah." I look down, fiddling with the handle of my coffee mug. "That's all true, and he probably knows it even if he'd have a heart attack to hear it spoken aloud. But seriously, Hayden. His work was so moving. I felt it here." I tap my chest and she nods. "I'm really proud of him."

She smiles at me, tilting her head to the side in a relaxed fashion. Suddenly a waiter appears, dropping off our plates in an unceremonious fashion. Hayden squeals and digs into her sandwich while I take a deep breath, inhaling the delicious aroma of my meal.

"I don't know how you do that." Hayden is eyeing my plate. "Breakfast for dinner is weird."

I shudder with mock offense. "What? How can you say that? It's my favorite. Nothing beats eggs, bacon, and waffles for dinner."

"Weirdo." She inhales a huge bite, sauce dripping down her chin. "So what's it like working with Mr. Mercier?"

I swallow, thinking. "Well, to be honest, he's not at all what I expected."

"What do you mean?"

"For one thing..." I start slowly, trying to figure out what I want to say. "He has a somewhat silly sense of humor." I think of his joke about Alex flirting, and a smile naturally forms on my lips.

She freezes, sandwich mid-air in front of her face. "Mr. Mercier? Silly?"

"Well, he's a bit playful. His smirk is kind of dreamy. And he makes the most ridiculous jokes out of nowhere that sort of catch you off guard."

Hayden's eyes tilt in surprise. "I never would have guessed. Whenever I see him around the building he's so straight-laced and uptight. That and..." She chews down another bite and nervously continues. "Alex kind of hates him now."

I pause, fork halfway to my mouth. "What? Why?"

Hayden shrugs and snatches a runaway crumb from her plate, popping it into her mouth with a satisfying crunch. "I guess Mr. Mercier was rude to him the other day when he took you up to your new office. Alex seems to think he was pretty dismissive of him. Called him an egotistical tight-ass."

"Ah. Well, that's not exactly false. About what he did, I mean. Not who he is." I fidget a little, remembering the exchange. "I don't know why he pushed Alex away, but maybe he was just really busy? He did kind of leave me right after he showed me around the office."

Her face morphs to an expression of surprise and before she can say anything, I cut her off. "He had a meeting, it's no big deal. He is incredibly busy, but he's never been anything but helpful and supportive. Really, I love working there so far."

Her eyes narrow skeptically, but her face eventually relaxes. "If you say so. I guess I can admit it now that you're really into it, but I was worried about you working for him at first. I thought he'd eat you alive."

"No," I counter. "He's surprisingly kind. Truly. He goes out of his way to make me comfortable. I can't argue that I was a little scared at first." Hayden's eyes sharpen and I sigh, admitting defeat. "Okay, a lot scared. I agree with you on being worried about working with him. But really, he's surprisingly fantastic as a boss. He doesn't waste time and I know he values productivity, but he takes the time to teach me what I need to know. And he's made me feel very welcome. He sent me a fancy coffee maker for my office, gave me his handkerchief when I was crying about my mother and Marcus, and he considered so many details that I was completely struck by how prepared I was - simply because of his foresight."

"Foresight?"

"He sent me all these files that I would need ahead of time, just like he knew what questions I'd be asking. And he set up my office in the perfect way to help me meet with clients and artists. Oh, and literally everything I could ever need is there."

"Huh," she mutters. "I guess when you have the kind of work ethic he's known for, you can really get things done."

I set my fork down and look at Hayden. "Hey. How old do you think Mr. Mercier is? He's obviously really young, but it's so hard to tell."

She makes a soft noise, like she is thinking. "I know what you mean. He has this almost regal aura to him and he seems so put together that it's difficult to guess. Based on his looks, he can't be that much older than us, I'd say, but he's really hard to pin down. An enigma, that one."

I laugh. "I bet he's in his mid-thirties, if I had to guess."

"I wonder what he did to get such a high-profile position at his age."

"I honestly have no idea, Hayden."

She smiles sheepishly. "Ah, you're right. I shouldn't speculate. Just tell me when you know!" She winks and I chuckle at her never ending search for the latest details.

"I'm glad everything is going well so far though. I really think you'll shine there in the new job."

"Yeah, but..." I trial off and Hayden cocks her head to the side.

"What is it?"

"Well, there's one thing that's bothering me. This whole thing is just so distant. The tickets START at a grand and go up to fifty! I can't even imagine what that looks like. How do I prepare for something that I don't understand?"

"Well, don't you think Mr. Mercier can handle that part? I mean, he's loaded, isn't he? Let him handle that scary stuff."

"I know that, but this is more like I'm doing the gala with some help from him, not the other way around. It's a little overwhelming and I'm not sure I like it."

"Did you tell him that?" Hayden's never been one for beating around the bush. She's direct and takes no prisoners in her way of doing things, a welcome contrast to my hesitance and awkward shyness.

"I tried. I just don't think I'm phrasing it right. Or I can't get my point across well. I mean, he's been very supportive, and he said that I could go to him at any time, and he said since we were going to be partners that I should call him Laurence so I felt comfortable coming to him with questions."

I know I should have seen it coming but Hayden's eyes fly open in glee and she grins widely at me. "What?! No way! You're on first name basis with him?"

"Yeah, is that weird?" I shovel some eggs into my mouth, hoping to ignore the awkward conversation.

"Weird? It's fantastic!"

"What are you even talking about?"

"Camry..." Hayden rolls my name off her tongue in an exaggerated fashion. "Are you seriously this clueless? He's your boss at work and he's trying to get chummy with you. This means something."

"I think you're crazy."

Hayden wiggles her eyebrows at me, grinning like the Cheshire cat. "Maybe."

I ignore her and take a deep breath, changing the subject. "Anyway, what's new in your life? Still doing that spin class every Wednesday?" I'm grateful to Hayden for taking it in stride, moving topics right along with me. After another half hour of chatting about everything and nothing, we pay the bill and head out into the night.

****

That night, while I'm brushing my teeth, my mind keeps wandering over to what Hayden said. I know Hayden reads way too many romance novels, and I know her over -active imagination loves to play out scenarios and circumstances. When I first started and got to know her, she had Alex and I dating in her mind before I even really knew him. I slip into bed, hyper-aware of the awkward feeling growing inside my chest. I close my eyes and the images that surface in my mind are ones of him here in my apartment, cuddling up to Shakespeare, calmly listening to me speak about my mother, helping me with the painting. My mind begins to recall everything I know about him.

Laurence is certainly handsome and he's very considerate. He treats me with professional courtesy yet he has hints of a wicked sense of humor. The rise and fall as he speaks with his accent is soothing. There is a comfortable presence to him and I have to admit, after hearing the way he spoke to Marcus and listened kindly to him, I respect him a lot more than I had realized. I groan out loud and roll over, smothering my face with my pillow. "God, do not let me fall for him!"

Somehow I fall asleep, with dreams filled with his smiling face.

****

The next morning I'm in the bathroom when a sudden thought strikes me. When was my last period? I quickly pull out my phone and figure it came more than three months ago. It's impossible for me to be pregnant. So what could make it take such a long hiatus? I stare at my reflection in the mirror and lean in to get a good look. Gently I press a finger to the dark circles around my eyes and prod at my cheeks, noticing a slightly pallid look to them. I grumble to myself and Shakespeare perks his head up from his place on my bed.

"I'm too damn stressed. And I'm not sleeping well. And I probably should eat better." The excuses keep coming, and soon I've justified my body's behavior enough to not feel any worry about it. I pay extra attention to my makeup and make sure to add some thick concealer under my eyes.

Fifteen minutes later, I am standing in front of my closet, frantically searching through my clothes. My room is a warzone and Shakespeare is having an improper amount of fun burrowing in the massive pile of discarded clothing on my bed, while I still can't decide what to wear. My eyes dart to the clock and I yelp in surprise, causing Shakespeare to perk his ears up and stare at me with concern. "I'm going to be late!" I grab the nearest dress off my bed and tug it on over my shoulders, straightening it out. Whirling around, I ask my closest friend and dearest confidant, "Shakespeare, do you think this is too sexy for work?"

His tongue lolls out of his mouth as he tilts his head inquisitively, then gives a few thoughtful 'rowl' noises before digging his nose back into the fluffy sweater in front of him. I scrutinize my reflection before deciding it's okay. The dress certainly doesn't hide my significant curves, but it comes to my knees and has a modest enough neckline so I'm pretty sure it won't hurt.

"Ugh, why do I even care what he thinks?" I glare at myself in the mirror but can't stop from carefully checking my makeup and hair over one more time before gathering my things, kissing my dog goodbye, and dashing out of the house.

The subway that morning is especially crowded and I squeeze myself into a small spot, gripping onto the rails for stability. I am not usually nervous on my way into work but my conversation with Hayden from last night keeps replaying in my mind. I sigh loudly, staring up at the ceiling. I should just admit it to myself. I'm developing a crush on Laurence and I feel as ridiculously giddy as the middle school version of myself when my eighth grade crush Jeffrey Raines joined the art club.

When I walk into the building, I wave at Michael the security guard, and step into the nearest elevator, already pulsing with workers from the various companies that house their offices in TMC Tower. A young man turns to me. "What floor?"

"Oh, um, fifty-six please." His finger freezes from its spot hovering near the mid numbers and coughs a little as he traces all the way up to the last button. He stares at me with a half-smile. "Going to see the big boys, huh?"

In no mood to put up with his ideas of just who belongs on the top floor, I snap back pretty quickly. "No, I'm going to *my* office."

His wide eyed gaze lingers a little too long like he's trying to suss me out, before he mutters "sorry" and turns around again, releasing me from the awkward tension. Slowly the elevator rises and I watch the crowded space empty until the last four floors are me riding by myself.

When I exit the elevator I nod to the receptionist and move down the hall to my office.

As I glimpse the door, I notice it is slightly ajar. Concerned, I slow my approach and hesitate outside the entrance. Looking back at Miss Davis to see if she shows any signs of alarm or interest, I find her quietly typing, absorbed in her own thoughts. Turning my eyes again to the door, I peek in through the crack.

My shoulders relax as I see the tall frame of Laurence leaning casually against the back of my sofa, half perched upon it. His crisp gray linen suit is impeccable as always and his hair catches the sun streaming in from my windows, lighting in a thousand colors of fire and crimson. Ankles crossed and one hand in his pocket, he's casually thumbing through something on his cell phone, no stranger to the new habit of waiting that has permeated our society today. I smile at the thought, enjoying the raw humanity of this moment. In so many ways, he is the untouchable man; seeing this mundane detail of his life that mimics mine makes me feel like he's not quite so far beyond my reach. I stand there, quietly admiring him from my hiding place.

Suddenly I realize, a moment too late, that I've been slowly leaning forward and my hand slips on the doorframe, sending me careening in through the door. It flies open under my weight and I tumble into the room, just seeing Laurence's alarmed expression as I stumble forward, barely keeping my balance. Before he can react or speak, I've stabilized myself and try to play it off like nothing's happened, straightening my clothes and hastily puffing my bangs out of my eyes. I'm tugging my necklace back center when I catch Laurence's face and he's squinting, cheeks stretched into a ridiculous grin that he attempts - and fails - to cover with his hand. His whole face is strained in his attempt to control his laughter but as I look at him and he catches my mystified expression, he guffaws and bursts into laughter, doubling over and resting his hands on his knees. He howls and snorts and I stare at him, stuck in the thought cycle of trying to brush off my entrance and fully giving in and laughing with him.

Finally he wipes the tracts of tears from his face and looks up at me, his face a mix of pity and adoration.

"Good morning, Camry. Quite the entrance you've had today." He cocks an eyebrow at me and smiles.

My cheeks burn crimson as the embarrassment finds me, and I trip over my words. "Uh, oh, yes."

He eyes me skeptically, taking me in and I can see concern in his gaze. "Was last night's late night too much for you? I know I did work you awfully hard." The innuendo in that sentence is not lost on me but I'm pretty sure that it was spoken in innocence, and he has no idea what he said. I stutter, trying not to fall into the trap he has so innocently set. "No, I'm fine. Thank you, again, though." In the end, self-preservation wins out, and I shift my eyes away and search around the room. "Did you bring the painting up here?"

He seems to come to his senses and leaps up, stepping over to the wall in the open space, showing me the painting there, leaning carefully against the wall. I follow him, staring at it.

Now that the time is ready to open it, I feel acutely aware of Laurence. Crush or not, this painting is personal, and it's the first time I've seen it since my mom died. When I open it, I'll see her again, and I don't really want an audience.

I take a shaky breath and turn to Laurence. "Thank you for bringing it here."

"Not at all."

I stare at him, trying to figure out how to ask for some privacy. "Could I..." I trail off and start again. "Do we have any work that needs to be done together immediately?"

"No, nothing that can't wait until later today."

"In that case, I think I'd like to get to work on the vendor list. Can we meet later?"

He quickly agrees, and from his behavior I don't think he's caught on to my agitation. "Absolutely. I'll come by in a little while."

"That'd be great." I muster up a smile and watch as he leaves the room.

I retrieve my letter opener from my desk and approach the painting again. After a few deep breaths, I press the tip of the blade into the wrapping.

But then I stop. My hand freezes and just sits there and I don't know why, but I can't get my hand to move at all. I'm standing there, motionless, a thousand emotions roaring in my ears, unaware of anything but the cool blade tucked into my palm. I blink a few times, trying to force my will. It's just a painting. You've seen it before.

The silver of the letter opener shines in the bright lights of my office, and it slices through the tape and bindings cleanly. As the last of the padding falls away, I let out the shaky breath I have been holding, viewing the canvas in all its glory.

The vivid reds and blues leap off the painting in three dimensions, palette knife strokes simple yet intentional, each slice of paint a note of affection felt between friends. The flutter of skirt tails, the grace of extended limb, the curve of spine all blend together, creating the one image of my mother that I wish to forever maintain, one full of life and passion.

I reach for it, not allowing my fingers to touch, but close enough that I wonder if I can feel the energy with which it was painted, tingling in the tips of my fingers. I close my eyes, concentrating on the minuscule vibrations.

"Oh, mama," I whisper, "Mama, I miss you."

A tear slips down my cheek and I pull back my hand, hurriedly wiping my face. My mind is full of the image of last time I saw her, lying pale and empty in that hospital bed before the nurse pulled up the curtain over her face. "I'm sorry, mama. I'm so sorry. I'm sorry I left you that day."

The tears are falling now, my attempt at controlling them a lost cause. Vividly, I remember the day she died as if it were yesterday. The day I was offered my position at TMC, I raced to the hospital to tell her the good news. She was so happy, but so, so weak. By that point, she had numerous tumors on her pancreas and the cancer had metastasized and we knew it wasn't long. But I had never expected it to be that same day. She dozed off and while she was sleeping, I stepped out of the room to get a drink. When I came back, she was gone.

She had been lying there with the same smile she always wore; I thought she was sleeping. I didn't even realize she was dead. But there was this strange sound coming from the machines next to her bed, and then a nurse came in behind me. She laid a hand on my shoulder and said, 'I'm so sorry,' before moving over and shutting off a monitor and recording the time of death on the whiteboard behind me.

I lost it. I had no idea what was going on. I started screaming and I jumped onto the bed. They told me later that I had pushed the nurse, but all I remember was holding mama in my arms, sobbing while I knelt on the bed.

Now, as I gaze at the portrait so lovingly painted of her image, my composure fades at these resurfaced memories. My shoulders shake and my breaths are shallow. I sit there hugging my knees, letting the tears freely fall, wishing that she was here, hugging me close.

All of a sudden, the door flies open and Laurence bursts through the door, head down to a folder and speaking hurriedly.

"Camry, I just realized. Before we decide on a venue it is crucial that we-"

He cuts himself off abruptly and I scramble to my feet, straightening my clothes and rubbing my hands across my face, trying to scrub the evidence of tears away. "Um, yes?"
I sniffle and tuck my hair behind my ears.

Laurence stares at me, eyes wide as they roam over me, assessing my current state. He opens his mouth to speak but I cut him off before he can ask what's wrong. "Did you need something? You said we needed to make a decision about something, right?"

There's a second or two of awkward tension in the room and I can see concern in his eyes. I send him a pleading look, and he closes his mouth and then forces an awkward smile, moving on to pretend like nothing is wrong.

"Yes. I realized that when I was reviewing everything yesterday, I neglected to include adequate kitchen facilities in what we need in a venue. If a caterer should need the space, we will need to have it. So any decisions about venue need to work with a caterer, and vice versa. If a caterer doesn't need any kitchen facilities, it's a non-issue, but it is probable they will need at least a simple staging area, so we will need to have that ready."

I mentally file all of that away, smiling weakly at him. "Yes, okay, thank you for telling me that. I'll be sure to make a note of it."

He looks at me for a moment before nodding. "Thank you. I apologize for barging in here uninvited." His eyes wander around the room and settle on the painting. "Is that it?"

I slowly bob my head, confirming his guess.

"May I look at it?"

"Sure." I shrug my shoulders and walk over to the painting.

As I feel Laurence move beside me, I hear him speak. "Truly, it is a piece of genius. And it serves your mother well."

"Thank you," I reply. "I think so too." A slight smile forms on my lips, even through the pain in my heart.

"I'll call the maintenance crew to have someone come hang this for you."

He stares at it in silence for a moment more, and then he turns to me. He seems to hesitate for a minute, but eventually he smiles and turns to the door. "I'll be back later this afternoon, as promised."

"Okay, thank you. I'll see you then."

And with that he quietly exits the room and I let out a sigh of relief. I rush into my bathroom and stare at my face, splotchy in complexion, with my foundation streaked by my tears. I hastily grab my makeup bag and touch up my look, hoping to hide most of the damage.

Not long after, the workers come and install the painting, and I sit at my desk, staring at it in across from me. I smile at it, and know that even though it hurts, I'll be able to see my mother, feeling of her with me every day now. And with that, I quietly pick up my pen and get to work.

****

The first hours pass quickly, checking email and reading more information from the files, trying to figure out what I'm looking for. I google places we've used recently and look at all sorts of pictures for inspiration. I have a list three pages long of ideas - but the fact is they're all ideas we have done.

Feeling frustrated, I push myself back from my chair and stand, stretching a bit and rolling my neck around. I frown at my notes. "Time for a break, I think." I moving towards my coffee machine when someone knocks on my door.

When I open it, Laurence inclines his head and I smile awkwardly, meeting his eyes and then quickly averting them. Between the realization that I'm attracted to him to the awkward interactions from this morning, my heart and mind are one big jumbled mess at the moment. Outwardly I force a calm appearance and invite him inside. "Come on in."

Laurence strides past and moves over to my desk, unashamedly peering at the notes and lists. "Vying for inspiration?"

I follow him, trying not to stand too close as I leaf through the pages. "Trying, more like. It's not working amazingly. I see what you've done, and I am getting the feel for things, I guess? But everything I'm putting on page is just what has been, not what could be. I'm not sure I'm finding the creative flow right now." I purse my lips as a sudden thought comes to me. "By the way, how did you do this in the past? Did you really do all of this yourself?"

"Not at all. As I mentioned before, I'd had the same assistant for quite some time. She left on maternity leave, and eventually decided she would rather stay home with her son. Her husband is also employed here. They are wonderful people." There is a fondness in his eyes as he speaks, and I learn more about Laurence's ability to truly see his employees as people, and not parts of a moving machine; something I admire as a member of the massive corporate landscape. I smile at him and he knocks his knuckles against the papers on my desk.

"This is all her work. She was excellent at her job and her absence is greatly missed. I suppose that once things calm down, I will begin the search for a new assistant. In the meantime, don't feel the need to compare yourself to anyone. You're doing well."

He winks at me with a genuine smile and I feel my heart flutter. Realizing my face is blossoming pink, I quickly look down at the page.

"Well I'm definitely grateful to her for all of this. It's made it incredibly easy to see the detail and break down the information I need. I just wish I knew what to DO with the information! I can't seem to move it forward into something new." I can feel the creases in my forehead from my frown and I reach up to rub at them.

"I understand. May I?" He taps the page beneath my finger, and I nod. Picking them up, he reads my notes for a minute or two in silence. "Well, looking at this, I think-"

He's cut off by a loud thumping at my door followed by the sound of chaotic voices outside. Laurence crosses the room, frowning, and opens the door to reveal Hayden and Alex standing there, goofy grins on their faces. They don't even notice Laurence behind the door as they barrel into the office. Stunned I stare at them.

They speak over each other at once, eyes drawn to me and the office. Hayden exclaims, "Oh my god, I love your office!" while Alex blurts out, "Holy shit. This is amazing!"

They look at each other and burst out laughing before the echoing sound of someone shutting the door behind them causes them to freeze in a comical timing.

Alex turns slowly, while Hayden whirls around. "Oh, hey, Mr. Mercier! How did I not catch the fact that you were standing... right there?" She quickly straightens her posture, shuffling her feet nervously.

Alex is obviously still under whatever unpleasant impression he has of Laurence. A curt "Hello," is all that comes from his lips before he turns back around to face me, coming close and gathering me into a firm embrace with a fond expression on his face. "Hey, you."

"Hey you too!" We exchange smiles and he steps back, looking at me. "Damn Camry. You look really cute."

Out of the corner of my eye I can see Laurence, staring at Alex with an unpleasant expression on his face. He speaks, his voice a calm bass timbre, but I can hear the slightest edge to it. "Mr. Epworth, do you often speak to employees that way while at work?"

My eyebrows raise and Hayden frantically looks back and forth between the two men. Alex tips his head a little, never taking his eyes off of me. His words come out smooth and easy. "No, but Camry isn't just any employee. She and I are close." His emphasis on the word 'close' is easily heard and I can only imagine what he's trying to insinuate.

I glare at him, stepping back and shaking my head in exasperation. What kind of bullshit male posturing is this? Having no desire to encourage whatever this mood is, I interject, returning the focus on the presence of my friends. "Alright. What's up guys? Why the sudden visit?" It's then I notice that there's a mug from my favorite coffee vending machine in Alex's hand. "And did you bring me something?"

Hayden scrambles into the conversation quickly, seeing my dilemma. "Yes, we did!" She smoothly removes the cup from Alex's grasp and passes it to me. "We were taking a quick break and I had the brilliant, if I do say so myself, idea to come and say hello and tell you not to forget about us."

"Well, thanks, guys, but it's not like I could ever forget about you!" I gratefully accept her offering and Hayden turns to Laurence.

"Mr. Mercier, I'm sorry for interrupting your time together."

Laurence's expression softens, but he doesn't smile. "It's not a problem, as long as the break is short." He looks at me. "Miss Hughes, you are welcome to enjoy a few moments with your friends. I'll be in my office. Come find me when you are finished, and bring the papers we were discussing."

That he referred to me as "Miss Hughes" in front of them is not lost on me, but my thoughts have no time to focus on that. He turns and exits in a flurry and Hayden lets out a low whistle once the door is closed. "Um, I thought you said he was kind of chill? That guy's as much of a hardass as I've ever seen him!" She whirls around and jabs a finger into Alex's chest. "And what the hell was that, Alex? You made Camry out to be your girlfriend or something, and you know damn well that's not true!"

All five foot two inches of Hayden swell as she glares up at the wickedly impassive face before her. Alex shrugs a little and sits down on my couch. "He's got no reason to care about how I talk to my friend. Besides, if he really knew Cam, he'd know she'd destroy any other guy who talked to her that way. He just had to step in and strut around, coming off like a benevolent ruler that 'allows' his employee to take a break now and then." He turns and sets his gaze firmly on me. "He doesn't own you, Camry."

Hayden looks at me pointedly and we roll our eyes in unison. It's not hard to see that this is less about either one of them, and more about giving an inch in a show of masculinity. "Guys are idiots."

"Agreed." We clink our coffee cups together and she giggles, effectively closing the matter at hand.

Peering over the work on my desk, Hayden makes little noises as she examines the pages I've drafted so far. "These are good!"

I reach over and pull the papers from her, turning them down on the desk. "Except they're not. They're just notes from what we've done in the past. Nothing original."

She looks at me and I puff out my cheeks, releasing the breath in a burst of hot air. "I'm going to do what you said and ask him for some more direct guidance."

"Atta girl!" Hayden smiles brightly at me, and Alex gets up and joins us by my desk.

"I know I already said this, but this is a really nice office. You sure you're not gonna get all high class and fancy on us now that you're up here in Swank-ville?"

"Rude. And no, I most certainly will not." I peer from face to face, furrowing my brow. "Besides, you guys are talking like I'm never coming back down to Copy. This is a temporary job. The Cinderella factor is small here."

Alex casually tosses his arms around our shoulders, pulling us close. "I suppose you're right. Gotta get the band back together eventually!"

We share a few more laughs before the two of them head downstairs and I wave as they walk down the hall. Once they've stepped onto the elevator, I grab the papers from my desk and set off for Mr. Mercier's office at the end of the corridor.

I tap lightly on the door and it pushes open under my touch. Peeking my head through the crack, I see Laurence seated at his desk, phone to his ear, one hand tapping keys on his keyboard and the other rolling a small stone around between his fingers. He looks up and meets my eyes, gesturing me to come in. Not wanting to intrude, I slip quietly through the door and take the time to unashamedly stare around his office.

The room itself stands in relative contrast to my own. Filled with warm hues, elegant furnishings, and gorgeous classic art, I smile at how unbelievably 'Laurence' the room feels. A fiery-hued oak desk, plush red chairs, and a gorgeous navy oriental rug encourage my assessment and I have to chuckle. What a posh space. Fitting for the image of Laurence at work; warm but a bit stuffy, comfortable, but not quite relaxed.

I wander towards the window, in love with the view stretching north from the financial district far up the island.

Though I can't interpret the French he is speaking, I can tell by the tone of his voice that he is trying to remain calm and composed but isn't pleased about what is being said. Though his voice appears to be neutral and polite, the tension in his jaw and crease in his forehead betray that he is restraining himself.

Finally the call ends and Laurence rises and stretches, giving me an apologetic look. "Forgive me for that. It was an unexpected call but an important one, I'm afraid." He looks wearily at his phone before turning his attention back to me.

"Is everything alright?"

Running his fingers through his hair, he sighs and says, "It will be." I haven't failed to notice that when he's nervous or shaky, he uses this gentle habit, and I am sure he's not letting onto everything, but I respect his privacy and choose to move on in the moment.

"I brought those papers you asked for. I think you were saying something to me about them before we were interrupted."

"Was I?" His normal commanding air is replaced by one distracted and not fully present, but he takes the papers nonetheless and asks me to repeat my concerns.

Nodding thoughtfully, he chews his lips while staring down at my notes and my eyes are drawn to the way his teeth curve over his lower lip, gently tugging it. This overwhelmingly sensual act robs me of my focus but his voice quickly calls me back to the present. "Ah, yes. Forgive me. I remember now where we were. Based on what I see here and from what you've told me, I believe a little real world experience would be beneficial."

"What do you mean?"

"I can show you some things that might help. Do you have plans after work tomorrow evening? I will take you to a few locations to help you get a grasp on things."

I gulp a little. Private time with Laurence, after working hours? "I'm not busy, no. I guess that would help some. What kind of places are you thinking?"

His fingers deftly stroke his chin, brow wrinkling in thought. "A few local venues would be good, and it wouldn't be bad for you to gain an understanding of the way money flows at events like this. Understanding fine wine and fine food will be important when we select caterers. When you come to work tomorrow, bring a dress to wear out in the evening. I'll take you to a tasting at a restaurant where I know the chef. He could work with a menu to show some different flavors and types of food. We'll head out immediately following work, so say 7pm?"

"Is seven o'clock normal for you?" I cock my head at him. "We worked until seven last night too!"

"Seven is... early for me. I am often here until nine or later." He looks mildly culpable as he admits his workaholic tendencies.

"No wonder you said you were never home! Don't you go crazy?"

He laughs softly. "Sometimes, I wonder." He hands the papers back to me. "Good work here, keep it up, but move it along now. Sit down with a cup of tea and relax and let your imagination follow the theme to something beautiful."

"Okay." I smile and take the papers.

He sheepishly stares at me for a minute. "I suppose I could make six o'clock work. Would that be alright?"

"Sounds good. Thank you! I hope I learn a lot."

"You're very welcome. Now, get to work! I'll see you later this afternoon."

****

The following afternoon has arrived before I know it. Almost as if I had been sucked into the executive's timeline, I worked well past dark on Wednesday as well. Looking over at the clock, I see that it's half past five pm. I stretch, pushing myself back from my desk and rubbing my eyes. I still have some things I want to do, but I know that I am meeting Laurence soon and I want to spend some time getting ready for our dinner. I stand and stretch widely above my head, reaching for the high ceiling. I crack my neck a few times, wincing as the tension releases in a few gentle pops.

I walk over to my private bathroom and take my dress down from hanging on the back of the door. I stand in front of the mirror, holding it up in front of myself. I hope this will be nice enough. I have no idea where we are going; no more than Laurence had said at first.

I admit, I do feel a little odd. My boss is taking me to dinner at a nice restaurant then taking me around the city to some of the finer locations in town. In any other situation, one could consider this a date. My heart flutters a bit and I swallow as my nerves spike. Why am I so nervous? *This is a business dinner*, I firmly repeat to myself.

I remove my clothing and pull the sleek black dress on. It skirts above my knees in the front, dipping lower in the back in modern style; the neckline sitting gently off my shoulders emphasizes my collarbone. I add a pair of sparkling crystal drop earrings, checking over my makeup, and touch up my lipstick to a slightly more dramatic shade. I carefully twist a section of my hair up, holding bobby pins between my lips when a few firm knocks ring on my office door. Muffled by the pins in my mouth, I attempt to shout "just a moment!" while I rush towards the door, hands still tangled in my hair.

I bend over and push my elbow against the door handle, the door sliding open as the lock disengages. I rise, and step back as Laurence pushes open the door.

He begins to take a step in but when his gaze comes to rest on me, he pauses almost comically. A second or two pass before he clears his throat awkwardly and steps inside a bit more, shutting the door behind him.

I blush a bit and tip my head toward the bathroom, indicating I need a few minutes.

"Ah, yes," he says, understandingly. "Take all the time you need."

I smile and return to the restroom. I quickly tuck the last few strands up, securing them into place. Lowering my hands, I rest them on the counter and take a deep breath. "Don't be nervous, Camry," I mutter to myself. "You got this."

I exit the bathroom, anxiously running my fingers over my ear. I gingerly meet Laurence's eyes, suddenly feeling far more shy than I normally am. "Um, am I dressed appropriately?"

His eyes sweep quickly over me again, and then a warm expression falls upon his face and his posture relaxes. "Yes, you look quite radiant this evening."

I study Laurence in return; he wears an elegant charcoal gray three piece suit and no tie, his shirt's upper buttons parted slightly. He looks so refined and polished that my gaze rakes over him a bit too long.

He swallows thickly, his adam's apple bobbing up and down. "Miss Hu- err, I mean, Camry. Are you ready to go?"

I suck in a deep breath and turn towards my desk, trying to hide the nervous blush in my cheeks. I pick up my clutch and turn, giving him a smile. "I am."

"After you." He moves to the door and holds it open for me, following behind me into the hallway.

We walk silently side by side, down the hallway and into the elevator. I take a few deep breaths to calm myself as the elevator descends to the basement level car park.

Laurence leads me to his car and opens the door for me. Watching him round the front of the car I notice that his posture seem much more relaxed and friendly than I've seen. He usually carries himself so stiffly, and even though he can be a bit teasing, he's always had a professional undertone to his words. But tonight he seems cheerful. I guess even the talented Mr. Mercier allows himself to relax a little bit now and then.

Once he takes his seat he turns on the car and we take off into the Manhattan night.

As the car weaves its way through traffic, it's chillier than I realized and I shiver a bit. Laurence looks over at me. "Are you cold?"

"Um, just a little bit. I think I was so nervous picking out my dress that I completely forgot to bring a shawl or a sweater."

"Here." He reaches in my direction and pushes a button on the center console. He leans back and smirks at me. "Heated seats. It'll warm you up in no time."

"Oh! Thank you!" I slowly run my hand along the smooth leather on my side, pleased.

We drive in silence for a few minutes but as the quiet stretches on, the easy mood I had before is replaced with suspense and worry. I sneak a glance at Laurence, but he seems calm and totally unperturbed in contrast to my anxious state.

I sigh a bit and settle for looking out the window at the passing bright lights and glamorous pedestrians, but my eyes seem to have other ideas. I keep stealing glances at Laurence's profile as we drive. He said he knows the owner of the restaurant we are going to, but with his connections I'm sure that could be any number of venues in the city. Will it be an energetic and trendy place? Or somewhere with a soft, romantic mood? I try to picture where he would be most comfortable and I spend some time conjuring images of him sipping wine at tables laid in crisp white linens. The more I think, the more I sneak peeks at him.

Finally he laughs, a genuine heartfelt laugh that I haven't heard before. It's almost youthful, and a bit frenetic.

"You're trying so hard not to ask me where we are going, aren't you?" A teasing grin lights up his face.

"No I'm not!" I blurt out defensively, crossing my arms across my chest. His eyebrow lifts, and it's clear he isn't buying it. I huff in defeat. "Alright fine. I am. Am I allowed to ask?"

Sliding a hand along the steering wheel as we make a turn, he flashes a devious smile. "You are certainly free to inquire."

I can't help but laugh a bit. "I suppose you won't tell me though, will you?" I shift in my seat to face him more. "I promise I'll still act surprised when we arrive."

"I highly doubt the quality of your acting skills, so the answer shall remain a mystery."

"It's a restaurant, right? You said we would be eating."

"Perhaps..."

"I am getting hungry, so that's good. Let's see... if you were picking a restaurant for me to learn from, I'd guess... Italian? Or maybe something a bit more trendy right now, like a super chic Pho bar?"

He laughs again, thoroughly amused. "Sounds like someone has been browsing the internet in anticipation for our outing today."

Laurence's good mood has loosened my lips and I find in my half nervous, half excited state that I can't stop talking. "Let's see here. Top 10 Manhattan restaurants right now..." I scroll through my phone, naming restaurants and quickly looking to see if he reacts at all, but at most my guesses are met with bemused chuckles or playfully exasperated shakings of his head.

He taps a finger against his lips. "I shall say no more. You will simply have to wait. However, that is good research, so don't lose that article."

I dramatically pout but can't keep from smiling at the atmosphere in the car as I lean back into my seat. "Fine then. Will you at least tell me how much longer until we get there?"

"Not long. In fact, I can see it now, so sit still for a few moments longer." His gaze drifts through the chaotic traffic patterns, navigating the car across the street. He pulls up to the curb and a valet immediately walks up and opens my door. Laurence steps out of the car and the valet greets him. "Good evening, Mr. Mercier. How was the drive?"

"No trouble at all, if you don't count this one," Laurence cheerfully replies, winking in my direction. "Kept this all a surprise and she wouldn't stop asking questions the whole way over!"

The valet laughs and takes my hand, helping me out of the car. Laurence hands him the keys and then extends his arm to me. "Shall we?"

Chapter 6

After slipping my hand through Laurence's arm, I take
a minute to look around. The visage before me is like
something plucked from a forest fairytale. A smooth
green awning is surrounded by ivy crawling up brick
walls. Large windows with brass framing reflect the
twinkling lights that peek through the creeping vines.
Soft candlelight dances on tables I see through the
glass, and inside the few patrons all wear expressions
of delight and comfort. Flowing music reaches my
ears, delicate strings coupled with the longing sounds
of an accordion's slower notes.

Laurence steps forward and we enter the beautiful
little restaurant. Its warm atmosphere lends itself to
the small space, and it doesn't feel cramped despite
the size. He leads me in, across a cobblestone floor,
past tables and a comfortable bar made of sleek wood
and brass. A stout man in a chef's coat emerges from
behind the door to the kitchen and greets us.
"Laurence! *Mon pote*! It's so good to see you." The
two men embrace and exchange a flurry of words in
French and finally Laurence steps back to introduce
me.

The man looks at me with a delighted expression of
surprise. "*Ah, et qui c'est?* Who is this,
Laurence? *Votre chère, n'est-ce pas?*" His teasing
countenance is not lost on me and I have a feeling that
this man knows exactly who I am, choosing instead to
give his friend some grief.

Laurence shakes his head and slaps his friend on the
back. "No, Leo, this is the woman I told you about.

She is working with me on the Met Hospital gala." He
squeezes his friend's shoulder tightly. "And you knew
that, you great goat."

The man, Leo, laughs with glee, not at all ashamed to
have been caught in his joke. He wags his finger
playfully at Laurence before turning fully to me. "Ah
mademoiselle, it is my greatest pleasure to make your
acquaintance." He takes my hand and makes a show
of kissing the back of my fingers. He stands up in a
snap, gesturing widely about the restaurant. "*Alors,
mademoiselle,* do you like my restaurant?"

"This is your place?" I let my genuine first impression
show and I nod vigorously. "I do! It's absolutely
charming."

"Ah see, Laurence! This girl, she has great taste. I like
her already." Leo's wide grin is infectious. "Let's be
off, eh?" He takes my arm and leads me through the
kitchen doors.

My eyes go wide as I see the hustle and bustle of the
kitchen in action. Though there are only five people
in the kitchen, they move with such speed and
precision it looks almost like a dance, shouts ringing
out as they call to each other, mixing bowls and pans
clanging and knives chopping loudly as they do their
work. "Wow, it's so busy in here!"

Leo stops for a moment and speaks loudly, leaning
towards my ear to be heard. "There are not many
here for the evening yet. The restaurant won't be full
until after eight. Right now these *asticots* are mostly
getting things ready for service *ce soir*." I hear
Laurence chortle behind me, and I steal a glance at

him. His relaxed face seems genuinely happy in this space. Following his gaze, I look again at the work going on in the kitchen, watching a few seconds more and then Leo tugs on my arm, leading me further on. At the end of the kitchen, Laurence pushes open a door and leads us out onto a small patio in the back. I gasp and my hands clasp in excitement.

The patio wraps around the side of the restaurant and as I look around, I see wrought iron tables set up in the space between buildings. But here in front of us is a table laid out with all sorts of food. Small servings of hors d'oeuvres and dishes to delight the eyes are dotting the white linen landscape. A young man in crisp white shirt and satin vest stands behind the table and gestures to me. "Welcome. My name is Andrew, and I will be serving you this evening." He lifts a small cocktail, holding it out to me. "*Un apéro, mademoiselle?*" I glance at Laurence, unsure of what I'm being asked.

"He means your drink." He winks at Andrew. "Very nice, Andrew. Your French is getting better. Do you have *mon couz* to thank for that?"

Leo puffs out his chest and slaps Andrew on the back. "*Oui, bien sur c'est moi!*"

Andrew laughs, but the joke goes over my head and I look back and forth between them. Leo reaches over and grabs the glass out of Andrew's hand. He leans in closely to me, lifting his eyebrows.

"Ah, a beautiful woman deserves a beautiful drink. Andrew has done well. Please accept this, Camry. I am so glad you have joined us this evening." He rests his other hand on my shoulder, stepping even closer, and holding the effervescent beverage up to my lips.

I hear Laurence clear his throat and he steps forward, lifting the glass away. "*Ça suffit*, Leo." There's a hint of warning in his voice, but his calm smile never leaves his face.

Leo stares at Laurence for a second, then bursts out laughing. "*Ah d'ac, d'ac!*" He wears a knowing smile and rattles off something in French so fast I can't follow along, but Laurence's eyes widen and he takes a half step back, looking caught off guard. Leo pushes along, though, and points at the drink now held in Laurence's hand.

"Give her the drink, Laurence."

Laurence starts, coming back to his senses, and awkwardly hands the glass to me, barely making eye contact. I take the stem between my fingers and hold the glass up, inhaling the aroma. The bubbles tickle my nose, the crisp citrusy smell begins to make my mouth water.

Andrew hands another glass out to Laurence. "*Monsieur.*" Leo picks up a glass himself and says, "*On trinque?*"

Laurence holds his glass out to me, firmly holding my gaze. "*Sante.*"

I smile and clink my glass to his. "*Sante!*" I also toast Leo and watch as Leo and Laurence clink their glasses forcefully, cocktail sloshing over the sides. Once they're finished, they drink, and I follow suit, lightly taking a sip.

The sweet effervescent quality of the drink is delightful and I close my eyes to savor it.

"You like it, *Mademoiselle* Camry?" Leo's eyes are twinkling as he peers at me.

"I do! It's so delicate and yet it feels... significant all the same. What is it?"

Leo claps his hands and cheers. "Laurence, where did you find this *chère belle*? *Elle est magnifique!*" He turns to me, touching my glass. "This is honeysuckle vodka, champagne, lemon zest, and a splash of limoncello."

"It's exquisite!" I lift my glass and peer at it, enjoying the way the curled lemon peel bobs in the cloudy liquid.

Leo smiles. "Now, do tell me. How did such a delightful woman as yourself come to work with this oaf over there?" He winks and points at Laurence, not bothering to lower the volume of his voice. I giggle at his comment, noting the friendship these two must have. Laurence is off to the side, leaning against the wall casually, watching us with a small smile on his face. I explain how I came to work with Laurence and Leo's smile grows with my explanation.

"*Ah, tres bien!* You are a woman of culture and intelligence. Perhaps you can teach him a thing or two. He needs a woman like you in his life." He slyly smiles, his grin full of playful mischief. His eyes dart over to Laurence and I see him narrow them for a moment, sussing out his friend. Then he turns to face me directly but keeps one eye trained on Laurence. "Or you could come and lend me your artistic sensibilities, *non*? I could cook you food fit for a queen, and we could be very happy." He waggles his eyebrows at me and takes a small step closer.

Before I can react, Laurence's voice cuts through the atmosphere. "Now, now, Leo, let's not forget the reason we are here." He pushes off the wall with one foot and walks closer, stepping between Leo and me, picking up a small piece of crostini from the table. He brings it closer and explains. "These shavings on top are smoked salmon, cucumber, and caviar, topped with fresh mint. Have a taste." He holds it up in front of me, clearly intending I eat it from his hand.

"Oh, um, alright," I say sheepishly, leaning forward and taking a cautious bite. He watches me intently, gauging my reaction. "That's amazing! I honestly have never had caviar before and I was a little nervous but those flavors are wonderful together."

Laurence casually pops the rest of the food into his mouth. A satisfied smile on his face, he turns to Leo. "Perfection as always, Leo." I blanch a little at his unaffected way of sharing food, but neither Leo nor Laurence seem to think anything of it.

Leo's expression is one of pure happiness and he takes a moment to look between the two of us, a wide smile on his face. "Just as I thought." He doesn't elaborate, but chuckles to himself and I have a feeling he isn't talking about the food. "Now, my dears, I simply must get back to it. Andrew here will take the most excellent care of you, and he will explain the rest of the dishes. Camry, do come and visit me again? You are an absolute delight! Best of luck to you both!"

He clasps my hands warmly, pats Laurence on the back, and returns to the kitchen. The warm air that escapes as the door opens is welcome on my skin, but with its disappearance I realize just how cold I am. I subtly rub my hands up and down my arms; the night has begun its chill.

Seconds later, a warmth descends upon me and I look up to notice Laurence is standing at my side, his jacket draped around my shoulders. He doesn't meet my eyes, casually moving closer to the table. "What do you want to try next?"

This subtle act of kindness touches my heart. I step up and look around, and we spend the next hour sampling food and drinks. I take a lot of notes on my phone; Andrew is a patient and thorough teacher, slowly talking about the current food trends, classics that never go out of style, and unexpected flavor combinations that pack a punch. He tells me what to look for from caterers, and buzz words to listen for when discussing menu items.

"Why can't we just hire you, Andrew?" At one point in the conversation I'm suddenly questioning the need to hire other companies. "You obviously know your stuff and all of this is so delicious."

Andrew's face brightens instantly. "I'd love that! But, as you've seen, we're a small restaurant. We only have capacity for around thirty diners at any time. We don't have the staff or the equipment to cook for the numbers you are expecting."

My face falls as I realize the truth of what he is saying. "I suppose you are right. I just got really excited there for a minute."

His sunny laughter rings out in the small courtyard. "I'll definitely tell Leo. But this should have helped you get an idea for what you need, so I hope it's been a good night?"

"Oh, excellent! It's been a fantastic night." I smile at him then look to Laurence, casually sitting in a nearby chair. "Thank you for all of this tonight. It's been amazing."

I approach him, holding out his jacket, and he smiles softly at me. "I'm glad it has helped." He peers around me at the well picked-over table of food. "Are you ready for our next stop?"

"Yes!" My answer is genuinely enthusiastic.

Laurence collects his suit coat from my hand, fingers casually brushing against mine. He walks over to Andrew and I can see that in their handshake, Laurence passes on a generous tip. "Thank you for everything, Andrew. We're running a bit behind schedule so please give our thanks to Leo as well, yes?"

"Of course, Mr. Mercier. It was my pleasure to serve you both this evening."

Laurence turns to me and once again offers his arm. This time I don't hesitate, and happily slip my hand around it.

Once we are in the car and making our way to our next destination, I can't stop chattering. "Oh my goodness, that was so great, Laurence! I can't believe I ate all that. I haven't ever even eaten half of that stuff and it was so good! I think my favorite thing was the spicy tuna thing. That was amazing. The tuna had such an amazing texture and there was that sauce: alley-sauce or... oily sauce?" I fumble over my words, trying to remember the name, when Laurence interjects.

"Aioli?"

"Yes! Aioli! That was so delicious paired with the avocado and the tuna. I think I could eat that all day! Which one was your favorite?"

I shift my focus to Laurence's face and I see that his eyes are narrowed to match the broad smile he wears.

"Call me simplistic, but the barbecued spare ribs with caramelized onions and bleu cheese was fantastic."

"Oh yes, that one WAS good." I conjure up the image of it in my mind and can practically feel my taste buds stir.

Thinking a bit back on the evening, I muse aloud. "Your friend Leo is adorable."

"Adorable?" Laurence shoots me an incredulous look. "I don't believe he's ever been called that before, even by his mother." He chuckles, continuing. "If he heard anyone say that he would die of shock and horror... except maybe for you. He was quite taken with you."

"I thought he was sweet."

Laurence looks at me skeptically, from the corner of his eye. "Did you now?"

I laugh at his question. "Absolutely. But aside from that, you can tell that he really knows and loves his craft." I'm suddenly struck by a thought and chew on my words for a few moments before continuing.

"It really is an art, isn't it? Not just in presentation, but in the taste, as well. I've always enjoyed food but I don't know if I have ever really experienced it before. The way the whole package was presented; the taste, texture, visual impression... it seems so much more complex and worth enjoying; like it's not just food, but an experience too. Does that make sense?"

Laurence strokes his chin thoughtfully. "Indeed it does. I know exactly what you mean." He gestures towards his stereo. "It is like a perfect symphony; when a talented orchestra plays a fine piece of music, you can both feel and hear it. The individual instruments are there and you can hear them each singing their own song, but collectively you also hear their melodies and harmonies combine. In turn, there is this beautiful piece that resonates in your heart and soul. It is the marriage of the individuals, without diminishing what makes the individual beautiful in its own right. Good food can be like this."

I nod slowly. "I hadn't ever really thought of it that way, but that's a beautiful way to put it." I lean back in my seat, thinking over what he has said. "You know, you can be awfully poetic at times. I think that deep down inside you're a closet romantic, aren't you?"

An amused, mirthful sound tumbles from his lips. "Am I now?"

"Well, that's my guess. I think you're a lot more than you let on, Mr. Mercier."

After a long beat, he speaks only one word. "Laurence."

The oddity of the response prompts me to look up. "What?"

"Laurence. You called me Mr. Mercier."

"Oh." The syllable falls from my lips. "I guess I'm still getting used to it."

He smiles gently at me. "It's of no consequence." He awkwardly scratches his temple, obviously embarrassed. "Ah, we're almost to our next destination."

Knowing our arrival will serve to sate my curiosity, I allow him to move the conversation on. "We've been driving for a while. Where are we heading?"

"Did I answer you the first time you asked me?" A teasing smile plays on his lips.

"I guess not."

"Do not worry. It's just ahead."

Once again we pull up to a valet station and I look up at the towering building before us. Standing in stark contrast to the quaint, cottage-like feel of the restaurant from earlier, this gorgeous stone building is detailed to the point that it approaches ostentatiousness. It reaches high into the sky and I'm a little overwhelmed at its looming presence.

I barely notice the car door open until a hand appears in front of my face. "Camry? Are you alright?"

My eyes focus to see Laurence standing before me with a concerned look on his face. "Oh, uh, yes. Sorry." I take his hand and he pulls me to my feet. Without even thinking I grasp his arm. He pauses for a moment, then gently lays his hand over mine, and gives a brief squeeze before letting go.

We walk into the building together, the gleaming marble floors and high ceilings giving an impression of grandiose sterility. Laurence leads me to a nearby elevator and we step inside. He leans past me, pressing the button for the top floor.

The ride up is silent; we are the only ones in the elevator. The gold-plated walls give a warm glow to our reflections and I close my eyes, feeling the comfortable warmth of Laurence next to me, my arm still linked with his.

The elevator finally completes its ascent and when the doors open I shrink back from the bright lights and loud music. When my senses return, I gasp at the visage before me.

Frail white trees, lit in vivid purples and blues, spring out of box hedges trimmed with precision. Colored lights flash through the air, and heavy bass thumps in my ears. All around me, people laugh and drink and eat, setting the mood as jovial and playful. Brightly lit tanks of water filled with colorful fish, beautiful glass sculptures, and stunning fire glass pits surrounded by lounge chairs complete the setting. And that's when I realize. "Oh! We're outside!"

Laurence chuckles. "Yes, we are. We are on the roof. You should be warm enough up here. Come this way. I want to show you a few things."

He leads me around, pointing out decor and design, as well as important functional choices like tall kerosene heaters and the ease with which the crowd flows through the space.

Arriving at a small table situated near the bar, Laurence leans over, speaking close to my ear to be heard over the cacophony of music and crowd. "If this looks familiar, you'll have seen images in your data. We held last year's gala here."

"Oh!" Suddenly the images and information I had read in the files came back to me. "Of course!" Immediately I begin to look around me, pointing around at what I can see. I ask questions; where was the DJ, where was the band? Tables, dancing, displays... I slowly develop an image in my mind of what this looked like under Laurence's careful direction.

Next to us, the bar serves people cocktails of various colors and styles. Patiently describing what he knows of each one, Laurence shows me the menu. "Look at the prices. The least expensive cocktail here is twenty-seven dollars. The average total at the end of the night per person is over two hundred. But see the craftsmanship, the presentation? It is exquisite."

He gestures to the drinks set before me on the bar, waiting to be whisked away to their awaiting clientele. "What do the colors, the tastes, make you think? Make you feel? Entertainment is a business, and maximizing euphoria is a big part of that. Anyone can make a martini, so what makes this one special? These are the things you must look for when you are planning this event."

I spend the next few minutes simply observing; drinks, food, ambience; the way people are dressed, the more popular areas. Taking random notes and photographs on my phone, I add to the inspiration and information I am collecting.

I hear a popping sound behind me and turn to see Laurence with a bottle of champagne in his hand. He quickly pours two glasses with a practiced hand, and offers one to me.

I slowly sip the champagne, letting the tart bubbles flow over my tongue. "This is really good."

He nods. "Yes, it is." We smile gently at each other and my heart is beating a mile a minute in my chest. The gentlemanly, caring side he is showing to me this evening is driving me wild. I am captivated by this sweet personality and it feels like he is doting on me in adoration. All his gentle touches, reassuring words, and thorough explanations have put my once nervous heart at ease and now its wild beats are for an entirely different reason. I'm grateful for the heavy bass in the music, knowing that he can't hear the frantic thumping.

As the minutes wear on, Laurence continues to walk me around the venue, describing any number of things and answering my never ending stream of questions. But the past few days of long hours, combined with the addition of alcohol begin to wear me down, and after the third stifled yawn, Laurence looks at me and apologizes.

"I am terribly sorry. It is rude of me to ignore this any longer. Let me take you home. You have been working hard all week and I can tell you are exhausted."

I try to stand up straighter and deny it. "No! I'm fine, totally fine."

He gives me an impatient look and I sigh, shoulders slumped. "Alright fine. But don't we have another place to go tonight?"

The concerned smile on his face warms my heart and I can't help but melt a little on the inside. What I wouldn't give for him to look at me like that every day...

"We did, but do not worry about that anymore. It is unimportant, and you have been a quick study, so I am sure you have lots of helpful information. Now, let us be going."

He takes my arm and leads me away.

****

A soft light touches my eyelids and I blink slowly, the gentle voice beside me pulling me from a light slumber.

"Camry? We're here." I feel a warmth on my shoulder and my eyes come to focus on Laurence's face, his caring gaze falling upon me. My eyes move around, taking in my surroundings and I shoot up in my seat, banging my head on the door frame in the process.

"Ow! Oh my god..." I clutch at my head, still trying to get my bearings. "Did... did I fall asleep?"

"Are you alright?"

"Ugh, yes... I just, I'm really sorry about that. I can't believe I fell asleep in your car."

"Please do not worry. As I said, you have been working long hours, and it is late. Why don't you take an extra hour tomorrow morning and come in around nine?"

I stare at him and slowly form words. "Are you absolutely sure? I feel like I'm letting you down."

His response is firm but gentle. "I insist you do. You are not letting me down in the slightest. Goodnight, Camry."

I slip out of the car and wave a little, enjoying the soft buzzing feeling from hearing him softly say my name. He waits patiently for me to open the door up to the apartments, and then he honks softly before pulling away into the cool Brooklyn night.

****

The next morning I'm sitting at my desk, hand to my chest, nervously waiting for the person on the other end of the line to return from putting me on hold. I'm impatiently tapping my pen against my desk when the line clicks and the voice returns. "Miss Hughes?"

"Yes!" I sit up quickly, nearly upending my chair in the process, and I hastily rub my hand across my face, wiping my hair out of my eyes. "Are you able to fit me in?"

"We are, but I'm leaving in a little over an hour. Can you make it here quickly?" I glance at the map I have pulled up on my computer screen, mentally tabulating the subway stops.

"I can be there in forty. I'm on my way!"

I slam the receiver down, grab my jacket and purse, and fly out of the office. Halfway down the hall I narrowly avoid a full-on collision with Laurence who steps out of the way at the last moment. "Camry! Where are you going?"

"Venue!" I shout, leaping into the open elevator and slamming the button. "Back soon!"

The doors slide closed and I anxiously peer at the descending numbers, praying silently that no one will be joining me at quarter to ten in the morning.

Luckily I make it down to the fourth floor before the doors open and one of the building's other tenants, a banking organization, begins to file a large amount of people into the elevator. Thinking it over, I slip out and make for the stairwell, racing down the last few flights and bursting into the lobby.

Sprinting for the subway station, I manage to make it to my train two minutes before it pulls in. Taking my seat, I pull up on my phone the place I am going to go visit, making sure I read as much as possible about it on my journey over.

Half an hour later, I step again into the sunlight, blinking and getting my bearings. I pin the location on my map and take off at a brisk walk in the direction. As the venue comes into view I practically squeal with excitement. It's everything I could have wished for and more; even better in person.

Looming ahead of me is an old gothic style church, its tall and ornate spires reaching to the sky. The church was purchased last year by a beloved art critic in New

York. He converted it to an elaborate venue space a few months ago, now called "Sanctuary". But before he could open its doors he died, willing it to his grandson. Since then it has hosted the occasional bat mitzvah or quinceañera and on Saturday mornings, it is home to a toddler ballet class. But Laurence told me to find a diamond in the rough, and here I am. The website was encouraging and I'm excited to see what this venue has to offer. If we could make this work, they could bail us out and relieve my greatest stress at the moment, and we could put them on the map.

As I reach the steps leading up to the grand entrance I lift my foot and suddenly a searing pain shoots through my lower abdomen. I cry out a little in surprise and pain and clutch at my side, leaning over the railing for support. It takes a few moments and my breathing is heavy but eventually the pain subsides, leaving nothing but a dull ache in its wake. What in the world was that?

I gingerly twist and turn, testing out my body, but no real pain lingers and I can feel no after-effects of whatever that was. Shaking my head to clear my mind of whatever freak pain that was, I walk up the steps, slowly quickening my pace as no further aches come to me.

When I reach the large oak doors with iron fittings, I pull hard on the handles and open the door. My breath catches in my throat and I stand amazed at the setting before me.

A foyer of grand design greets me, polished marble floors reflecting the intricacies of the wooden carved walls and decor. I look around, taking in all the beauty when I see someone walking towards me from the main event space.

"Are you Camry?"

I quickly extend my hand in greeting. "Yes! Thank you so much for meeting me here. I am really grateful to you for squeezing me into your busy day."

"It's not a problem. I'm Antonio Vasquez, the owner of Sanctuary." He slips me a business card and I return the favor.

He reads it over and looks at me. "So how can I help you? You said you wanted to view the space and it was urgent. You work for TMC?"

"I do, and this is in regards to this year's charity gala."

His eyebrow lifts; I can tell I've piqued his interest. Any event space would love to get their hands on a company like Travers-Moreau as a client, especially for their biggest event of the year. I muster my most professional tone and explain to him the details of the project; our needs for space, catering, and ease of access for artists to display their work.

He listens patiently, and we walk through the facility. I snap photos with my phone, taking notes and recording Antonio's thoughts as we go. There is a large open space that houses a beautifully detailed stage that was once a chancel. Balconies frame the nave, and the architecture contains more detail in every single inch than I have in my entire apartment. It is beautiful to behold. He shows me photographs in a slideshow of decorations they've used for small events. A lower level kitchen has ample space for food preparation, and there are plenty of restrooms. I am reminded of accessibility upon seeing the many levels, and Antonio shows me the location of elevators to facilitate access to all of the floors.

At one point as we are looking over the floorplans, Antonio sheepishly scratches the back of his head. "We've had parties of a hundred or so people here before, but never something on this scale. This would be a first. Are you sure TMC wants to take the risk on a venue like us?"

I nod firmly, not willing to back down. "Absolutely. Everyone starts somewhere, don't you think?"

He purses his lips in thought and turns back to the blueprints. "Do you know how we could do the seating? You might need to -"

"-Put people here, here, and here as well as in the main gallery, I think." I cut him off, tapping locations on the map. "If we immerse the art in the experience, instead of making one or two locations where 'viewing' is set up, it will make it feel more organic and cohesive, help keep the crowd flowing from piece to piece, and lower any costs for decorating since the art will then serve a double purpose." I take a slow breath. "I can really see it."

Antonio smiles. "I agree. You have a good eye for this. It will be truly beautiful."

I chew on my pen cap and then smile at him. "I'll have to speak to Mr. Mercier about this, but please - wait for my phone call! I know you're in a hurry and need to leave soon, so could you email me the lighting plans you have in place already, as well as what supplies are provided? I'll call you if I have any more questions, or if he wants to see the space."

Exchanging a firm handshake with Antonio, I exit Sanctuary and feeling proud of myself, I return to work.

****

I'm just entering the building when my cell phone rings. It's Marcus. I step off to the side, my breathing turning shallow, and answer the phone.

"Hello?"

"Camry, it's me."

"You called!"

He laughs gruffly from the other end. "I said I would, no? I'm one to keep my promises."

"I know. I'm really glad. Did you make a decision?"

"I did. I'm not sure how I feel about it, but I'll do it. For you."

I thought I had been so confident in his decision, but now that I heard the truth from his lips I let out a dramatic breath and I realize how unsure I had actually been.

"Oh Marcus, thank you, thank you, thank you!" I practically shout into the phone I'm so excited and I see heads turn in my direction. I tuck back into a small alcove even more. "I'm so, so happy. You won't regret it, I promise."

"I hope so. Listen, I have to go, but I wanted to tell you this morning and it's almost noon, so you've got your answer."

"Okay." I giggle at his literalism. "I'll be in touch with you to tell you all sorts of things, but I'd also like us to have dinner together soon, no work, just us, okay?"

"Sounds good, *querida*. I'll talk to you later."

He hangs up and I clutch my phone, puffing my chest up with a heaving breath. Then I race into the elevator and head for the top floor.

The second the elevator opens, I practically fly down the hall to Laurence's office. I burst through the door without knocking, and find him sitting in an armchair, eating a salad propped on his knee and reading a book. He startles as the door flies open and barely catches the bowl of greens before it tips. He looks up at me, takes one look at my face and frazzled excitement and sets down his food. "Yes?"

He's barely gotten out of his seat before I'm standing in front of him and I grab his hands in my excitement. "I found us a venue AND Marcus said yes!" I squeeze his hands and let them go, pacing around his office, rambling in excitement. "Marcus said he'd do it, so he's in and I feel so good about that, and I was out this morning and found the PERFECT place to host the gala. I'm so excited! It's the most beautiful place I've ever seen and I can picture the gala in my mind. It's like a switch went off and everything just clicked and I'm completely visualizing the whole thing!"

I spin to look at him and find Laurence with a hand in front of his mouth, eyes wrinkled and shoulders shaking. I straighten up indignantly. "Are you laughing at me?"

Caught, he lowers his hands and his bemused chuckles vibrate through the air. "I see you have found your enthusiasm. I suppose the extra sleep last night helped some?"

He cocks an eyebrow at me and I feel my cheeks flame with embarrassment. "Uhm... Maybe?" I frown at him and pout, my hands on my hips as I glare at him. "Anyway, that's not the point! Don't you see? I've DONE something and now we can move forward!"

"*Oui, oui, d'accord,* this is all very wonderful. Come, sit." He gestures to a nearby chair and I do as I'm told, while he walks over to the phone on his desk and presses a button on his intercom. "Miss Davis, please bring Miss Hughes' lunch to my office."

He hangs up and returns to his chair. Not a moment later, the door opens and the receptionist enters, carrying a tray of food. "Here you are," she says softly, setting it down on the tufted footrest before me. "Would you like anything else?"

My eyes scan the food in front of me. A lunch that makes my mouth water sits before me; a bowl of tomato basil soup, sliced turkey on rye, and a sparkling water, along with a small piece of chocolate cheesecake. "Oh, this looks amazing! No, thank you, I'm all set."

Once she exits the room, I quizzically look over at Laurence. "What's with the lunch?"

He doesn't meet my eyes, keeping his head down to his book, but he answers casually. "When you flew out of here earlier, it was about time for Miss Davis to collect the lunch orders. I simply ordered something for you in your absence, anticipating you'd be back eventually."

"That's so thoughtful of you. Thank you!" How is one man this perfect?

"If anything is not to your liking, you are free to - "

"No! It's perfect. This looks amazing."

He finally looks up, meeting my eyes, and smiles. "I am glad to hear that."

I stare at him for a few moments before his expression changes. "Are you going to eat?"

"Yes! Yes I am!" I quickly look away, embarrassed by my complete transparency. I pick up the sandwich and take a large bite. "Mmm!"

I make a happy sound as I chew with my eyes closed, head towards the ceiling and I hear a laugh from beside me. "You never cease to entertain."

I shoot him a sideways glare. "I can't help it. This is delicious!" I take a sip of the sparkling water and sigh. "This feels heavenly. I finally feel like I've done something right, and now here I am eating this lovely meal with you. Thank you so much for thinking ahead and ordering me lunch. I hadn't exactly considered that when I flew out of here earlier."

Laurence nods quietly. "No need to thank me. Seeing you enjoy it is thanks enough."

I look over at him and bite my lip. When he says things like that I can't help the burst of heat in my heart and it makes me nervous. This casual flirting that he does... does he realize he is doing it? Is he like this with everyone? Or am I special?

Realizing my thoughts are taking me down a spiral I certainly don't have time for right now, I turn back to my food, enjoying every last bite.

Once I have finished, Laurence turns to me. "So tell me about the venue you have found." He sets down his now empty bowl, and leans back into the chair, casually crossing one leg over the other.

"Have you ever heard of Sanctuary?"

His face falls pensive, thinking for a moment, before I see a glimmer of recognition in his eyes. "I do believe I have. It's that old converted church, isn't it?"

"Yes, it is. It's absolutely fantastic. I have a copy of blueprints if you want to look, but I spoke to the director and had a tour, and we were able in just a short amount of time to plan out the layout and flow. Laurence, it was stunning, and it really felt like it fit the theme we were going for. I know we said 'timeless' in the theme and I'm totally in love with the idea of pairing this almost ancient feel of the building with modern art. Don't you think that would be amazing? The combination of the two would marry them together and I could really see how beautiful the place would be in my mind."

Laurence's forehead creases for a moment, deep in thought, his fingers steepled before his lips. "If done well."

"Pardon?"

"The old and new would marry nicely in that space, if it is done well. Put together poorly and it would look tacky or dissected."

I chew on his words for a moment before agreeing. "You're correct. But I think I can do it."

He focuses on me directly and I want to squirm a bit under his intimidating stare, but I don't let myself. "You think you can?"

Squaring my shoulders, I sit up a little straighter. "No. I know I can."

He stares at me for a few minutes longer, then acquiesces to my request. "Alright, if you can do it, we'll move forward."

My head shoots up. "Really?!"

"I presume you have looked at budgets and space and are one hundred percent sure about this? I would hope you had no doubts before coming to me with your final proposal."

"I am totally confident." I nod firmly, staring at him with every ounce of determination and grit I can muster.

A beat passes and then a smile blooms on his face. "Well then. It looks like we have a venue."

"Thank you! I'll bring you everything in a few minutes. Is that alright?"

He rises too and collects his dishes. "Yes, that's alright."

I go to pick up my empty plates as well and he extends a hand, placing it gently on my forearm to stop me. "Do not worry about that. I can take care of it."

"Thank you!" I spin on my heel and dash out of the office, his laughter following me out the door.

Chapter 7

The next few weeks pass in a flurry of activity. I spend my days booking artists and vendors, making design and decor selections and every decision requires hours' worth of research. Some visits to artist studios take full days of work but no matter how busy he is, Laurence always comes to each and every one. I suppose he really listened when I made my first impassioned plea.

It's Friday afternoon and he's just left my office to take a phone call. I sit in my office chair, mindlessly thumbing through papers when I notice he left his mug on my desk. I gently pick it up, looking it over and I notice the place where his lips had been. My fingers brush over the imprint before I startle and shake my head, putting it back down on my desk. I groan a little to myself. I knew when I fell for him that it was a mistake but I suppose the heart does what the heart wants.

Nothing much has changed in the past few weeks between us. He still speaks formally, and while he continues to have his moments of teasing me, he maintains a distance that I feel like I cannot cross. It may be pointless to hope for something more than a professional relationship with him, but I can't help it. My dreams at night are filled with him; his eyes, his graceful hands, the relaxed and beautiful way he looks when he drives. I have stared at him so much I know every detail of his face. I know which words he always speaks in French, and I know how when he's nervous he rubs his chin, pushes his hands through his hair, or plays with his cufflinks.

I lay my head down on the desk and close my eyes. What am I even doing? I really need to put a stop to this. Falling for my boss, who is so obviously out of my league, is a disaster. In a few months, I'll go back to the Copy Department and our time together will exist of nothing more than randomly spotting him in the building or somehow ending up in the same elevator.

I stand up, taking a determined breath. *Put an end to this. Nothing good will come of it. It's affecting your work. Time to move on.* I shove the feelings I have for Laurence deep into my heart and lock the door, throwing away the key. That was fun, but it's time to face the music.

I look at the clock on the wall: 4:30pm. I wonder if I could go home early tonight. I'm so tired and I can't help but yawn, stumbling a bit as a wave of exhaustion overtakes me.

"Camry? Are you alright?"

I look up to see Laurence has returned, files in hand. "Oh! Yes, totally. I'm just tired. It's nothing."

He frowns but doesn't push the issue. "Alright. I have brought a few papers I would like you to look at. Please input them into the ongoing spreadsheet. These are florists we have received quotes from, and this," he hands me a flash drive, "contains their design submissions. All of this needs to go into the working document under a new tab."

"Yes, of course." I collect the papers and flash drive from him and set them down on my desk. I move over to the coffee maker and begin to brew another cup. As the coffee drips into the awaiting mug, I feel eyes on me and I turn to see Laurence looking at me, a mixture of concern and disapproval on his face. He rolls his lips to keep from speaking, and gradually he loosens his lips and smiles at me, pretending as if nothing is bothering him.

"What? You look like you want to say something."

He pushes his hands through his hair and huffs a bit. "How many cups of coffee is that today?"

I shoot him a severe look. "And how, pray tell, is that any of your business?"

His face crumbles and I let loose a loud laugh. The expression he wears closely resembles a puppy caught doing something they shouldn't have. It's so purely adorable that I can't help but smile at him, and he scratches his head in confusion.

"I'm not sure what you're laughing about, but I didn't do anything."

"You looked just like a scolded puppy there, for a minute, Laurence."

He coughs awkwardly, caught unawares by my comment. I walk back over to the desk and pick up the new items he brought me, leaning over to insert the flash drive into the computer. Just as I am about to do so the papers are taken from me, and warm fingers close around the hand holding the drive.

"Stop."

"What? Why?"

"Stop here for today. You can do this Monday. Go home, rest. You look exhausted." He sets the items down on my desk and picks up my sweater. I stare at him, hesitantly, and he repeats himself. "Go home, rest, have a good weekend, and I'll see you Monday."

I can barely blink, I'm so in shock. Mister Workaholic, telling me to go home early? I nervously glance around to make sure this isn't some sort of prank. "But I have so much more to do still!"

"Camry. I'm serious. Go home. Sleep."

I hesitate, but the exhaustion wins out. "Alright, I will. I still want to get as much done by next week as possible, though."

"Next week? Is there a deadline I missed?"

I blink at him stupidly. "No, but the week after that is the week of Thanksgiving."

"Oh, yes, of course..." he trails off and I am distinctly of the mind that there is nothing 'of course' about it.

I stare at him, and smirk. "You had no idea, did you?"

The tips of his ears begin to turn crimson and I can't help the laughter that bursts from my lips. As his embarrassment grows, so does my amusement and I can't help but laugh more and more. His look is abashed and he tugs at the hair on the back of his head. I am so lost in my laughter that I do what feels natural to me and I reach out and clutch at his arms, falling over him in laughter. Eventually he begins to chuckle as well and we laugh together for a moment, me with my fingers wrapped in his shirt and he with his arms around me. The laughter dies down and we stand there silently. Suddenly I realize the position we are in. His hold on me is firm and my heart takes off at a gallop, thundering in my ears so loudly that all other sounds cease to exist. I study his face, claiming every detail for my own. His cologne tickles my nostrils and I take a slow deep breath, savoring the warm notes. I swallow, gazing into his eyes before he suddenly clears his throat and relaxes his arms, moving away from me. Awkwardly, my hands clutch at my necklace and step back, dropping my eyes to the floor. "I'm sorry..." my voice comes out strained and awkward. Realizing I don't need to apologize for standing so close, it take me a minute to remember what I'm apologizing for. And then I remember - forgetting Thanksgiving. In an attempt to erase my embarrassment and the situation we have just found ourselves in, I square my shoulders and look up at him, training my expression into an insouciant smile. "I shouldn't have made fun of you like that. My apologies."

He sighs and shuffles his feet, looking perfectly childlike and adorable in that moment. "I suppose I deserve it. I get so lost in work that I..." he trails off, unwilling to finish his thought. He straightens up and I can quite literally watch the mask of professionalism settle on his face. "Enjoy the weekend. Rest well. You certainly need it, from the looks of the coffee you have there."

I can't contain a small chuckle, watching as he leaves my office. As the door closes behind him, I exhale with the remaining strength I have and then collapse into my chair. My mind is consumed with what just happened. The feel of his arms supporting me, his scent, the smooth lines on his face, and the wrinkles between his eyes from concentrating too much. Knowing I won't get any more work completed now, I gather my things and head for home.

****

My laptop sits open on my kitchen counter and I stand before it, leaning over the counter to scroll through my emails, while keeping one eye on my kettle, warming on the stove. Tonight is the perfect night for tea, and I decided I'm going to relax and work on my blog. Shakespeare is laying on the ground next to me, and I'm using one of my feet to absentmindedly rub the top of his head.

I open up my blog and find, nestled amongst the comments, a small note from a reader I haven't seen before.

"Go to @goldenfinchart on photo+. You won't regret it."

I check the blog and see no other comments from this reader, and the username yields no search results. Intrigued, I do as the comment instructs and as the first page loads, my interest is peaked... by page ten, I am totally hooked.

The variety this artist puts forth is astounding. Mixed metals, glass, acrylics, watercolor, charcoal sketch... I'm mesmerized by their work.

After another ten minutes of browsing and another five minutes of research on google, I'm staring at my phone, the number I've found ready to be dialed. I pour my tea, chewing my lip deep in thought. It's 8:30 on a Friday night, and I don't particularly want to leave a message, but my curiosity gets the better of me and I connect the call.

The line rings three times and a sunny voice picks up. "Hello!"

"Good evening. My name is Camry Hughes, and I'm interested in speaking with the artist who is known as Golden Finch Art about their work."

"Oh cool! That's me. What's up? What do you want to know?"

"Well, to begin with, let me say a few things. I'm an art blogger." I tell her about my blog, and she says she knows of it and calls it 'savage'. "I suppose the next thing I should ask is, what's your name?"

"I'm Lucy. Lucy Finch."

"Thank you, Lucy! If it is possible, I'd love to find a time to come and view some of your works in person. If you don't mind me viewing your pieces, do you think you can check your schedule for me and let me know when I could come visit your studio?"

I hear her click her tongue once. "That's fine, but unless you can wait a few weeks, it'll have to be tomorrow. I'm not available on weekdays and next weekend we're leaving for my family Thanksgiving trip."

"Oh! Okay, I can do tomorrow. Where are you located?"

"Hang on one sec."

The sound cuts out, leading me to believe she has muted the call. A moment or two later, she's back on the line. "You can meet me tomorrow at noon, if that works?"

"Yep! Just tell me where."

She gives me an address and I thank her before hanging up.

I type it into a map and see the building her apartment is in is a gorgeous four story walk-up in Sugar Hill. Curious about who this Lucy Finch is, I google her name, but nothing comes up.

Chewing on the end of my pen, I decide that I'll quickly finish my work on my blog for the evening, then relax with a book and my now well-steeped cup of tea.

****

The next morning I'm riding the train along to upper Manhattan. When the train pulls to my stop, I wrap my coat around me tightly. The fall weather is boomeranging around, winter's grey fingers claiming what hours they can as warm weather slowly slips away. Huddling up, I make my way a few blocks north until I see where I'm heading. Sure enough, the top floor apartment in the brownstone has 'Finch' written on the tag, and I push my finger into the buzzer.

A few seconds later a happy voice calls out. "Yes! Camry?"

"Yes, it's me."

"Great! I'll buzz you up."

The door unlocks and I climb the four flights of stairs before reaching the apartment. I knock on the door and it is wildly thrown open by a young girl of maybe thirteen, bouncing up and down like an excited Pomeranian.

"Hi! I'm Lucy!"

I blink a few times in surprise. Quickly gathering my manners I grin and extend a hand to her and she grabs it and yanks, dragging me into the house.

Her incessant chatter never ceases, telling me all about her father and mother, how she's an only child, and how art was the only thing that ever felt real to her within the pages of a storybook. I follow along, secretly trying to focus, while inwardly I'm dissecting my brain as to whether she told me her age last night when I called. I had missed this detail somewhere along the way.

"Come on, my room's this way!" She bounces down the hall and I suddenly feel very awkward.

I pause in the hall and she looks at me expectantly. "What's wrong?"

"Are your mom and dad here?"

"Oh totally." She turns and shouts at the top of her lungs, loud enough to make me shrink back. "MOOOOOM! DAAAD! That art lady is here!"

Promptly a door at the end of the hall opens and a confused looking woman sticks her head out. "Art lady?" She spots me and her eyes flash through concern, confusion, and then remembrance.

"Oh, yes! The art lady!" She ducks her head back inside the room and reappears a few seconds later, drying her hands on a towel. "Good afternoon. I'm Sarah, Lucy's mom."

"It's a pleasure to meet you. My name is Camry Hughes and I'm here to interview your daughter about her art for my blog."

"Welcome, welcome! What a great thing, huh, kiddo?" She smiles warmly and reaches out to pat her daughter's head.

"Anyway," Lucy ducks and steps aside, "I'm showing her my room."

Sarah cheerfully comes along with us, laughing at her daughter's skilled maneuvering.

When Lucy opens the door to her room, I am gobsmacked. If a normal teenage girls' room is messy, this room is downright catastrophic. A loft bed stands in one corner, and a dresser underneath, but that is all there is to hint at this being a bedroom. The rest of the space is filled to bursting with jars, jugs, boxes, bottles, and more canvasses than I think I have ever seen in my life.

Multiple easels stand around the room, half-finished canvases sitting on each, and piles of completed canvases are strewn around in corners wherever they fit. Lucy tiptoes over piles of paint tubes and boxes of brushes and begins flipping through canvases and pulling a few here and there out of the piles.

Wordlessly she props them up in front of me, setting them out so I can get a good look.

I step closer and bend down, shifting side to side to follow the light's pattern in the artwork. I study them carefully. Again, I'm struck by the sheer variety of style, size, and color.

"How did you craft this? What were you thinking as you made this one?" I point in particular to an abstract piece; dusty rose, grey, and soft creams layered in thick bands across the canvas. It has some shiny, sparkly coating, flexing and flowing in a third dimension, leaping off the canvas. It looks like crystal or glass, and it gives a touch of harsh deception on such a calming, gentle canvas.

Lucy frowns for a bit. "I've got depression, you know? My doctor told me. I guess it's true. I painted this one afternoon after school. My friends all see me as this cheery, bubbly type and everyone talks about how nice I am. Most of the time I don't mind, but sometimes I hate that. Sometimes I want to be mean or angry or crazy. But I can't, honestly. School sucks enough as it is, and I don't want to be branded as the one who went crazy. So I put on a smile and get through it, never letting anything negative show. When I painted this, I was imaging beautiful, soft, comforting colors, neatly laid out so there's nothing complicated about them. They're simple. They're easy. They don't threaten or make people think too hard. People like easy. So I painted them like this, but then I crushed glass and just before the paint was dry, I poured it over the painting and then shook off the excess. I collected whatever fell off and poured it over three or four times until most of it stuck. It's beautiful and calming, but it's also deceptive and dangerous."

I can't help but be impressed with her vision of the world. "Do you have a name for it?"

"Nope. Sorry. I don't name my stuff."

"No, it's fine. I love it, and I love the story behind it. It's exceptional and I can really see your message. It's beautiful."

Lucy nods, almost unconcerned with my thoughts.

The next few hours are spent with me looking at various pieces of her art, listening to many stories, and observing her as an artist and a person.

Before I leave, I sit down with Lucy and her mother over tea. I clear my throat, intent on broaching the subject that's been hovering in my mind for so long. "May I tell you something?"

Lucy shrugs, and her mother lifts her eyebrows, waiting for me to go on.

I shift in my chair somewhat awkwardly, but keep my posture professional and slowly begin to speak. "It's true that I'm the one who writes this art blog. And I'm really excited about the piece I'm going to be writing about your work!"

Sarah looks at me seriously, then slowly sits up a little straighter. "But?"

I look her in the eye, and then Lucy, before continuing. "I'm also an employee at Travers-Moreau, the big French marketing firm, and I'm working on this year's fundraising gala for the Metropolitan Hospital System. This year, the focus is on art as healing. I'm gathering artists to showcase work at the event and... I was wondering if you would like to be one of them."

I slowly let out my breath and study their faces. Sarah looks wide eyed, at me, then her daughter, then back to me. She speaks, her voice hesitant and disbelieving. "You wish to exhibit my daughter's works at your fundraising gala?"

"I do." The words are simple and to the point.

Lucy looks on for a brief minute then leaps up, chair legs scraping along the floor noisily in her exuberance.

"Hell yes! I want to do it!"

Sarah looks at me with a cautious smile. "Tell me what it entails, and if it's okay, she can participate."

I grin and pull a folder out of my bag, explaining the details and securing this artist that is so fascinating to me.

****

Leaving the Harlem brownstone apartment, I squint in the bright sunlight and tilt my head upwards, feeling the warmth on my face. My time with Lucy is still fresh in my mind, and I don't want to lose the photos, materials, and information I collected today. Deciding to head to the office to input the data and save the photographs there, I begin to walk towards the subway station. I check my watch and see that it's already almost 5pm... the sun will be going down soon and the already brisk temperature will get even colder. I shiver a bit at the thought of it, and quickly make my way for the station.

When I reach TMC tower, the lobby is quiet and I show my badge to the security guard working in the desk. He waves at me and I make my way to the elevator.

When I arrive on the top floor, I quickly make my way into my office. I deposit my papers on my desk and upload photos to my computer, before gathering my things to go home. As I leave my office in the dark hallway, I notice a light creeping out from underneath Laurence's door.

Puzzled, I make my way down the corridor until I reach the entrance to his office and then I lift my hand to softly knock on the polished wooden door.

I hear a muffled voice say "Come in," and I slowly open the door. Laurence sits at his desk, on the phone, rubbing his brow in frustration. He looks up and we make eye contact, his eyes widening in shock. Staring for a moment, he finally shakes his head out of his reverie, and tilts his head towards a nearby chair. I give him a small smile and quietly take my seat, gazing around the room to avoid staring at him.

He listens intently for a while, and then he begins to speak, rapid flowing French coursing through his thin lips. The conversation is quickly paced, I can tell, based on the tones coming through the receiver, and Laurence is getting more agitated as the conversation continues.

Finally at one point, he gets very loud and shouts a word even I know: *merde.*

There is a long pause and the voice on the other end begins again slowly, and I sneak a glance at Laurence, who looks completely and utterly defeated in that moment. I turn away slowly, and settle for staring at my hands.

Laurence answers the voice on the phone calmly now, and there are a few more minutes of quiet conversation before he finally places the phone down. I turn again to look at him, and he is sitting stock still at his desk, staring at a note in front of him. After an uncomfortable amount of time, I gently call his name. "Laurence?"

He looks up at me and sighs, tugging his hands through his hair. "I apologize for that. I was so consumed by the conversation that I began to forget you were here."

"Are you alright?" I venture unsurely.

"Yes, I was just... dealing with something." He looks around and it's as if my presence finally fully clicks in his mind. "What on earth are you doing here?"

I raise an eyebrow at him, hoping a little light teasing will pull him from his melancholy. "I could ask you the same thing. Really, Laurence? Office hours at 6pm on a Saturday?"

He at least has the decency to look somewhat chagrined before he hangs his head and mumbles something I can't quite make out.

"What was that?"

He lifts his head and stares at me for a second. "Nothing of consequence. Have a seat. Would you care for a drink?"

I blink, caught off guard by both his complete avoidance of the question, and the abrupt change of subject. Quickly I clamp my jaw shut and agree. "Okay, thanks."

He walks over to a small shelf set into his wall of cabinets and collects a few glasses. He lifts a decanter and pours a fragrant amber liquid into each glass, the wave of bourbon curling up the walls of the glass. He hands one to me and stands, staring out the window, gazing at nothing.

I sit on the sofa, staring at his back, speaking nothing. Taking small sips of my drink, I can feel its heat fill my stomach and warm my body from the inside out. Eventually, Laurence speaks.

"I was trying to get ahead."

I purse my lips, trying to figure him out. Before I can ask what he means, he continues.

"You said Thanksgiving was next week, but I had forgotten. I'm here today trying to get ahead on my work so I can take some time off for the holiday."

I take a moment to soak in his words. "Oh, alright. Do you have anything in particular planned for your trip?"

"No, nothing. I thought that perhaps it would be wise to force myself to relax once in a while."

I snort in laughter and his eyes dart to me, accusing and bearing a small amount of hurt. I bite my lip and apologize, trying to rein in my smile. "I'm sorry, I shouldn't have laughed. You're here being all sweet and sincere, sharing this with me, and I'm mocking you. It's really terrible of me. I'm sorry." I meet his eyes, trying to convey my feelings of sympathy and understanding. "Forgive me?"

He stares into my eyes for a while before nodding, the hint of a smile appearing at the corners of his mouth.

"Yes, of course."

I grin widely. "Okay! So what are you working on?" I rise from my seat and walk around to the side of the desk to look at his papers. He quickly steps in front of me, sliding into the small space between me and the desk. I'm so close to him that the fingers around my glass of bourbon are brushing up against his chest.

"Nothing important. It's the weekend, and I don't intend to make you work." He stops suddenly, remembering. "You never did tell me why you were here."

"Oh! I secured the most amazing artist today!" I quickly tell him all about my odd discovery of Lucy and her art, as well as my visit. He listens intently, watching me as I enthusiastically share of my day.

When my tale winds down, Laurence is staring at me with a carefree grin, thoroughly enjoying my passion and happiness. He gently pokes my bourbon glass with an extended finger, laughing softly. "You could teach me many things about passion for your work, and for life as well."

I grin happily for a second. "You should try it for a time. Life's better when you *live* it, not go through the motions."

He twists his lips in thought and I realize he's seriously considering my words. I lay a hand on his arm and peer into his eyes. "Oh, don't be like that. You certainly live, don't you? Look at how comfortable you are when you drive your car, and how much you enjoy fine food and wine. You love music and art and you're capable at your career. You aren't living a half-life, you're just not pursuing what really makes you happy. You have all the passion and excitement, you just need to use it."

He stares at me for a few moments, and I feel like I'm suffocating under his stare. Cursing myself, I quickly backpedal on my words. "Oh, I'm sorry, I've put my foot in my mouth again, haven't I?" I turn my back to him in shame and walk slowly towards the window. "I always do this; say too much imagining I know everything."

"You're... you're not wrong." A soft voice curls over my shoulder, making me look curiously at him, hope sparking in my heart.

My eyes meet his momentarily. He continues, slowly.

"Do not worry. I'm not angry with you."

"You're not?" My voice betrays more emotion than I realize; I'm oddly tense and nervous.

"I'm not. I think that with you I feel vulnerable, more than anything. Somewhat exposed, perhaps."

I can't help but search his face but what I see there is no ruse. There is a mixture of embarrassment and uncertainty but no anger or malice.

"It has been both a pleasure and a never-ending roller coaster with you these past weeks. And for that I am grateful."

I'm struck by his sincerity, and I feel my heart swell. I respond in kind. "And I am grateful to be here. I'm learning and growing so much, both in art and in my working life. And..." Suddenly aware of what I was going to say, I clamp my lips tightly, unwilling to go on.

"Yes?" Laurence's eyes seem sincere and welcoming, and he invites me to continue.

"Well, I'm glad I got to meet you too. You've taught me a lot and I really enjoy your company."

"I am glad to hear that." Laurence shuffles his feet slightly. He looks almost nervous, and my curiosity is peaked. "Though, I'm afraid I owe you an apology."

I frown, wrinkling my forehead in confusion. "I don't understand. You've never done anything to apologize for."

Laurence's hand aggressively pushes through his hair, and a cold sweat forms on the back of my neck. His nervousness is infectious, and I find my own anxiety growing. He straightens his back and hesitantly begins to speak.

"When I first was looking for someone to hire, Jameson approached me, saying he had the perfect candidate. He showed me your blog and I was, in fact, impressed. The work you had done at the company to that point was solid, and as eccentric as Jones might be, he's got a keen eye for talent."

I peer at him cautiously, waiting for the 'but' that feels ready to follow.

"That being said, I didn't see anything truly remarkable that made me want to hire you. I was ready to hire another person from a different department when Jameson came into my office. He pleaded your case with passion. He promised me I wouldn't regret hiring you, that you were the one who would make this the best gala yet. And I honestly couldn't imagine that he was right but the determination with which he spoke left an impact on me, so I went ahead and appointed you."

My heart sinks at his words and I lower my gaze, feeling all too uncomfortable. I don't think I could feel any smaller than I do in this moment. My fingers tighten around my glass as I attempt to contain the anguish I feel at this sudden bombshell.

Of course. I knew it all along, somewhere in the back of my mind. Why would I have ever really been a serious candidate?

Out of the corner of my eye I see Laurence reach his hand toward me, but then he quickly retracts it and drops it again to his side. "I do not say all this to make you doubt yourself. You may not have stood out as an exemplary employee, but you have always been consistent, reliable, and you produce solid work. You should feel proud of that."

I can feel his eyes search me but I can't bring myself to look up at him.

A heavy sigh tumbles from his lips. "I am terrible at this. I'm trying to say that even though I was hesitant, you have fully proven yourself and I am very glad that I listened to Jameson's advice."

I slowly raise my head. "What?"

"My first impression of you was downright comical. You were like a bewildered little puppy and your clumsiness is record breaking. But Camry, you are gifted. You speak with such passion and understanding. You don't appear to be afraid of much. Or at least, you aren't afraid of me." He takes a deep breath and swallows down a large sip of bourbon. "Not many people would have told me 'no' so quickly. You wanted something and I tried to take a shortcut and you stood your ground and said no... and not only that, you backed it up and you changed my mind. Not many are capable of that. That meant something."

Stunned at the complete turnaround, I blink a few times. But I realize what he is saying is all too true. Slowly I begin to speak. "To be honest, you're right. I've always been accident prone but those first few days were particularly so. I know I didn't make the greatest first impression. I'm sorry if I made you doubt me."

"No need to say that. It is I who must apologize to you. I should not have let such insignificant issues affect my opinion of you."

He exhales deeply, then walks away a few steps.

"That phone call just now... it was my uncle."

"Your uncle?"

He nods. The hand not holding his drink flexes, opening and closing into a fist. Another long draw of bourbon and he lowers his eyes.

"I am thirty-three years old. I am the youngest branch manager that Travers-Moreau has ever had by almost fifteen years. And... my uncle is Jacques Moreau." My eyes widen, connecting the dots as he tells me of his relation to the CEO. He offers a self-deprecating smile, continuing with his story. "My father was French, my mother American. While I lived much of my childhood in Paris, I came to America at the age of fourteen when my father died and my mother returned to the United States. I started working for my uncle ten years ago, fresh out of Columbia's College of Business, returning to Paris and taking an unimportant entry level job within the company. But I heard all the whispers. I was just some foolish child, hired only because of my uncle's influence. I was young and stupid and had a lot of pride and I hated that. So I worked. I worked four times as hard as any other young and stupid man in that company. I worked so hard I made myself sick. But I got things done. I had results. I practically flew up the corporate ladder, I was so good at what I did, and after only seven years I had gained the promotion to head up the New York branch and I returned here to this city."

I listen intently. I'm not sure if it's the alcohol that's encouraging him to open up, but I don't dare make a sound.

"I had thought that earning such a promotion would have finally shut down the rumors and the accusations of nepotism, but it's never stopped. My uncle hears all the rumors and his only response is work harder, be stronger. He gives no leniency nor room for error. If I want to rise above all of this, I can't stop. I haven't yet and I don't know that I ever will. If I fail, everything they say will be true. Or at least, I know it will look like that."

He slowly lifts his head and meets my gaze. "You're the first person I've met in ten years who has taught me something about work and about myself. And I think that now, I am somewhat less afraid."

He averts his eyes nervously and begins to pace around the room. "You're one of the most observant people I've ever met. Your understanding of art is beyond me and part of that is because you don't just see what's in front of your eyes, but you see beneath and throughout. It's almost like you can feel everything buried underneath the surface, whether it's a canvas, a sculpture, or a person."

Suddenly he looks around and I feel like the magic is broken. He sighs and his feet still, stopping next to me at the window. Then he begins to laugh softly. "*Mon Dieu.* What am I even saying?" The words fall in a whisper and he slides his hands along his face.

Slowly I reach my hand over to him and rest it on his arm. "Thank you. For telling me all of that."

He raises his eyes and looks up at the ceiling. "You weren't wrong."

"About what?"

"What you said, in the car. What did you say I was? A closet romantic with a poetic side?"

"Oh please don't repeat that." It's my turn to feel embarrassed and I lower my eyes. "I never should have said that to you. I can't believe I was that presumptuous. I've spoken to you so many times as if I truly know you and... I'm sorry."

I begin to pull back but he suddenly grabs my hand. He stares at our connected hands while my eyes are fixated on his face. The dull warm lighting from his desk lamp dances along his smooth skin, playing in his eyelashes. When he speaks again, his voice is raw and hoarse.

"I... don't think I would mind that."

"Mind what?"

"You knowing me."

I stare at him a while, and he slowly pulls his hand away. "Maybe that's why I told you all that. About me. Maybe I wouldn't mind you knowing me."

I suck in a breath at his words, searching his face. My heart is racing. Emboldened by this new development, my fingers reach for his face and gently I touch the side of his cheek. "Laurence?"

Laurence meets my gaze and we sit there, eyes locked for a few brief moments. I can feel his breath on my skin. His irises seem almost liquid, a stormy gray like the sky above the ocean before a squall. His voice cuts through the quiet, a low rumble echoing through the space between us.

"May I... would you mind if I kissed you?"

Words fail me in that moment. I barely manage the smallest of nods. Seconds pass like molasses, as if both of us are afraid to cross the line between. I don't know how long we hover here, the inches between our lips taking eons to cross.

Then all at once I feel the warmth of his lips on mine. Barely brushing together, it's full of hesitation and uncertainty and it ends almost as fast as it has begun. A small noise of longing curls in the back of my throat as I feel the distance grow between us.

He pulls back and looks at me, a thousand emotions in his eyes. Confusion, hope, fear, passion, bewilderment; his eyes betray so much and as we stare at each other, I can see them cloud over and he begins to move away. He clears his throat and opens his mouth to speak. Sensing an apology, which honestly, I could not bear to hear, I grab his face with my hands and pull him forcefully in for another kiss.

He momentarily seizes up in surprise but that quickly fades, and our lips melt together in warm, fervent kisses, over and over again. My fingers curl into his hair and I tug him even closer. Laurence's lips feel hot and full as they move against mine and I feel his tongue slip inside my mouth. A small moan escapes from me and I return this embrace.

I feel his fingers tentatively search my face, and after a minute, slowly we separate, gazing into each other's eyes. I can't keep silent, but it seems my words have failed me. "Um..."

Laurence lowers his head and sucks in a deep breath. "Camry..."

I gently press a finger to his lips. "Don't. It's okay. I said yes. I wanted this."

Laurence twirls his fingers around mine and I close my eyes, feeling their warmth. His voice floats to my ears, soft and purring with emotion. "I wanted to do something nice for you."

"What do you mean?"

"You've been working so hard and blowing away my expectations, and I've..." he awkwardly clears his throat, "...cared for you for some time now. I hoped that if this happened, it would have been somewhere a little more romantic. My office isn't exactly the place to be."

I can't help but giggle a little. "So I *was* right. You are a closet romantic."

He laughs softly and pulls me close to him. "I don't think there's much closeted about it now."

I relax into his touch, inhaling the dark aroma of his cologne. I sigh a little, content. "You're warm."

His hand glides over my hair, smoothing it out. My mind wanders through what Laurence confided in me about his family, and I begin to imagine a young Laurence, fiercely determined and working to the bone. "You know... I think you're amazing to be here, and I don't think you got your job just because of your uncle."

His hand pauses briefly, reflecting his momentary surprise. I blurt out more words before he can say anything else. "I've seen the way you work. When I got here, you had everything figured out, down to which files I'd need to look at. You're considerate of other people in a refreshing way, going out of your way to anticipate what someone will need. You took the time to teach me that ridiculous coffee machine."

His feather-light laugh brushes past my ear, prompting a small shiver but I continue, gently squeezing him in my arms. "I see how hard you work. I know how late you stay; your office light is always on when I'm leaving. You're not here because of someone else." I turn to meet his eyes. "But I also think you do as well as you do because you're simply good at it. You have a talent for leadership, and your aura attracts people. You don't need to prove anything to me, alright?"

He swallows and I can see emotion building in his eyes. "I'm so glad you hired me for this. When I first saw you in Jones' office and he told me what was going on, I was terrified. Of the work, of you... but I couldn't help but eventually see you as this beautiful, wonderful person. I'm really glad we are working together."

He runs his hands up and down my arms. "I'm glad we work together too."

I smile and then suddenly stiffen, as realization dawns on me. "Wait. Oh my god. We work together! We work together and we just kissed and I really like you, and are we even allowed to date? I mean, you're my boss! What do we do?"

A second thought hits me and I lean away a little, suddenly aware. "I mean, that is... Do you want to? Date me, I mean?" I avert my eyes, painfully aware that I may have been reading way too much into things. His words and kisses may have been sweet, but I am suddenly insecure as to whether it was just what he wanted in the moment, or if he actually feels something for me.

Laurence gently places a finger under my chin, pushing it up until our eyes meet again. He looks at me with calm, clear eyes. "To answer your questions... we are allowed to date. You don't need to hide anything. HR policy states that employees may be in relationships as long as professionalism at the office is not affected, and if it is, it's dealt with on a case by case basis. Secondly, I am your direct supervisor, but I like to think I am a decent man. I won't be using anything to gain favor with you, or force you into any work, and if you want to do well, you will have to earn it. I will not promote or encourage anyone unless they deserve it."

I nod slowly, and he continues, tracing a finger gently around my lips. "And thirdly... I don't kiss people without good reason. I thought you were beautiful from the start, but I had no idea who you were as a person. It did not take me long to realize how special you are. I want to see what things are like between us, and where things might go." He pauses and purses his lips, offering me a chagrined smile. "I'm not good at being with people, but I am willing to try. Have I answered your questions?"

I offer him an exaggerated frown and for a moment he looks taken aback, but when I mutter, "How are you so goddamned perfect?" his face relaxes into a laugh and he sheepishly strokes his hand over his chin.

"I am not perfect, in any way, and I'm not sure it's a good thing that you think so highly of me, but... I am glad you think positively of me, in any case."

"You're cute," I say to him, tapping his forehead with my finger. I can practically see the blush rise in his cheeks and I press a kiss to the rosy glow.

I tug his hand and lead him over to the sofa where we sit side by side in companionable silence, enjoying each other's warmth, fingers gently toying together, stroking each other's hair. I'm over the moon, smiling happily to myself as I think of this change, how I feel cherished by this man who so quickly stole my attention and my thoughts. I make a mental promise to myself to never let the details go; I want to learn more about him, and I want to make him proud.

"This really has been a great day. I learned so much, about work, and about you. Thank you."

He smiles down at me, and kisses me gently. "I feel the same. Thank you for sharing with me about your day. I'm glad you found a wonderful and unique artist for the gala, as well."

"I wish you could see what her art looks like in person. I suppose you'll just have to wait until February."

Not wanting to forget any details, I slowly slip out my phone and bring up all my notes and images from the day. I look over them, nestled in Laurence's arms, feeling like all is right in the world for just a few minutes. I feel his breath against my hair before I hear him speak. "Keep that up and I might think you're more of a workaholic than I am."

I laugh, squirming as he pokes my side. "I want to do a good job for me, but also for you and for everyone that will be helped by this gala. I think we could do good things here, not only for the hospital and its patients but for the community as well. I really want to make this great, so I don't want to forget anything."

After a few seconds of silence, I hear a small noise of frustration. I pull back and look up at Laurence's face, noticing an odd expression; half pleasure, half pain. He looks at me with worry and happiness, and mutters softly, "I'm done for, aren't I?"

I purse my lips in confusion. "What do you mean?"

He gathers me back into an embrace and softly kisses my hair. "Nothing, *ma chère*. Nothing at all."

The rest of the evening passes in comfort and happiness, and I spend the night feeling as if I am on cloud nine. Soft kisses, creative discussions, and all the while the warm touch of the man behind me.

Chapter 8

I convince Laurence to order in some of my favorite
Chinese takeout for dinner and we spend a few hours
picking out areas in Sanctuary to showcase
artists. After my fifth yawn, Laurence stands and
holds out his hand to me. "Alright, time to go home.
I'll drive you."

He helps me to my feet and glances at the clock on the
wall. "It's after nine. I'm sorry for keeping you this
late."

"Please don't apologize. I'm not sorry you did." I
perch up on my tiptoes and plant a kiss on his
cheek. He smiles and picks up my coat and bag and
handing them to me, we leave the office together.

****

When Laurence's car pulls up in front of my
apartment, he is nothing but the kind gentleman I
know he can be. He runs his hand through my hair
and says goodnight softly. "Enjoy the rest of your
night."

"Thank you. I have to take Shakespeare for a walk,
but after that I'm going to relax. It's been a long day.
Good - *really good* - but long."

I smile at him but Laurence frowns. "Would you mind
if I joined you for your walk?"

My mouth falls open and I stutter for a moment. "I suppose..."

"I don't mean to imply anything, but it's awfully late and I'd feel better if I came along."

I think for a second then purse my lips. "I'm not a child, and I'm not a damsel in distress either."

"I know, I know. I don't doubt you. But it would make me feel better knowing you were going to sleep safely tonight."

I nod slowly. "Alright, but don't make a habit out of this. I've been an independent woman for a long time."

His expression falters and he sends me an apologetic look. "I'm sorry. I'm honestly not good at this. I don't really know how to act or what to do. I don't want to coddle you or smother you, and I know that you can take care of yourself. But I also want to be dependable and I want you to come to me when you need someone for anything. I want to support you."

Melting a little inside at his embarrassed confession, I gently poke his forehead, grinning at him. "That's alright. I'll tell you when you are being an idiot." He offers a weak smile. "Go park. I'll get Shakespeare and we'll be down in a minute."

He agrees and I slip out of the car.

I change my clothes into some cold weather walking gear, unashamedly picking out the pair of leggings that my butt looks best in, laughing to myself. Shakespeare is a bundle of boundless energy and I apologize to him. "I'm sorry I was gone so long, buddy. I know we got a good run in this morning, but I bet you're itching for some exercise!"

After gearing up, we head downstairs, Shakespeare already straining in his harness.

When we emerge from the foyer onto the street, Shakespeare makes a beeline for Laurence, dragging me along with him. Laurence kneels down and laughing, ruffles Shakespeare's neck and strokes his fur. "Well, it's lovely to see you too."

He stands, and after an appraising look in my direction, offers me his arm. "Ready?"

I grin and accept it, comfortably sliding in next to him. We walk quickly along the streets, pausing for brief stops for Shakespeare to enjoy himself. The air is quiet and cool, and neither Laurence nor I speak. The silence between us is comfortable and easy, and after a few blocks, I snuggle a little closer, settling my head against his shoulder for a moment.

The arm I'm holding slips from my grasp and curls around my waist, pulling me closer. I tilt my face up to look at him and he steals a quick kiss. "Don't want you getting cold."

I giggle and wrap my arm around him too and we continue our walk in happiness. Shakespeare runs back every now and then to lick our fingers or prance before us, happy and feeling content in the brisk air.

"He loves this." I admire my animal as he thoroughly enjoys his time frolicking along, skipping down the sidewalk in pure bliss.

"He does. I'm rather enjoying myself as well."

"Even though I'm being quiet? We can talk, if you'd like."

He chews on his lips for a moment. "No, I am quite content. I don't need the air filled with any distractions or noise, and even though I love to hear your voice, I am happy to simply share the silence with you."

I'm so touched that I can't think of any response, and a dull heat spreads through me. I gently squeeze him closer, kissing his shoulder through his thick wool coat.

Eventually we arrive back in front of my building and make our way into the alley to Laurence's car. He leans back against the door, pulling me close to his chest. "Thank you for indulging me," Laurence whispers into my hair. Shakespeare, in the age-old wisdom of animals, settles down at our feet with a soft contented whine. We stare into each other's eyes for seemingly endless moments, until the web of the universe tightens its strings and we are drawn together, a delicate kiss exchanged between us.

The pounding of my heart competes with Laurence's soft breathing and the dull sounds of the city at night. My teeth curl over my bottom lip, tugging it backwards as I try to control the wild emotions rolling through my mind. Laurence's hands cup my cheeks, gently stroking my face with his thumbs and I close my eyes, savoring his touch.

Suddenly he pulls my face forward, his lips capturing mine in a feverish kiss. I return it in kind, sucking on his lower lip and pressing my hands against his chest. I let my fingers roam, feeling out the lithe body beneath. Tongues intertwining, my breathing becomes ragged and I clutch at him, desire burning through me in a rush of heat.

Laurence pulls away and a whimper of disappointment slips from my lips. He chuckles and gently tucks my hair out of my eyes. "It's..." he takes a breath and pauses. "It's probably time for me to say goodnight."

I don't want to be clingy, so I reluctantly plaster on a smile. "Okay. Be safe going home."

"I will." We stand there for a second longer, neither of us moving. The absurdity of this as we stare at each other for a moment longer suddenly makes us both burst out laughing.

"God, I feel like you're my middle school crush."

He grins at me, ruffling my hair. "I know what you mean."

Finally he huffs out a breath and drops his hands to his side, pushing up off the car. "Have a good day tomorrow. I'll see you Monday. Goodnight."

I step back and Shakespeare stands up, pushing his nose between Laurence's fingers. Laurence scratches my dog's ears and then slips into his car.

"Come on, boy." I tug on the leash and we head inside to a night of sleep filled with happy dreams.

****

The next morning, sunlight streams in through my windows in gentle rays, catching dust motes like sparkling fairy wings in the air. Squinting my eyes, I groan and roll around, covering my face. My body feels heavy and knowing it is Sunday, I make no moves to rise from my nest of pillows and blankets. I shift in bed, only to find Shakespeare's warm body lying on his back, legs in the air, puffing breath and softly whining in his sleep. I snort out a laugh, clumsily reaching over to ruffle his belly when suddenly a vicious wave of nausea hits me. Reeling backwards I all but fall from my bed and scramble to the bathroom, reaching the sink at the last moment.

"Oh God." I wipe the back of my hand across my face then turn my lips under the faucet and hungrily gulp down water. I shakily stand up, feeling like my knees are weak and unable to support me. I slowly move back into bed and pull the covers over my head. What is going on? I take a mental checklist of my body, trying to come to a sensible conclusion. I don't feel ill in general and I don't have fever or chills but my body feels like lead and my head is pounding. Deciding that I simply need more sleep, I close my eyes and let my exhaustion carry me under again.

****

My cheek tingles and I reach up to scratch it, half awake, but instead my fingers make contact with my phone, buzzing away as it vibrates with an incoming call. Struggling to pull myself awake, I bring the phone to my ear, answering the call.

"Hello?" My voice is almost nonexistent and my throat is scratchy and raw.

"Camry?" The voice on the other end is hesitant and unsure. My brain slowly comes to life and I put the pieces together.

"Laurence?"

"Are you alright? I tried to call you today but you haven't answered your phone all day."

"I... think I'm sick."

"I'll come over. I'll be right there." He hangs up before I can protest, but exhaustion quickly pulls me back under, my phone falling limply to my side once again.

The sound of someone knocking on my door wakes me from a deep sleep. Shakespeare leaps out of bed and bounds for the living room, whining. I slowly blink open my eyes and notice the golden light of the day's gloaming. I stumble out of bed and make my way over to the door, peering through the peephole.

Outside of my door I see Laurence, wearing a look of concern. I can hear his voice softly calling my name as he knocks on the door again. Weakly I reach up and disengage the locks and open the door.

Laurence steps in, eyes darting around the room before settling upon me directly in front of him. A great sigh tumbles from his lips and he pulls me into his chest. His momentary relief melts into worry and he pulls back to gaze at me. He carefully looks me over, running his hands around my face and arms. He peers into my face, concern written on his features. "Come with me."

I can only mutter a small whimper as he guides me over to the couch. As we walk along I wrinkle my nose. "Ugh. What is that smell?" My voice is raspy and hoarse from hours without speaking and as Laurence leads me to sit, I lay my head down on the cushions. Shakespeare rests his head in my lap, whining softly.

Laurence brushes his fingers along my face then stands and looks at me. He speaks in a voice both gentle and concerned. "Camry... what happened to you? I tried to reach you a number of times, and now that I'm here, it looks like you haven't taken Shakespeare out all day. He's had a few accidents in the kitchen."

"Oh..." I close my eyes softly, stroking Shakespeare's head. "I'm sorry. I woke up this morning and I threw up. I felt so weak and tired, I just climbed back into bed." I close my eyes and rest my head.

Laurence makes a frustrated sound and steps away. I hear noises in the kitchen, and smell the stringent scent of cleanser. "What are you doing?"

"Cleaning up a bit. Don't concern yourself. Just rest."

"No, please. I can do that."

"Don't be silly. Rest." Still feeling disoriented, my objections die in my throat, and I settle back into the couch cushions.

Not long after, Laurence steps closer and kneels, giving me a large glass of water, placing a hand upon my head. "Do you have a thermometer?"

I lift my hand and point towards my bathroom. "In my medicine cabinet." He leaves me and I slowly lift myself to a sitting position. He returns quickly and after reading my temperature, exhales a relieved breath. "You don't have a fever." He rubs his jaw, clearly uncertain. I lift my head and attempt a smile.

"It's alright... I'll be okay." I reach out and squeeze his hand. "I'm sorry I worried you. I must not have heard my phone."

He bends down and kisses my hand. "I'm glad you're alright." His gaze sweeps over my face, concern evident in his features.

"Have you eaten today?"

I shake my head side to side.

"Give me a moment, then." He rises and moves towards the kitchen.

I turn and watch him over the sofa, as he peers through my refrigerator and cabinets. "What are you doing?"

"Feeding you." He pulls out some items and lays them down. I watch as he chops fruits and vegetables, tossing them into a large pot. Apples, winter squash, onion, and broth. Soon a delicious aroma fills the air and my stomach rumbles loudly, enough so that Laurence lifts his eyes to look at me, a humored smile playing upon his lips. "Not much longer."

He takes some bread out and before long he sets a steaming bowl of soup in front of me. "Here you are."

I lift the spoon carefully, blowing softly on it before taking a sip. The food warms me and it isn't long before the bowl is empty. I sit, drinking water and nibbling on bread, and eventually Laurence speaks.

"How do you feel?"

"Much better. Thank you." I frown a bit. "I'm honestly not sure what happened to me earlier. It was like all the energy had been sucked from my body."

"And the nausea?" Laurence calmly looks at me.

"I don't know. I feel much better now, regardless. Oh, and I know I'm not pregnant." I make the joke, but in the back of my mind my thoughts drift to the noticeable lack of a period in my life.

Upon hearing the word *pregnant*, Laurence chokes a bit on his tea, eyes wide on me. A quiet laugh tumbles from my lips. "You're too easy," I tease him, slumping back in my seat. "I feel better now. Thank you again for the soup. It really helped."

He dabs at his lips with a napkin, the picture of elegance. As I look him over I become aware that Laurence is not in a suit but rather a pair of light chinos and a navy sweater. I don't think I've ever seen him in anything other than a three piece and I blink, staring at him.

"What?" Laurence looks at me in confusion.

"I don't think I've ever seen you in casual clothes before. They suit you." I smile at him and he appears embarrassed.

He clears his throat and stands, avoiding my eyes and taking my empty dishes. "I'll clean up." Before he can get a step away, I reach out and grab onto his sleeve.

Looking up into his eyes, I give him a pleading look. "Sit with me awhile?"

He stares at me for a moment before setting down the dishes and moving into the spot next to me on the sofa. He shifts to put an arm around my shoulders and I lean into him, resting my head against his chest. A contented sigh escapes my lips and I snuggle a little closer.

His fingers gently comb through my hair and we sit in silence for a while. Shakespeare rolls on the floor, gnawing on a toy and I laugh at him a bit.

Laurence's voice echoes in his chest beneath my ear, deep and reassuring. "Are you sure you're alright?"

I tilt my head and kiss his cheek. "Yes, I'm feeling better, thanks to you. I'm really grateful you came. I don't know what happened. I can't believe I slept all day."

There is a long period of silence before I hear him speak up again, his tone full of frustration. "I'm afraid this is my fault."

I sit up a bit, peering into his face. "Your fault? How could it be your fault?"

"I... believe it was exhaustion. You were also dehydrated. You've been working too hard and it's because of me. You're getting swept away by my terrible habits, and you're under a lot of pressure, so I-"

I cut him off by placing a finger firmly to his lips. His body stiffens and I give him a serious look.

"Don't you dare."

He stares at me, sorrowful eyes focused on my face and I continue before he can object. "This is not on you. Even if I got sick from working too hard, you've never required me to stay late and you've never forced me to work too hard. And if you think I'm trying to emulate you, you are giving yourself way too much credit." My glare sharpens, and I try to force all my emotions into my eyes. "Don't go blaming yourself. Something happened, I'm fine now, and you're amazing for coming over here and cleaning up and cooking for me."

His eyes slowly soften as my words sink in. I decide to add one last point. "*And,*" I emphasize the word, "you are such a caring boyfriend that you were worried about me and came all the way here to make sure I was alright. So, don't guilt trip yourself, okay?"

Pressing on the finger I have against his lips, I push his head up and down in a forced nod. This finally earns a smile from him and I relax, smiling in return, releasing my finger.

"Good." I lean in and give him a light peck on the lips. Then I rest against him again, reveling in his closeness. "I still can't believe it."

"Believe what?"

"Believe that you're here with me. And not just as my boss, but as you and me, together."

He gently kisses the top of my head. "I can."

"Can what?"

"Believe it."

"Oh."

He slowly traces a finger over my face, his delicate touch soothing. "You are a wonderful woman, Camry.

You are intelligent, hardworking, capable, and true to yourself. I am honored and humbled that you would care for me."

I blush a little at his words. Trying my best to sound nonchalant, I admit the truth to him. "I had a crush on you for a long time." I bury my face a bit into his chest, trying to hide my embarrassment.

"Oh did you, now?" I can hear the humor in his voice. "And just when was it that you fell for my dashing personality and debonair good looks?"

I giggle and lightly punch his chest.

He plays along, clutching at the point of contact. "You wound me, madam. Are you trying to avoid answering the question by way of violence?"

Another punch, a louder giggle. "No. You're just being absolutely adorable." I shrug my shoulders a bit, thinking it over.

"I think... it was the night after we went to see Marcus. You were amazing that day. You went with me to an unknown place to see an unknown artist, you patiently explained everything to me as I was learning, and you were so kind to go out of your way to help me with my painting."

I hear Laurence suck in a deep breath. I poke him a bit, laughing. "What, are you that touched?"

"No, you just have surprisingly low standards."

I sit back, affronted. "What?"

"What will I do when the next person who comes along is nice to you? Are you going to fall for them instead?"

My mouth falls open in silence and I try to come up with words: any words, to assure him that it's not so simple, that he touched my heart, that it was his thousand thoughtful gestures and the way he looked at me and how he opened up to me; that those were all why I fell for him. But I'm too shocked and startled at his words that I just sit there, gaping like a fish.

Suddenly he bursts out laughing and I realize I've been had. I try to get up in frustration but he grabs my waist and pulls me down again, firmly planting me next to him. "Don't go. I'm sorry. It was too perfect."

He laughs through his apology and I pout at him, the annoyance I feel mixing with laughter at the joke. I can't really stay mad at him, but I don't want him knowing that!

He tugs me into his arms, the laughter slowly - very slowly - dying down and I grumpily stare up at him. "You're terrible."

"Perhaps. But you are such a delight to tease. That, my dear, is one of the first things I discovered that I liked about you."

I make an unhappy noise but relax all the same, resting my arms on his shoulders. "You're lucky you're cute."

Now it's Laurence's turn to look offended. "Cute? A man of my age, status, and familial heritage is not cute."

I snort. "First of all, you're only, what? Five or six years older than me? Secondly, as your employee, I am definitely going to be calling my boss 'cute', so go see HR if you feel it is necessary. And third, Laurence Jonathan Mercier," I emphasize the French pronunciation of his first and last names, "I couldn't care less about your 'familial heritage.' You are you, and that's who I want to be with, whether you're the son of a noble or a pauper on the streets."

I wink at him. "Don't stop being cute. It's really your only saving grace."

He playfully grabs my waist and tickles me, an eruption of giddy screams and giggles tumbling from my mouth. When he finally pulls his fingers back, my laughter dies down only to be met with a gentle kiss.

The kiss is far too brief for my liking, but he gently takes my hand and laces his fingers with mine. "I'm not going to kiss you like mad. You're still getting over something, so for now, this is what you get."

I pout a little but I can't blame him. "I'm sure you were worried. I am really sorry."

He squeezes my hand. "Would you like to watch a movie? We can put something on and snuggle up together."

I begin to giggle uncontrollably. "Did you just use the word 'snuggle'?" My laughter robs him of any chance to retort, and I lean over, pulling a blanket up over the two of us.

He knows I'm teasing him and allows the scowl to slip from his face and picks up the remote, handing it to me.

I grin at him happily. "It's almost Thanksgiving. There's a few channels already running Christmas movies!"

He freezes and looks at me in shock and horror. "What did you just say?"

"Christmas movies!"

"No. No, no, no. We do not watch Christmas movies now."

I cross my arms. "Yes, we do. And the cheesier the better. This is my house so I make the rules here, and you are going to cuddle me and make me feel better, right?" I look up at him with coyly pleading eyes, and he admits defeat.

"I suppose I must concede this one."

"Smart man." I slip under his arm and as our movie begins, I have already forgotten about the reason he is here to begin with.

****

When I wake up the next morning, I'm snuggled in my bed. It takes me a minute but then I remember the movie and Laurence. I sit up straight and flip on a light in the dark room...A note lies on my bedside table.

> Good morning *ma chère*. You fell
> asleep last night so I tucked you into
> bed. I took Shakespeare for a quick
> walk before heading home. I hope that
> was alright. Take your time coming
> into work this morning. I'll see you
> soon. - Laurence

I stare at the letter for a few minutes, overwhelmed at the gesture.

Slowly I extract myself from my covers and rise, stretching noisily as my joints pop and creak. "Ugh. I feel like an old lady."

Glancing at the clock I see it's a full hour before my alarm is set to ring, the sun barely lighting the sky.

Shakespeare is apparently not quite ready to wake because he rolls over noisily, grumbling in his sleep like a cranky old man. I giggle and stroke his fur. "Sorry about yesterday, buddy. I promise we'll have a good long run this morning." I kiss his wet nose before I make my way into the kitchen. Clumsily I get my French press together and begin working on a cup of coffee. While I wait for it to steep, I send a quick text to Laurence. "Good morning. Thank you for taking such good care of me last night. You are amazing."

I set my phone down and sift through my cabinets, trying to find something to eat for breakfast. "Hmm..." Eventually I pour myself a bowl of my favorite cereal and sit there quietly munching and enjoying the silence of the morning.

After a few minutes of sipping on coffee, Shakespeare waddles into the room, nose in the air. "Are you hungry boy?" I pour him some food which he greedily wolfs down then turns to paw at the wall where his leash is hanging. "Alright. Let me get dressed."

I check the weather - it's cold! Pulling on my best cold weather running clothes, the desire to stretch my legs after a day in bed is growing in my veins and I can't sit still. I secure Shakespeare's harness and we set out for a long morning run.

As I jog along, my body seems to be coming alive again. All of the stiffness, exhaustion, and pain from yesterday is melting away and each breath of frosty air fills my lungs with life.

Shakespeare is enjoying the weather, fully in his element. He seems as jovial as I am, and as we run, people laugh at his exuberance and pure joy. The run feels good - too good - and I keep us going longer than normal. After a solid hour we return home, out of breath and coated in sweat that freezes in the frigid morning air.

In the shower, I feel the hot water soak into my bones and muscles. There's nothing more satisfying than a hot soothing shower after a winter's morning run.

Selecting my clothes is a struggle. I want to look nice today. It is my first day at work now that Laurence and I are together, and I'm a bit nervous over how things will go. I'm still not as confident as he is about how all of this will work out, but that is to be expected. Laurence oozes confidence, while I lack it in spades.

Mindful of my nerves, I fuss over my outfit. Eventually I settle on black tights, a grey tweed pencil skirt and light pink sweater, with the beautiful gold necklace that my mother gave me. I pin my hair up and carefully do my makeup.

Staring at my reflection in the mirror, I smile, determined to make this a good day. Just one week of work before taking days off for the holiday! I'm excited and I can't wait to relax next week. I enjoy work, especially now, but there's nothing quite like the happiness of days spent lounging around in pajamas.

I give the now snoring Shakespeare a quick peck and grabbing my coat and scarf, leave my apartment.

****

When I step into the glass doors to the lobby, I carefully remove my coat and scarf and drape them over my arm. As I do so my eyes land on Jameson Jones, my former boss, standing nearby and saying goodbye to someone. He finishes shaking their hand and then lifts his face, eyes lighting up when he sees me.

"Camry! My god, it feels like it's been ages! How are you?" He comes over and tosses his arm around my shoulder, squeezing me tightly. I barely wriggle out of his arms, plastering on a smile.

"I'm doing well, Jones. Thank you! How about you?"

"All is well. We are really missing you though."

"I'm sorry to be gone. I am having a great time though!"

"Well that's great to hear. I knew you'd be the perfect person for the job." He puffs out his chest a little, obviously preening over his role in my life right now. If only it hadn't been him who had suggested it! I admit to myself that I'm extremely grateful to Jones, what with how well things have turned out. But his ego certainly needs no additional stroking, so I keep my mouth shut.

Seeing my pursed lips, Jones gestures to the elevators and changes the topic. "May I escort you upstairs? I need to speak with one of the junior executives about an initiative we are promoting."

I nod politely, hiding my weariness at being stuck in an elevator with him. "Of course."

We make our way into the elevator together and I stand as far from him as possible. After pushing the button he comes closer. "So I know you said you're enjoying your work, but tell me what you're up to, working in the clouds of the 56th floor."

"Well, right now I'm recruiting artists for exhibition, and I've been securing vendors. We hope to have the official brochure at the printer's next week. It hopefully will be distributed immediately following the Thanksgiving break."

"Good, good. Do I know the designer?"

"Probably? I suggested my friend Hayden in print media, and Laurence gave the okay for her to handle the promotion."

His eyebrow raises somewhat. "You say Laurence gave you the okay?" He emphasizes the word *Laurence* and I feel my cheeks pink in response. Jones isn't stupid and I'm sure he's caught onto something. I suppose I should be still calling him Mr. Mercier when speaking to colleagues and inwardly I grimace at my foolish mistake.

I stutter out a response, trying to make it seem like a non-issue. "Yes, that's right. She's really very talented."

He eyes me with the hint of a smirk on his face but says no more. Thankfully, the bell rings and the doors open and I try to slip out quickly. Jones, however, moves with alacrity, pressing one hand to the door and the other to the small of my back.

"After you, Camry."

"Oh, of course," I answer awkwardly, plastering a smile on my face.

"Which way is your office?" He looks down the hallways on either side of the lobby.

"It's just over here to the right. Thank you for escorting me."

I try to dismiss him but Jones' cheerful countenance isn't so easily swayed. With a small amount of pressure against my back, he encourages me down the hallway. "It's been my pleasure! Perhaps I will say a quick hello to Laurence while I am here, as well." Again, the emphasis on the name has me caught off guard but this time I'm less embarrassed and more wary.

Jones doesn't have to wait long. We get to my office and he opens the door, revealing Laurence inside. He is leaning against my desk and flipping through a folder in his hand. He looks pristine as always, wearing a brown suit. Today he has glasses on and I'm taken aback by how handsome he looks in the thin wire frames, light reflecting off of them and accentuating the tints of his red hair. His eyes light up upon seeing me, but then he notices Jones, and the way Jones' hand has now snaked its way slightly atop my shoulders.

I stand there awkwardly for a split second, then quickly step out of Jones' grasp and walk over to Laurence. "Good morning!" I speak cheerfully, trying to pretend like none of this is going on.

Jones casually makes his way over to us and reaches a hand forward in greeting.

"Good morning." Laurence accepts his handshake with practiced countenance.

Jones clasps Laurence's hand firmly, then looks around, taking in the office. "It's good to see you today, Mr. Mercier. I see you've been treating our dear Camry well. Why, this office is a step above mine!" He laughs it off but I can tell he actually considers this a minor slight and I roll my eyes at the absurdity of it all.

Laurence's eyes are trained directly on me, but eventually he tears away his gaze and forces a laugh in response.

"You've always had an excellent sense of humor, Jameson." He pushes his glasses up his nose, looking around the space. "To what do we owe your presence here today?"

"Oh, I'm here to see Rodney for a moment, but I caught Camry in the lobby and I decided to escort her up." He smiles broadly, seemingly content. Laurence clears his throat and turns to me. "Well, Miss Hughes. Shall we?" He holds out the folder in his hand and I accept it, grateful for the excuse to avoid this awkward situation. Sensing the finality of the conversation, Jones turns to Laurence and bids him farewell. "Mr. Mercier." He nods to Laurence then looks back at me. "Camry, if you're ever feeling lonely up here in the sky, come down and visit us again."

I say a clipped farewell, and Laurence walks him over to the door, holding it out for him. Once Jones is gone, I let out a sigh of relief. Then I open the folder in my hand and begin to read over the data within.

"These are statistics on the artists we have secured?" Puzzled, I question Laurence as he crosses the office to my side. But instead of an answer, I am greeted by Laurence pulling me into an embrace, lips pressing against mine. The kiss is what one might expect from distant lovers reunited; strong, affectionate, slow and tantalizing but full of passion. When we separate, I take a deep breath.

"Wow, um, good morning to you too. What was that for?"

Laurence smiles down at me and places a quick kiss to my forehead before lowering his arms and walking around my desk. "Nothing in particular. Now, what were you saying?"

I blink, still caught off guard at his behavior, but allow myself to be steered in the new direction.

"I was wondering about the data you have here. It's information about the artists, correct?"

"Yes, in case you can identify any gaps in representation that you feel we might best fill."

"Well, that's awfully thorough..." I trail off, concentrating on what I'm seeing in front of me. Pleased with my recruitment so far, I can't help be chuffed with myself, but Laurence's voice cuts into my self-congratulations.

"Did Jones often touch you like that while you worked for him?"

I look up from the folder, confused and suspicious. "What?"

Laurence's head is down, attempting a casual posture as he sifts through the papers he is holding. He clears his throat again, and I notice he moves his hand to his sleeve, twirling the cufflinks between the tips of his fingers.

"Never mind. It is unimportant."

Not believing him for a second I drop the folder on the desk and move to stand in front of him.

"I'm sorry, no. What did you say?" His behavior is irritating me and I have a strong suspicion of what is behind it; something that I am not going to let slide.

"As I said, it was an offhand comment and it is of no concern. Now, have you-"

Noticing his attempt at a change in subject, I cut him off. "Dammit, Laurence. You don't have any reason to feel threatened by Jones. He's like that with everyone. He's a massive flirt!"

Laurence stiffens. "You think I was threatened?"

I glare at him. "Yes, I think that's exactly what happened. Good god, Laurence. I chose you, don't you see that?"

He stares at me for a few minutes while I sit there, fuming. Finally he groans and shoves his hands into his pockets. Staring down at his desk, I hear him mumble something.

"What was that?" I put my hands on my hips. He is not getting away that easily!

"I'm sorry."

"For what?" This isn't a question; I want to hear him say it.

He shoves his hair back and removes his glasses, tossing them on the desk. "I'm sorry for that. I... apparently, I'm a jealous lover."

I snort in mild disdain. "I highly doubt this is a new discovery."

He chews his lips. "Well..."

I blink at him momentarily. "What? You were never stupidly possessive of your past girlfriends?"

"Camry..." he trails off, looking embarrassed. "I haven't had a real girlfriend in over ten years. I honestly don't remember much. I was in college."

My anger quickly melts to shock, and before I know it I am laughing. Laughing so hard that I can't stand up and am clutching my sides.

He shoots me a bewildered, frustrated glare. "Why are you laughing?"

I rush over to him and throw my arms around his neck. "You are unbearably adorable." I give him a big kiss, catching him completely off guard. "And yes, I'm still calling you adorable."

"Why is it adorable? It's embarrassing."

"I don't think so. I know how singularly you were focused all that time. And I think you're just going to have to learn. I don't have eyes for anyone but you." I step back and look at him directly.

"But listen to me now - being possessive and jealous? That's a huge no. I am not an object you own and I am more of a person than just your girlfriend. If you want me, we're partners, and we trust each other. I can take care of myself and I have a life of my own. You're going to be okay with that because I am with you and it's a requirement and that's all there is to it. Alright?"

I serve him a pointed glare and his face flashes through a myriad of emotions; shame, guilt, sadness, and finally, acceptance.

"Alright."

I nod firmly. "Good. And yes, I am well aware that Jones has his issues, but he's unimportant. You are."

"Are what?"

"Important. To me."

Laurence presses fingers to his temples, obviously deep in thought. "You're right," he finally agrees. "I'll try."

"Thank you." I smile at him and plant a kiss on his cheek.

He grins and kisses me back. "Are you feeling alright today?"

"I am. Thank you again for yesterday."

"It was my pleasure." We stand there for a moment, before he releases me.

"I guess I should get to my office."

"Can I walk with you?" He laughs, but doesn't object, and like that night weeks ago, I slip my arm through his. Side by side, we walk down the hall and I follow him to his desk.

He looks around, still seeming a bit unsure of himself. I peek at the daily schedule displayed on his monitor, and chide him a bit.

"Getting forgetful, are we?" I tap the screen and his eyes follow, a look of recognition flashes across his face as he glances at the clock. I step to the side and pull out his chair.

"Looks like you're getting company in a few minutes. I'd better go."

"Thank you, *ma chère*. This meeting may last all morning. Would you care to join me for lunch?"

"Not today, I've got plans. But I'll see you this afternoon!"

I saunter over to the door, purposefully swaying my hips. When I reach it I place my hand on the doorknob, and cast a seductive gaze over my shoulder, summoning my best Marilyn Monroe impression. "Have a wonderful day, Mr. Mercier." Using his last name feels so funny in this moment but it has the desired effect. I notice him swallow thickly before I exit the room, smiling to myself.

Chapter 9

The morning flies by and before I know it, the alarm I
have set begins to ring loudly, alerting me to the
time. Hayden and I are having lunch today, not
uncommon for a Monday. We find it helps to break
up that unending feeling of the first day back after the
weekend.

Today, however, I'm a little nervous and I twist my
mouth in thought as I stare at the time on my clock. I
want to tell her - I really do, but Hayden's penchant
for overreactions means this probably won't be a short
or easy conversation. I suppose I'll have to get this
over with; she'll never forgive me if I don't tell her
right away.

Deciding that 'grin and bear it' is the best policy, I set
down my pen and grab my coat, getting ready to meet
Hayden for lunch.

When I arrive in the lobby, Hayden meets my eyes
and waves enthusiastically. We quickly work our way
to our favorite little lunch spot, making small talk as
we hurry through the brisk November chill.

The warmth of the cafe is welcome against the
weather outside, and we duck into our favorite booth
and order some warm drinks. Staring at the menu, I
am reminded of the main responsibility of the week.
Venue in hand, the one booking I've been really
dragging my feet over is the caterer. Feeling like food
is still my weakest area of expertise, I've been unable
to wrap my mind around what I'm looking at while I
stare at the bids I've received. So every day my
decision has been bumped back and after a firm "get

this done" from Laurence last week, I know I need to act, fast.

My shoulders slump and I sigh, looking up to find Hayden eyeing me curiously. "I have to pick the caterer this week. I am so lost."

Hayden frowns for a minute, nodding thoughtfully. "Still stuck on that, huh?"

I admit as much and she shrugs. "I think you're making it way harder than it is. Don't overthink it. You always do this, you know."

"Do what?"

She clicks her fingernails on the table, thinking for a moment. "You get discouraged easily. You're pretty confident when it comes to things you know and know well. But if you think you don't know something, you tend to shut down a little. You clam up, thinking you're not good enough, just because you never learned something."

I scowl at her but she continues. "You know I'm right. But you're not stupid, so instead of freaking out, do something about it. You have all the information in front of you. All you have to do is take a careful look at the bids from the catering companies and go with your gut. It's not that hard, but you convince yourself that it is."

I know she means well, but I can't help but be a little put-out by her always optimistic attitude.

Hayden cocks her head and smiles brightly. "You're smart; I'm sure you'll figure it out. If you're really feeling lost, why don't you ask Mr. Mercier for his thoughts?"

"Oh, sure, I guess." I avoid her gaze, trying not to encourage that topic. On one hand, she's right. I should ask him. But on the other, he already has tried to help me with this exact issue the night he took me out to learn about food at Leo's restaurant. I remember what Andrew told me, and recently I've been staring at my notes from that night so much that I can't even understand what I'm reading any more. Can I really ask Laurence to keep stepping in and helping me? I feel like I haven't done much on my own yet, which fills me with guilt. I may have booked the venue and secured some artists, but those were things I felt comfortable with to begin with. I was supposed to have been the person to take the responsibilities away from Laurence, not add to them. I want to show him I'm growing and learning, and I'd like to be able to do this on my own.

Seeing my reluctance to agree with her, she clears her throat and shifts the conversation's gears. "On another note, you should know I'm almost done with the brochure. So that will be one less thing on your plate!"

I follow her change of topic eagerly. I knew Hayden would be the perfect person for the job and I'm excited to see what she has come up with.

"It's basically perfect." She laughs at her own self confidence and I follow suit.

I grin back at her. "I believe you. You're amazing at what you do. Once Laurence gives it the okay it will be ready for publication. And you're right. That will be a huge relief."

The waiter comes and takes our orders and Hayden leans forward and props an elbow on table, perching her chin in her hand. "Speaking of Mr. Mercier...."

I look up at her, trying to play it coy. "Yes, what about him?"

"So?" That's all she says, but her voice is pitched high in excitement and she is leaning forward, eyes wide with glee.

Willing myself to get this over with as soon as I can, I suck in a deep breath and say it. "Laurence and I are together." I see her raise her eyebrows in a knowing fashion, a devious smile on her lips. Suddenly I realize that *somehow* she knows, or at least has had her suspicions, and she isn't going to let me get away with this until I say the word. I grimace and keep going. "As in, dating."

That must be enough for her, because she screeches in delight and claps her hands together. She takes a massive breath and I can tell I'm about to be met with a barrage of rapid fire questions. I quickly speak up before she can gather steam, effectively cutting her off.

"Yes, I'm happy. Yes, we have kissed. Yes, he is wonderful." I lower my voice and look around before answering what I am confident is her next question. "No, we haven't had sex yet."

She sits there looking at me, agape at my strategy, then sits back and pouts, her brows drawn together in irritation. "You're no fun, Camry!"

I smirk at her exasperation, happy that I foiled her plan. Her disappointment doesn't last long though and she grumbles, repeating back to me the basics. "Happy, kissed, wonderful, no sex. Got it."

I snort in laughter at her. She glares at me, but suddenly sits up straighter and fixes her eyes on me with burning intensity.

"Go on then. What are you waiting for? Tell me what happened!"

I give her a very brief rundown, detailing my Saturday visit to the office. I leave out the details of Laurence's family and work history, but explain that he confided in me and wanted me to know him better. Her eyes widen when I tell her that he asked if he could kiss me, and how after our short kiss I went back for more.

She sends me a sly smile. "Just how long were you into him before this?"

I clear my throat awkwardly. "A while." A reluctant grin tugs at the corner of my lips and she scoffs at the sight.

"Ooooh, you clever girl!" She laughs happily, slapping her hand on the table. "I'm so happy for you."

"Thank you, Hays. I'm over the moon." This time the smile that blooms on my face is genuine and unrestrained.

"Yes, I can certainly see that. I hope he keeps you this happy." She stirs her cup of hot chocolate, blowing softly through the whipped cream to help the steam escape.

Eventually her eyes meet mine and her face turns momentarily serious. "Are you sure, though? He's not too much of a hardass? He always seems so... cold, to me."

I shake my head and lift my hands up, gesturing her worries away. "No, really. He's amazing, even more so than I told you before." I take a moment to find the right words. "It's like he sees me on a deeper level, beyond whatever lies on the surface. He is clever and kind, and he isn't above admitting when he's wrong. He wants to be a better person and he's willing to listen to what others have to say. Honestly, I don't even know why he's interested in me. I'm pretty normal and well, he's amazing. Oh! And Shakespeare loves him. So to answer your question, yes, I'm sure. I'm happy and I'm sure."

After a few brief seconds, Hayden covers her face with her hands and lets out a frustrated groan.

I look at her confused, with some measure of alarm. "What? Did I do something?"

She peeks at me from between her fingers. "You are so hopelessly into him already!" She pulls her fingers down, revealing an exasperated look.

I stutter quite a bit, knowing it's true but feeling like admitting it directly is too much. "I -"

She rolls her eyes, then shifts and perches on her knees so she can reach across the table, resting her hands on my shoulders. "I just want you to be careful. You've had a hard year, what with losing your mom. Don't get sucked in just because it looks like something good is coming your way, and don't forget that you're allowed - no, welcome - to come to me if or when the shit starts to hit the fan. I'm here for you, okay? I'm obviously happy to hear all the juicy bits, but please remember that I'm your friend, and you can tell me the hard parts too, okay? If you need to scream, or punch something, or go dancing, or drinking, or cry, I'm here, even if I have to stand up to Mr. Mercier. I'll do anything for you, okay?"

She gives my shoulders a firm squeeze, emphasizing her point. After a few slow seconds her words sink in. "I will. I know. I'll try not to get carried away and I'll come to you if things get bad."

"Promise?" She sends me a hopeful look, full of more emotion than I've seen on her in years.

"Promise." I lean forward and press my forehead to hers.

She lets out a long breath and, satisfied, releases my shoulders and scoots back down onto her side of the booth. The mood for a moment is reserved, but after a few seconds, Hayden looks up and gives me a sly grin. "So you and the big boss, huh?" She wiggles her eyebrows at me before breaking out into a fit of laughter.

"Yeah, I guess so." I can't help but laugh along with her, and I know in my heart that I'm grateful to have her as a friend. "Thanks, Hays. I love you."

She winks at me. "You're damn right you do. And I love you too."

****

My head is spinning as I'm standing in front of a massive whiteboard in my office. It's once pristine face is now a mess of scribbles and lines, peppered with sticky notes and clippings from brochures.

Upon returning from lunch I tried to take Hayden's advice, and the disaster in front of me was intended to be an organized way of comparing and contrasting the bids from the multiple catering companies. The reality is that I've confused myself more and I can't comprehend what I'm looking at. After spending an hour trying to make sense of the information and attempting to compare entrees and appetizers, the frustration is mounting. Fed up, I ball my fists and stamp my foot in frustration, before chucking a marker at the white board and shrieking at it loudly. "I hate this!" I slump dejectedly into the chair nearest me and cover my face with my hands.

A sound from across the room causes my head to jerk up, and I stare wide eyed at Laurence who is standing in the doorway, looking at me with a dubious expression.

"Camry? What in the world are you doing?"

Guilt and embarrassment flood through me and I shrink back into my seat, lowering my eyes to my clenched hands in my lap. "I don't know if I can do this."

Laurence frowns, stepping into the office and closing my door. "That is an unusual thing to hear, coming from you. Talk to me. What is bothering you?"

I glance over at the whiteboard. "That."

He walks to the whiteboard, peering at its contents. Rubbing his fingers across his forehead, he pulls his glasses down and looks at me.

"Come here a moment?"

I huff and push myself off the couch. As I approach, he pulls me to stand in front of him, facing the tangled mess of disorganized information. "Look at your hard work." It's a directive, not a comment, and I lift my eyes to take in the details before me. "You're putting so much time and energy into this, and I can tell." His words are soft and gentle, and I almost wish to cry at this recognition.

He makes a soft sound, lifting a finger to point past my peripheral vision, gesturing to some of the notes closer to the middle of the web I've created. "I see what you are attempting with this, and you have the right idea. Comparisons help. But at this point you're looking too deeply. You've made it more complicated for yourself. It's time to take a step back and return to the basics."

I can't help but pout a bit as I turn to face him. "I know, you're right. You're right! I still feel like this is the biggest area of shortcoming for me and I don't feel qualified to make a decision. So I have analyzed the details to the point that they no longer mean anything and I've backed myself into a corner."

He smiles, his eyes crinkling at the edges. "Yes, you have. And now that you know, how can you change that?"

"I..." I trail off, trying to come up with the answer. "I don't know. I don't know, other than go back to the beginning, and start over."

"Then that is what you shall do." He picks up the eraser and hands it out to me. I send him an incredulous look. How can he ask me to simply abandon so much work? But before I can say anything, he opens my palm and places the eraser in it, then turns and begins to pluck the papers and clippings from the board, stacking them in his hand.

A small sound of horror curls in the back of my throat as I watch my work disappear. But I can't ignore the odd way that tension leaves my shoulders with every piece of paper he removes, so begrudgingly I admit defeat and step over next to him.

We make short work of the mess of notes and soon the board is sparkling white again, ready for a new round of thought.

"Okay, show me what you have so far."

I pick up everything I have and spread it out on the coffee table. His eyebrows raise, and he looks at me, bewildered. "This is your first problem. How are you working off of so much? How many caterers do you have in this file?"

"Ten."

"That's twice as many as you should be looking at. Give me a list of your five most important criteria, and we will narrow it down to five companies immediately."

Unsure of what he means, I bite my lip. "But, what are the five most important criteria?"

"That is for you to decide. I am on my way down a few floors but I'll be back up within the hour. Can you have that ready for me by then?"

"I'll do my best." Outwardly I am confident, but inside I'm reeling. I have no idea what he's asking for!

"Excellent. I'll be back in an hour."

He quickly steps out of the office, but pauses at the door and turns around to face me again. He looks at me intently for a few moments before he speaks. "Camry, you are so much more capable than you understand. You can do this. Just take a few deep breaths and be calm. It is only five things, alright?"

I smile at him a little more. "Alright."

He quickly leaves the room. Frustrated but determined not to be beaten, I sit at my desk and think. What is most important about catering? I decide to start with experiences I've had. Remembering my brother's wedding and the issues there, I add in what I know of former galas and the blueprints of Sanctuary. Slowly, cautiously, the ideas begin to flow and eventually I've got the five criteria on which I want to focus. Laurence returns after his meeting and within the first ten minutes we've got it narrowed down to five companies. I stare at our list, amazed at how quickly that went by. Of the five we eliminated, one company was now booked, two served a limited menu, and two were way over budget once all the extra factors like travel and service fees were calculated. Looking at it now, I feel foolish for tripping over myself so much. It seems so easy and I can't believe how wrapped up in my own head I was. Nervously, I steal a glance at Laurence's face, expecting to see exasperation or condescension, but his face bears a pleasant expression, seemingly content. With kindness I don't deserve, Laurence breezes on by as if it is nothing.

"Now," he says, "take a look at what you have in front of you. There may be variety in some of the offerings, and of course it's hard to compare apples and oranges, but think outside the box. Not the 'what' necessarily so much as the 'how'. How will the food be eaten? Do you want a seated dinner with servers? Do you want serving stations where people can visit and select their own food? If so, how heavy will the main courses be? If they are lighter you can go for appetizers that are more complicated to the palate, but if the food is heavier, go for a lighter starter. Do you remember our conversation in the car after we left Leo's restaurant? We spoke about how food can be more than something to eat, but something to experience. Keep that in mind."

Starting to understand, and I pick up a whiteboard marker again. Laurence smiles warmly at me and lifts my hand, brushing a gentle kiss across my knuckles. "*Ma colombe*, I need to go. It appears we are close to wrapping up this long overdue acquisition deal. I'll be rather busy this week, I'm afraid, but I am confident you will come to me soon with an answer. All you must do is focus and think more simply. Do not let your insecurities bring you down. Do your best work and look for what calls to you. Come and find me when you are finished."

He squeezes my fingers before letting go and exiting the room.

Slowly and carefully I focus in on what I imagine the gala to be. Soft jazz music, warm lighting, people in elegant dress chatting happily with one another as they mill about the room, taking in the exhibits. I mull over the artists I have selected so far and mentally place them around the venue. I picture the kitchen below, bustling with catering staff, and the images of food my thoughts create. My mind fills with vivid imagery and I sit once more in front of the pages that have pained me for so long.

In almost no time at all I am standing in front of my desk, having chosen a caterer. The price is right, they can prepare the food on site, the appetizers are complex in flavor but not too overbearing, and the entrees are served via serving stations that we can set up around the event space, encouraging movement between the artists' exhibits. Even better, the dishes are age-old favorites but with a twist, and I feel that fits well with the gala's general theme of being timeless and yet, new.

But what really tipped the scales in their favor was the presentation of the dishes. Even the smallest dish was extravagant but not ostentatious; true works of art.

For as sure as I am about my decision, I cannot help but feel somewhat nervous as I walk down the hall to Laurence's office. The details and bid from my chosen company are clenched tightly in my hand.

Knocking lightly on Laurence's door, I almost pray that he doesn't answer, but instead I hear him invite me in. I open the door and step in, shocked to find not only Laurence but three other executives including the New York branch's financial director and the heads of two departments. I swallow nervously and step into the room, my steps timid and unsure.

Laurence looks up and smiles at me. "Ah! Camry. I take it you have come up with a selection then?"

I stumble a bit as I approach his desk but quickly right myself, silently praying no one noticed. Laurence's eyes flicker for a moment and I see him roll his lips together in an attempt to fight a smile. Nothing gets past him, so I can't say that I'm surprised. But with grace and every air of professional courtesy, Laurence steps forward, meeting me halfway. "Tell me, which company did you choose?"

I look at the other executives. Are we going to do this here, now? They look at me with neutral expressions - it doesn't appear I am interrupting, but they don't appear altogether interested in what I am here for either. One offers me a quick smile and I return it awkwardly.

Shifting my eyes back to Laurence, I tell him the company's name and he smiles. "I see. And what was it that led you to this choice?"

I don't want to look foolish but at this point, if I don't answer I feel I'm in danger of appearing more unprofessional than if I give a jumbled answer. So I slowly begin to speak, detailing my choice. First, the basics, the practicalities that fit the criteria, and then how I was excited by the look and feel of the food, the unique twist on classic fare, and the flow through the venue, encouraging guests to explore the event space. Once I'm finished, I've forgotten my nerves and the words have flown freely.

There is a brief pause as I finish, broken by the voice of one of the other executives. She looks at Laurence and gestures to me, a broad smile on her face. "You've secured yourself quite the assistant here, Laurence. I have high expectations for this year's gala."

I gape a minute before beginning to blush. Laurence laughs heartily. "I certainly am lucky to have her." He winks at me, outside of their view, and my eyes widen momentarily. "I believe this year's gala will be one of our finest."

"Oh, goodness, I..." I laugh nervously, then clear my throat and straighten my back, making eye contact with each of them in turn. "I will do my very best."

The executives laugh, clearly at my expense, but I don't sense any malice. Laurence gestures to the door. "Camry, I'm afraid I need a bit more time here with them, but let me walk you back to your office." He turns to the others. "Sorry to step out for a moment. Please continue where we left off and I'll return shortly."

They nod, relaxed, and turn back to their documents, and Laurence leads me out of his office. If they find anything odd about Laurence walking his assistant back to her office, none of them show it.

When we get to my door, he opens it for me and once we are through, he shuts the door. I look at him, slightly confused, and he beams at me, his whole face lighting up. "How do you feel now?"

"Good. Really good. Though, I couldn't have done it without you- or Hayden. You both gave me advice today and I really needed it."

He looks at me with a soft expression full of adoration and praise, and I find myself blushing again under his intense expression.

"Laurence, don't look at me like that."

He rubs the back of his head, a nervous chuckle escaping him. "You impressed Ms. Kinsley. She is not the easiest person to win over. I'm sure the others were thinking as she was. But best of all, you have accomplished the task that has been troubling you. Well done."

I can't help the small smile that spreads across my lips. "Thank you."

I look at him and feeling somewhat embarrassed, try to change the subject. "You should probably get back. They're waiting for you."

He smiles ruefully. "Indeed. But I'd very much like to kiss you before I go."

My eyes widen momentarily but then I grin at him and he pulls me by the hand into an embrace. I tip my face to meet his and he kisses me tenderly.

When we separate, I laugh. "Perks of dating the boss, I guess. Maybe I should act incompetent all the time, because then you'll be this proud of me every time I accomplish something menial!"

"Unfortunately for you, I know you are joking." He laughs but bends to kiss me again before stepping back, still holding me in his arms. "I wasn't lying when I said I would be very busy this week. I might not have any time to give you in the evenings, either."

"That's alright, I know you're working hard." I straighten out his clothes, tugging on his collar and pulling his lapels taut. "Just take care of yourself, okay?"

He dips his face and grants me one last kiss. "I will try." Eventually his arms drop and he points to the papers on the desk. "Now, go book that caterer!"

I grin and watch as he leaves, feeling light and at ease in my heart.

****

Thursday morning rolls quickly around. No more odd illnesses, no strange pains, and unfortunately still no period. (Or is that fortunate? I don't even know.) I'm feeling better, but the long hours, late night dinners, and restless nights are taking their toll on me. This entire week I've been working overtime, pouring over minute details and trying to get ahead of the curve so when I get back from Thanksgiving break I don't feel overwhelmed. I can feel my stamina waning, and the break can't come fast enough.

I'm up to my ears in paperwork sometime in the morning when my office phone rings. "Hello?"

"HEY!" A bubbly voice bursts forth on the other line.

"Hayden?"

Raucous laughter erupts from her side of the phone. "Yes! It's me, it's me. How are you?"

"I'm fine, I guess. What's got you so excited?"

"Oh, just because yours truly has finished the brochure and if you're free I'm going to run the proof up to you!"

I push back from my desk and stand in surprise. "You have? Oh my gosh! I'm so excited! Yes, yes, come now!"

Hanging up, I grin, excited and absolutely terrified. What if it's terrible? What if it's amazing? This is real, and this is happening. I'm so filled with nervous energy I barely know what to do with myself.

A few minutes later my door flies open and Hayden practically leaps through the doorway. "Here!"

She shoves a folder in front of my face. Laughing, I accept it and with a deep breath, slide open the cover.

Two things immediately grab my attention: inside is the brochure, and taped to the cover of the folder is a flash drive. "What's this?" I ask, tapping the flash drive.

"It's for later. For now, take a look."

I let my eyes linger on the cover for a moment: simply put, it's beautiful. The contrast of navy blue, silver, and gold make small highlights of color stand out even more. I carefully open the pages and see selections of art from some of the artists who are holding exhibition at the gala. There's even a small paragraph on Marcus, our featured artist. I bite my lip. I never called him for that dinner. I should do that...

Continuing on, the design and the details are polished and professional, elegant but imaginative. I'm rather impressed at my descriptions and taglines, smiling to myself in happiness as I read over my words. The true beauty, however, is in Hayden's design work. It is top notch and I'm amazed. The imagery is timeless and her understanding of color is fantastic.

"It's damn near perfect, Hayden."

She smiles, cracking a joke. "That's why they pay me the average bucks!"

I join her in laughter. "Seriously, though, this is really great. How did you do this? I mean, you've perfectly balanced the funky art world and the formal presentation of a gala, and your eye for design is amazing. I could stare at this all day." I flip the brochure back and forth in my hand, looking over it again and again.

She shrugs. "Eh. You gave me good material. I loved your write ups."

I give her a grateful smile. "So what's the flash drive?"

"Ah," she says slyly. "This is all the digital rendering, plus posters, print ads, custom letterhead and more; whatever you want, really. I had a lot of fun doing this for you."

"Hayden, you're amazing!" I wrap her into a big hug. "I want to see!"

Looking over the items is enthralling. Hayden's prepared multiple sizes and types of each item and there are versions for print and for digital broadcast.

Feeling content and satisfied, Hayden and I make some coffee - or rather, I make coffee, and Hayden spends almost ten minutes making some extravagant espresso drink, her small frame even standing on my counter to fully search out the upper cabinets in search of the perfect 'drink accessories'.

Once we are finally past that hurdle, we settle into the seating area and relax for a moment.

"Are you loving it here?" Hayden asks, sipping her drink, foam sticking to her nose.

I snort and gesture to her, and she quickly wipes it off. "Yes, I'm very happy. I'm really feeling fulfilled. This is far more than I ever imagined it would be. I'm getting to do so much, I've met some amazing artists, and I'm really pushing my skills and learning new tools."

She seems genuinely pleased at my answer. "I'm really glad. I can tell, you know. You're really looking happy."

"Thanks, love. I have no complaints."

She takes a deep breath. "Okay, good. But, Camry, answer me honestly. Are you feeling okay these days?"

My cup freezes on the way to my lips. "Yes?" The answer is more a question than a reply and she lifts an eyebrow in my direction.

"Well, it's not that I don't love you, but honestly, you look like shit."

I visibly blanch at her words and she smiles. "Just don't go overworking yourself, okay? I know how you get, and you're an easy read. Monday you looked a bit peakish and today you look exhausted."

I stare at my friend for a moment or two. "Yeah, thanks. I'm okay. I'm just not sleeping well and I've been here really late this week."

"Okay. Please take care of yourself, though. Rest a lot during vacation."

"That's the extent of my plans!" I laugh it off, trying to sit a little straighter and smile brightly.

We continue our talk for a few more minutes before Hayden slurps the last of her drink down and rises. "Well, back to work. See you later, Cam."

As I close the door behind her, I take a deep breath. The brochure is amazing. The work is coming along. Finally, for the first time since taking this job, I really feel like I'm accomplishing things.

Chapter 10

Friday dawns and with it, the complete lack of focus known well to students before school vacations. My pajamas and I have made thrilling plans, including lounging on the couch, reading books, and sipping steaming mugs of tea. I'm sure Shakespeare will want a run or two every day, but the only other wish I have for my time off of work is to spend time with my new beau. I haven't seen Laurence since Tuesday, as we've both been working extra hours. He has sent a few emails and texts, and they've all been supportive and sweet, but I'm feeling somewhat lackluster. After the chaotic start to our relationship, it's almost nonexistent since.

Allowing myself a small amount of self-pity, I throw on a pair of dress slacks and a big comfy sweater as I get dressed. Today I'm prioritizing my own comfort over that of Corporate America.

When I arrive in the lobby I see Alex and my heart swells. I've been so busy I have barely had a second to think about the lack of his presence in my life but now that I'm looking at him again, I realize I've deeply missed our witty banter and warm laughter. I shout his name and wave at him. Eyes lighting up, he rushes over and gathers me up into a massive hug. "Cam, I've missed you! How are you doing up there in the ivory tower?"

I roll my eyes and squeeze him tightly before letting go. "I'm fine, and shut up."

He grins. "Hey, do you want to have lunch today? We should totally catch up."

"I would love to! I'll check my schedule on what time works best, and then shoot you an email."

"Sweet."

We get into the elevator together, and chat about his sister, his boxing club, and his new favorite pub until Alex gets off on his floor. "See you around, kid." He winks and heads off to his desk. I gaze wistfully out into the bustling cubicle zone, remembering back to the happy days working there. I am definitely happy now, but I enjoyed that work a lot too.

The doors close and when I reach the top floor I exit and wave to Miss Davis at the desk. She's on the phone and looks overwhelmed, but she still spares me a smile and a wave back as she tries to convince someone on the other end of the line that whatever they are suggesting is a bad idea. Her eyes are smiling but weary, and I grin at her, pressing palms together to convey my gratitude for all she does for us.

I smile to myself and walk down the hall, pushing open my office door.

Something's different and it takes me a moment to figure it out. But then I notice that on my desk is a large vase with the most gorgeous purple calla lilies inside. I delicately stroke the petals and observe from all angles, breathing in the light scene filling the air. There's a small note attached to the vase.

"A little something to get you through the final day. -L"

I purse my lips, trying to subdue the smile on my lips. Just when I thought he had all but forgotten about me, an endearing gesture arrives to reassure me.

I sit at my desk and go through the morning motions: coffee, email, schedule review and completing any leftover tasks from the day before. When I finally have a chance to sit down at my computer to bring up the digital promotional files for their final review, it's almost noon. I keep plugging along, scanning every inch of the images and text carefully. Eventually my phone pings and I look to see a text from Alex. "What's up with lunch? Are we going?"

Guilt floods over me and I sheepishly pick up the phone and type out a reply. "Yes! Give me fifteen minutes. I'll meet you in the lobby."

I set my phone down, rub my temples, and save my file.

Standing and stretching, I am yawning widely when my door gently opens and Laurence pokes his head in.

"Camry?"

I start at the sound, surprised and then excited to finally see him. "Laurence!"

He smiles and slips in the door, closing it quietly. I walk over to him and he gathers me in his arms, squeezing me tightly.

"It's been too long. I am so very sorry that I have not been available for you."

My cheek rests against his chest and I breathe in his scent, relishing the feeling of his embrace. "It's alright. I know you've been working hard. I have too."

He tucks a strand of hair behind my ear and gently touches my cheek. "I have heard. But please continue to take care of yourself. I worry, you know."

"Yes, I know. And I'm fine. So you have nothing to fret over right now." My gaze shifts to my gift from this morning. "Thank you for the flowers, by the way. I love them."

"I'm very glad to hear that." He presses a soft kiss to my forehead and steps away, leaning against my desk. "I have some news, darling."

"Oh?" I admit I am curious, but the pet name, in English, makes my heart flutter.

"I took your advice." He paces back and forth around the room, seemingly too excited to stand still. "It's true that I've been working quite a lot this week, and some of that was necessary. But I also had a new goal in mind."

"What goal is that?" I encourage him, wondering what has wound him up.

"I've decided I'm going back to Paris."

"What?!" I shriek the word out, feeling distraught and panicked. Leaving for Paris? How can this be?

My face must betray hurt and confusion, because he looks taken aback by my reaction. His face falls and he rushes over to me.

"I apologize. I phrased that incorrectly."

"You... did?" My eyes lift up to his, anxiety and worry painted on my face. He gently strokes his fingers across my cheeks, pushing lightly at the corners of my eyes.

"I'm not going back permanently. Do you remember how I said I was working hard in order to take some time away from the office? Once I got word that the deal is more or less completed, I booked a flight this morning. I want to go see my mother, my brother. They are back living in Paris now, and I haven't seen them face to face for a few years." He runs his hands up and down my arm, shivers prompting goosebumps to appear in their wake. "It's thanks to you, you know. I took what you said about making time for myself to heart, and I'm going home. I never go back, but it feels right. I have the time, and I want to see them again."

A whirlwind of emotions flows through my mind. I had been so hopeful to spend time with him, but the look of elation on his face is so genuine that I paste on a smile for him. "Oh, Laurence, that's wonderful news!"

I embrace him tightly and wrap my arms around his neck. "I'm so happy for you."

He closes his eyes and rests his forehead against mine. "You're happy for me, but not happy with me, aren't you?"

I jump back, startled. "What? No! I'm really glad you're taking time to be with family while you can, and I'm glad you're not planning on working all week, alone here while everyone else is gone."

He tugs on my shoulders and pushes my cheeks with his thumbs. "Perhaps. But you're stiff, and your smile is tight. I can tell."

My eyes lower to the floor, able to admit my true feelings with my eyes downcast. "A little. I wanted to spend time with you this week."

"Did you?"

My head rises and I offer a weak smile. "I haven't seen you for a few days, so..." I trail off, feeling a bit pathetic.

"I know. You're right. I should have made more time for you."

My eyes fly to his, a stern look on my face. "No! That's not what this is about. I can appreciate you working hard, and you spending time with your family. It's just me being lonesome and wishing to spend more time with you."

"I promise I'll make it up to you. But thank you for understanding."

"Of course. I want you to be happy." I pull him back into my arms, trying to memorize the way it feels for him to hold me.

He smiles and returns my embrace, pulling my hips against his. "You'll be alright while I'm gone?" I think he means it as a statement, more meant to reassure himself than me, but it comes out like a question.

I laugh a bit, bumping heads again. "Of course I will. I'll be fine." I pause, and ask a question that comes to mind. "Will I be able to talk to you while you're gone?"

"I'm sure we will be able to."

I feel so much warmth in this moment that for a moment I let down all my guards and my true feelings escape me. "I'm going to miss you."

His eyes search mine and he stares into their depths for a while before bringing our lips together. The kiss is captivating, filled with longing and adoration. All the pent up stress and desire to see him seems to burst forth and I strengthen our kiss, whimpering softly with each new angle. "Laurence..." I whisper into his mouth. Hearing his name encourages him and the kiss takes on even more intensity. He steps forward, pushing me back against my desk, and my knees buckle. My hands move with a mind of their own, yanking up his shirt and running my hands along his abs and chest. He gulps and his tongue twists into my mouth, making me gasp for breath. I desperately try to keep quiet, but any sounds I make Laurence stifles in his lips. My mind is blank and lust consumes me. Almost lost to the moment, the small nagging part of my brain suddenly kicks in, reminding me that we're here in the office, and of course, I'm supposed to be meeting Alex!

I pull back and push against his chest. "Wait, Laurence..."

He immediately separates, his eyes wild and full of passion. He pulls away to search my face and makes a slightly strangled noise as his eyes regain their focus. He shakes his head as his expression melts to one of guilt. "Forgive me. I don't know what got into me all of a sudden." He looks at me for a moment, and then sighs. "Ignore that. I know exactly what got into me." He taps my nose affectionately, his smile tender.

"I'm sorry. I got nervous. We're at work and I have to be somewhere." I busy my hands straightening out his disheveled shirt. "I'm having lunch..." I trail off and bite my lip before I fix my eyes on him deliberately. "...with Alex."

I give him a neutral look, trying to portray this as the non-event that it is, at least where he is concerned. I catch the slightest flicker in his eyes, but he schools a casual expression onto his face and smiles politely. "You don't need to apologize. You are right, we are indeed in the office. I lost myself for a moment there." He scratches the side of his face and straightens his wire frames. "As for lunch, have a lovely time. But, my lady," he says, picking up my fingers and leaving lingering kisses on each knuckle as he stares over them into my eyes, "would you allow me to escort you home this evening? I'd like to spend time with you before I leave for Paris tomorrow."

I nod and reach up to kiss his cheek. "I'd like that. Thank you."

He leans in once more for a kiss, then stands up and leaves the room, waving gently at me over his shoulder.

****

I meet Alex in the lobby, five minutes late after a full wardrobe adjustment, but I'd rather be delayed than have him see me in the state my little escapade with Laurence left me in.

He lifts an eyebrow in my direction and clears his throat. "I do not want to ask why you're late."

He turns and begins to walk, a faint smile on his lips. I skip a little to catch up, trying to keep an embarrassed smile off my face.

We make small talk on the way to the restaurant, Alex catching me up on the gossip and news from the copywriting department. A new pregnant coworker, someone fired for coming in smelling strongly of - and testing positive for - marijuana, and yet another who's been coming out of Jones' office every few days, looking rather pleased with herself. He regales me with tales of swapped folders, computer glitches, and a coworker's private email that was sent to the whole department. I laugh and enjoy the conversation, fondly reminiscing about my time there. Copywriting was always a lively environment and it seems like little has changed.

"If I end up there again, I'll be happy," I say softly.

Alex looks seriously at me. "What are you saying? I mean, I'll be glad if you come back, but don't sell yourself short. Try to work for something bigger. If you can keep a job working on assisting with the big projects, why not?"

I chew my lip in thought. "I'm not sure that's even an option. There's been no mention of it."

A teasing smirk settles on Alex's features. "Are you sure your French lover hasn't mentioned anything?"

My eyes bulge and I cough. "Do you lead a network of undercover spies or something? What in the world, Alex?"

He laughs jovially, obviously content in his deduction. "A gentleman never reveals his secrets."

I playfully smack his arm and he has the good grace to look seriously wounded.

"Did Hayden tell you?"

"Hayden? She knows already and you didn't tell me?" He fakes a look of anguish then grins cheekily. "No, she didn't say anything. You're too obvious, Cam. All your emails were Laurence this, and Laurence that, and you smile like a lovesick puppy whenever you see him."

I wrinkle my nose in disgust and irritation. "I do not!"

"Sure, sure..." He winks and wraps his arm around my shoulders, pulling me close.

"Anyway, Camry, I'm glad you're happy." He lifts an eyebrow at me. "You *are* happy, aren't you?"

"Yeah. I am. It hasn't been long at all, but really, I'm happy. I got sick and he came over to my house and took care of me and cleaned up after Shakespeare and everything. He really is great."

Alex's face falls for a brief moment but assumes a casual expression quickly. "You were sick?"

"Tired, I think. I slept all day and once I ate, I felt better." My shoulders shrug as I think back on the night spent watching Christmas movies with Laurence.

"Alright. Promise me you'll take care of yourself, though."

Rolling my eyes, I smirk a bit. "Yes, mother hen. I shall."

He scoffs and playfully lunges for me but I duck and run, laughing the rest of the way.

When we reach the restaurant, Alex leans over dramatically, bowing deeply as he opens the door for me. "And now, my lady, your lunch awaits."

****

Finally, the day draws to a close and I snap shut my notebook with finality. Vacation is here!

I quickly look around my office, mentally ticking off my list and deciding that I'm ready to go. I fly out of the door and down the hall to Laurence's office. I barely skid to a stop and gently rest my ear against the door, listening to see if he's busy. I don't hear much, so I knock gently.

No response, but soon a text chimes on my phone. "Come on in."

I push the door open a crack and peek my head in. Laurence meets my eyes, sitting behind his desk, phone to his ear, and quickly returns his focus to his computer screens. He seems to be verifying something with someone, as they converse quietly together, Laurence following along, speaking 'correct' over and over again to the person on the other line. Once in a while he will ask the person to wait, and enter something on his keyboard, before continuing. After a few minutes of this, they conclude. Laurence bids them farewell and wishes them a Happy Thanksgiving.

When he finally replaces the receiver, he heaves a massive sigh and runs his hands over his face, pushing them up through his hair and resting his face in his hands.

Finally he looks up and smiles at me. "Forgive me for that. I had hoped to be done by now."

I walk a little closer, moving towards him at his desk, and he pushes away a bit as I stand in front of him. "It's alright. Are you all finished? Is the deal complete?"

He glances around, frowning in thought, before settling his gaze back on me. "I do believe so." A smile steals across his thin lips and he rises from his seat, tugging the corners of his suit vest down.

"Laurence, that's fantastic! Congratulations!"

His laughter is light and airy, more youthful than I've yet heard. "Thank you, *ma colombe.* I presume you are as well, seeing as you're standing in my office, buzzing about with so much energy that you might very well go supernova any moment."

I bounce on my toes a little. "I'm just so excited! You have no idea how much I've been looking forward to this. An entire week of minimum responsibilities and time to do whatever I want! Long runs, art exhibitions, a million cheesy Christmas movies, and so much junk food. I'm in absolute heaven."

This time, a hearty laugh sounds throughout the room, Laurence leaning back in amusement. "I'm quite glad you're so enthralled. Congratulations, *ma chère,* you'll be living a life of luxury this week." He winks at me and I scowl playfully back.

"Yes, I will!" I retort with gusto but my heart is light, laughing along with him. He wraps his arms around my waist and places a gentle kiss against my forehead.

"Now, I do believe that you promised me the rights to your return trip home?"

I grin at him, and we gather our things and exit the office together in high spirits.

****

The car pulls up to the curb in front of my apartment. I look at Laurence and offer a sad smile. Now that we are here, I don't want him to go. "I'm going to miss you."

He gently reaches out and runs a finger down my cheek. "I will miss you too."

I stare at him headlong, searching his eyes for clues, but seeing none, I lean across and kiss him gently. Then I turn and reach for the door handle.

But it isn't enough; it's not enough and I turn to face him again.

"Would you... Would you like to have some tea?" I blurt out the lamest excuse I can, my voice fumbling over syllables.

Laurence's eyes widen and he freezes in momentary shock before clearing his throat awkwardly. Slowly he slides the gear shift into neutral and applies the parking brake. Laurence focuses on me intensely and I feel like I'm shrinking under his scrutinizing gaze. Finally he speaks somewhat sternly. "Camry."

"Yes?" It comes out as a squeak, timid and unsure.

He closes his eyes and lifts his head toward the sky, rapping his knuckles lightly on the steering wheel. "I am trying to be a gentleman."

"I don't understand what you mean."

"After today at work..." he trails off, his tone hinting enough that I know exactly what he's talking about. "I'm trying to treat you with respect. That was too much of me. So here, now... I wasn't going to come up."

"Oh," I say. "Oh!" It hits me and my face burns with the heat of a thousand suns. "Oh my god, no, I didn't mean it like that, I -"

He cuts me off my taking my hand and squeezing it gently. "I know. But I wasn't going to ask. Now you've so casually come up with a reason for me to go up there and..." He affectionately taps my forehead. "I'm a bit hopeless with you, aren't I?"

"I guess that was a little forward of me. I wasn't trying to insinuate anything, I swear."

"I know. And truly, I'm happy to spend time with you." He pauses in his speech to gather his thoughts before shifting in his seat to face me more fully. "Are you sure you want me to come up, though? I'm happy to join you for tea but I'd like to ensure you aren't going to have some inner explosion of self-consciousness once you realize I am about to walk into your apartment."

"Technically you've already been in my apartment."

"True, though the first time I was simply lending a hand to a work colleague. And the second, all that was on my mind was making you better."

Two words fall from my lips, seemingly simple yet full of meaning. "And now?"

Entwining his fingers with mine, his next words are quiet and spoken while he stares at our connected hands. "Now, you are the most amazing woman in the world to me - and that means that I will share a cup of tea with you, if that is what you want."

"I would. Is it okay if it is just tea?" My awkward question hangs in the air for a moment but Laurence as always steps in and calms my worries.

"Please know that I will never pressure you into anything and I'll endeavor to never make you feel awkward, as long as it's within my power. 'Just tea' would be my pleasure."

I force down a swallow and breathe deeply, pressing my hand to my chest. "I'm really glad to hear that. Would you mind if I went up first and made sure I didn't leave anything embarrassing out?"

He laughs, letting go of my hand. "Send me a text when you're ready."

"Okay!"

Halfway out the door, I pause, ready to offer an amendment to our prior agreement.

"Laurence?"

"Yes?"

"Tea, and maybe some kissing?"

I bite my lip, trying to hide a smile but also because I'm nervous for his answer.

"Miss Hughes, I do intend to kiss you thoroughly." He sends me a slightly wicked grin and the butterflies in my stomach feel like they might explode from my chest at any moment. I leap from the car and grin at him before dashing up the stairs.

When I step inside, Shakespeare comes bounding over to me. "Oh, sweet boy, how was your day?" I bend down, wrapping my arms around his neck, and glance over on the counter to read the note left by the dog walker containing the usual happy remarks about what a delight he is. I pat his head. "What a good boy you are! I bet you want to go outside soon!" I stroke his fur. "After tea, okay? Laurence is coming up." He seems to roll around in happiness and I laugh at this adorable approval.

I hang my coat and glance around the apartment, quickly tidying up and lighting a candle. I check over things a few more times, completely nervous, and when I finally feel satisfied, my phone pings off. I rush over to it and see that Laurence has messaged me. Three words. "Did you die?"

I guffaw at Laurence's joke and quickly text him back. "Alive and well! Apartment good. Come on up."

A minute later, a gentle knock raps on my door and I open it so quickly Laurence's hand is posed midair as if he was ready to knock again. He looks a little taken aback, but then lowers his hand. "May I come in?"

"Yes, of course!" I step to the side and let him in, awkwardly shutting the door behind me.

Shakespeare shoves his way between our legs, begging for attention. Laurence bends down, and gives him a few generous ruffles of fur. *"Bonsoir, Monsieur Shakespeare.* It's good to see you again."

I stifle a giggle as I move into the kitchen and fill my kettle with water. After setting it to boil, I begin to reach into an upper cabinet for tea leaves, when suddenly hands wrap around my waist from behind and a kiss is planted on my neck. I shiver in delight and surprise, nervousness coursing through my veins.

"Um, what kind of tea would you like?"

He murmurs into my neck between kisses, not stepping away. "Whatever you like."

I squirm a bit as his lips brush over my skin. "Can you grab that green box for me?"

He steps back and follows my gaze, keeping one hand firmly on my waist and lifting the other to retrieve the box. He sets it down on the counter and smirks at me.

"You're terrible." I pout at him and playfully bump his shoulder.

"I'm acting that way, aren't I?" Laurence reaches over and squeezes my hand gently, then pulls me close. I rest my head on his chest, listening to the steady beat of his heart. Arms tighten around me, and a soft kiss is placed to my hair. "I feel I must take in as much of you as I can, to remember you when I am in France. I'm going to miss this, miss you. It's only a week, but I will."

I nod, tracing the buttons on his vest with my fingers. "Me too."

I set the tea steeping and we take our cups to the sofa, relaxing together. I pull a blanket over me and offer it to him, and we cuddle together, sipping tea and making small talk. His fingers are constantly running through my hair, stroking along my shoulders, but never anything more. It's as if he needs to be touching me, connecting to me, but never wanting to go too far. It's comforting, him seeking this link between us, and I'm feeling blissful.

Finally, Laurence extracts me from his arms and stares down at me. My eyes are drowsy, giving away the long hours and late nights. Knowing he can't stay forever, I ask the question I know is coming. "Time to go?"

"Time to go." We stand and he kisses me once, twice, over and over, his kisses growing almost worshipful. He whispers my name between, the repetition of syllables becoming like a song that I will keep - the sound of my name upon his lips. Finally pulling away, he gently touches my tingling lips.

"Take care, and enjoy your week."

Pressing my head to his chest, I take in the sound of his heartbeat, trying to memorize its rhythm. "I hope your visit is everything you want it to be."

A sonorous chuckle meets my ears. "I doubt it will be, but I'm sure I will enjoy myself."

We hold hands over to the door and it takes multiple kisses and a few quick rubs of Shakespeare's head before he steps out and turns down the stairs. Shutting the door, I sigh loudly and stare at my faithful dog, who looks up at me with the knowledge only animals can have.

I wait a few minutes, change my clothes, and take Shakespeare on a quick walk. Now that he is gone, I realize that my week of lounging around seems more like one where I'll be bored and thinking of Laurence. I stare at my ceiling feeling fed up with myself. How have I fallen this hard, this quickly? Praying that the week flies by, I fall into a restless sleep.

Chapter 11

The next morning, I drag myself out of bed sometime after ten, to find a text from Laurence sent hours before. "Flight preparing to depart. Enjoy your day, *ma chère*."

Once again the feeling of nervous attraction fills my stomach and I swallow, trying to calm down. I've got a week to go without him. There's no sense fussing over him now.

Since it's the weekend, Shakespeare and I go grocery shopping, and I'm halfway through the cheese aisle when my phone rings. It's my brother!

"Ciaran!" I answer excitedly and his cheerful voice rings through.

"Well, big sis, you *did* answer!"

I laugh, knowing full well how busy I've been lately. We have barely talked in weeks. "Yeah, yeah. I know, I'm sorry. What's up?"

"I'm just calling to check in. Asher and I are headed out to his parents' tomorrow in Cali, so I wanted to call today before we go. Are you sure I can't convince you to come along? You know you're always welcome." He takes a deep breath. "Plus, I don't want you to be alone this year, you know? Without mom, who are you going to be with?"

"Thank you for the invitation, but I'd rather stay here. I'll be alright. I'm going to spend a quiet week alone. I'm looking forward to that. I love Asher's parents but work is absolutely frantic right now so a house full of people sounds exhausting. You guys have fun though. Give Mr. and Mrs. Butler a hug for me, okay?"

"Absolutely, Cam. When are you coming up to visit again? Boston in beautiful in December, and our door is always open."

"I know! But this is your first Hanukkah with the kiddo and I don't want to get in the way of that. This will be special so enjoy it. Maybe I'll come up for a long weekend once the gala is over."

"Gala? What are you talking about?"

"Ah." I stretch out the word, embarrassed and guilty at my lack of communication with Ciaran. "I guess it's been a while since we've talked."

I can hear him snort on the other end of the phone. "You mean, it's been a while since you've answered my calls? If not for your blog postings, I'd wonder that you were dead."

An apologetic murmur rolls off my lips and I grimace. "Okay, how about this. I'm at the grocery store now, but when I get home, I'll call you and tell you all about it."

"I'm going to hold you to it. I'm giving you two hours, tops, then I'm driving down to steal you away if you haven't called by then."

"Deal! Talk to you soon, little bro."

I hang up and quickly finish my shopping. This week I let my hand naturally gravitate towards the comfort food I'd usually refrain from buying, convincing myself that this is a cheat week and that snacks will help fill the loneliness of a long week without the excitement of a new beau and the distraction of a busy office.

When Shakespeare and I arrive home, I settle in on the couch and call up Ciaran, giving him a detailed description of the gala and my responsibilities and accomplishments thus far. He sounds appropriately impressed, giving encouragement and praise. Then, the conversation turns to his favorite "not-so-little-brother" topic: me and dating.

Ciaran is the younger sibling only in years - everything else about him reflects an older, more experienced person. He moved to Boston for college and secured a job at an engineering firm immediately following his master's degree. There he met his now husband and they just had their first baby nine months ago. Her birth, though a joyous occasion, was followed quickly by the death of our mother and I've only been to see them once since Genevieve was born.

Due to all of this, Ciaran's 'little' brother status is a bit of a joke. His steady job, marriage, and parenthood, as well as his overall maturity level, have surpassed me by far. At any given chance, he launches into the over-protective, when-are-you-going-to-get-married speech left behind by my mother. I know he doesn't mean to be demeaning, but he definitely has the concern and care of a mother-hen.

Deciding there's not much to be helped, I tell him about Laurence. I know if I don't, and slip up in conversation another day, I can imagine the lecture I'll face.

Slowly I unravel the story of how working together turned to romance, and the excitement on the other end of the phone is almost palpable.

"Well, I'll be damned." He finally mutters. Then, I distantly hear him shout. "Asher! Camry's finally got a boyfriend!"

Somewhere on the other end of the line I hear an "oh my god", and Ciaran chuckles a bit. He follows it up with, "and he's her boss!"

I shrink down into the sofa, trying to disappear, even though we're not in the same room.

Quickly, I wrap up the conversation, wishing a happy Thanksgiving and making a promise to call on Thursday.

The rest of the week passes as hoped. Shakespeare and I get in lots of long runs, I spend too much money eating takeout from my favorite Thai restaurant, and the Hallmark movie channel and I begin a long-term relationship over our mutual love of farcical romantic Christmas films. I spend my Thanksgiving holiday baking cookies, reading, and blogging - desperately trying to feign normalcy. But no matter how busy I am, I can't keep the tears from falling as I drift off to sleep that night, wishing that my mother was with me.

Finally, Friday afternoon arrives and the number of times I pick up my phone increases with every passing hour. Laurence is set to arrive this evening, and though I'm certain that he will be exhausted, I'm also convinced that he will at the very least call me tonight after he has landed. Nine o'clock passes, then, ten, then eleven, and I drift off to sleep on the couch, book in hand.

Sometime later, I'm woken by a strange noise. My eyes slowly drift open and I realize that the noise is Shakespeare whining, pawing at the door. I rise and walk over to him, checking the clock. It's just past midnight.

I peek through the peephole but there's no one there. Curious, I push my ear to the door to listen. There is no sound, but that's when I notice it; peeking out from under the door crack is a small note. I pick it up and the heart inside my chest begins to beat faster, the smile that creeps over my face cannot be contained.

> "*Ma chère,*
>
> *I suppose now that my attempt at being romantic has been foiled. I decided that instead of calling, I wanted to come surprise you, but it appears you are asleep. When you see this in the morning, call me. Let's spend the day together. I've missed you.*
>
> *Yours, Laurence.*"

Heart melting, I open the door and peek out onto the landing, but he's nowhere to be found. I softly call his name, hoping he may hear me, but there is no response, and I hear no other sounds.

Shakespeare is sniffing the door frame, tail wagging frantically. "You miss him too, don't you boy?"

I scratch his ears and the two of us head into the bedroom and fall asleep.

First thing in the morning, I dial his number. It rings a few times and finally a sleepy sounding Frenchman answers the phone. His accent is much more pronounced than usual and I laugh a little at the sound of it.

"*Allo, oui?*"

I giggle, feeling somewhat shy now that I'm finally able to speak to him again. "Good morning, Laurence."

"Good morning, Camry."

My fingers play with the buttons on my shirt, filled with nervous energy. "Did I wake you?"

There's a long pause, followed by a soft grumble. "Perhaps."

"I'm sorry, I didn't mean to. I found your note. I know it is early but I wanted to hear your voice."

I hear a content sound on the other end of the phone before he speaks. "It's quite alright. I am glad you did. Would you like to get together today?"

My grin stretches wider and I'm sure he can hear the excitement in my voice. "Yes, I'd love that!"

I hear a soft, sleepy chuckle. "*Ma chère*, would you do something for me?"

"Of course, how can I help?"

"I'm going to need a bit more sleep. The flight took a lot out of me. Would you be willing to meet me at my home? We can spend the day doing something together. Perhaps we can drive to Hell's Kitchen and visit the Flea Market for a little holiday shopping together."

I can barely breathe from my excitement. "That sounds wonderful! Do I have time to take Shakespeare for a walk and shower?"

"You've got all the time you need. I'll be here, asleep."

We finalize the details and I am already halfway out the door with Shakespeare before our phone call ends.

****

I check my text message again. When I punched Laurence's address into my GPS I almost fainted. He lives in a massive brownstone situated in the Upper East Side, steps from Central Park. From my seat on the bus, I'm googling the address to see what I can find. The more I read, the more amazed I am. I know Laurence is wealthy, but I'm not sure I am prepared for this level.

When I arrive at his home I swallow thickly, looking up. A four-level gorgeous 1880's structure stands before me, tucked among similar homes. I can see the tips of trees above it, making me wonder if there's a rooftop garden. Checking the address one final time, I step up the stairs and push the doorbell.

I hear a shrill ringing from inside and after a while I can see motion from behind the mottled glass in the side lights.

The door opens, and there is Laurence. He's dressed casually in gray chinos and a burnt orange sweater, but based on his appearance, he hasn't been awake long. His undershirt is untucked and while one sock is on his left foot, the other sits in his hand. Glasses look hastily pushed on and his wet hair is sticking up sideways on the back of his head - a cowlick he apparently tames every morning since I've never seen it before. The sight of him in this disheveled state takes me by surprise. His clumsy appearance is endearing, and I break out into a grin.

He returns my smile with one of his own that is loving and kind; it is obvious he is not yet well rested. Pushing aside his fatigue, I am offered an enthusiastic greeting and he invites me inside. "You found it! Welcome!"

I step inside and the moment I hear the door close behind me, I am in his arms. I breathe deeply, filling my lungs with the scent of him. My hands reach around the back of his neck and I gaze into his eyes, so filled with adoration. We waste no time in reaching for a kiss, and he bends me backwards slightly. Giggling, I smile against his lips and I can feel him do the same. The kiss is gentle, loving and simple, but it fills me with warmth all the way down to my toes.

When we separate, I rest my head on his shoulder. "I'm glad you're back."

"As am I." He strokes my hair before releasing me from his embrace, stepping back and chuckling lightly at the sock still in his hands. "I'm not quite ready for the day. Please give me a moment?"

I nod, reaching up to flick the wayward hair and he ducks his head, laughing. He takes my coat and hangs it in the closet before leading me inside. We walk down a hallway, past a staircase, and into his living room. The floor to ceiling frameless window at the back of the house takes my breath away. Through the glass I see a small green space filled with small trees and planters, sheltered to protect them from the cold.

"Will you wait here for me?"

"Absolutely!" I exclaim, while looking around.

He laughs, and retreats up the stairwell.

I settle comfortably into a large white chair. Gazing around, I notice that the space feels very much like Laurence. The furnishings and warmth of the space remind me of his office but with a more relaxed and comforting feel. The room carries more personal touches and a slightly more eclectic aesthetic than his orderly and formal workspace. A beautiful orange and navy oriental rug, well worn with age and love, accents the furnishings of similar hues. A large canvas hangs on the wall behind, a beautiful landscape of rolling hills and sunset.

Soon come his footfalls as he hurries down the stairs. Watching as he walks down the hall to me, I notice that his hair is now orderly and he has changed out of his glasses into contacts.

He stretches his neck back and forth, then extends a hand to me and I take it, allowing him to pull me to my feet.

He doesn't let go of my hand and brings me close, holding me tightly. He studies me, twirling his fingers through my hair.

"Tu es très jolie aujourd'hui."

"What does that mean?"

"You look very beautiful, today." There is no hint of teasing in his eyes; only softness and adoration.

I try to fight the wry smile that twists my lips around, but before long I'm grinning like a fool and looking down at the ground. "You look good too."

His bemused chuckle hits my ears before he takes my arm and twirls me like a dancer before dipping me back into a kiss. When he rights us, he hugs me and murmurs into my hair. "Shall we be off?"

"I'd love that."

He leads me towards the stairs and we descend to a lower level and into his garage. He opens the door to his car for me, and as we pull out into the alley, I squint in the bright sunlight.

The drive to the Flea Market is spent with Laurence asking about my week. "I spent a day or two Christmas present shopping, and I decorated my apartment for Christmas and baked a batch of snickerdoodles."

"All while watching cheesy Christmas movies?" He sends me a slightly mocking smile.

"Yes!" My enthusiastic shout echoes through the car and Laurence can't stop from laughing at my response.

He gently rests a hand on my shoulder for a quick squeeze before returning it to the shifter, and a fondness in his expression crinkles up the corners of his eyes.

"You really love Christmas, don't you?"

"I do," I reply with no hesitation. "It was always a very special time for my family. My mother loved it as well and she did so much to make wonderful memories for all of us."

"That's probably all the more treasured now, isn't it? Will this be your first Christmas without her?"

I nod my head a few times and when I speak my voice comes out quietly. "Yeah."

"I hope you will share some of those memories with me this year as a way to remember her. And will you allow me to make new memories with you as well?"

His words are gentle and I realize he's not trying to cover my pain, nor is he trying to overwrite the old with the new; he's wanting to share in my past and be a part of my future. A slight prickling in my eyes from the emotion I feel in that moment makes me blink rapidly, but I turn my face to him and tell him my true thoughts. "I would really love that. And thank you for saying that."

"No need to thank me, *ma douce*. I'm glad to know more about what makes you who you are."

There is a small moment of silence in the car before Laurence clears his throat and speaks again. "How was the rest of your time off?"

Assuring him that it was otherwise rather uneventful, I grimace while I tell him that Ciaran is now aware of his promotion from boss to boyfriend. His laughter fills the car as I explain the reactions on the other end of the phone, and we talk a bit about the part of my family that lives in Boston. He listens aptly, asking questions and clarifying details as he commits them to memory.

When we find a place to park, Laurence suggests a quick brunch in a nearby restaurant and I eagerly agree, my stomach rumbling its support of the idea. Fresh daisies on the table, crisp linen napkins, and the best hollandaise sauce I've had in years are certainly a pleasant part of our breakfast, but my appreciation for them is restrained. My attention is instead captivated by Laurence recounting his trip to France.

Leaning back in his chair, he crosses his legs and runs a fingertip along the rim of his water glass. "I was too long away from home. That much is certain. I have had the luxury of seeing with my mother and brother occasionally through video calls, and of course I keep up with them through phone conversations and social media, when I have the time."

His eyes are somewhat distant, lost in the memories of his time spent in Paris. "But Camry, it was almost startling, being home once again. My mother looks..." He trails off and closes his eyes. "She looks older. Much older. I don't think video chatting revealed the tiredness in her eyes."

He offers a weak smile and I can tell that he's feeling the separation keenly. I lay my hand on his and squeeze gently, and his eyes soften and his shoulders relax. "My brother is doing well. He's a physician with a practice near my mother's home in Trocadero. That's new as well. He's only had it a few years but his ability to speak English so fluently has made him quite popular with the Expats living there."

He heaves a weary sigh and takes a sip of his coffee. I don't speak, almost afraid to end this vulnerability that Laurence is showing. Keeping my attention firmly on him, I try to show him that I am listening and happy to hear all the things he is sharing with me. He must still be comfortable because when he sets his cup down, he purses his lips and begins to speak again.

"It's not only my family. Everything has changed so much. Even in the three years since I left Paris, the city feels like a new place. Patisseries I have known and loved are no longer there. The neighbor who was like a second mother to me is now gone to heaven. The whole city feels darker, and more crowded. It was disappointing but it also reminded me that things change quickly."

His fingers curl back and forth around the coffee cup and he tilts his head, making solid eye contact with me for the first time in a few minutes. "I admit that I am questioning myself now."

I can't help the small amount of surprise on my face. "How do you mean?"

"I regret that I have been away too long. I need to take more time to go home and see them, or invite them here when they are able."

I smile brightly at him. "I think that's a great idea."

"Oui, je m'en doutais." He smiles openly at me. "That seems much like something you would approve of, *n'est-ce pas*? Me taking more time to enjoy life instead of working."

"Oh, I definitely do." I agree quickly, then catch myself. "Though, you're absolutely brilliant at what you do, and it shows, so I don't think you should back off too much." I wink at him, and he laughs, curling his fingers through mine.

"Darling, you flatter me too much. I'll become an unbearable ogre if I listen to more of your praise."

I giggle and tighten our intertwined hands. "I really doubt that."

Our brunch finishes quickly, Laurence sharing more about what he did and where he went, and I ask about the food he ate. He finds this amusing, teasing me about my new obsession with food since the caterer decision catastrophe, and I give him a glare or two, prompting a sincere apology from him, as well as a few delicate kisses across the table. Ordinarily I'd be timid, aware that we were sitting in broad daylight in a restaurant, but I just can't seem to bring myself to care today. Once satisfied, we leave the restaurant, holding hands. "I'm really happy that you told me all that. Not just about your trip and what you did, but I'm glad you opened up to me about how it felt to be there and see things change. I can imagine that would be hard to process, and I hope that talking with me helped at least a little."

His feet come to a sudden stop and I pause as well, looking back at him. "Laurence?"

He moves to meet me, pulling my fingers to his lips. "Thank you, truly. I am so lucky to have you."

A confused look settles on my features. "What did I do?"

"If you must ask, *ma colombe*, it is even sweeter. Do not ever change."

****

A thorough day of shopping later, Laurence drops me off at my apartment. "Forgive me, *ma chère.* I'm sorry to cut our day short."

"It's alright. I'm sure you are exhausted. Jet lag is no joke."

"Thank you for understanding." He reaches over from his seat and runs his fingers through my hair. "I have something I need to do tomorrow, so I won't be able to see you. But Monday at work, alright?"

"Well, alright." I try and force a smile but he pushes on the corner of my lips, giving a groan of amusement and frustration.

"Don't do that, please. Don't ever make yourself smile. Be honest with me."

There's not much I can say to the significant look in his eyes so I purse my lips and agree. "Okay."

"Now. What do you really want to say?"

Searching my memories, I know it's been a long time since I dated anyone who had been so mindful of my side of a relationship. It's not easy, being that vulnerable to someone, but something about the way Laurence has always been so supportive of me, both in work and in our newly budding relationship, is encouraging me to speak up.

"I know you have your own life, and for that I am actually pretty grateful. But I'm just a little bit selfish that I can't spend tomorrow with you and the next time I'll see you is at work. I'm not quite ready to act like your girlfriend there, with other people around. Maybe when it's just the two of us, but I wish there was a little more time for us to be together as a couple, since you were just gone for so long."

A deep breath draws my brows together and Laurence smiles at me. "That's good to hear. I missed you while I was gone, and today has felt much too short." He takes a moment to think, and continues. "May I take you out on a proper date soon?"

My whole face lights up at the proposal and I find myself enthusiastically agreeing. "I'd love that!"

"Consider it done, my dear." He leans across and kisses me, but it slowly morphs into a yawn and he pulls away, covering his mouth in embarrassment. I burst out laughing, and he flushes red.

"Ah, I-" He stutters and I shake my head in humor, waving away the awkwardness.

"Go. Get some rest. Sweet dreams."

He stifles another yawn, an apologetic look on his face. "How could they not be?" He places a quick chaste kiss to my lips again and I step out of the car. "Goodnight!" I shout at him, hoping he can hear me through the glass.

A wide grin splits across his face and with a wink, he drives off into the night.

Late the next night, I get a text from Laurence. "Wednesday night. Don't make plans."

Chapter 12

The first days two back from the Thanksgiving break have been busy, the beginning of multiple weeks spent in back-to-back meetings with artists and vendors. In the end, Laurence and I have selected just under thirty artists from the New York metropolitan area to exhibit at the gala, and we have chosen artists from almost every known medium.

The last artist on the schedule for today shakes my hand and bids me farewell. Once my door closes, I flop down on the couch. I should be tired; these past few days have been a whirlwind, and last night I dreamt that all night long the receptionist kept calling me, saying, "Mister Smith is here to see you," over and over again.

Exhausted though I should be, I'm sitting not from weariness but because the nervous energy running through me is enough to make my knees weak and my fingers tremble. I can't get over the quality of these artists; I'm getting to do more interviews than my humble blog could ever afford me, and the work that I've seen in the past few days from just a handful of artists is mesmerizing. I have more than once imagined the feeling of being in Sanctuary, surrounded by stunning works of art and beautiful people. The images floating in my brain are captivating, and I am desperately hopeful that the night itself will be electric.

This anticipation has filled my stomach with butterflies. I hate this. Patience has never been a virtue of mine, and the fact that there are still nine weeks left until the night of the gala is an irritating thought. I realize that being on edge for nine weeks is less than healthy, and with a determined slap on my knees, I stand again, pushing my excitement and nerves aside.

No sooner have I stood up then my phone chimes with an incoming message from Laurence.

"I can't wait for tomorrow night."

And just like that, the butterflies settle into my stomach again.

****

It's hard to apply mascara when not standing still, but I'm currently leaning over the sink in my bathroom trying to pass the mascara wand through my eyelashes. The precision required is failing me miserably with the way my whole body seems to vibrate in excitement. Tonight is the night of our date, and as many times as I had begged him, I never got an answer out of Laurence as to our plans for the evening. The only tip he gave me was to wear a nice outfit. I gulped a little at hearing this, knowing my wardrobe is not exactly being filled with much but running gear and business clothes. Sensing my internal struggle, he suggested the black dress I'd worn on our first night out together, telling me it was beautiful. Laurence's ability to always see through to what is hiding beneath the surface is a little unnerving, but I must admit that it has its benefits.

I'm wearing that same dress and since we are leaving straight from the office, and I'm repeating the motions of doing my makeup and hair in my office bathroom. When I'm finished, I find I can wait no longer, and walk down the hall to his office. I push open the door with no hesitation, unable to contain my excitement.

Laurence has changed his clothes and I find myself slack jawed at his appearance, now wearing a solid black three piece suit with an ornately textured vest. He looks absolutely stunning and I'm internally screaming about how this man is my boyfriend. Sensing my presence, he looks up and greets me warmly.

"Camry, there you are. You look absolutely stunning tonight, my darling."

I blush a bit at his compliment but casually return it. "And you look smashing, my dear Frenchman."

He laughs, eyes twinkling. "Are you ready to go?"

"Yes, but when am I going to know where we are going?"

"The same as always, my dear. When we arrive." The sexiest look I've ever seen on Laurence is the face he makes when he's got a trick up his sleeve. This mischievous side is not one he shows often, and it gets my heart racing seeing it on his face now.

I open my mouth to try and plead my case once more but he casually changes the subject while pulling on his coat and scarf. "Is that your coat?"

I nod, lifting my arm to show the long pea coat draped over my bent elbow. "Excellent," he says, then pulls out a small gift bag from his desk drawer and hands it to me. "A gift, for you."

I'm caught off guard, but accept it, curious. I peek inside and gasp. "Laurence, this is fabulous!"

The soft cashmere scarf I pull from the bag shimmers in the evening light, deep purple in color. Gold silk threads expertly woven into a delicate pattern flash as they catch the sun's dying rays. I rub it along my cheek before wrapping it around my neck.

He tugs on it gently, straightening it out, and rests his hands on my shoulders. Peering down at me, the corners of his eyes wrinkle as he happily smiles.

"It suits you." He gathers my hand in his warm one. "Shall we?"

"Absolutely," I say, and we move off into the night.

****

The drive takes much longer than I had expected, but finally we pull up to a valet and are ushered through two large glass doors. I'm vaguely aware of which part of Manhattan we are in, but I have little time to ponder it; almost immediately we arrive at a security checkpoint and present identification. Curious as to what sort of place this is, I try and peek at the tickets Laurence produces and notice that they contain our names. The off-duty officer returns our identification and tickets and after stepping aside, he says, "Welcome to the Rockefeller Tree Lighting Gala."

My eyes widen in surprise and delight. "Laurence, are you kidding me?"

His eyes sparkling, he leans over and whispers in my ear. "Not in the least. *Joyeux Noël, ma chère.*"

I punch his arm, staring at him. "I DVR-ed this!"

His laughter is full and absolute, drawing stares from those around us. "I wondered if you would. I'm honestly shocked that you didn't say anything about it to me. But this is an altogether different vantage point. Let's enjoy the evening, and we can watch it together later, *n'est-ce pas?*"

Dumbfounded but filled with elation, I let him take my hand and lead me further into the venue, unable to wipe the expression of wonder from my face.

Clean white lines and modern style give the space an avant-garde look, but uplighting in gorgeous hues of blue and purple soften the space. Impeccably dressed people are milling about, and a jazz band plays soft music in the background, some couples dancing nearby. Mouthwatering aromas fill the air and I glimpse food stations set up around the room. I can see at least two bars serving various cocktails, wine, and champagne. Laurence smoothly takes my hand and guides me through the many people, and orders drinks from the bar. Handing me a glass of champagne, he lifts his own, toasting with me. "To memories, both old and new."

His words draw deep emotion from within, and I bite my lip as I touch my glass to his. "Thank you," I say, voice hoarse with a mess of feelings. Laurence gathers me to his chest with one arm and places a kiss to my temple, and I close my eyes and allow myself to be comforted. Eventually I draw back and stare into his calm grey eyes. "Thank you."

Gentle fingers brush against the side of my face and he kisses me sweetly. "Now, let's go find our seats."

Dinner is an extraordinary affair. The largest sea scallops I've ever seen, beef roasted to perfection, crisp haricots vert, and other delightful dishes dance across my palate all night long. The wine I've discovered has left my cheeks pink and my mind at ease.

Throughout the night as guests mingle and move about the space, Laurence receives many a visitor. Some try to talk business, others attempt small talk; all offer inquisitive looks in my direction. With each and every person, Laurence politely but efficiently waves them away, stating with unabashed directness that he is on a date with his girlfriend and "would like to focus entirely on her". The first few times I try to insist it is alright, but he will hear nothing of it. "I don't often get to take you out. Please allow me this moment." Finally understanding, I selfishly indulge in claiming his attention for the night, feeling touched and honored by the singularity of his focus this evening.

Our private night ends eventually when we meet one person whom Laurence doesn't dismiss; at least, not a first. As we mingle near the bar, a large man, perfectly flushed from the heat and alcohol of the evening, seems to spot Laurence and begins to make his way toward us. Though the room is filled to capacity, he parts the crowd with the mere threat of his girth. He moves quickly for a man of his size, and is soon standing in front of the two of us, wheezing slightly and dabbing at sweat on his forehead with a yellowed handkerchief.

"Laurence, you old rascal!" He slaps a firm hand across Laurence's back, speaking loudly. "I'm absolutely delighted that you came!" The man shakes his hand vigorously, gripping fingers tightly, wringing Laurence's hand along for the wild ride. I have to chuckle a bit; the man is quite entertaining to watch, and anyone who refers to Laurence as 'old rascal' must be someone whom he has known for quite some time. Eventually Laurence extracts himself as much as possible, and smiling, pulls me flush against him.

"August, may I please introduce you to my lovely date for the evening? Camry, this is August Rudolph, this evening's organizer. August, this is my girlfriend, Camry Hughes." The slight emphasis on the world 'girlfriend' isn't lost on me, though I can't tell if it's spoken with pride, a hint of warning, or both.

August's eyes fly open, excitement flooding his face. "Girlfriend?! Why Laurence, you've done well!" He openly ogles my body, quickly glancing in multiple angles, before he conspiratorially leans in to me, and speaks in a loud whisper, obvious to anyone who's nearby, "He's done VERY well." He chuckles loudly, finding himself hilarious.

Outwardly I giggle and smile but inwardly I'm torn between exasperation and anger at yet another man who acts like this. Thoroughly disgusted by his behavior on the inside, I take a careful step back. Laurence notices my behavior and steps forward, wrapping an arm around August's shoulders and steering him away.

"Ah, August, you old dog, you embarrass me. Thank you again for allowing me to purchase tickets at such late notice. It's very much appreciated." Laurence inclines his head and tips his glass at August, who beams with pride.

"Ah, well, anything for an old friend of the family, eh? Now get along and enjoy yourselves! It's not too much longer until we head outside!"

He swings around, red faced and moves on to his next target. I relax my shoulders and let out a deep breath, and Laurence returns to my side, looking at me apologetically.

"I'm terribly sorry about him. I knew we'd run into him eventually tonight, but I had hoped it would be only from afar."

I eye him from across the room, trying to keep my expression neutral. "How do you know him?"

"Some connection between our parents. Not of my choosing, but being acquainted with him certainly was advantageous for this evening. He's unfortunately a high profile event promoter in this area, and he runs quite a few large scale events in Manhattan every year. This is one of them. And," he turns his eyes from August back to me, "I happen to have a girlfriend who adores Christmas, and I thought, what better way to begin celebrating it, than to be a part of a private event for viewing the lighting of the Christmas tree?"

I smile up into his eyes, adoration swelling inside. "You, sir, are absolutely amazing. Did you know that?"

He sheepishly runs his hand through his hair, his bangs becoming disheveled and sticking up in the front. I stifle a laugh and lift my hand to straighten them. Before I can lower my fingers, he reaches up and gently grasps my wrist. We lock eyes and meet suddenly for a kiss.

It's a short kiss, but it isn't chaste either, and my cheeks are burning crimson fire as we pull away. I tuck my face into his shoulder as I wait for my cheeks to cool, smiling all the while.

A minute or so later, August takes the stage and announces it's time to move outside to the area private to the event. We bundle up and I pay extra attention to my new scarf as I drape it around my shoulders. Outside, the large tree towers in front of us, and I can't help but gasp at the amazing site. Even unlit it is beautiful, and I clutch at Laurence in excitement.

The announcer calls us to attention and the countdown begins. We all chant and cheer as we count down together, and when the time is come, the lights come on and I practically scream with glee. I'm jumping up and down, tugging on Laurence's arm, pointing and exclaiming and so wrapped up in the magic of the moment that I barely notice the smile on his face, watching me the whole while.

The party moves back inside after a few minutes and the crowd disperses but I remain, quietly staring at the tree in wonder. Laurence stays by my side, nodding hellos and one word greetings to people that pass by, until we are almost alone.

The silence around us gradually calls me back to reality, and realizing I am without the press of bodies nearby, I grow cold and I shiver. Laurence wraps his arms around me from behind, and whispers in my ear. "Are you alright?"

I nod, pressing my cheek to his. "I'm more than alright. I think I'm perfect." I close my eyes and absorb his warmth.

I hear him humming along with the musical group performing on the other side of the spectacle, and I focus on the sound of his soothing voice.

The song ends, and his voice sounds low and gentle in my ear. "We can stay here, go back inside for another hour, or we can go somewhere else for a nightcap. What do you say?"

I turn in his arms to face him. "Any particular ideas?"

"I happen to have received a fantastic vintage from my family's winery while I was in France, and I was thinking tonight would be a lovely evening to enjoy a sip or two. Would you care to join me?"

I nod, returning his smile. "I'd like that."

We bid farewell to the other guests and narrowly avoid bumping into August again, before we slip out into the cold winter's night.

****

Inside its frame of white marble and gold tile, the fire crackles merrily and I kneel before it, warming my hands. It's the second time I've been to his home, but this time, Laurence has shown me around a little bit. Sensing I was cold, he started up the fireplace and is pouring us wine, a beautiful red forming crystalline waves in the glass as it cascades from the bottle.

I rise and return to the sofa, sliding off my shoes and feeling the warmth of the flames on my toes. I sit back and accept the glass he offers to me before sighing contentedly and snuggling up to Laurence.

We sit in companionable silence for some time. My eyes half focus on the dancing flames before us and my mind is empty of most coherent thought. It's blissful, being somewhat detached. Long minutes pass before I withdraw from my empyreal state and venture to speak.

"Laurence?"

"Mmm?" He makes an inquisitive sound, glass to his perfect, thin lips.

"Thank you for tonight. It was incredible. I can't imagine a better evening."

"You are most welcome, *ma chère*. Spending this evening in your company was my joy. Watching your eye sparkle and your face light up were reward enough for me for a lifetime. I could never tire of seeing you happy."

I stare at him, trying to decide where he comes up with lines like these. It's almost embarrassing to hear someone say such things with such sincerity. "You're awfully romantic this evening."

"Is that a bad thing?"

"No. It's just... intense."

He levels his gaze with mine, its consuming heat causing a prickling sensation to spread across my neck and cheeks. "Is intense a bad thing?"

Caught in the crosshairs of his fervid look, I'm torn on how to answer. Finding no words, I shift to face him directly, and I tilt my face up to kiss him on the cheek. He raises an eyebrow at me, and I kiss him again, this time, a slight bit closer to his lips.

I stare into his eyes, and then shifting carefully, half-mindful of the glass of wine in my hand, I slide onto his lap, facing him directly. From this angle I can look down into his face and the unusual perspective is intoxicating to me.

I lean in again, kissing on one corner of his mouth, then the other, and as I move forward again I can feel Laurence's fingers close around mine, removing the glass from my hand and setting both his and mine down on the table beside us.

I kiss his face, his neck, his ears, gently lifting my lips again and again, until finally I bring my lips just above his, hovering a hair's breadth away.

My eyes seek his, unfocused with proximity, but I can feel his gaze and with that I gently brush his lips with my own.

Once the contact is made, something snaps within me, and the hands that were resting on my thighs suddenly grasp his face, pulling it to mine. I melt our mouths together, meeting in unrelenting kisses of frenzy. The kisses he returns are hungry, filled with passion and desire. His hands rest on my hips and I can feel his fingers tensing into my sides, as well as the pulsing rhythm of his hardness straining beneath me.

I'm barely breathing and I have to pull back for a second to catch my breath, but our eyes connect and he surges forward, capturing me in another kiss. A moan tumbles from my lips and his hands slide up my back, playing about my shoulders.

"Mmm, Laurence, please..." I murmur into his lips. "Please, I want you."

With each word I utter, the tingling sensation of carnal desire grows stronger and I feel my body wanting him. In between kisses, he asks me a question. "Are you sure?"

"Yes," I sigh into his lips. "Yes, I'm sure. Please."

Even as I speak, my hands are actively working my way down his chest and undoing the buttons on his vest. Once they are free, I tug his shirt free from his pants and begin to grapple with his belt buckle.

"Camry, if you're at any time unsure, say something. Tell me and I'll stop, so speak if you change your mind."

My hands stop moving for a second and I look up from my work to meet his eyes. The reality of his comments hits me and for a moment, a feeling of warmth and comfort swells in my chest, momentarily displacing the lust surging through me.

"Wow," I say.

He suddenly looks nervous. "What? Did I say something wrong?"

"No," I say, smiling at him. "You are doing everything right."

His wary expression melts into one of passion and adoration, and our lips meet again.

His fingers dance up my back, tugging the zipper down, and I shiver as my skin meets the cool air and his feather light touch. I shrug my arms from the dress, letting it fall to my waist and Laurence pulls back to look at me.

"I always find you beautiful, but you look absolutely radiant lit by firelight, like the goddess Hestia at her altar."

I half roll my eyes, half close them in giddiness at the flowery compliment. Keeping one hand behind my back, he reaches with the other and traces along my collarbone from one shoulder to the next. He leans forward and runs his lips in light kisses along the same path, causing me to shiver and gasp as he makes his way across my sensitive skin.

His fingers find my bra clasp and as he hooks one finger behind it, he looks at me. "May I?"

I nod, and a few seconds later, the familiar sense of relief courses over me, my back, sides, and breasts now unbound. Slowly, Laurence pulls the bra away, massaging gently at the red marks left along my skin. Then his fingers gently move along my body, cupping my breasts and gently squeezing them, massaging them, holding them. His eyes close for a second as if he is trying to remove all distractions, memorizing the feel of their weight in his palms. The gentle tugging and pushing is stimulating me and I whimper a bit, arching my back into his touch. I tilt my head back and close my eyes, taking in the feeling of his touch on my skin, when suddenly I feel his lips kissing down my breast and taking my nipple into his mouth.

I gasp a sound of pleasure as his tongue twirls around it, softly sucking and licking along my skin. The other breast receives the same reverent treatment and I'm quivering with pleasure, almost vibrating with it.

His hands glide across my back, gently massaging sore muscles, and between the two pleasures I'm feeling impatient.

It takes a monumental effort, but I manage to lift my head and once the blood rush has subsided, I resume my work. I strip him of his shirt and vest completely and stare at his body, feeling over faint ripples of muscle and soft skin with my fingertips. I lean forward and suck on the skin of his neck, causing his body to tense under my touch. His fingers sneak into my hair, toying and tugging, and I work my tongue along the side of his neck, deviously filled with satisfaction as I feel him squirm beneath me. My fingers mimic the movements of my tongue as they trace along under his waistband and that same familiar pressure beneath me pulses again.

I scoot back and pull down his zipper, forcefully yanking on his pants until they sit below his hips. Sliding down onto my knees in front of him, I flash him a mischievous smile as I slide his hardness from cover and place my lips around it.

A sharp breath from above tells me I'm doing something right, and as I swirl my tongue around, move up and down, and flick along the tip, his groans and grunts fill me with excitement and satisfaction. I make eye contact with him at one point and he stares hard into my eyes, gray irises a storm of passion and need.

All at once his arms surge forward and he lifts me from my seat, flipping me around to lay me down onto the soft rug. He kicks his remaining clothing out of the way and kneels before me completely naked, as a priest before his goddess. He's no eunuch though, and I can't help but stare at the intensity of his erection, so tight and hard that the skin along his inner thighs is taut with the strain.

He lowers his lips to my chest, once again taking my breasts in his mouth. I hold my breath as one of his hands creeps lower along my abdomen, finding its path down. His fingers slip under my panties, impatiently tugging them down and I lift my hips so he can easily remove them. I can't help but cry out as his fingers find the hard nib of my clitoris, swollen with need. Gently he strokes it, slides a finger around it, before he lifts his head and kisses me softly again. The gentleness of his kisses make me feel like putty, but suddenly my head snaps back and I cry out as I feel his fingers slip inside.

They run along my inner walls, gently finding their way, until he strokes my sensitive spot and my body convulses beneath his touch. He murmurs into my lips as he continues to kiss me, "*Oui, ma chérie, je sais*", curling his fingers back and forth.

After a few seconds of pushing me nearly to the edge, his fingers withdraw. My disappointment is short lived, as he moves quickly, replacing his touch with his lips and tongue.

My cries are loud and my fingers grip the fabric beneath me, as my back arches and my knees bend, unwittingly angling myself up to him. The soft swirl of his tongue inside, the way he sucks on my clitoris, and the gentle hums that vibrate through me bring me to the brink quicker than I can imagine, and I'm left heaving and quivering on the floor, pleasure rocketing through me like a lightning bolt.

Barely able to catch my breath, I slump against the floor, feeling my strength leave me.

"Oh god, Laurence..." I can barely get the words out, but he smiles and rises to meet my gaze, looking down on me in adoration. He gently kisses my forehead. "Tell me when you're ready."

I nod and take a few minutes to catch my breath, and we exchange countless soft kisses. Eventually, I know I'm ready, but I'm unsure how to say it so I begin to deepen our kisses, holding him tighter. He takes this as a sign and slides again above me. I hear a condom wrapper open, and after a moment, I feel a pressure against me.

The slight touch below ignites me again and I nod at him, slowly lifting my hips and wrapping my legs around him.

He moves his hips gently, and though he is being as tender and loving as can be, I can't help the sound that I make when he presses inside of me. His eyes meet mine, concerned, and I smile. "It's alright, keep going..."

He looks down again and slowly moves his hips closer, pushing deeper. Bit by bit, he glides inside, until we are neatly fit together. He lets out a breath: he'd been holding it, I can tell, and after gazing at me again, he begins to slowly rock his hips into me.

He reaches under me, lifting my hips higher. He slides deeper still and my eyes cloud over with a renewed sense of pleasure. Slowly he moves, just the right pace to let the feeling build up again within, and I clutch his arms as they help keep me in place.

We moan together and in time, he speeds up, finding his rhythm. A soft grunt comes from his lips and I look up at him, studying his face. He seems to be concentrating, focus laser sharp, eyes furrowed and brow taught. I slowly reach up and stroke his face and he snaps out of his stupor, looking at me with bewildered eyes.

"Laurence," I call his name. "It's okay. You can let go."

It's as if that was what he needed to hear. His rhythm picks up, increasing in speed, and I can feel him pushing deeper, stronger. His movements become more erratic, as does his breathing, and he grips me tightly, sweat gleaming on his forehead. I cry out in a soft voice, speaking the words that fall naturally from my lips. "Laurence, yes, Laurence!"

I can feel my own wave coming and my walls clamp down upon him, squeezing him tightly as he lets out an animalistic roar, pushing hard within me in two, three, four deep thrusts, then slowing his movements as the calm settles over us both.

Finally he collapses to the floor beside me and we lay there, naked and spent, bodies glistening and inhaling the air filled with sex and sweat.

I almost purr as I curl up next to him and he slides an arm around my shoulder, pulling me flush to his side. Our ragged breathing and the crackling of the fire are the only sounds in the big room as we lay there, bodies wrapped in one other, skin melting into skin.

Chapter 13

A softness settles on my eyelids and I wrinkle my face as I am roused from slumber. As my senses return, I realize I'm dozing in Laurence's arms, lying on the floor in his living room. I groan a little, stretching out the aches in my joints before I slowly open my eyes and find Laurence, still holding me close, gazing fondly at me from just inches away. The same sensation touches me again as he leans forward and kisses my eyelid once more.

"*Tu as bien dormi?*" he whispers softly, reaching over to brush hair out of my face. I wriggle a little closer to him, breathing in the scent of his skin.

"What time is it?"

"Late. You dozed off."

"I'm sorry, I was just so comfortable." I can feel his cheeks pull into a smile as he rests his chin to the side of my head.

"Were you now?" There is the smallest hint of teasing in his voice, but he kisses my hair and murmurs softly. "I'm glad. You looked quite peaceful while you slept."

I push back a little and look into his face, studying the shallow wrinkles that line his eyes. "Did you not?"

"No, I was not yet tired. And to be honest, my thoughts are flying a million miles an hour, so I've been content to lay here, with you in my arms."

"Mmm." I make a soft sound, and sleepily curl my fingers through the faint line of hair beneath his belly button. I'm feeling content enough to stay here forever but then reality returns and I mumble in frustration. "Damn. I just realized. We have work tomorrow."

"Indeed we do." His answer is indifferent and I lean back and look at him.

"And I'm here, and I need to go home."

He smiles at me mischievously and cocks an eyebrow. "Do you?"

"I most certainly do. I have no intention of going to work in the same outfit as the one I wore yesterday."

"I suppose not." He sighs and admitting defeat, rolls over and sits us both up, keeping a steadying hand on the small of my back to support my still languid body. "Come on, get dressed. I'll take you home."

"Really? I can call a cab."

A pointed look crosses his features. "No, I think not. Not only would the fare put a serious dent in your bank account, I would much rather take you home myself than trust you to an absolute stranger at this time of night."

I pinch my face together, annoyance at his overprotective side coming out.

He must have sensed my trepidation because he stiffens for a moment. "I apologize. You're right.

You're not a child. But..." he links our fingers together, rubbing his thumb across my knuckles, staring at our connected hands, "I'm not quite ready to let you go yet, either."

Between my weariness and the afterglow of our first time together, I decide not to argue. I squeeze his hand in return and place a chaste kiss on his cheek. "As long as that's your reasoning."

Softly, he leans in and we exchange the gentlest of kisses. When he pulls away, his voice is soft and low, a rumble from deep within his chest. "By the way, that was even better than I had imagined."

An itchy burning feeling roars across my skin as I blush from his words. I try and tease him to cover my embarrassment. "You imagined it, did you?"

"Often," he says directly, looking me straight in the eye. My plan backfires and my blush deepens until I look away, fighting the smile on my lips.

"Well, we'll just have to do it again sometime." I try and sound coy, but my voice squeaks a little, and I can hear him snort in amusement above me.

His lips find the back of my neck and what I think is going to be a soft kiss is instead a sharp prick of pain as he nips my skin playfully, then soothes it with his tongue. Then he pushes against my back, rising to his knees, and offering me a hand up.

"Time to get you home."

Sure that my face resembles a complex mix of a pout and a wry smile, I allow him to pull me to my feet. We kiss once more, then gather our clothes, setting aside our passion for the practicality of a new workday soon to dawn.

Once dressed we slide into his car, and a small smile creeps over my face as I secretly thank the stars for giving me a boyfriend with heated leather seats for middle of the night December car rides. Kissing the back of my hand with a tender look, he then takes my hand and rests it gently on top of his atop the gear shift. Along the way, at every stoplight, his fingers gently entwine with mine, twisting and twirling, weaving together, always in motion. Then as the lights change to green again, he pulls our fingers apart and settles his hand atop the shifter again, resting my fingers once more above his own. I get the distinct impression that he's craving physical contact, never wanting to be apart, as some way of continuing the bonding after our first love-making. It's a gesture that sends my heart trilling within my ribcage, flitting along listlessly with every curl of his fingers around mine.

When we pull up in front of my building, the bar on the lower floor is emptying of its last patrons and the bar owner gives me a sly wink as Laurence holds open my door and helps me step out. Hoping the street is dim enough to hide the blush blossoming on my cheeks, I give her a sly smile before a gust of frigid air causes me to shiver, pulling my coat tightly around me. Laurence's arms weave around me, lending me his warmth, and he whispers in my ear. "I hope you had a good night?" His voice carries hesitation and uncertainty. My embrace tightens around him, and I lean into his chest, a sweet sound curling from the back of my throat.

"I did. It was all wonderful. I had such a wonderful time with you at the gala, and..." I trail off but force myself to finish the sentence with clarity. "... and with you after." I'm glad my head is tucked against his lean frame, because I can feel him exhale deeply, his muscles relaxing under my touch.

"I did as well. You were magnificent, you know."

"Oh my god, Laurence..." I squirm at the directness of his compliment, and he pulls his head back, long fingers bringing my eyes up to meet his.

"What?" His voice is wondering, unsure of my reaction.

"You can't just say stuff like that!" I playfully punch him in the chest and he chuckles, soft sound waves caressing my ears.

He leans down and rests his forehead against mine, before gently taking my hand.

I cock my head and grin at him, allowing myself the momentary teasing. "You know, you are surprisingly touchy-feely."

I feel his muscles tighten and his posture tense, hands quickly dropping my fingers but I reach out and snatch his fingers back. "I didn't say it was a bad thing. I like it."

I kiss his knuckles and peer at him over his hand,

trying not to burst into laughter. For such a prim and confident man at the office, I never could have guessed that he would be so affectionate and uncertain with me in this way.

My eyes must fail at a good job of hiding my amusement because the next thing I know he's tugging me into his arms, leaning against the car and kissing me thoroughly. He pulls back and smirks. "If it's not a bad thing, *tu n'avais qu'à pas faire le malin!* Don't be a smart ass."

Offended to the quick of my satirical core, I stare at him in mock horror. But eventually our matching wits crumble and we both burst out laughing. Then Laurence pulls himself to his full height and peers down into my face. "I think it's time I go. We both have to work tomorrow. And it is... quite late." One glance at his watch and we both realize just how few hours there are until we have to be awake and in the office again.

I pout but step back, accepting the truth. Stretching up on my tiptoes, I place a gentle kiss on his lips. "Goodnight, Laurence."

He returns the kiss. "Goodnight."

He moves away and with his absence, the December air whirls around me. He gets into his car and once he's sure I've opened the door to my stairwell, he waves and disappears into the streets of Brooklyn.

****

Whether I can blame the quick passage of time on my newfound relationship bliss or the excitement and fast pace of work, Friday has come and mostly gone before I know it. I'm standing behind my desk, drumming my fingers against my hips, glaring at the clock. There's one last artist to come in today, and he's late. Eight minutes late, to be exact, and I'm biting my lip, trying to decide whether I need to call. But then as if by magic, my cell phone lights up on my desk and I lunge for it, frantically accepting the call.

"Marcus?"

I hear his bright, warm laughter on the other end of the line. "Worried about me, were you?"

I pinch my forehead and close my eyes, stuck halfway between exasperation and relief. "Of course I was! You have never been late for anything in your life! Where are you?"

"*Querida*, don't fret. The subway was running late. I'm a few blocks away but I figured I'd call because I knew you'd be fretting."

My mind does a few cycles before I finally put together what he's saying. "The subway?"

He pauses, then speaks slowly, a question in his answer. "Yes?"

"Aren't you bringing one of the statues?"

"Absolutely not. I've got a portfolio of images of them, but I'm not moving a single one of those until absolutely necessary."

There's a moment of silence while I think, brows drawn together in concentration. If I think about it, I can't say that I'm surprised. Marcus has always been a little headstrong - something that both benefited and held him back in his time in the Army. I know he got the same contract form that I sent to all the artists, and I know I was specific about making sure I mentioned that artists needed to bring at least one of the items they would be exhibiting, unless they alerted me ahead of time and made other arrangements. I know he read it; he's never been one to shirk responsibilities or details. I roll my eyes, knowing I may never get a concrete answer from him.

Finally I heave a relenting sigh and agree with him. "Okay, okay. I'm glad you're okay. You'll be here soon?"

"*Si, querida.* See you soon."

"I'm so excited! I can't wait to show you around."

"Aren't I coming on a business visit?" His voice is amused; I know his game. He's trying to trick me into admitting that I'm excited to see him, but he should know that no deception is necessary.

"Absolutely, this is business, but I see no harm in enjoying your company while I'm at it!"

"Then let's make the most of it and do dinner together after. We have yet to get together, in spite of all your promises." His voice is teasing but I can't help the guilt that tugs on my heart. I really do miss him, and I want him back in my life. I agree and with a smile, hang up the phone.

When my office intercom finally buzzes, and Miss Davis clues me into Marcus' arrival, I find myself racing out my door and down the hall. His imposing figure seems to be somewhat intimidating the petite receptionist and she's unsuccessfully hiding her nervousness, fingers twisting into the sides of her skirt.

"Marcus!" My steps quicken and I fly into his waiting embrace. Lifting me off the floor, he hugs me so tightly I feel my joints pop.

The booming laughter that rumbles in his chest is loud enough that a junior executive from down the other hall peeks his head out of his office and gives us a bewildered look. I squeal a little, and bang my fists on his back. "Don't suffocate me!"

The receptionist's eyes are wide, and as Marcus sets me down, I turn to face her, laughing breathlessly.

"Miss Ashley Davis, this is Mr. Marcus Carrera. He's the featured artist for the gala, and a very important person to me."

I can only guess what sort of thoughts are running through her head, but she smiles awkwardly and greets him once more. Now that introductions are out of the way, I grab Marcus' hand and drag him down the hall toward my office.

Just as we near my door, Laurence exits his office, his ear to his phone and speaking rapidly in French. His head is down and a look of focus is written on his features but he briefly glances up, and seeing Marcus and I, breaks into a wide grin. Unable to speak, he quickly crosses to us, gives Marcus an enthusiastic handshake and blinding smile, and leans over to plant a quick kiss on my cheek before continuing down the hall and into the elevator.

Marcus turns to me, eyebrows comically raised, humor and curiosity set upon his face as he waits for me to explain the interaction and a nervous sound escapes my lips. Quickly pushing open the door to my office, I usher Marcus inside.

"So, this is my office! Isn't it amazing?" My voice squeaks a little, betraying my attempts to keep it calm and even.

He gives me another teasing look but thankfully allows the conversation to be steered away from the words I am sure are burning on the tip of his tongue.

"It is impressive." He wanders around the room, observing details and making thoughtful humming noises of approval as he looks around. "Yes, this suits you." His eyes give way to warmth and he pats my shoulder. "You've done well, and this space looks like it is serving you well."

"Definitely! I love working here, and I am loving what I'm doing." I point over at the coffee maker and his eyes widen before he chuckles at the ridiculous contraption on my counter. "Would you like a coffee?"

"Can it make real coffee? Or just those silly drinks all you millennials are obsessed with these days?"

I scowl at him. "Of course it can make real coffee!" I point at the sofa, playfully glaring at him, and he sits while I get to work brewing a pot of the darkest roast I have.

Coffee in hand, we sit down and pour over the images that Marcus brought. The statues are finished and I'm completely in awe. Though the images are brilliant, I can't wait to see them in person once again. Minutes pass devoted to each photograph, as Marcus carefully describes the detail and inspiration behind each individual piece. When he finally turns to the last page of the portfolio, I gasp at the image.

"Wait, Marcus, are these the same statues?" He nods and I run my finger over each figure. They stand all together in one image, but with their staging, I find that it's impossible to tell where one begins and one ends, or that any are missing any parts. The arm of one looks like the arm of another, the leg behind takes place of the missing leg in front. The complexity of the bigger picture is stunning and I'm captivated, staring at the image before me. Individually the sculptures are mesmerizing but now I realize that this is so much bigger than I had ever imagined. They're meant to be part of a whole, not seen on their own, and the complexity of the planned pieces is almost inconceivable.

I let out a slow breath and look up to meet his eyes. "I cannot even comprehend how you pulled this off. I am absolutely blown away!"

His eyes wrinkle and he smiles broadly at me, nodding in satisfaction. "I'm glad you get how they fit together."

"Did you plan this? It's seamless!" Literally stunned into speechlessness, those words are all I can muster.

"Yes, from day one. It's not just about the individual, but the way we're all part of the larger community." He rubs his chin, eyes narrowing in thought. "That was a rather difficult thing for me to see, for a long time. I felt alone and isolated, hurt and confused, and not even the VA would do more than the bare minimum for me."

He taps the photo with a little more force than necessary and I realize that he's still loaded with heavy emotions about all of this.

"At first I was miserable. But after a while, I just wanted to move on. I knew I was different, but I never wanted people to treat me with pity. Everyone would go out of their way to make things easier on me, and they never talked to me the same anymore. It was always like they could only ever see the loss of my legs, and not me, as a person. Kindness suddenly felt like distance, like I was too different to be a part of the world anymore. I know I'm different, and I know I changed, but I still wanted to be me. Your mom was one of the only people who understood it. She was the perfect mix of sympathy and refusing to let me wallow in a woe-is-me attitude. She'd look at me, straight faced, and tell me, 'Marcus, this fucking sucks,' and hug me tightly while I sobbed, but then she'd turn around ten minutes later and give me a look full of sass when I'd try and get something out of the kitchen cabinet. 'Figure it out yourself,' she'd almost taunt me. It maybe seemed two faced but she was trying to show me that she'd both be here for me but also make sure I could take care of myself. If I really couldn't do something, she'd just walk over calmly and help me like it was no big deal. She was true and absolute love; hard on me when I needed it, but her kindness was never mixed with pity. I was still me, and she didn't act like I was this needy, dependent person."

A fond expression settles into his features and he looks up at the painting hung proudly on my wall. "Your mother was the first one to help me make me realize that I was still me, no matter what I looked like or what body parts I had. She reminded me that I belonged to the world just as I am. I started these sculptures not long after your mother got cancer. It felt right, in that moment, because it was people who were changed; on the outside, they look like they're missing parts. And they are, there is no denying that. But inside, they're still alive and full of vitality, and together they're part of a bigger picture, part of the world, and they get by just fine."

I can't help but lay my arm across his broad shoulders, squeezing tightly. Sitting quietly for a few minutes, the mood relaxes and the tension slowly leaves his body, rigid posture giving way, and he leans back into the sofa.

"You're a lot like her, you know," he speaks quietly, finally lifting his eyes to meet mine. "I'm really proud of you." He rubs his hands over his knees, exhaling loudly. Standing, he gestures widely around the room. "And look at this! Here you are, working in the arts and in philanthropy, and doing well. It looks like everything is coming together for you."

I grin and rise to stand alongside him. "Thanks, Marcus," I say, trying to convey a million words of comfort, support, and genuine thanks.

He stretches, his fingers reaching close to the high ceiling, before looking at me. "What else do you need from me now?"

I pout at him a minute, a suspicious look crossing my face. "Are you trying to leave that quickly?"

He chuckles, the honeyed sound filling the air between us with warmth. "More like, I'm wondering when we can blow this joint and go grab a bite to eat together."

Laughter lights up my face and I beam at him. "Definitely! In that case..."

We spend some time talking about the venue, the square footage of the stage for his exhibit, and some ideas on lighting. When we are finally finished, I peek at the clock. It's a bit earlier than I'd usually leave work, but seeing the opportunity before me, I quickly punch out a text message to Laurence, letting him know I'm leaving to grab a bite with Marcus. We grab our coats and leave the office together, bickering out the choice of restaurant as we go.

******

Finally settling on a little Vietnamese restaurant over in Brooklyn, I find myself sitting across from Marcus, fidgeting under his penetrating gaze. He stares at me for a few minutes before leaning back against the booth, tossing an arm up over the back. "So..." he trails off, a teasing smirk settling on his lips. "Are you finally going to tell me what's going on?"

Recognizing the mood of the man before me, I decide to respond in kind. Carefully I sip my tea, replying with an innocent smile. "Whatever are you talking about, my dear Marcus?"

He snorts in laughter, shaking his head as his teasing look gives way to one of sincerity. "You and your boss, huh? Can't say I saw that one coming."

"Well you have only met him the once. And he was very much in 'work mode' at the time."

Marcus' eyes narrow a bit, studying my face. "He certainly seems quite taken with you. That little affectionate display in the hallway this afternoon did more than pique my curiosity." He laughs softly, running his hands along his legs as he breathes out a deep breath. "You're happy, though, yes? And he treats you well?"

I'm more than touched by the way Marcus is acting. Always stuck somewhere between friend and father, his opinions of and actions towards my boyfriends to date have been a mix of intimidating presence towards them, and doting affection for me. His straightforward questions and respectful demeanor make an important point: in his eyes, I'm no longer the young person whom he watched grow up, clumsily and passionately pushing my way through life. Now I am a grown woman and he'll respect my choices even while maintaining a concern for my wellbeing.

"He treats me very well. Almost more than I deserve, actually. And I'm very happy."

He reaches out and takes my hand. "Then I'm happy too, *mijita*."

My fingers squeeze his gently, and a pleasant sensation floods my senses. Since my mother died, I can count the number of genuinely wonderful moments in my life on one hand, and this one joins the collection. Pledging to always remember the fullness I feel right now, I consciously internalize every detail around me, engraving it all into my heart.

Marcus' fingers tap gently against mine, and I look up, meeting his gaze. "Your mother would be happy, right here, right now. And I know she's proud of you."

"Thanks, Marcus. I'm glad you're here with me."

The night wears on, comfortably slipping into easy conversation, warm laughter, and cheerful smiles, and before I know it, our food has long been eaten and night has fully enveloped the city.

Marcus leans across the table, a yawn drawing out the subtle lines in his skin. "*Mijita*, time for me to go. I need to get out of these damn legs and relax."

"Okay. Thanks for spending time with me tonight." I reach into my purse to take out my wallet, but Marcus puts up his hand, stopping me.

"No, let me pay. Let this old man treat you to dinner tonight."

"Are you sure? I'm making a decent salary right now." I frown a bit, knowing his income is less expendable than my current one.

"*Si, chica.* I can handle dinner this evening. Go call your new boyfriend. He might want to see you." He winks and flags down our waiter, handing over payment for the meal.

An unseemly yawn stretches my face wide, and I quickly shove my hand in front of my face to hide it. "I don't know, I might just go home and pass out. It's been a long week."

He snorts in amusement. "And I thought I was the old one here." Slowly he rises to standing, working with the joints and connections of his hardware until he's filled his legendarily tall frame. Leaning over to kiss my cheek, he places his hand on my head and ruffles my hair a bit.

"Goodnight, Camry."

"Goodnight!"

We leave the restaurant, and after one final hug, move from each other into the night, going our separate ways. I turn around to see him turn the corner, hailing a taxi. He gives me a wave through the window, then the car sets off, and I clutch my coat around me, tucking myself into its warmth.

****

When I step into my apartment, Shakespeare greets me enthusiastically, sniffing up and down my clothes, his tail wagging fiercely. "I saw Marcus today, boy!" He chatters away, howling his approval, and I laugh. "Who's ready for a walk?"

Zooming around the apartment in excitement, he trips me up as I make my way into my bedroom. "Yes, yes, I know! Give me two minutes." He flattens on the floor, covering his nose with both paws, looking up at me with pouting eyes.

"Don't think that will work on me, mister," I laugh, quickly changing clothes. When I'm finally reading for a cold late night run, I grab his leash and we take off at a fast pace, racing through the streets of Prospect Heights.

The run is brisk and quick but Shakespeare is bounding exuberantly down the sidewalks. I'm about to turn the final corner when my vision fades and I feel a sudden fog in my head, stealing away my senses and coordination. Shakespeare pulls on his leash, unaware of my struggle, and I stumble to the ground, wincing as my knees scrape the pavement. My legs buckle and my hip hits the ground hard, and I can practically feel as the bruise begins to form with each throb of pain. Shakespeare, tugged back to me by my fall, frantically licks my face. Brought somewhat back to my senses by his behavior, I blink, trying my best to hold back the rush of blood in my ears. My vision exchanges blurs of color and movement for sharp focus, and I shake my head trying to find myself again. Forcing myself into a crouch, I rub my skinned palms over my knees, shivering from the sudden cold I feel sweeping over my body. Slowly, pulse settles and my vision clears. I look around, and notice a few people staring at me cautiously. One person makes eye contact with me. "You okay, honey?" she asks, peering curiously at me as I kneel on the ground.

I nod my head, rubbing loose gravel from my palms and pushing hair from my eyes. Shakespeare forcefully presses his nose against my temple and I twine my fingers through his coarse fur, inhaling deeply. The familiar scent of his fur comforts me, and after a few deep breaths, I gingerly rise to my feet.

Once back in my apartment, I peel away the layers of my clothing, assessing the damage. I wash my palms, hissing as I brush dirt out of the scrapes. When my pants are off, I groan in frustration. The knees of my favorite winter running pants are totally ruined, and blood, fibers, and gravel are firmly caked into the scratches on my knees. Only a few seem deep; most are superficial. The hip bears the telltale signs of a bruise about to form, and I grunt in pain as I try and shift around. Knowing this will hurt for a few days, I grimace as I finish treating my wounds. Finally I curl up on my couch, dressed in cozy pajamas and curled under a blanket. Shakespeare curls up at my feet, and emits a low whine in his drowsy state.

I pick up my phone and see a text from Laurence.

"*Bonsoir, ma colombe.* How was your night?"

I shift uncomfortably, trying to avoid my sore hip, and type out a reply. "Marcus and I had a great meeting and grabbed dinner together. Told him about you."

Not much time passes before a reply chimes and I chuckle at his nervousness. "Do we have his approval?"

I wiggle my fingers around, trying to stretch out the sores on my palms, before I type my response. "Not that we need it, but yes. He's happy for me."

"I'm so glad to hear that." The first reply is almost instant. A few seconds later, another follows. "How is the rest of your evening?"

I frown a bit, torn on how much to share. I know I should tell him what just happened, but based on what I've seen from Laurence so far, overprotective seems to be an accurate word to describe him.

Tapping my fingers against my screen, I tell him I tripped and fell during my jog with Shakespeare, but that I'm alright.

No surprise, a response arrives immediately, asking if I need anything, or if I hurt myself. I feel a sliver of remorse in my half-truths, but weariness wins out over a longer conversation of reassurances and I tell him I'm fine, making sure to thank him for his concern.

"I am glad to hear you are alright. Let me know if you need anything." His reply is short but still carries his concern. I thank him, telling him truthfully that I'm tired and ready for sleep.

A sweet goodnight text arrives, and I respond in kind, adding a few emojis to my text, then get up and slip into my bed, pulling the covers up around me.

I wince at the movement, feeling the sting of taut skin on my knees and the pressure of bruising on my hip, but eventually I settle into the mattress and close my eyes, a night of restless sleep ahead of me.

Chapter 14

For the first time in my life, the weeks leading up to Christmas are not filled with my favorite traditions surrounding the holiday. My workload has increased, with Laurence eliciting my organizational skills and assistance on some of his other ongoing projects. While I appreciate the ability to be of support to him and see more about the work he does on a regular basis, my hours at the office stretch later into the evenings and more than one dinner a week is spent in my office or his, pouring over spreadsheets, letters, and even French lessons. Most of the staff at our Parisian headquarters speaks English, but it's come in helpful for the occasional phone call or files that arrive in French. I'm not great at languages, but Laurence's superhuman patience levels have been a steady support in my learning.

TMC consistently earns recognition for being a wonderful employer and the upcoming week of vacation between Christmas and New Year's is a hot topic of conversation now, just a few days before the break. Hayden and Alex have been stopping by my office on their breaks more often these days, helping me disconnect for a little while, a welcome respite for my overburdened brain. Hayden's spending the holidays with her family in the city, but Alex is heading with some friends to catch some sun - and hopefully the eyes of a few people - at a resort in Mexico.

Laurence and I have yet to discuss our plans. These days, our private time together has diminished, but we have a date coming up tonight and I'm eager to finally have some time to relax together and not think about work.

Before that time can come, I have a meeting with an artist I am most excited to spend time with: Lucy.

When Miss Davis chimes in on my intercom, I can hear Lucy's bubbly voice cutting across the speaker. "Hi Miss Hughes! Hi!" Her mother's voice follows, chastising the young woman, but a poorly disguised snicker is evident in her tone.

"I'll be right out!"

When I step out into the hall, Lucy yelps and zips down the hall to me, her mother following along with an apologetic smile written upon her lips. They're each carrying large paintings and I help out by carefully taking the one from Lucy's hands, greeting her warmly.

Welcoming them into my office, I look back to Miss Davis and ask for a snack or two to be brought over, then we sit down and take a look at the most recent works that Lucy has brought me.

"These are two of what I want to present. You said I can exhibit five pieces, correct?"

"Yes, that's right. Are these new?"

"They are! I painted these this last month."

I grin at her enthusiasm, and eagerly unzip the cover of the paintings. "Let's take a look!"

Two paintings sit before me, so similar and yet so very different. The first one is a swirling mix of darkness along the bottom, then the blackness gives way to soft shades of green, yellow, white, and blue; a hesitant light blossoming along a horizon bringing the colors into focus. The colors are fluid, carefully blended to seamlessly stretch into one another but each holding their distinctive identities. There is something raw and almost violent as the darkness first gives way to the freshness of the cool hues, harsh lines bursting into the softness of color.

The second painting is similar in its artistic structure but the colors in this are vivid, almost shocking in such close proximity to the delicate shading of the first. A burst of yellow light sits along the horizon, striking shades of pink, purple, and orange extending out in ripples of light. The horizon is stained in reflections of the light above, mirroring the light on its shimmering surface.

She points to the painting on the left first. "This one is morning." Then she directs my gaze to the other. "And that is evening." Without waiting, she plunges ahead in her descriptions.

"You told me this was about art as healing. And I thought a lot about healing and I finally figured out that I really feel a lot of healing when I'm watching the sun rise, or the sun set. I wanted to capture the way the sky feels when it is most alive - its birth and its death, every day. There's a cycle to every day, just like life. Those are moments that the sky is its most chaotic but also its most beautiful. I think that's pretty healing, and real, you know?"

I turn to face her, taking in the expression on her face. I can only sense that she is totally unaware of how brilliantly she sees the world, finding art in the everyday around her.

"I do know." I give her a genuine smile, overwhelmed at her ability. "These are absolutely perfect, Lucy. I love what you have to say about them. It's incredible. Your perception of the world is one to be envied."

I look at her mother, conveying my respect for her daughter, and Sarah shrugs, looking pleased, but also wearing the expression of one who has grown accustomed to the wonder and amazement she holds for her daughter.

"I'm glad you like them! I was really excited to show them to you today." Lucy beams at me and I grin back. Miss Davis knocks on the door and brings in some snacks, and we sit chatting and eating for a few minutes before another person stops by.

Laurence pops his head in, and realizing I have company, stops short. "My apologies. I'll come back later." He ducks his head out the door but I call out to him to stop him.

"Wait! Come back here a moment, Laurence."

He enters the room, looking at me curiously. "I want to introduce you to Lucy Finch, and her mother Sarah. Lucy is the artist behind Golden Finch Art that I told you about! Lucy, Sarah, this is Laurence Mercier, the executive director here in New York, and the one overseeing the charity gala."

He greets them warmly, exchanging handshakes and pleasantries. "Are these some of your works, Lucy?"

She nods proudly and quickly runs over the descriptions for him again. I watch with a sense of satisfaction and excitement as Laurence's expression morphs into one of marvel at the spectacles before him.

"You are a true artist, Miss Finch. Your work is impeccable." His sincere comment is said earnestly, and Lucy blushes and shakes her head at his direct praise.

She stutters a bit in her thanks, unaccustomed to the intensity of Laurence's look and I step in to help her, laughing at his straightforward compliment.

"Don't worry about him, Lucy. He's always been a very direct person and it takes some getting used to. Be proud though! He doesn't always give praise so easily."

I smirk at him a bit, watching his eyebrows lift in mild confusion. Lucy peers at us closely for a minute, eyes narrowing. "Are you guys dating?"

My eyes fly open and I look at her in surprise. "I, uh..."

Laurence bursts out laughing, resting a hand on my shoulder. "Indeed we are, Lucy. Your insight is impressive!"

Lucy's whole face lights up, excited with her discovery. "You guys are adorable together! Are you going to be at the gala together?"

Laurence nods, looking into my eyes. "I'm very much looking forward to it."

One look at the expressions on the faces in the room with me is all it takes for me to want to die of embarrassment. Sarah looks fondly upon us, Lucy excited, and Laurence's gaze is full of adoration. Not used to this, especially in my office, I squirm and shift out of his grasp, stepping forward. "Yes, I am as well. Anyway, I'm really glad the two of you could meet! The gala will be an amazing night, I'm sure of it."

Lucy seems unperturbed by my change in subject but Laurence and Sarah exchange knowing looks and I stare at the ceiling, breathing deeply as I try to recover my composure.

Laurence clears his throat and announces he must be going. "It was a pleasure to meet the both of you. I look forward to seeing you at the gala in February! Happiest of holidays to you."

They say their goodbyes, and I walk Laurence to the door. I open it for him, but before he leaves, he leans over and kisses me quickly, a teasing expression written on his features. I glare at him and he laughs, ducking out the door before my hand can push him through it.

I shut the door, ready to apologize to my guests but they have none of it. Sarah comments on how much she enjoys seeing expressions of 'young love' which elicits a flood of heat across my face and neck, and Lucy laughs at me. "Why are you embarrassed? It's just a kiss!"

A few minutes later it is time to say farewell and after they've gone, I lean against the door, shaking my head in exasperation at Laurence, but I can't stop a smile from creeping over my lips and I groan at the realization that I liked the exchange. Pushing off the door with my heel, I straighten up and make my way over to my desk, determined to not let my flustered mind get in the way of finishing my work for the day.

****

Laurence and I are sitting side by side, squashed together into a tight booth at a tiny Italian restaurant. Empty plates and wine glasses are strewn about the table, evidence of my overly full stomach. With one arm casually resting across the back of the seat, Laurence shifts his body to mine and looks into my eyes.

"It's almost time for the winter break, *n'est-ce pas*? You've been working so hard and I'm sure you must be ready for some relaxation."

At the mention of my extra workload, I roll my shoulders, tilting my head from side to side. His fingers reach across and slowly massage my neck, and I close my eyes, leaning into his touch.

"I apologize for dropping so much work into your lap these past few weeks. You've impressed quite a lot of people, however. You're exceptionally capable at your work and you handle details flawlessly. I'm very proud of you."

I lean forward to sip my wine, feeling somewhat shy at his praise, but I thank him, smoothing out the napkin on my lap.

"I'm just trying to do a good job."

"And you are." He carefully tucks some hair behind my ear, gently running his fingertips along my cheek. "Do you have any plans for your week off?"

"No, I hadn't really thought about it. Sometimes I spend time with Ciaran and his family but this year they're traveling... again. He invited me up sometime after the gala, though, so maybe I'll take some time off then to go and see them."

Laurence gives me an encouraging look. "You will deserve a break by then, *ma colombe*. I imagine that would be nice. You have a new niece, *oui*?"

"I do. She's delightful. But growing so fast!"

He laughs, then his expression falls more serious and I see him tug at his cufflinks, twirling them around. Instinctively I sit up a bit straighter. What could have him nervous?

"Camry..." His fingers play with the stem of his wine glass and he takes a deep breath before continuing.

"I realize this is last minute, but would you consider a trip with me? An acquaintance was recently

314

discussing their vacation in Telluride, and after doing some research, I wondered if perhaps you'd be interested in traveling there with me for a little trip."

My jaw goes slack and I stare at him, bewildered. "Telluride? Like, in Colorado?"

His sheepish smile gives way to a small chuckle, confirming with a nod. "Yes, in Colorado. Would you care to join me? We could spend a week or so. What do you think?"

It takes a moment for my brain to catch up but quickly I find myself grinning from ear to ear, and I throw my arms around his neck. "Are you kidding? I would love to go!"

He slides his arms around me, awkwardly twisting to embrace me in our cramped quarters. I eagerly plant a kiss on his lips and he meets me in it, taking in my sounds of happiness.

After a moment or two, I slink away and stare into his stormy grey eyes. "You are too good to me."

His posture stiffens and he presses his hand to my lips. *"Non. C'est pas vrai."* He speaks with strength, conviction in his words. "Why do you believe you are not worth the world? I would give anything to see that smile on your lips but it never lasts, because you worry that you do not deserve such things."

Shocked, I stutter a moment. I'd honestly never thought about it like that before but deep within I know he's right. I do question my worth, my abilities, my value. I tear my eyes away, looking down at the ground, feeling hurt and confused, and more than a little shameful.

His index finger carefully traces a line along my face and I hear him speak, soft as a whisper. "You are beautiful. That much is true. But you are so much more than that. You are passionate, and dedicated. You work harder than many I know and yet when you are struggling you are not afraid to ask for help. You are eager to grow and learn, and you are devoted to the people in your life. Tell me why I am too good to you! There is no reason, because it is simply not true. I adore you, for all these reasons and more. Do not say such things. You are too wonderful for that."

His forehead rests against mine and I close my eyes, soaking in his words. A silly sound escapes my lips as I process all of that. I take in a breath, ready to respond, but he moves quickly and cuts off any words with a kiss.

"No need to say anything. Frankly, I am somewhat embarrassed. I didn't know I had that sort of impassioned speech within me."

I giggle a bit and he presses another quick kiss to my temple before signaling to our waiter for the check.

As we exit the restaurant, pressed together against the cold winter wind, I sneak a glance at his face. "Telluride, huh?"

He grins at me, and we walk together hand in hand into the night.

****

I'm standing slack jawed at the entrance to our hotel
suite. Warmth and comfort seem to fill every square
inch of the space, from the gleaming hardwoods to the
plush white furniture. A stunning view of the
mountains faces me and I squeal, running over to it
and looking around.

"Oh my god, Laurence! Just look at that! And all
those people skiing!" I laugh, delighted, and Laurence
steps up behind me, wrapping his arms around my
waist and settling his chin on my shoulder.

"I'm glad you're thoroughly enjoying yourself, but we
have just arrived. Save some enthusiasm for the rest
of our week together." His voice is warm and teasing,
with just a hint of passion below the surface and my
cheeks flush at his mention of our spending an entire
week here, alone.

He gently nips at my ear and I let out a yelp in
surprise. Long fingers pull my hair off my neck, and
he begins to kiss down its side until a loud knock rings
out upon the door. With one last lingering kiss, and
slightly annoyed sigh, Laurence steps away and opens
the door, greeting the man standing there with our
luggage.

The young steward pulls the luggage cart into the
room and Laurence wastes no time in handing him a
tip. He gestures towards the bedroom for the luggage
and then without a second thought, crosses the room,

returning to me, and once again takes me into his arms.

"Do you have any ideas on what you would like to do this week? I know it was such a last minute trip that you probably have not considered it."

"Actually..." I shift in his arms, turning my back on the wintry landscape to see his face. "I may have done a little research ahead of time. Once you told me the name of the hotel, I looked into it, and-"

"Now you possess an entire list of things you'd like to do?"

I laugh, smoothing the travel-worn lines out of his collar. "Perhaps."

"Tell me, *ma colombe*. What have you decided upon?"

I sneak a peek at the form of the steward, leaving the bedroom after depositing our luggage. Laurence's eyes follow suit and the steward inquires if there's anything else he can help us with.

"No, not at this time. *Merci, monsieur.*" The young man gives a polite bow, then exits the room.

Laurence turns back to me, and taking my hand, leads me over to one of the sofas. "You were saying?"

"I want to go skiing. I have absolutely no physical coordination but I figured I could try the baby slopes. Can I take a lesson or two?"

"*Absolument.*" He kisses the knuckle of my pinkie finger, keeping his eyes trained on me.

"Okay, great." Trying to avoid becoming flustered by the weight of his gaze, I quietly clear my throat. "I was also thinking of visiting the spa here. I read that it was really good." His lips move to my ring finger, caressing my skin with another gentle kiss. I sputter out my next words, struggling to link together coherent trains of thought while trying to figure out what is going through his head at the moment. "B-but I'm not sure how much money it costs. They didn't list the prices on the website and you know what that means..."

Lips moving to the next knuckle, his kisses are accented with words. "No reason to worry. This trip is my gift, and I am happy to treat you."

I swallow, unable to stop looking at the way his lips are dancing across the back of my hand. "Um, and... I was thinking about doing a little shopping along the Main Street here. It looks very quaint and charming and the view of the mountain from it is breathtaking." My own words are now jolting, coming in fits and starts as his gaze becomes more intense and his tongue flicks across my fingertips.

"Laurence?" I ask sheepishly, knowing I can't continue like this.

"Camry, *ma chérie*, while I do love listening to your voice while it is speaking, I would very much like to hear it making different sounds in this moment."

A strangled noise escapes me at his comment and I feel myself swallow again, then close my eyes and gasp as he slides his tongue up and down one of my fingers.

"Tell me more later?" He whispers, his voice laden with sensuality, and I give a small nod, staring at the workings of his lips.

He smirks suddenly then scoops me up in his arms and carries me over to the bed, dropping me quite spectacularly into the sumptuous bedding.

He makes quick work of his own shirt and sweater, yanking them over his head and tossing them behind him in a move that is sexier than one might imagine the calm and collected Mr. Mercier capable of. He leans over me, a sly look in his eye, and I can't help but giggle at this side of his personality. "My, my, Mr. Mercier. Whatever has come over you?"

"You." He whispers in my ear as his lips leave a scorching trail along my neck, skin lighting under his touch. "Do you not realize how you turn me on? How you leave me thinking of you, wanting to touch you, to feel you?"

He kisses me roughly, fingers working under my shirt and creeping along the edge of my bra. He sneaks inside and begins to softly rub against my breast, and I moan as my nipple hardens beneath his touch.

"Laurence, I think I need you, now."

I push myself up onto my elbows and he quickly unbuttons my shirt. When I try to shrug it off of my shoulders, he whispers, "don't," and moves his lips along my now exposed bra line.

He pulls back the fabric, taking my breast into his mouth and my whimpers soar to the ceiling, filling the room.

Hands snaking their way up my legs, he pushes my skirt up around my waist, running his hands along my thighs again, breathing out in admiration. "You are incredible."

My eyes slide closed in ecstasy as I feel his fingers below, tantalizing and teasing with every touch. I hear his trousers fall to the floor, and the telltale sound of a wrapper opening. A gentle pressure moves against me and I suck in my breath. "Please, don't be gentle," I beg him. "I want you."

In an instant he has filled me, both of us crying out together at the feeling of our union. I lift my hips and wrap my legs around him, and he settles further, pushing me to the brink of what I can take. I let out a shaky breath, opening my eyes to stare into his own and he smiles down at me. I push up to kiss him, trailing my lips along his own before nibbling playfully on his ear. Then, knowing I've caught him in my spell, with one monumental effort I push against his shoulder and using momentum, flip us over until I am straddling him.

His eyes are wide, pupils blown to black holes ready to suck me in. I press a hand against his chest, keeping him flat against the bed and begin to move, enjoying the feeling of our bodies intertwined. I start slow, but realizing how much I need release - and quick - I increase my pace and Laurence lifts his hips to meet mine, skin coming together loudly. I press my wrist to my mouth, trying to hold in my voice, but he pulls my arms down and stares straight into my eyes.

"I want to see you. I want to see it when you find your release."

Turned on even more by his words, my head rocks back but he holds my neck fast, pushing my eyes back down to him, keeping our heated gazes focused on each other. I can feel myself getting closer and no sooner do I think that I'm nearly there than I feel the spasms overtake me, my body pulsing around him with each continued stroke. Quickly he follows, face contorted in the pain and pleasure of release, and as our bodies still, he pulls me down to lie on top of him. I can feel the throbbing of my body with his, my mind a white blur of sensation and fantasy.

Once my ability to make coherent thought returns, I lift my head slightly and gently poke his cheek.

"You naughty boy, getting carried away like that."

Smirking, he toussles my hair. "Tell me you did not enjoy it."

The tone in his voice is teasing and I grumble, knowing he is right, and settle back down. "I liked it."

I feel his chuckle deep within his chest, and I curl into his arms, letting the waves of pleasure flow around me.

Laurence sits on the sofa, feet propped up on the coffee table, quietly reading a book. Outside of our magnificent window, a vivid orange sun hovers beyond the mountain, filling the room with a warm golden glow.

His silver framed glasses catch the light, casting bright flashes across my field of vision as I lay curled up beside him, my head resting in his lap. With my eyes closed, I can attentively feel the rhythm of his breathing and hear the sound of his fingers flipping pages back and forth.

Now, as I feel the wax and wane of drowsiness, I'm struck in this moment how completely at odds this experience has been with the Christmas Eves of my past. Many of my memories center around *La Noche Buena* celebrations at Marcus' home; loud, busy, and full of energy. When he was stationed overseas, my childhood holidays were still bustling, with mama filling our cramped apartment with as many friends, family, and people off of the street she could find.

Everything about this surreal environment is different. Not bad, but not the same. The realization this is my first Christmas without my mother brings forth a sudden burst of insecurity and sadness. Instinctively I reach for Laurence, and I twist my fingers into his shirt, seeking an anchor against the waves of emotion.

His eyes leaves his book and settle on me. Sensing something of my inner turmoil, he moves methodically, closing his book, setting it down beside him, and removing his glasses.

"Darling, are you alright?"

Looking into the storm of color in his eyes, a million thoughts fly through my head. Visions of people I hold dear float across my mind and a new understanding dawns; though I have lost the woman who held me in my darkest moments, listened to my deepest secrets, and shared my most profound joys, still I am surrounded by people who care for me. Friends, family, and this man whose affection for me is a living and breathing presence in my life.

"*Chérie,* what's wrong?" Laurence's voice is concerned, and he traces his fingertips along the hair around my brow.

I answer genuinely, more sure of my answer than I knew I could be. "Nothing. I'm okay."

He stares at me a minute more and I can see the infinitesimal narrowing in his eyes as he examines whether my words are truthful or whether I am hiding something. In the end, his eyes return to their typically pleasant air.

"Alright." He pauses again, rubbing his hair and glancing at the setting sun. "It looks like we should be getting ready soon. The dinner begins at eight."

I stretch, yawning, and sit up. "You're probably right." I give him a quick kiss, then follow his advice and head off for the bathroom.

Once primped and polished, I step into the bedroom, eyeing the long red dress laid out on the bed. Given only a few days to pack, Laurence had informed me on the plane on the way over that he had secured reservations for a special dinner at the resort on Christmas Eve. This is quite the affair for the wealthy families who spend their holidays at Telluride every year, and he was able to snag a few tickets through one of his many connections.

The event was black tie, however, and my serious lack of anything other than the warm and comfortable clothing in my suitcase quickly dampened my enthusiasm. Not to be deterred, Laurence quickly brought out his laptop and we spent much of our flight browsing websites, picking out a dress for me to wear. We both were drawn to one in particular, but I quickly pushed it aside and moved on. It was more the kind of dress I wish I could wear, not one I ever would; Laurence disagreed. We argued; my opinion being the color and cut made it too dramatic for me, and he'd politely pushed back, challenging the idea that basic and safe were not common words to describe me, a smile on his face the entire time. In the end I relented, and with expedited shipping directly to the hotel, I now found myself staring at the long gown with more than a little nervousness.

"I suppose I should just go for it." Muttering to myself, I lift the dress and slip it on.

"Oh." My breathless whisper tumbles out from my lips as I stare at my reflection. I know it's me, but I've never seen myself look like this before, and it takes a few minutes for me to come back to my senses. I slowly spin, examining myself in the full length mirror.

The dress is simple in design, but that doesn't stop it from being utterly stunning. Deep burgundy fabric runs up over my left shoulder, leaving the other bare, and a slim fitting bodice transforms into folds of sheer fabric that pool against the floor. A deep slit runs up my right leg, its pinnacle mid-thigh, giving the otherwise modest dress a distinctively sexy flair. Each full curve of my body is proudly displayed, and I straighten my back, rolling my shoulders into a relaxed posture. I do one more small turn, twisting this way and that as I gaze at myself. I feel incredibly beautiful, and I grin at my reflection, excitement for the party beginning to take over.

After sliding into my heels and picking the right shade of lipstick, I enter the living room to find Laurence sitting in an armchair, clad in a crisp tuxedo.

"Wow, you look incredible in a tux!"

His eyes snap up, his focus breaking from his phone and settling onto me. I can see various expressions cross his face until his eyes settle firmly on me. "*Mon dieu*, Camry."

We both stare at each other for a few seconds, taking each other in, before bursting out laughing together. "You're looking especially dapper tonight, *Monsieur Mercier*," I giggle and walk towards him, lifting my skirts in an exaggerated curtsy.

He takes my hand and kisses it, rising to meet me in a formal bow. "And you are looking more stunning than usual, Miss Hughes."

With one last look, he steps backwards and from under the table pulls out a large box wrapped in silver paper with a beautiful ribbon tied round its center. "Before we leave, I would like to give you your Christmas gift."

He hands it to me, rubbing his hands through his hair, bashful and anxious. With the box settled into my hands, I am shocked at how heavy it is, and I give it a curious look. "What is it?"

He barks out a nervous laugh, and playfully taps me on the head. "You need to open it. Gifts are best as surprises, *n'est-ce pas?*"

With a gentle touch, I pull the ribbon free, then slide a finger under the edge of the wrapping. "Did you wrap this yourself? If so, bravo."

"No, most assuredly I did not. The clerk at the store from which I purchased it wrapped it. He did an exquisite job, if I may say so myself. I was mesmerized watching him."

My fingers pause and I look up at him. "When did you have time to go out and buy this?"

"I made time." His statement is simple and honest, and I smile to myself, enjoying the effort he put into this.

Removing the rest of the wrapping paper, I pull open the lid on the box. Inside sits something that reminds me of a coat, but its build isn't quite right. I lift the heavy garment, noticing how soft it is. Even I can tell this is quality craftsmanship, based on the texture beneath my fingers.

I stand and hold it up to me, realizing that it is a thick wool poncho in a deep midnight blue, with beautiful covered buttons banded together across the front. A satin lined hood lays gently across the back, and some well-placed banded buttons give the cloak's shape some flair.

Eagerly, I slip it over my head and a comforting weight settles on my shoulders, surrounding me in warmth. It looks incredible, and I slide my arms through openings in the sides just near my wrists. I do a little twirl, my skirt and cloak swishing about and I laugh happily at how it makes me feel. I jump and wrap Laurence up in a hug.

"Laurence, I love it!"

His arms wind around my waist, pulling me closer, then he pushes me slightly away to take in my full appearance. "It suits you."

"You did very well. Thank you so much! But wait just one moment." Dashing into the bedroom, I pull a gift of my own out of my suitcase, and return to Laurence.

Red satin ribbon is tied artfully around the small ivory box, even if it is a little smashed from traveling in my suitcase on the flight over. "This is my gift for you."

"Merci, ma chérie. May I open it now?"

I nod in encouragement and he smiles before tugging gently on the red ribbon. Opening the box, he folds back the tissue paper and runs his fingers alongside the gray cashmere scarf within. "I thought it might keep you warm, and it matches so nicely with your favorite coat." I reach up and twist a small bunch of his red hair in my fingers. "Plus, this color looks amazing with your hair!"

He laughs and pulls me in for a kiss. "I love it. *Je la chérirai toujours.*" Laurence slides the scarf neatly around his neck, tying it into place, then kisses me thoroughly once more. *"Joyeux Noël,* Camry."

"Joyeux Noël, Laurence."

****

After a few more days of relaxation, shopping, skiing, and even taking in live music from a local band on New Year's Eve, we board a plane and fly home to New York. The week's respite from the constant noise and fast pace of my city was quite welcome, and though the magic of feeling like Laurence and I were in our own little world was intoxicating, I cannot help but be delighted to be returning home.

Hayden assures me that Shakespeare was quite happy with her during the trip, but I can't wait to snuggle up into his fur and take him for a run around my neighborhood.

When we finally touch down and Laurence's car pulls up in front of my apartment, he honks the horn in a few short blasts. I look at him questioningly, and grinning, he points up to my windows on the third floor.

The blinds fly open and I can see Hayden's sunny smile appear in the window. Not even thirty seconds later, she and Shakespeare come bounding out of the ground level door and Shakespeare comes flying for me, dragging Hayden's petite frame along for the ride.

His frantic licks and thrashing tail are coupled with playful husky chatter and lots of bouncing around. Laurence gathers my suitcase and we all make our way up the stairs and into the apartment.

"Welcome home, you two!" Hayden's cheerful greeting and Shakespeare's excitement are contagious; I am ecstatic to be home.

"Thanks!" I let Shakespeare off his leash and he takes off, zipping around the apartment in a frenzy of happiness.

"Well, I'll let you settle back in, but let me watch him again sometime! He was awesome!" Hayden calls Shakespeare over and he gives her some enthusiastic kisses before she stands and gives me a quick hug.

"See you later, Cam! By Mr. Mercier!" With a brief wave of her hand, she's gone.

Laurence shuts the door and carries my bag into my bedroom, setting it quietly on the floor. "You must be tired, *ma colombe*, so I will leave you here. I have a few things I need to see to before work begins tomorrow, but I will call you later this evening to check in with you, alright?"

"Yes, alright. Thank you so, so much for this trip, Laurence. I had a wonderful Christmas thanks to you."

We exchange one last lingering kiss, neither wanting to part, but finally he pulls away with a chuckle. He taps my nose gently, and with one last press of his lips to my forehead, he steps into the hall and closes my door behind him. With a wistful sigh, filled to the brim with memories of our trip together, I go to the window, watching as he drives away. I smile happily, letting the feel of his embrace wash over me for a few minutes more.

Eventually, Shakespeare nudges his nose into my palm and I laugh, scratching his ears. "Okay, boy. Let's go for a run." And just like that, I'm back to my life as normal.

Chapter 15

The numbers on my budget spreadsheet are beginning to blur together, so I take a minute and push my chair back from my desk, rubbing my eyes. There are only a few weeks left until the gala and from the moment I walked into work on my first day back from my vacation with Laurence, things have been flying at a breakneck speed. Laurence's office is handling an acquisition deal, and I am helping him out with whatever tasks I have time for as I navigate the final details for the gala. I am spending more time out and about making final selections, or at Sanctuary with various vendors and artists, discussing displays, placement, and decor.

My fingers work slow circles around my temples, trying to push away the headache I can feel coming on, and I'm leaning back in my chair, eyes closed, when the ominous 'ping' from my email lets me know that a new message has come in. Sighing, I open my eyes and lean forward, peeking at the notification on my monitor. When I see the name listed in the sender field, I practically fall out of my chair in surprise, yelping as I grab my mouse and open the email.

Mme. Hughes,

I have received reports from multiple executives at our New York branch that your work in recent months, acting in the role of Monsieur Laurence Mercier's executive assistant, has been of both quality and efficiency. Your contribution does not go unnoticed, and I commend you for your exemplary service as to date.

Thank you for your continued efforts on both the project for the Legacy of Health Gala, as well as in assisting M. Mercier in his work for Travers-Moreau.

Veuillez agréer, Madame, mes respectueux hommages.

M. Jacques Moreau
President
Travers-Moreau

I read over the email four or five times in rapid succession. At first I was alarmed, wondering why I would be receiving an email from THE Jacques Moreau, but panic quickly gave way to bewilderment, disbelief, and now utter confusion.

Before I know what I'm doing, my fingers smash the button for the intercom to Laurence's office.

"Oui, qu'est ce que c'est?" His voice is lazily calm, distinctly the opposite of what I'm feeling in this moment.

"I need you! I got this crazy email and I am totally freaking out!" I can faintly hear him call out to me as I hang up as quickly as I call.

Not twenty seconds later, Laurence flies in through the door, looking frazzled and caught off guard. "What is it? Are you alright?" He glances from me to my computer and all I do is point at it.

"Read it!"

He sits at my desk and as he reads, his rigid, frantic posture melts a fraction, until he finally swivels in my chair to face me.

"Is that all?" There is an edge of irritation in his voice for reasons I don't comprehend.

"What do you mean, 'Is that all'? It's your uncle, Laurence! And look what he wrote!"

"Yes, I see what he has written. It appears to be a lovely note, complimenting you on your fine work- which, might I add, he has heard not only from me, but other executives as well." He pauses, staring at me, and when I don't say anything, he tosses his hands up in frustration.

"I fail to see what the problem is here, Camry. Why did you call me in here like this? I thought something awful had happened; that someone had sent you a threat or something unseemly."

Suddenly understanding the reason for his annoyance, my shoulders slump and give him an apologetic grimace. "I'm sorry. I got carried away. I was so surprised and it made me nervous so I called you because..." I trail off, not even sure how to finish that sentence.

"Because?" He doesn't seem willing to let this one go, and I awkwardly wring my hands together behind my back.

"Because... I want to share things with you?"

His scowl gives way to a mirthful laugh and he looks at me the way one looks at an adorably disobedient child. "A pleasant answer, even if I do not believe it to be a wholly truthful one. That being said," he stands, slapping his knees and rising to his impressive height, "I am very pleased to see such a letter has come to you from *le vieillard*. You are a talented, hard working woman, Camry. Why are you surprised that you would be recognized for your efforts?"

His question gives me pause, forcing me to face a hard truth. "I suppose I'm not used to it. Outside of my mother, brother, and Marcus, I've always been extraordinarily average." I smile, though it feels somewhat forced.

"Mon oisillon..." He speaks softly, taking my hand in his. He sounds disappointed, almost sad.

"What?" I link our fingers together and look into his eyes.

"You are far beyond extraordinarily average. Be joyful, be honored, be encouraged that you have received this praise. He would not make the effort to send a note like this for just anyone. You are doing well, and I am proud to have you working here with me."

I swing our connected hands back and forth a little, staring at the ground below them. "Is that all?'

"What do you mean?"

"You're proud to have me working with you."

"Yes, I am."

"Is that all you're proud of?" I meet his gaze, and he shakes his head in feigned exasperation, then leans down and kisses me on the forehead.

"I am proud to have you working with me, and I am proud of my girlfriend, who has received impressive accolades from her company president. I cannot wait to spoil her later tonight."

The serene smile growing across my face at his words is suddenly shocked at his last sentence, as a wicked grin settles onto his features. "Congratulations, *ma colombe*. Now, I must be getting back to work, as should you. But do not forget, we have dinner arrangements at seven o'clock at Leo's!"

He quickly kisses my temple, then leaves like a storm, rushing back into the chaos of our employ.

I take the next hour crafting a careful reply to the president, fingers practically vibrating with nervous excitement at the unexpected praise.

****

A few hours later, I glance at the calendar. Not long, now. We have only two weeks until all my hard work comes to fruition. The buzz of anticipation is increasing day by day, my excitement and nervousness all approaching their crescendo on a February winter's night.

"Deep breaths, Cam," I tell myself. "Calm down. You're not there yet, and you don't want to overlook any details."

But hard as I try to focus, I cannot get anything to come together. My brain feels totally fried, as details are failing me and simple bits of information can't be recalled.

Deciding I must need a small snack, I push back from my desk and stand up quickly. In an instant, my vision clouds over and darkness engulfs me.

****

When I open my eyes, the view takes a few moments to come to focus, and I can't help but wonder why everything looks so strange. That's when I feel my shoulders are on something hard, and I blink a few times to clear my vision.

Why am I on the floor? I start to sit up but bright light flashes and a searing pain rips through my head, causing me to reach up and clutch my skull. My hand lands in something warm and wet. Startled, I pull it back to stare at it. Blood stains the palms of my hands and tips of my fingers. Panic floods my mind, a small sob of worry escaping my mouth. I push myself slowly along the floor, using the edge of my desk to ease myself up, propping my back against the drawers. Vision comes and goes and it feels a monumental effort to stay awake. Forcing myself to stay coherent for fear I'll succumb to the darkness lapping at the edges of my consciousness, I take an inventory of my current state.

I touch my head again, feeling gingerly along the hairline. My breathing is ragged and my whole body tense. What happened to me?

I sit there with no idea how long I've been leaning against the desk, until finally thought and focus begin to return. Slowly, using furniture around me for support, I bring myself to my knees, then to my feet. I move across the office, bracing my hands along the back of my sofa for extra strength. A small glimmer of guilt washes over me, seeing the bloody handprints staining the upholstery. I grimace but continue on towards my lavatory, feet moving like molasses. Finally I slump against the counter, exhausted from the journey.

As I bring my face up to stare into the mirror, I can't help but gasp at what I see. Blood, dried and fresh, stains one side of my face in tracts that mimic tears. My face is covered in a sheen of sweat and my hair is matted in blood along the top of my head. My blouse is soaked along the collar and shoulder, droplets splattered across my breast like a Jackson Pollock painting. The sight steals away the last of my strength and I slump to the floor, leaning against the wall as I try to piece together what has happened.

That's when I hear my office door open.

"Camry, I apologize for taking so long. It should have been a five minute phone call at worst, not-"

Laurence's voice cuts off and his feet come into view. "Camry?" I watch his feet and legs pace across the room, stepping this way and that as he looks around. He moves to the right of my desk, looking past the seating area, then turns; when his eyes fall upon the space behind my desk, his feet freeze mid step.

"Mon dieu."

I try to summon my strength and I call in a hoarse whisper from my place on the bathroom floor.

"Laurence..."

His gaze snaps to me and his eyes widen. In seconds he is kneeling beside me, gathering me into his arms. He cradles me gently, almost as if he might break me. "Camry! What happened? Where are you hurt?" His panic builds and his touch turns almost aggressive, his hands racing over my body checking for injury. He pulls back a bit and I feel more than hear his sudden intake of breath.

"Your head. You've hurt your head." His composure is shot... he's mumbling words and frantic, his normally collected persona crumbling before my eyes. I reach up weakly to him.

"Laurence, I... I don't know what happened."

Those words steal away any strength I had built up and I feel my body sag in his arms again. He nods, coming to his senses. "I'm calling the doctor."

I rest limply in his arms as he shoves a bloodied hand into his pocket and digs out his phone. I can't help but notice that his hands are shaking as he tries to press the keys. Once or twice he has to backtrack, and he curses under his breath.

Finally he pulls the phone up to his ear.

I close my eyes, listening to the gentle thrum of his voice as my head rests against his chest. I can feel his heartbeat thundering in his chest like a herd of wild horses. His voice finally cuts out and I feel him wrap his arms around me again. He whispers into my hair, "I'm sorry, I'm sorry," on repeat. It takes monumental effort, but I lift my hand and gently touch his face.

"Why are you apologizing?" I murmur my words, perplexed at his distress.

Before he can answer a loud banging noise causes us both to jump and immediately a pair of shoes comes into view. Suddenly, a kind face appears in my vision, an older man with a gentle smile. "And what has happened to you, dearie?" He pulls a small flashlight out and shines it in my eyes. I recoil, shutting out the bright light by firmly pushing my eyelids together. I hear him murmur approving sounds and I feel gentle fingers running through my hair and along my scalp.

After a few moments, the touch disappears.

"Well, she definitely hit her head on something around here, and she's going to have a wicked bruise on this arm when she wakes up. This is a decent gash she's got here along the side of her head. You said you saw blood behind the desk?

Laurence's voice floats through my ears and I instinctively relax into his touch. "Yes, I saw blood on the floor behind it and then she called to me from the bathroom." His voice seems strained, almost choked.

If the doctor notices, he doesn't say anything. He gets up and walks over to where I fell. Bending down, he looks carefully around, gently using the tip of his pen to poke at something on my desk. Once satisfied, he rises and returns to us.

"It looks like she fell and hit her head on the edge of the desk. There's evidence of blood and tissues on the corner. I'm guessing the bruising on her arm is from contact with something on the way down." He turns to look into my face, gently touching my arm. "Do you remember what happened before you fell?"

I squint my eyes, trying to pull memories back from nowhere. "I was sitting at my desk, and then I..." I trail off, finding a blank spot between sitting at my desk and waking up on the floor. "... and then I woke up."

He nods, understanding the situation. "Alright. I'm going to call an ambulance and have her sent over to the ER. She needs to get that stitched up. She will need to have some x-rays done to assess a linear fracture, and they'll need to check her over for a concussion and rule out any more severe problems." He looks at me. "That was quite the fall, little lady."

Laurence raises his head and asks the doctor a question. "Would it be alright if I drove her instead?

The closest hospital is not far from here and I have a good rapport with the hospital director."

The doctor frowns and tilts his head, shaking it slightly. "I'm afraid not. Make whatever calls you need to, but she needs to be transported in an ambulance. The EMTs can keep an eye out for any complications that could arise. When I contact them, I'll make sure they take her to New York Met. Okay?"

Laurence is torn, but obviously unable to argue, so he nods and agrees. "Alright." The doctor exits into the hallway, already beginning his call.

Laurence takes out his phone again and dials, this time his hands calm and determined. "Jack, this is Laurence. Yes, well I am afraid not at the moment. I will be coming in soon and my assistant will be arriving with paramedics shortly. She's had a fall and needs to be checked over for TBI. Yes. Thank you."

He ends the call and shifts his weight around underneath me. "Just stay here with me, darling. I'll sit with you until paramedics arrive."

I touch my face to his chest, eyelids feeling heavier by the second.

"No, Camry, stay awake, alright? You need to stay awake." He speaks loudly, enough to pull me back into the brightly lit world around me.

"Tell me, *ma chérie,* what are you most excited about during the gala? Tell me what you are imagining. Tell me what you see when you close your eyes."

The next few minutes pass by, with me slowly talking, trying to pull images and ideas out of my clouded mind. His murmurs are gentle and encouraging, keeping me talking until finally I hear the telltale squeaking of a stretcher's wheels roll into the room, along with the pristinely white sneakers of two paramedics.

"Hello there, Miss Hughes. I'm Rodney, and that's Ben, and we're going to take care of you now, okay?"

The man gives me a smile as soothing as cool rain on a hot summer's day. "And who's this handsome man here?" He points at Laurence, still holding me protectively.

"I'm her boss. And her boyfriend." His answer is concise with no hesitation and Rodney laughs warmly, winking at Laurence.

"I see, I see! Looks like you've caught yourself a good one, Miss Hughes." After a few quick questions and examinations to determine my spinal cord's status, they gently lift me from Laurence's arms and place me on the stretcher. A shock of pain lances through my skull and I hiss, rolling my head to the side to avoid it.

Laurence takes my hand, his expression a mask of barely hidden emotion. "I'm here, *ma colombe*, I'm here."

Rodney stands next to him, taking a few readings with various instruments. "Alright miss, we're going to get you to the hospital. Now, your boyfriend here, is he going to ride with us?"

Laurence cuts me off before I can say anything, squeezing my hand in his. "I'll be going in my own vehicle. But I'll be right there, just a few minutes behind. I'm sorry I can't go with you."

I try and nod my head, but the truth of the situation hits me like a freight train and I feel my eyes begin to water.

Ever since the first visit with my mother, I've abhorred hospitals and doctors' offices. Every anxious feeling, negative bit of news, and paralyzing fear I've felt while sitting beside hospital beds or at a doctor's desk comes back to me in a flood, overwhelming my senses. I don't want to go. I am terrified of all the negativity and the pain that could be awaiting me... and deep within my heart, every weird and confusing medical issue that's been happening to me recently comes back to haunt me, piling up into something I'm no longer able to ignore.

A solitary tear trickles from my eye and down onto the stretcher, pink with the blood stained across my face.

Laurence notices and a grimace of pain and guilt settles into his face as he kisses my fingers.

Rodney speaks up quickly. "Don't you worry, either of you. We'll take good care of you, and he'll be right behind, okay? You just tell me what's wrong and I'll listen. I may not be a dashing French beau, but I can stand in until we get to the hospital, yeah?"

Rodney slaps Laurence on the back and then he and Ben begin to push the stretcher into the hall. Laurence follows closely behind, stopping at the front desk to speak with Miss Davis. She is standing to the side of her desk, worriedly looking on at the sight of me being wheeled into the elevator. Laurence grabs a notepad from Miss Davis' desk and begins to frantically scribble onto it, speaking to her in a quick voice.

"Call a custodian for Camry's office, Miss Davis. They'll need the fluids kit... She fell and hit her head. I'm going with her to the hospital now. Hold all my calls. Also, please send copies of incident report forms to my email. Lastly, would you please contact the names on this list, and tell them that Miss Hughes has suffered a head injury and is being taken to NY Met. They will want to know." He hands her the list, thanks her briefly, and rushes into the elevator beside me just as the doors close. Gently, he takes my hand again, thumb smoothing gentle strokes over my skin the ride down.

When we reach the lobby, the eyes of everyone fall upon us and I keep my sight trained on Laurence's face. I can hear the whispers of curious onlookers, eager to know what catastrophe has befallen an employee of TMC. When they notice Laurence, many straighten and lower their gazes, surreptitiously observing from their places. He is unbothered, keeping our hands clasped and his eyes on mine, an expression of affection and concern on his face. Quietly, he coos reassurances to me as we cross the open space.

Once out on the street, a few jolts and bumps have me loaded into the back. Rodney hops in alongside of me while Ben rushes into the driver's seat. "Say goodbye to your man, Miss Hughes," Rodney says.

"Camry, I'll see you shortly. Don't fret. They'll take good care of you."

I nod my head at him, and force a smile, before Rodney pulls the doors shut and the siren kicks on, the ambulance pulling away from the curb.

Rodney's small talk on the way over keeps me awake and calm, and I watch him fiddle with all sorts of gadgets as he takes readings and enters information onto a tablet. The ride finishes quickly and when we pull into the ER parking lot, the doors open and some nurses pull my stretcher from the ambulance. Rodney smiles at me and bids me farewell.

"I hope my company hasn't been too lacking!" He winks and a small laugh tumbles from my lips. "Ah ha! There we go. You're going to be alright, you know." He waves to the nurses. "Take good care of my girl, you hear?" They take a moment to grab data from his tablet, and before I know it, I've been whisked away into the ER. We march past intake and directly into a private room for examination. The nurse begins to ask me a bunch of questions and she takes various readings, marking details into her tablet as she does so. She's a cheerful woman with a kind smile, maybe even younger than me, and she speaks to me kindly, like I imagine a sister would.

"We need to get you changed. I'm going to undo your buttons now, okay?" She helps me undress and slip into the hospital gown, then lays me back down into the bed and pulls a blanket up over me. "These rooms are always so cold. This should help."

The door flies open and Laurence steps into the room, his hair wind-blown and his appearance disheveled. "Ah, *ma chérie!*" He moves to my side and picks up my hand, thumbs running across the words printed on my ID bracelet. The look on his face tears my heart in two, and I gently squeeze his fingers in mine.

"I'm sorry. This is such a mess. My office... I got blood on my sofa."

A long finger presses against my lips, ending my moment of self-pity. "Hush. You have nothing to apologize for. I'm just glad you appear to be alright."

He gently rubs some of my hair off of my forehead, careful to avoid my injury. "Excuse me, nurse? When can she get cleaned up?"

Before she can answer, the door opens and two men enter; one in scrubs and white coat, the other in a suit and tie. Laurence turns to the more formally dressed man, releasing my hand and taking the man's in a firm shake. "Jack, thank you so much for getting this ready."

Jack turns and looks at me, his voice low as I can tell he's trying not to be obtrusive. I've only met him once in our preparations for the gala, but he had always spoken well of Laurence and I was sure they might consider each other friends. "My God, man. What happened? You said you were at work?"

Laurence shuffles awkwardly. "I wasn't there. I found her after." He clears his throat and I wonder if he is even more terrified than I am. "It looks like she fell and hit her head on her desk."

Jack nods, looking on, his grey haired temples shimmering in the bright lights of the room with each movement.

The other man walks over to me. He peers into my eyes and affixes a kind smile on his face. "I'm Doctor Hansen. I'm here to get you all fixed up. First we will take a blood draw, and run a few easy tests. We are going to figure out why you fell, if we can. And I'm going to stitch up this big ol' hole in your head too." His casual tone makes me feel at ease and I offer him a lopsided grin. "Are you in any pain?"

The moment the word falls from his lips my brain reacts, suddenly registering what I'd been unable to feel before and I wince, sucking in a sharp breath. He mutters a few things to himself and makes a note on my chart, before casually stepping outside. Mere seconds later he returns, accompanied by the same nurse from earlier. "Are you allergic to any medications?"

"No," I mutter weakly.

"This is going to pinch a little, alright? We're just getting an IV started."

I don't know how long it lasts, but my time is filled with being poked, prodded, and bandaged. The bright lights and constant touching make me feel oddly funny, my senses all out of whack. All the while,

Laurence stands in the corner of the room, speaking quietly with Jack, the older gentleman reaching out at times to lay a hand on Laurence's shoulder.

The nurse comes into view again and updates me with what's next on the agenda for me. "We're going to take you in for some x-rays and a CT scan, okay?" She turns her gaze to Laurence. "You're going to have to stay here. We'll be back in no time at all."

Then quickly, she wheels me through the long corridors, until we get to the radiology department. For the next hour I'm laid in multiple awkward positions, commanded to keep perfectly still, and subjected to various embarrassing moments as the techs handle the necessary imagery. Once the technicians in charge of both the x-rays and the CT scan are satisfied, I'm brought back to my room. Much to my relief, Laurence is still here, leaning against the window sill and talking on the phone. I know how busy he is with work at the moment and I can't help but feel guilty over how I'm dragging him down. Noticing our arrival, he quickly ends the call and comes to my side.

"It will be a little while before we have any results for you, so you just rest here. Can I get you anything?"

I ask for another blanket and the nurse obliges, then leaves the room to the two of us. Time passes by slowly. Laurence's phone is ringing constantly, and he grimaces apologetically every time, answering but keeping his conversations short. He sits on the bed with me, never once removing his hand from mine, and I allow myself to close my eyes.

"Camry?" His worried tone is evident and I smile a little, hoping to console him.

"I'm not sleeping. Just... resting my eyes. This headache is a nightmare."

A few more minutes pass in silence, and I feel anchored to reality only by the touch of Laurence's hand in mine. My brain slowly begins to come into focus again, and the fluids from my IV help me feel less worn and empty.

Eventually I hear the door open, and Doctor Hansen enters the room. "Alright Camry. Short story is you're going to be just fine. You've suffered a small linear fracture in your skull, but its a minor one. You bled a lot due to the fact that you popped an artery running along the side of your head but it was a superficial one, so your brain is doing alright and there's nothing to indicate you're in danger of developing anything serious from here out. At this point, the best we can guess is that you suffered a sudden drop of blood pressure, perhaps due to standing too fast, or from being exhausted and not having proper nutrients in your body and not enough sleep. We're going to run your blood work over a few more things to test for hormonal and dietary deficiencies, but for now, I'm going to do some sutures in your head, and then we're going to let you get some rest."

He turns to Laurence and gestures to my IV. "I'm giving her something to help her sleep and someone will come in to check on her in an hour or so. You're welcome to stay with her as long as you'd like."

Laurence tilts his head, a gesture of gratitude. "Thank you."

The doctor faces me again, continuing with his explanations. "You're going to be moved to a regular room and will probably be here a day or two, but then you'll get to go home, as long as you promise to stay at home, resting for the rest of the week."

Absorbing all the details that I can, I nod my head and mutter a brief thanks. "Okay. Thank you."

Laurence steps aside but keeps my hand in his, while the doctor applies some numbing gel to my scalp. It's cold and stings and I wince, squealing in pain. "Sorry about that, but trust me. The worst is over now."

He gets to work and while I can feel a light tugging, there is no pain. After the sutures are in place, the nurse cleans my head with a warm washcloth and swirls lengths of my hair into a small bowl of water, rinsing the blood as clean away as possible.

Finally, the doctor and nurse smile at me and say their farewells, with promises of paperwork and the transfer to a new room.

Jack returns to the room at that point, taking their place, and Laurence firmly shakes his hand. "Thank you, Jack. I owe you."

Jack shakes his head. "Laurence, for all you do for us, you couldn't possibly. Get some rest as well, alright?"

Laurence agrees begrudgingly, and then Jack comes to stand by my bed. "It's good to see you again, Miss Hughes. I'm sorry it is under such circumstances."

"I am too, but thanks." I smile shyly, unsure of the protocol of greeting one's client in a situation like this.

He clicks his tongue, a teasing admonition. "Don't worry about formalities now. At this time, I'm just an old friend of a man who cares very deeply about you."

I must be feeling better because I can feel a tingling blush creep up into my cheeks and I smile at him. Has Laurence told him about us? "Alright, thank you."

"I'm afraid I must be returning to my work, but keep me updated, Laurence. I look forward to hearing of your full recovery, Miss Hughes!"

With a final wave, he exits the room.

As soon as the door closes behind him, the strength seems to leave Laurence and he practically falls into the chair near my bed, head in his hands as he stares at the floor. I sit there, looking at him, wondering what is going on in his head at that moment.

Eventually he sighs and looks up, offering me a small smile. "I'm sure you are exhausted. Would you like me to turn out the lights?"

I study him for a few seconds but find I don't have the energy to sleuth out his behavior, so I nod slowly, and he does so. Only the small lamp in the corner of the room remains on, casting a dull golden glow over the room. Laurence returns to my bedside and pulls the chair closer. He sits and gathers my hand in his, his thumb moving in soothing strokes, carefully avoiding the IV inserted on the back of my hand.

After a few minutes of silence, I can hear his voice, quiet in the dimly lit room. "I'm afraid this is all my fault."

"How can you say that? You didn't do anything wrong."

"No, perhaps not directly. But you have been so enthusiastic about your work and the tasks we have taken on that you are throwing your life out the window. I know you are not sleeping well, and though you eat lunch regularly, what about your dinners? Your breakfasts? You work overtime every day in an effort to keep pace with me and I fear I have overworked you to the point of.... this." He gestures to my state on the hospital bed.

"Don't be silly." The concoction of painkillers and sleeping medicine are starting to drift through my head and my filter is slowly slipping away, honest thoughts tumbling out of my drowsy lips. "I just want to make you proud of me. I like working hard. I like the way you look at me when we get things done, or when I accomplish something important."

"That is exactly what I am saying. You should work hard for yourself, not me or anyone else, and you should not work *this* hard, *this* long. I am used to it. I have lived like this for ten years, and it has taken its toll on me. But I let myself get swept up in your enthusiasm and I did not enforce limits. I have failed you as a supervisor, and as a partner."

I sigh and lift my fingers, tracing them along his knuckles. "You're wrong."

He doesn't reply.

"Laurence?"

"Yes?" His voice is weary and withdrawn and I'm suddenly fearful that he will pull away from me. I grasp his hand tightly and whisper to him in the darkness. "This isn't your fault."

"Perhaps."

A long stretch of silence extends between us, and I cannot keep my eyes open any longer. "Laurence, I'm tired."

He gently squeezes my hand. "Then you should rest."

"Will you stay with me?"

"I will," he says. "I'll stay for as long as I am able."

I close my eyes, feeling his hand wrapped around mine. His fingers dance in circles across my palm, gentle and soothing, and just before I drift off to sleep, I mutter one final thing. "I like it when you touch me like that, Laurence..."

And then I am surrendered to the darkness of deep sleep.

Chapter 16

My eyelids flutter open. I'm in a dimly lit room, and
slowly the memories of yesterday return to me. In the
low lighting I see it's not the same room I was in
before. They must have moved me from the ER to a
regular room while I slept. Another glance around the
room reveals that I'm also alone. Unsure of how long
I've been asleep, I reach around the side of my bed
and fumble until I feel the buttons I know so well
from my mother's many hospital stays. I press the call
button a few times and soon my door opens.

"Hello, Camry. You're awake! I'm Alice and I'm the
nurse on duty right now."

I nod and attempt a small smile. "Um, do you know
where the man I was with earlier is now?"

She nods. "He went home, sweetheart. Did you need
me to call him?"

I shake my head. "No, that's okay." I know it's
unrealistic but my heart sinks at this news. "I'm glad
he's getting some rest."

She smiles. "Alright dear, it's only one in the
morning, but now that you're awake for a bit, I'm
going to do a little check over on you."

For the next few minutes, she takes various readings
and makes notes. I answer all her questions as best as
I can, but the late hour soon catches up to me and I
begin to yawn again.

She rests a gentle palm on my head. "I'm sorry,

Camry. I'm almost done and then you can rest again. Just one last question - they never filled it out earlier. When was the date of your last menstrual period?"

I open my mouth to answer automatically, then shut it because I realize I'm not sure.
"Umm..." I think hard, but realize it's been quite a while since I've had one. "You know I'm not sure. I think it was two or three months ago."

"Are you sexually active?"

Her question is phrased entirely business-like but I can't help but still feel uncomfortable. "Yes, within the last month or so."

She scribbles a few notes. "So your period had stopped before you became sexually active?"

"Yes, I figured it was stress related, honestly."

"Is your period normally regular?"

"It was always pretty regular until last year or so. But since then, my mother died and I started a new job and now I'm on a huge project and it wouldn't be a stretch to say I'm stressed right now."

Her eyebrows lift a moment and she studies me. "How old was your mother when she died?"

"Fifty-seven. She had pancreatic cancer."

She makes a few notes. "Okay. I'm going to go ahead a draw a little more blood."

I nod and she attaches a new tube to my IV, pulling blood into the small plastic container. I watch it fill up and shudder some, remembering the experience in my office yesterday.

I speak up, tiredness momentarily set aside in favor of curiosity. "Do you know anything more about why I fell? They said something about my blood pressure, but still wanted to do a little more research to find out."

"I promise we'll tell you anything new as soon as we know, alright?"

I nod. "Okay."

She smiles and says, "Alright, go ahead and get some more sleep now. I'll be around in the morning when you wake up."

"Thank you." I drift off quickly.

****

I'm just rousing from sleep the next morning when the door to my room suddenly flies open. Standing in the doorway, out of breath and looking utterly disheveled is the last person I ever expected to see: my brother. "Ciaran?!"

"Camry!" He runs over to me and hugs me so tightly I feel like my ribs are going to crack. Then he releases me and glares at me. "What the hell, sis?"

"Isn't that what I should be asking you? What are you even doing, barging in here? Why aren't you in Boston?"

"Well excuse me for not being a terrible brother!" He huffs at me and when I shoot him an exasperated look he lifts his hands feigning innocence. "Your boss, er, boyfriend called me."

The blood drains from my face. "You're kidding me. Laurence called you?"

"Yes, yesterday night, and I took the first Acela train down."

"I can't believe you did that. It's not such a big deal, Ciaran. I just fell. I was exhausted. I've been working too much and I just fainted, so it's-"

He throws down his bag with a loud thud, irritation plain on his face. "Can you imagine what I felt like, getting that phone call? It hasn't even been a year since mom died, and here you are, pulling a stunt like this! If you think I hesitated for even a second before coming here, I'm insulted at how little you must think I care. Jesus, sis! I felt like the ground had dropped out from under me!"

His impassioned speech now over, he stares at me with a desperate expression on his face and I burst into tears on the spot.

"Oh god, Cam, I'm sorry. I'm sorry." He moves to sit with me on the bed, wrapping his arms around me and holding me tightly, absorbing the shudders of my sobs.

"I bet you were scared too. I'm sorry. I..." he cuts himself off, squeezing me tighter. "I need you, okay? I was terrified."

I nod my head roughly against his chest, letting the tears fall. The stitches in my head throb with each heaving breath and I force myself to get my sobs under control.

In time the tears cease, and with that the cathartic but wearying feeling that follows a meaningful cry. I lie down on the bed and Ciaran curls up behind me. We lay there, not speaking, for a few minutes, before the door opens and Alice pokes her head in.

She smiles brightly at us, seeming completely unsurprised to see Ciaran there. "Thought I'd give you two some time for a happy reunion before I had to come in here and break up the party."

I can't help but return her smile, and slowly extract myself from my brother's arms, sitting up in bed. Ciaran rises as well, stretching. It's only now I can see the dark circles under his eyes, and I realize how exhausted he looks. "You look like hell, you know."

He rolls his eyes. "So says the girl with the Frankenstein scar."

I feign indignance. "I'll have you know I worked hard for this!"

Alice laughs from her place at the counter, thumbing through some paperwork. "Alright, Camry. One of the doctors is going to be by in a few minutes and she's going to go over some important information with you. But first, let's get the fun stuff out of the way."

She takes readings of blood pressure, pulse oximetry, temperature, and a few more, scribbling away at her notepad and typing into her tablet.

Once satisfied, she turns to me. "Your boyfriend was here this morning at the crack of dawn. Visiting hours were nowhere near time yet, but I hear he's got some special privileges here, seeing as he's Mr. Mercier, and all!" She winks, laughing at her own joke. "Your gala plan for this year sounds really lovely. I'm looking forward to hearing about it after it's over."

"Oh! Did he tell you about it?"

"Yes, came down to the nurses' station after he snuck in here to give you a quick kiss while you were sleeping. He told us all about how you're the one in charge of the gala this year and he was gushing all about you."

I look down, trying to hide the smile I can feel on my face. "I'm glad he came by. I wish I had been awake though!"

"He'll be back later. Don't you worry. Now I have to scoot! You're not the only patient I have here!" She winks and waves goodbye to both of us before exiting the room.

There's only two seconds of silence before Ciaran begins to chuckle.

"Don't say anything." I glare at him and he puts his hands up in innocence.

"I didn't! I didn't!"

Begging for a change in subject, I ask Ciaran to give me the latest updates of his family, and we spend the next hour browsing the hundreds of pictures and videos that Ciaran has of his daughter on his phone.

Eventually there's a knock on the door and a doctor sticks her head in, accompanied by a nurse I am unfamiliar with.

"Good morning, Camry. I'm Doctor Allen, an endocrinologist here at NY Met." She shakes my hand, and reaches out to Ciaran.

"Ciaran Hughes, Cam's brother."

"Nice to meet you." The doctor pulls up a stool and sits down in front of us on the bed. The nurse hands her a file and she opens it a bit, taking a few seconds to glance over the information, before resting it across her lap and looking at me.

"After taking a look at some of your symptoms and running your blood and urine, we've been able to come up with a solid diagnosis for what you are experiencing. Based on the endocrinology reports, you're dealing with hyperparathyroidism, which is when one or more of your four parathyroid glands are producing too much of their hormone. We're confident this can explain some of what you've been dealing with lately."

I take in a deep breath. "Okay." I don't really know what or how to feel, my mind still trying to grasp what the doctor has said.

"The most basic treatment for this is surgery to remove the affected glands. Most of the time, the surgery is outpatient, and doesn't require anything but localized anesthesia. It's generally a minimal procedure, and has a 95% success rate, so we'll start looking into scheduling that for you. You'll meet beforehand with the surgeon, and he'll go over the details of the procedure with you at that time." She looks at me directly, a kind expression on her face. "You with me so far?"

"I think so." The sight of my mother comes to mind, laying in a hospital bed, tubes and wires attached to her sickly frame, and before I know it, I'm imagining myself in a similar situation. I rub my palms along my thighs, wiping the thin layer of sweat forming on them off. Ciaran notices my behavior and lays his arm across my shoulders.

"Does the surgery have to be soon?" I bite my lip, trying to think of how this could all affect the gala. "I've got a big event coming up in a few weeks at work, and-"

The doctor taps her pen on the folder in her lap. "It doesn't have to be urgent, no. But it should be taken care of in a timely manner. We can hold off a few weeks, if needed."

She pauses, and her eyes flicker to Ciaran's face for a moment, then return to mine. "That all being said, we'd like to do a little more investigation. The symptoms you described and the different results we have from your blood tests are leading us to believe that your hyperparathyroidism is secondary; meaning, it's stemming from another cause that needs evaluation and treatment."

"What?" My eyes widen as worry and fear settle from her words. "There's something else wrong with me?"

Doctor Allen leans over, a kind yet stern look on her face. "First off, don't think of it like that. There isn't anything 'wrong' with you; it's just that your body is working a little differently than normal, and we're here to help it do a better job. Secondly, there could be an underlying factor here, yes, but remember that learning about your body and what it is doing are good things. We want to know what we can so you can live as healthy of a life as possible."

I swallow, unable to process what she is saying. Ciaran asks the next question, cutting off my spiraling thoughts.

"What kind of testing are you talking about?"

"It's straightforward and simple. It involves taking a swab of the inside of your cheek. We're doing this to see if we can't gain some more insight into some of your other symptoms and a little more about why you lost consciousness. So we would like to run some genetic testing in order to see if there's something hereditary that might clue us in."

Ciaran nods along, listening intently. "Sounds simple enough. You in?"

I meet his eyes and he seems confident, so I turn to the doctor and agree. "Okay."

She pulls a small vial out, accompanied by a cotton swab wrapped in plastic. "Just open your mouth and say, 'ah'."

I comply, and she sweeps the papery dry tip across the inside of my mouth, before taking it and placing it into the vial.

"All done. Now, what questions do you have for me?"

****

My initial shock and irritation at Laurence's decision to call Ciaran quickly morphs into gratitude. His presence alone is a monumental help to me today, and with lots of conversation, hugs, and laughter, I'm feeling much better about all of this. Still conflicted about being stuck in a hospital, Ciaran's reassurances are invaluable to me. He promises to come and be with me for the surgery, and during a long phone call with Asher, Ciaran's husband, we settle on some tentative dates. Once I receive input with Laurence, we will go ahead and schedule the surgery.

Feeling a bit more relaxed, we are now making our way through the questionable food items on our hospital cafeteria meal trays during dinner in my room. The nurse comes in with more medication to help with the pain and to fend off any possible infection, and Ciaran does a remarkable impression of the way the pudding on our plates wiggles with each bump of the tray.

I'm trying to stifle giggles, so that my wound doesn't hurt any more than necessary, when my phone chimes with an incoming text. Laurence is almost at the hospital!

I tell Ciaran as much and he quickly sits up straight, a serious expression settling onto his features.

"Ciaran? What's up?" I eye him curiously, wondering what could have changed him so quickly.

He doesn't respond, but stands and distractedly smooths out his clothing, tidying up the dishes on his tray, and glances around the room.

"Good grief, what's gotten into you?" I speak a little louder, causing him to stop and give me a severe look.

"Your boyfriend is about to be here, and in case you've forgotten, I've never met the man."

"So?" I tilt my head and give him an odd look, which seems to frustrate him.

"Don't worry about it, Camry. It's nothing for you to freak out about."

I stare him down for a few seconds more before I shrug my shoulders. "Whatever."

Ciaran finally returns to the bed, sitting beside me, but his posture is rigid and he looks as if he's about to face a villain in a fantasy novel. I lean over and whisper, "Why are you so tense?"

"I'm not tense," he replies, rolling his shoulders.

Suddenly it all clicks and I can't keep a giggle from bubbling up. "Pfffft! You're nervous!"

The look he sends me could stop anyone else in their tracks. I've seen him use it before. But this is me he's dealing with and it only fuels my laughter. I cackle, pressing a hand to my head as the pain ripples through it. "Ahhh dammit, don't make me laugh!"

"I am doing no such thing!" He pouts at me and I wheeze a little, trying to get my laughter under control.

Finally calming down, I notice his shoulders relax a fraction, but he's still sitting with impeccable posture and I can't help but smile.

Not two seconds later, Laurence bursts into the room and freezes momentarily, seeing Ciaran beside me.

I watch his eyes carefully, observing him as he works out all the details in his brain.

He shifts awkwardly, then seems to find his composure and crosses the room, extending a hand. "You must be Ciaran." Ciaran stands, accepting it with a firm shake.

"I am. And you must be Laurence."

"Indeed. I cannot thank you enough for coming all this way to be with her. I'm sure she has found your presence invaluable today."

Ciaran gives Laurence an appreciative smile. "I'm grateful you called me last night. Knowing this one," he jerks a finger over his shoulder at me, "it would have been days before she called to tell me anything."

At that, Laurence walks over to me and places a gentle kiss upon my forehead, careful to avoid the wounded area.

He kneels in front of me, running a hand along my cheek. "How are you doing today?"

"Better. But, I have news."

"Oh?" He pulls a chair over toward the bed and sits before me. Ciaran takes his place beside me and slowly I explain everything, from what the doctor told me, to what Ciaran and I discussed. Laurence sits quietly, and he doesn't speak at all until I draw a slow and shaky breath.

"And you have decided on the third week in February?" His voice is quiet and he speaks slowly. I nod, and he lets out a deep sigh.

"I cannot say I am happy about that. If it were up to me, you would do this sooner. I want you healthy now - not eventually. But..." he pushes a hand through his hair, signs of resignation on his face. "Something tells me that you would stage a full *coup d'etat* if I asked you to have your surgery before the gala."

I grin at him, brimming with happiness at his understanding. "You're damn right I would." I lean forward and kiss him on the cheek, then rest my forehead against his. "Thank you. I'll work hard for you until then."

Laurence sits up quickly, a look of incredulity on his face. "You will do no such thing! I will welcome your presence at the gala itself as the primary organizer, but you are going to otherwise rest until you are completely healed from this injury, and then to limit further risks, you'll take a leave of absence until the surgery."

My emotions do a complete one-eighty, frustrated with his typical overbearing and protective mindset. "Absolutely not! They want me to rest for a few more days but there is nothing about my healing or my diagnosis that says I cannot return to work. If none of this had happened-"

Laurence cuts in, hand up to stop me. "But it did happen!"

My words plow over his, voice raised. "This is my project, Laurence. I'm going to finish it!"

He grunts in obvious irritation and Ciaran, sitting as a spectator this whole time, speaks up. "Look, I can tell you care deeply for my sister, but you need to know something about her. She's never been one to stay quiet, back down from a fight, or behave the way others wanted her to. She's her own woman, and she runs her own show. You can forbid her from coming into work but she'll resent you for the rest of her life for it, and to be honest, nobody's going to do as good of a job as she will. She's been on this project the whole time and she knows the artists, the vendors, everyone. Once she's able to go back to work, you'll be within a week of this thing happening. Are you really saying you'll get by without her?"

I stare at Ciaran, touched by his defense of me, before I look at Laurence, scowling with determination. "He's right, you know."

Laurence's eyes waver and he lets out a shaky breath. "But what if something happens; what if you fall again? What..." His voice falters, raw with emotion. "Camry, do you have any idea what it felt like for me to find you like that?" He places one hand on my knee, the other he lifts to my cheek. "Camry, I-"

"I do know, Laurence." Softly, I place my hand over his and take it into my own. "I do, because I dealt with things like that with my mother. Don't take this away from me, please. I want to do this, and I want to finish this. With you."

I watch his face, turmoil of his thoughts raging a silent storm inside his mind. Finally he hangs his head and speaks, softly.

"Alright." He shakes his head back and forth slowly. "Alright." Lifting his head, he looks me in the eye. "But you monitor your hours every day. No more working late into the night."

"Okay." I agree, and smile. "You're so stubborn, Laurence."

"As if you are not?" Finally a slight smile edges on his lips, and he kisses my fingers. Turning to Ciaran, he purses his lips. "You are obviously her brother. What your mother must have been like to have cut the two of you from the same cloth."

Ciaran and I smile and laugh, and he shakes his head in humor. "You have no idea, Laurence. You have no idea."

****

Two days later I'm getting ready to leave the hospital, feeling very much back to normal and my head is healing nicely. In the few days I've been here, I've had visits from Alex and Hayden, who brought a small vase of daisies, and from Jameson Jones, who came carrying an obscenely large flower arrangement. His visit was short, but I was very grateful that Laurence was not there at the time. While cheerful and bearing entertaining stories I was glad for, Jones was also true to form, his flirty demeanor not subdued by the sterile environment. He kissed my hand, winking at me, as he made his exit. As the door finally fell shut behind him, I breathed out a sigh of relief, both grateful for and immensely irritated by his visit.

Laurence has spent a fair amount of time with me during the evenings, but during the days he returns to work. Now, as I'm waiting for my discharge paperwork, he is promised to arrive and take me to his home. After a rather fierce argument between us, I finally gave in to him that I should stay at his home with him during my week of bedrest. He was fretting immensely about my being alone for days on end and with Ciaran returned home to Boston, Laurence asked me to stay with him so that he could at least watch over me in the evenings. After complaining that I'd already asked Hayden to watch over Shakespeare enough, he stated with conviction that the dog could come too, and I relented. He left last night satisfied and I left our conversation exhausted.

My door slowly opens and a nurse enters, cheerfully bringing me a few pages to sign. "Here's your discharge paperwork!" He hands me the stack and I sigh in relief, entirely ready to be leaving this place.

The nurse sits with me, going over my wound care, pain medication, and activity limitations, when Laurence arrives. The nurse pauses to say hello, but Laurence waves him on. "Don't mind me. Please, continue." I can tell Laurence is listening carefully to what the nurse is saying, a look of concentration settled on his brow. Finally, the nurse hands me a pen. "Sign here, here, and here."

With the business side completed, the nurse brings in a cart for my bags and flowers. Then another nurse arrives with a wheelchair and I groan, staring at it. "Sorry, but it's procedure. Have a seat and let us spoil you just a little bit longer."

Begrudgingly, I take my place in the wheelchair and Laurence walks behind us as our little caravan moves through the hallways and elevators until we arrive at the entrance.

Laurence runs off to bring his car around, and the nurse with my wheelchair smiles at me. "Thank you again for what you've done for the gala this year. We're all looking forward to hearing about it when it's over!"

My cheeks flame with embarrassment and I duck my head. "Oh sheesh. I'm not doing anything all that special."

"I highly doubt that, but keep up the good work."

"Okay," I acquiesce, still feeling a mix of awkwardness and pride.

Laurence's car saves me from further discussion, pulling into the portico and gliding to a stop. He steps around and takes my hand. "Are you ready, *ma chérie?*"

I nod and Laurence opens the door for me, helping me sit, then takes the various flower arrangements and my bags and places them in the backseat.

He turns to the nurses waiting there and offers them a grateful bow of his head. "I am truly grateful for all you have done for Miss Hughes. I cannot thank you enough."

They smile at him and each other. "No need to thank us, Mr. Mercier. We hope the gala goes well!"

He shakes each of their hands, then turns to the car. I send each of them a little wave and they return it, one giving me an enthusiastic thumbs-up which earns a burst of laughter from me.

Once in the driver's seat, Laurence glides the car away from the curb. "Let's stop by your home first. We can collect any more of your things that you might need, as well as Shakespeare."

"That sounds good. I can't wait to see him."

He smiles and takes my hand in his. "I am sure you are happy to be leaving. Thank you for agreeing to stay at my home. I will do everything I can to make sure you are comfortable there."

I sigh a little, not wanting to rehash the same argument but I am unable to hold my tongue. "It's not comfort I am worried about, Laurence. It's boredom, and feeling helpless. There's nothing to do there, and I'm losing out on so many things I need to do for the gala. I'm supposed to be in charge of this; I want to do it. I feel like I'll just be sitting around on my ass all the time." My irritation brings out a crass attitude and I am met with an inscrutable expression on Laurence's face.

There's a few seconds of silence before Laurence speaks. "I'm sorry."

He faces forward, eyes focused on driving, but I can see the muscles of his jaw clench for a brief moment before he slowly drags a hand through his hair. He begins to speak again, haltingly, weighing his words. "I'm sorry. I do not mean to smother you. I know you value your independence, and truth be told, that is one of the things I most cherish about you."

He stops to draw a slow breath. "I worry that you will get hurt again, or that I might lose you. I am not used to uncertainty. I've led a privileged life but it was not without trials. I've struggled and faced difficulties. But everything I have ever wanted has been attainable with focus and determination, and every challenge I have met I have overcome by the work of my own two hands. This is the first time I've had anything precious to me that I cannot fix with these!" He pulls his hands away from the steering wheel, clenching them helplessly around air. His emotional moment is over quickly, a deep breath easing his shoulders back to their natural position. He returns his hands to the wheel, gripping it ever so lightly. When he speaks again, his voice is subdued, almost wistful.

"It is hard enough convincing myself that I am not to blame for overworking you and causing your loss of consciousness. It is worse to feel that I am helpless, unable to protect you or take away your pain and worry. I have no recourse and I hate that I can only stand and watch as you suffer!"

A pained expression is etched on his features and I reach out, laying a hand on his arm. "But you're not."

"Not what?"

"You're not only standing and watching. You're here. And that means the world to me. I'm really touched that you care so much for me, and that you wish you could change the world to make everything better. But you can't, Laurence. I can't either. Don't beat yourself up so much over it."

His eyes flick over to my hand resting on his forearm, and then to my face. I smile softly at him and he sighs, blinking slowly before bobbing his head in surrender.

"I will try."

"And I'll try to be patient and mindful of my health more."

He chuckles, his normal calm demeanor sliding back into place. "That is all I can ask."

I squeeze his arm gently and send him a significant look. "But that doesn't mean I'm converting to being a pampered princess. I am not going to sit back and let things happen around me. I'm going to be a part of my work and my life. I can do this, and I need you to trust me."

His teeth rake over his bottom lip, a sign of his internal struggle. Finally he nods once, and turns his eyes back to the road.

The rest of the ride passes in silence but the atmosphere is more comfortable, now that we've each said what we needed to. At the last stoplight, I press a kiss to his cheek and he smiles at me, a little less weary than before.

Pulling up to my apartment, I'm struck by how long it feels since I have been here. I eagerly scramble out of the car and hand in hand with Laurence, climb the steps to my front door. With a click, the lock turns, and within seconds there's a blur flying across the room towards me.

"Whoa, boy! You've got to be careful with me! I'm damaged goods, you see." I turn my injured side away from him, holding him close and burying my face in his thick fur. "I missed you too, buddy."

Laurence steps around us, careful not to interrupt the reunion. After a few more minutes of furry snuggles and dog kisses, I extract myself from my place on the floor and give Shakespeare's head a few more loving pats.

"Hey boy, we're going on a little trip together. You're going to come stay with me at Laurence's house!"

He cocks his head, giving a few Husky chatters, before trotting along beside me, nose pressed to my hand as much as he is able.

"He's missed you," Laurence observes. "I'm glad he'll be coming along with us."

I look down into the pale blue eyes staring up at me, and smile. "Me too."

We pack up a few more bags of my things and a box of Shakespeare's favorites, piling into the car together.

Shakespeare's boundless energy seems amplified in this moment and a sudden thought occurs to me. "I just realized. He's going to make your car all disgusting. He doesn't often ride in cars and I'm sure his hair and slobber is going to go everywhere."

Laurence pauses for a minute, wearing an inscrutable expression, before he smiles softly at me. "It's nothing that cannot be cleaned. Not to worry."

True to my prediction, the excitement from a rare car ride for Shakespeare proves incredible, and he bounds back and forth across the backseat, nose to the window cracks, insatiable curiosity and infectious joy bringing a smile to my lips.

As the car pulls into the garage, I turn and look at my dog. "Shakespeare." I use a firm voice and he stops mid-flip and looks at me. "You need to be a good boy, okay? This is Laurence's home and you're a guest, so no chewing and no accidents."

He makes a noise that sounds almost like a solemn agreement and I burst out laughing at the entire exchange.

"You need not worry, Camry. I am more than delighted to have you both here with me and I am confident that Shakespeare will make for a fine housemate." Laurence helps me out of the car, one hand gently placed on my back.

The fingers of his other hand reach out to gently cup my cheek, and he stares softly into my eyes. "There is no need for you to consider yourself a guest, Camry. You are my girlfriend, are you not? You are welcome here at any time, day or night, for as long as you need." He bends down and places a soft kiss against my lips and I practically purr at his gentle touch.

"Thank you, Laurence. It means a lot."

He winks at me, then opens the back door and Shakespeare leaps out, nose to the ground, sniffing and examining his new environment.

"Shall we?" Laurence offers me his arm and we make our way into the house.

Once I'm settled onto the sofa, Laurence turns toward the kitchen. "I'll put a kettle on for some tea, then bring in everything from the car. You relax here for a moment."

I watch as he goes, looking around. The familiar room helps to put some of my anxieties to rest, and I enjoy watching Shakespeare roam, investigating all the sights, sounds, and smells of his new space.

When Laurence is finished with the luggage, he walks to me, holding something behind his back.

"What do you have there?" I ask, full of curiosity.

What he sets down in front of me is something I would never have expected: a sleek silver laptop. "What's this?"

He rubs his chin and shrugs a bit, a sheepish look settling on his features. "I know that you would rather be at home, or even at work. But since you are staying here, and not allowed back to work yet, I thought you might appreciate a little work being brought to you."

I gape at him, piecing together his words. "This is a work laptop?"

"*Oui*, it is linked to the server in your office so you can access all of your work remotely. While I wish you would simply enjoy the time off, I know you; and that instead of sitting still, you would wind up reorganizing my spice cabinet or dusting my furniture, so I thought that it would be a better idea to give you something to do that would at least be stationary." He pushes his hair back off his forehead as he often does, and I smile at the gesture. "I know you care about your work, and you hate to miss it, so hopefully you won't feel like I've shut you out too much."

I soften at his words, realizing that he is - and has been - well aware of my thoughts regarding all of this. "You sure know how to make a girl, swoon, Laurence," I joke, and I see his shoulders relax somewhat. "I do feel better knowing I can work from here. Truly, I do. Thank you so much! This is really thoughtful. Now I don't have to worry, and I can keep helping you out."

He frowns a little, staring at the computer. "Camry, you have somehow convinced yourself that you have to do everything alone and that you can't slow down or take a break. You are a force to be reckoned with, but that doesn't mean you can't ask for help when you need it, or rest when you are tired. Please, pay attention to yourself. I need you at your best, both for work..." he sits beside me and pulls me close, fingers twining with mine, "...and for us."

I giggle a bit at his expression but nod my head in agreement. "Yes, sir."

He sighs in mock exasperation, but kisses my temple. "You'll be the end of me, Camry. I am simply no match for you."

I laugh again, snuggling closer to him, and a murmur of contentment slips past my lips. "Thank you."

His arm curls around my shoulder, pulling me close. "You're welcome."

Chapter 17

My fingers tap against my phone nervously, writing, deleting, and writing some more. Stepping onto the subway, I press the button to send off the text before I can lose my courage. The rumble of the train as it races through the tunnels picks up my heart rate, and I fidget nervously bouncing back and forth between my feet.

When I finally face the sunlight again, I take in a deep breath, smiling to myself. The quick walk to my apartment is lively at this time of day, school children shrieking in happiness at the escape onto city sidewalks.

I scuttle past a small group of them and make the final dash up the stairs to my front door. With Shakespeare still at Laurence's house, it's quiet inside, and I take a quick inventory of the place, hoping everything looks okay.

Now that I'm finally cleared to return to work and other activities, the 'other' has been buzzing in my mind and abdomen since I left the doctor's office an hour ago. Once I've picked up the few things laying around, I sift through my lingerie drawer, untouched for an embarrassingly long time. Finally I pull out a black set that I think still fits, and take my time putting it on, carefully tightening the laces on the corset. For the next half hour, I style my hair, apply some light makeup, and light candles around my apartment. I'm giddy with both excitement and uneasiness. I really hope he likes this. It's been a long time since I've been both so forward and so daring, and Laurence has yet to see me like this.

A moment of panic seizes me up, wondering if perhaps I've made the wrong call. What if he's not into this? What if this is weird?

I don't have time to worry. Someone knocks on my door and I creep over to it, pressing my ear to the door. "Hello?"

"Camry? It's me."

"One second!" I race into my bedroom and toss on a bathrobe. I hadn't thought this part through and suddenly I'm more nervous than ever! Am I really prepared to go through with this?

Knowing I can't leave him on the doorstep, I slowly open the door, an embarrassed smile on my face. "Come on in."

He takes one look at my coiffed hair and subtle makeup and lifts an eyebrow. His eyes sweep over my appearance and while he looks slightly confused, he doesn't say anything. Stepping inside, he sets his briefcase down and stretches, then bends down to kiss me sweetly.

"Hello, darling."

"Hi," I say, my voice a shy attempt of its usual animation.

"Are we going somewhere and I have forgotten? You are all done up."

An awkward, high pitched giggle escapes my lips and I stutter. "No, I..."

My eyes flit around the room, searching for a distraction. My kettle catches my eye and I latch onto that idea. "Would you like some tea?"

He's not deterred, barely listening in his perplexion. "Camry, why do you have candles lit everywhere? Did your apartment have an odor after being gone for the week?"

Realizing this is not going as I planned, I huff a little in annoyance. Subtlety isn't working. Grabbing his hand, I drag him over to the sofa and with a little push, send him backwards into the cushions. Mentally shoving all my anxiety aside, I untie the sash of my robe and it slips from my shoulders onto the ground at my feet.

Laurence blinks at me for a few moments, unmoving, then a noise of confusion gets caught in his throat. He clears it awkwardly, shifting his eyes to the side. "Camry, what are you doing?"

A flare of frustration rises but I quell it, focusing on what I want. "Laurence, I'm as good as new. The doctor said I'm good, and I can go back to work and... everything." He still avoids eye contact but his Adam's apple bobs with the word and I smirk to myself.

"I want you. Please?"

I watch as his eyes slowly climb up my body, taking in the black lace and satin. "Camry, I don't know... This is so soon, what if-"

I cut him off, moving closer. "It's fine. I'm fine! Except I'm not fine because it's been too long and god, Laurence, please for once ignore that voice of caution in your head and listen to me instead. I need you."

His eyes flash but he still seems hesitant. Slowly, I lower myself to sit beside him and run my fingers up along the insides of his thighs. He shudders a great breath and clamps his eyes shut. I lean forward and press a kiss to his lips and I gasp at the feeling. Always afraid of hurting me, he had barely touched me since my fall, and I had near forgotten what it felt like to have his lips against mine. I drag my tongue along the space between his lips and he moans into my mouth. Taking advantage, I slip my tongue inside and run my fingers along the sides of his face. His heart is beating a million miles a minute and before long he pulls me onto his lap, fingers curled around my waist, holding me fast to him. I begin to move against him slowly, rocking my hips to his.

Suddenly he pulls back. "No."

"No?" I can't help the hurt in my voice.

"Not here. If we are going to do this, we will do it right." He slides me off his lap and stands, taking my hand and tugging me after him. When we reach my bed, he sits and slinks out of his suit jacket, tugging his tie loose. I can't help but bite my lip at the gesture. Watching the always put together Mr. Mercier become just the opposite - completely undone - by my hand is tantalizing and powerful. "Come here."

He pulls me close and I stand before him, bending down to kiss his lips. His hands ghost along my sides, playing with the strings crossing the corset. A smile pulls at my lips as I realize he's undoing my laces and before long he tugs on it, pulling it up over my head. "God, you are beautiful," he whispers against the skin of my stomach, breath sending a shiver of pleasure through my body.

Feeling high and powerful, I murmur a question. "Did you miss this? Miss me?"

His reply is instant. "Every day." Following his words with a quick nip on sensitive skin, my gasp is cut off by his hands guiding me around until I'm laying on the bed under him. Soft kisses find their way across my skin, and I reach my hands down to his hair. I try to pull him up to me, but he slinks away, placing a soft kiss to my forehead. "Gently, *ma colombe*, gently. Let me be careful with you."

I nod, relishing the worshipful way he touches me. My eyes fight a battle to close in pleasure but I force myself to keep them open, recording everything of this moment. My right hand reaches out and tugs open the drawer on my nightstand, sifting through trinkets until I find what I'm looking for. I set the condom on the pillow beside me then reach down and work the belt off his trousers, tugging them down with my toes. He smirks at me for a moment, noting my impatience.

We make quick work of the rest of our clothes until I'm lying beneath him, bare and vulnerable. His breath is ragged as he looks at me, toes to crown, and then he slides up and places the gentlest of kisses against the scar on my head.

Then, with boyish exuberance, he grabs the condom and slips it on, eyes fluttering closed at the contact. I can tell he needs this as much as I do.

I pull him back to me, head tipping into the pillow as I feel him fill me. The sound of pleasure we both make at the contact is exhilarating, and I pull him down for another kiss. Slowly he curls his arms around my shoulders, keeping us close as we move together. The room is quiet, save the sounds of our love-making, and it turns me on even more. I squirm a little under him and he moves up again, pulling one of my legs up over his shoulder. "Is this alright?"

"More than. That feels incredible."

His hips rock into me, strong and tender, and his hands roam my breasts, covering them as if he is recording them to memory. The consistent, fluid strokes build in my belly, a quivering excitement growing with each movement. I can feel release coming, and fast, and I barely have time to get the words out before the waves crash around me, like bolts of lightning under my skin.

Laurence grunts at my tightening around him and his tenderness evaporates, giving into his need. He pushes into me with strength, pace quickening with his urgency. A few jerking movements later and he exhales sharply, brows knit together as he stills.

He heaves a great breath and collapses on top of me, propped on both elbows to avoid settling his weight on me. He peppers small kisses on my brows, laying mostly still as our breathing calms.

A minute later, he sighs and chuckles to himself, a mocking smile on his lips.

"What?"

"I am powerless against you."

I giggle madly, lifting up just enough to place a quick nibble against his jawline. "And don't you forget it."

Laughter rumbles in his chest pressed to mine and he kisses me to silence my teasing. "As if you'd ever let me."

****

The rest of the night is spent with us returning to Laurence's home and collecting my things. Shakespeare is excited to see us, and on the way home he's practically frantic when his nose picks up familiar smells in the frigid January air. The first thing he does when we open the door is race into my bedroom and leap onto the bed. Burrowing his face in the sheets, he lets out a contented whine and begins to roll around happily.

Giggling at his behavior and blushing at remembering what happened there just hours before, I shake my head. "Silly dog."

Laurence, insisting on carrying up all my bags, steps into the apartment with a solemn expression. I tilt my head, observing him. "Why the long face?"

He looks around, gently setting down my things. "I suppose I shall miss you."

I straighten up, eyes brightening. "What do you mean?"

Laurence clears his throat, eyes on his shoes. "I enjoyed having you there. At my home."

His sheepish behavior makes me laugh and he pouts a little which only spurns my giggles more. "I'm sorry. I'm sorry! I don't mean to laugh at you," I say, though the smile on my face betrays me. "It's just really adorable."

He glowers at me mockingly. "Adorable?"

Teasingly, I tap the end of his nose. "Adorable." Sneaking a kiss on his lips, I slip my arms around him. "I'll miss you too."

"But it's good to be home." He finishes my sentence for me and I smile.

"Got it in one!"

Bending down, he returns my kiss, though this time it lingers. When he pulls back, he traces a finger along my lips. "We should get you settled in again. After all, someone has work bright and early tomorrow."

****

The following days of work go well - too well. The gala is coming together with precision and skill and my confidence is the highest it has been. Unfortunately, the weather outside as I make way down the street stands in stark contrast to my internal mood.

Tucking my shoulders down beneath the collar of my coat, I grip my umbrella tightly. A frigid rain pelts passersby and cars alike as they rush through the streets of Manhattan. I glance behind me just in time to see a taxi come barreling down the road, heading straight for the puddle beside me.

"Shit!" The taxi splashes right through, creating a fountain of dirty water that I only half avoid with a quick movement of my umbrella. The cascade I don't manage to block ends up covering the side of my face and shoulder, muddy splotches bringing my chill to new heights.

I mutter a few choice words under my breath and try to shake off as much as I can before continuing through the streets on my way to the doctor's office.

The office where I'm headed is in exactly the wrong location. If it had been a few blocks more I would have splurged on a taxi, but at exactly three blocks away, it's not worth doing anything but walking, even in this abysmal weather.

Finally making it to the lobby, I knock my umbrella against the door frame a few times before stepping inside.

I hurriedly make my way into the bathroom and observe the damage. Worse than I had originally thought, my first inclination is to strip my shirt off, quickly rub out as much of the mud as possible, and dry it, but memories of that morning I started work with Laurence surface and I burst out with nervous laughter. Recalling the embarrassment in Jones' office, I grab a few paper towels and try to discreetly clean up as much as I can.

Once I've decided I'm as good as I'm going to get, I leave the bathroom and take the elevator to the fourth floor where the doctor's office is.

I check in and take a seat in the farthest corner of the room, staring at my phone. Losing myself in social media, I manage to shake a lot of the discomfort I feel at being inside the waiting area, but I can't quite stop the sensation of my skin crawling as I sit and wait to be called back.

Finally a nurse too cheerful for her own good calls my name, and I hesitantly follow her into the back. But instead of taking me to an exam room, she leads me into a large office at the end of the hall.

"Have a seat," she says, bubbly voice ringing in the open space. "The doctor will be right with you."

With the sound of the door closing, I suddenly feel isolated and alone. Every ounce of anxiety I have is coming back tenfold, and I shakily pull out my phone, sending a quick text to Laurence.

"I'm kind of freaking out."

The second I send it, I regret it. Coming up with the perfect apology, I quickly send a follow up message, telling him I'll be fine, and that I'm only upset because I've been waiting for a long time, letting myself get anxious. I assure him I'll call as soon as I can, and tuck my phone back into my bag.

I know he wanted to come. He'd asked a few times but in the end didn't push, more understanding now of my displeasure with his coddling and unreasonable sacrifice. His presence for some work with the Los Angeles branch was necessary and I didn't want him putting me in front of his work commitments. In the end, he bade me farewell with a lingering embrace and countless kisses, leaving me just a little breathless as I left his office.

Recalling his goodbye spreads a heat in my cheeks, and in an effort to calm my reddening face, I peek curiously around the room. Along with the large wooden desk I'm facing, plaques and diplomas litter the wall, along with shelves of books and artifacts. The room isn't cold or unfeeling and I find myself calming.

Finally the door opens and the doctor comes in. "Hello Camry, it's nice to meet you." He reaches out and shakes my hand. "I'm Doctor Park. I've gotten the results of your tests and we're going to discuss some of your genetic markers today."

He takes a seat behind his desk, tucking the tails of his long white coat under him. Then he looks to his computer and turns the monitor towards me so that I can see.

He opens patient software and locates my file, bringing it up. I can sense from him a gentle aura, but he also has an air of directness to him, not willing to temper bad news. I can respect that, and I sit up a little straighter, ready and willing to hear what he has to say.

He goes through a series of clicks and opening new things until I can see a graphed image of DNA - presumably, my DNA.

He folds his hands and looks at me. "At the hospital, the blood work we ran indicated parathyroidism. You've been scheduled for surgery, correct?"

I nod and he continues. "Excellent. After that, your cheek swab was sent to our office. We used your cells for genetic mapping and we've been specifically looking here." He indicates part of the DNA strain, zooming in and highlighting it. "This is the 11q13 locus; it's the long arm of chromosome eleven, in position 13.1."

He pulls up another graph. This one is full of colored blocks, stacked in rows and columns, with complicated labels on every axis. He points to a specific part with the tip of his pen.

"This is the indicator we are looking for, and this tells us that you have the MEN1 gene."

"MEN1?" I repeat the name back, questioning.

"Yes. Multiple Endocrine Neoplasia Type 1. I will walk you through what this means."

He takes his time, slowly describing all the details, patiently answering my questions. "You possess a rare gene; the MEN1 gene. This means that your body has an increased likelihood of overactive certain endocrine glands; most notably, the parathyroid, the pancreas, and the pituitary glands. When these overactive glands are not regulated, they flood the system with these excess hormones, and often develop benign tumors called adenomas. In general, these adenomas are not harmful on their own. But it is these adenomas that are overactive, thus causing problems within your body."

He pauses, looking at me to make sure I'm still with him. "Okay." I look back at the screen before returning to meet his eyes.

"This syndrome is a bit of a wild card. There are not many things that apply to all cases. But I can tell you what we in the medical community feel confident saying regarding it. You inherit this from one parent, not both, and the chance is about fifty-fifty. About one in every thirty thousand people have this MEN1 gene. The majority of people with the MEN1 gene live over 65 years of age, even longer. But sometimes the adenomas can lead to malignant tumors, most of which occur on the pancreas.

He speaks slowly, deliberately. "You'll need regular blood testing for the remainder of your life, as well as periodically determined scans. The tests will look for elevated endocrine activity; that is, parathyroid hormone, calcium, prolactin, and gastrin. These blood tests will need to be conducted every six months. Right now, I'm also going to order a scan on your pituitary gland. You're experiencing a high frequency of symptoms that lead me to believe you may have an adenoma there as well. I'll have our office schedule that with you."

I swallow, taking it all in. I close my eyes, trying to replay his words in my mind. Live past sixty five, some malignant tumors, blood testing every six months... it feels like the rug has been pulled out from underneath me and I'm struggling to process all of this. One question comes quickly to my mind.

"Can you cure it?"

Doctor Park shakes his head. "No. Since this is a gene that is malfunctioning, the issue lies in every single one of your cells. It can be managed, however, with careful observation, and in most cases, surgical removal of the adenomas."

I take in a shaky breath. "Do I..." I trail off, clear my throat and try again. "What do I have to change? What can I do? I need to be able to work and I've got my brother, and my dog, and my boyfriend, and-" my voice has escalated in both volume and speed and I cut myself off, realizing my behavior. "Sorry," I murmur, shrinking back into my chair.

"There's no need to apologize." His gentle eyes calm a small portion of the storm brewing in my head, but I draw a deep breath.

"This is a lot to take in. I'm not sure what to think."

"Start with this. Wrap your head around what's going to change in your life. We will set you up with a nutritionist who can help you with some dietary changes that may help you when you're feeling worse or weighed down. You also may find that you benefit from keeping a sort of journal that tracks your health. That often helps patients feel more in control. You can expect to get to know us here, as we will be the ones who help handle your treatment and adenomas removals if you are in need of them while under our care. And you can make sure that you find room in your schedule for bi-annual blood testing."

My molars are grinding together but I relax my jaw, letting go of the tension. "I see. What do I need to do now?"

"For now? Stop and schedule your pituitary scan on your way out. Then go back to work. I'll see you in a few weeks for the removal of part of your parathyroid."

"You?" I open my eyes widely, noticing his choice of words.

"That's right. I'll be the one performing your surgery. I have privileges at the Met Hospitals." He smiles, and it lights his entire face up. "After that, you'll have some typical post-op evaluations, as well as a blood test, but then you'll be free to enjoy life for another six months until your next visit."

I chew my lip, and slowly nod. "I just need one second."

"Understood. Take all the time you need."

Sitting in silence, my mind races over everything, trying to piece together the details. I feel both terrified and relieved. All those moments of brushing off what I'd experienced, all those health scares, all those odd happenings: I finally have a name to what was behind them all. And yet, that knowledge doesn't soothe me. Why couldn't I be healthy? Why did this have to happen? First mom, now me.

I lift my head and roll my shoulders, breathing deeply. "Okay. Thank you for your time."

I begin to stand up, but the doctor lifts a hand, gesturing for me to wait, and I silently sink back into my seat. He shifts his eyes to my face and the smallest flash of emotion wavers in his gaze, before he returns his expression to one of neutral perspective.

"Camry, before you go, I feel it's only right to tell you... It is highly likely that your mother's pancreatic cancer was caused by this same gene, so -"

His voice continues on. I can see him speaking, hear a murmur of a voice in the background, but my focus is destroyed. I no longer clearly hear him, see him. A suffocating grip claws its way around my lungs and I feel each beat of my heart pounding sharply in my head. Unable to grasp at reality, I take large, gulping breaths, trying so suck in the air vital to my lungs. My mother. My mother! She died from this? This is what killed her? What stole her from the world?

My hands shakily secure themselves around the arm of the chair and my body rises to standing. I can feel myself speak, reach across the desk, shake hands. But I feel trapped within my own mind, screaming and crying in pain.

My feet move me down the hall, out of the building, onto the street. I don't even notice the rain as it pelts me, soaking me to the bone. One by one, step by step, my feet begin to walk, carrying me forward. The world outside seems silent, only because it is being drowned out by the raging storm in my head. Every single minute of fear, anger, sadness, anxiety, and grief that I felt watching my mother grow sick and die flood my brain, overwhelming my senses. My body moves on its own, as if my brain is held captive by the past. Before I realize it, I'm entering the lobby and stepping into an empty elevator. With the lurch of the lift coming to life, my mind and body snap together abruptly. I stumble from the force I feel, covering my eyes. The lights are too bright, the noise too much. I'm clutching my hands to my ears, hunched over in the corner, when the doors open and Alex steps in.

Two seconds of staring at me are all he needs before he is down on his knees before me, looking up into my eyes. "Cam! Camry, what happened?" His strong arms encircle me and hold me close, soft shushing noises curling from his lips. Tears burst forth from my eyes and I sob uncontrollably into his arms as the doors close around us. Alex leans back, keeping one arm around me, and jabs a finger into the emergency stop button and the lift shudders to a halt.

We sit there together for I don't know how long. He doesn't push me, doesn't say anything, just sits there holding me closely, letting the sound of his steady heartbeat bring me back around. Anchored by his arms, the noises in my head begin to quiet and my thoughts begin to clear. As my cries begin to slow, and my breathing evens, he squeezes my shoulders and speaks softly into my ear.

"What happened?"

"I..." I try to speak, but realize I can't. I cannot bring myself to admit the words. The only thoughts in my mind are irrational and distraught. I have what killed her. I'm going to die. My mind is stuck on repeat, cycling through my brain like the skips on a record.

Sensing my inability to speak, Alex rubs a hand over my forehead, gently pushing my hair away from my face. "You're soaking wet. Let's get you to your office so you can dry off."

He starts the elevator up again and we arrive much too soon on the top floor. Alex helps me to stand, then tucks me under his arm, guiding me down the hall. Miss Davis gives us an incredulous look, but I keep my eyes down and Alex shields me with his body away from her curious eyes. "She's fine. No need to worry. Bring her a cup of hot tea, though, please?"

He quickly takes me down the hall, shutting the door firmly behind us. He leads me to the couch and sits me down, then runs to the bathroom and returns with some towels. His touch is gentle and caring as he pats my hair and my shoulders, slowly lending me warmth. I close my eyes a little, desperately trying to latch onto the weight of his hands, when I hear a knock on the door.

Alex leaves my side, and returns with a cup of warm tea. Lifting each of my hands, he places it between my fingers. "Drink this. It will help."

The room is silent as Alex carefully helps to dry me off as much as possible, and I'm grateful for both his attention and his silence. Once he's moved me to the other couch and a dry seat, he crouches down in front of me.

"Do you want to tell me where you were?" His eyes are full of concern and genuine affection, but I can't look at him. I cast my eyes down, staring at the swirls of steam rising from my half-drunk cup of tea. It hurts too much to think about it, let alone say it.

Alex sighs, pushing to his feet, and lays a hand on my shoulder. "I've got to get back to work. But call me for anything. If you're not okay, or if you need anything, let me know." He bends down and presses a gentle kiss to the crown of my head, then exits the room.

Silence stretches around me and suddenly, I feel very alone. Conflicted and confused, I try to grasp at logic. Why can't I say it? Why couldn't I share with him? He's a good friend and someone I trust. I don't have an answer, and I don't know why. I'm grasping at straws, wondering what to do. When he was here, I wanted him to leave. Now that he's gone, I'm desperate for him to return.

Unable to bear the stillness and silence of my office any longer, I move into the bathroom and slowly peel off the wet clothes, hanging them over my sink. "He did a good job," I say to no one, as I notice how my skin, though still cold and clammy from the rain, is better than it had been.

I grab the oversized sweater I keep hanging on the back of my door for when I'm cold and slip it around my shoulders, snuggling tightly inside.

Numbly I go and sit at my desk, desperate to fill my mind with something. Opening my email, I notice a few have come in since I left for my appointment. I check the clock and see it's still only 11:30. Knowing there is a full day ahead of me, I get to work, beginning to email the final placement arrangements and meeting times for the artists to install their work at the venue. My fingers begin to tremble against the keys, and I pull my hands back, wringing my fingers together in an attempt to calm the feelings of unease. I look up, staring at the painting inspired by my mother. It's hard to imagine someone who could inspire such life, such color, could have been drained so thoroughly of the passion that she once had. The vivid hues and bold paint strokes on the canvas now seem only a mockery of me, proving how far I could fall. I turn my head away, unable to bear the sight of the image any longer.

As I sit there clutching my fingers together, my door quietly opens and Laurence peeks his head in, a cautious look on his face. He spots me, his eyes going wide at my appearance, and I smile weakly. Stepping inside, he closes the door gently behind him before approaching me. "Why are you -" His question cuts off as he figures it out, shaking his head with mild exasperation. "You were caught in the rain." He doesn't wait for a response, taking my hands and encouraging me to stand. When I rise, he wraps his arms around my waist and shoulders, pulling me close.

Feeling him so close to me, so full of warmth and life, I let out a deep shuddering breath. I fill my lungs with the scent that grounds me so well and my muscles relax one by one, like a lock disengaging its pins.

We stand there in quiet for some time, while he gently strokes my back. Eventually he pulls away and still holding my hands, he guides me over to the sofa where we sit together. He angles his body toward mine and looks me directly in the eyes. His gaze is gentle, searching. And yet, he's not pushing nor prodding, just waiting calmly.

I take a deep breath and begin to speak, but the words that fall from my lips surprise even me.

"They didn't find anything new." I continue to speak but I don't even know what I'm saying, aware only of the fact that this feels... easy.

Apparently whatever I've said convinces Laurence because a relieved sigh tumbles from his lips and he squeezes my hands. "You will have your surgery in a few weeks, and they think that is the end of it?"

I find I can't agree to that, and my mouth forms a half-smile. Stroking my hair with a gentle touch, he speaks in a tender voice. "Oh, my darling. You are so very strong, to go through all of this." He leans forward, placing a soft kiss on my forehead. "Let me call for a change of clothes for you, and then we can get back to work."

****

Throughout the day I sense something odd about Laurence's behavior. On the surface, his behavior is the same, but he's unusually attentive and close by. He maintains some variation of physical contact with me almost all day, from our legs touching as we sit near each other, to his fingers idly tracing lines up and down my back as we work. I catch him stealing glances in my direction frequently, and at one point, he brings some of his work into my office, sitting beside me on the sofa while flipping through documents or typing on his laptop. I silently question whether this is problematic for him, studying his posture and facial expressions, but it doesn't seem to be bothering him in the slightest. If anything, he seems content to be close by. His efficiency and focus are second to none - and yet, I can tell that a portion of his mind is trained on me, studying my every move, ready to leap to action at the slightest sign of trouble.

Most days, this hovering would bother me, but his presence today is comforting. He doesn't speak more than necessary, nor does he let his presence smother me. Silently I question his behavior, wondering if he can sense my earlier turmoil. But no - there's nothing to worry about.

Logically, I know the truth. We are two different people. The more I think about it, the more conviction I feel. There's simply no way that I can have what killed my mother. She died from cancer, plain and simple. We're not connected. This isn't the same. I repeat this over and over in my head, convincing myself of its truth. It's not the same. We aren't the same. Forcing my mind back into the workload before me, I push the anxieties and concerns far from the forefront of my mind.

When the new alarm signaling five o'clock rings, Laurence stands and stretches, yawning in an uncharacteristically casual manner. "I am unnaturally exhausted today." He smiles ruefully at me and glances at my workload. "It's time to finish up. Are you at a stopping place?"

I take in the scene before me, and frown in thought. "I think so. I guess I'm ready to go. I'll be here for an hour or so every morning this week before spending the rest of my days at Sanctuary, meeting artists and getting the installations completed."

"Alright, I'll drive you home."

I lift my brow at him, eyeing him dubiously. "Are you sure? You really don't have to. I can take th-"

He cuts me off by wrapping me in his arms and dropping a gentle kiss quickly to my lips. "It's no issue. I want to."

"Okay."

We clean up a bit and take a few things back to his office. Laurence holds my hand through it all and as we leave, he makes no attempt to separate our intertwined fingers. Miss Davis lifts an eyebrow at our hands but otherwise her expression doesn't change. She bids us farewell and after one more glance at our proximity, returns her eyes to her computer screen.

In the elevator we stand together, hands clasped, but silent. Laurence seems comfortable and at ease, but my eyes are darting back and forth, fidgeting in the silence. Laurence's eyes shift to me and a small smile blooms on his lips. He lifts our linked hands and gently kisses my fingers.

Then he lowers our hands and returns to looking at nothing in particular, seemingly content as the elevator begins its descent.

A small ping from his phone encourages him to dig it out of his pocket, looking at the screen. Nimbly using his thumb, he navigates responding to an email with ease and my gaze follows the fluid movements of his finger across the screen.

Not even three floors down and the doors open, other employees filtering in. With each addition of people, my fingers stiffen in his hand's embrace, but he makes no attempt to move nor release them. Slowly, even, I feel his thumb gently stroke over the line of my hand. I jump a little and I can hear him chuckle quietly but otherwise he shows no other indication of acknowledging my hesitations.

I sigh, admitting defeat, but I can't help stealing furtive glances at the faces of those in the elevator with us. The people are either deep in conversation, or laughing together, or they are mimicking

Laurence's attention to their devices, lost in the technology wonderland that invades their mind. Really, no one is looking, are they?

As the elevator arrives on the ground floor, most scuttle out, but we continue to the car park with a select few. As usual, Laurence opens the door for me when we arrive at his car, and I settle into the seat. The drive home is quiet, and Laurence seems deep in thought. When we pull up in front of my building, he speaks quietly, not turning to me.

"Do you want me to come up?"

I press my lips together in thought, but in truth the day's events feel as if they are weighing heavily on my soul. "I do, but..."

"But you are exhausted." He finishes my sentence for me, turning to look at me.

I nod slowly, an apologetic grimace on my face. "I am. I really would love to invite you to dinner, but, I just want to sleep."

He pauses for a moment, then asks another question. "Do you want me to walk Shakespeare?"

Surprise, quickly followed by guilt, flood my emotions. I'd forgotten all about my dog, and walking him in the damp, cold weather on a night when I feel like I've been pushed through hell is the last thing I want to do. Before I can say anything, he adds, "I will not bother you at all, only take him for a quick walk, and bring you home some soup for dinner. I know you need to rest."

Even hearing the word 'rest' weighs my eyelids a bit, and knowing it is the smart choice, I agree. He quickly pulls the car into the space in the alley, and we make our way up the stairs.

When I open the door, Shakespeare's boundless energy greets us full force, tail wagging and nose sniffing as he takes in our day. "Hey buddy." I offer him a weary greeting, and drop my bag onto the table by the door.

"*Ma colombe,* go and take a shower. I'll take care of the walk, and bring you something to eat." He kisses my forehead, then turns to the energetic ball of fur before him. "*Allons-y,* Shakespeare!" With an enthusiastic reply, Shakespeare allows Laurence to attach his harness and leash, and after grabbing the doggie bags and a set of keys off the shelf, they disappear into the hall.

I lock my door, then make my way into the bathroom. As I peel away layers of my clothing, I stare at my body in the mirror. Now, the sight of myself is almost frightening. I study myself in detail; every curve, every line, all the veins and bumps and hair. This body looks so... normal. How can such a thing that seems so harmless contain something so malevolent? The longer I look at myself, the more revolted I feel, and I turn away from the mirror, wishing I could remove my soul from this shell, banishing the darkness from its hold over me.

I scrub my skin almost raw, desperately trying to make up for my feelings. Tonight, the shower's heat does nothing to soothe the ache I feel deep within my bones.

****

As I'm toweling off and getting into some pajamas, I hear the front door open. "Do not worry, it is only us," calls Laurence from the entryway. Shakespeare comes flying into my bedroom and leaps upon my bed, nosing a toy at me. He looks at me with adoring eyes, but I narrow my own.

"Not now, buddy. I'm tired." I toss the toy to the floor and slip under the covers, ignoring the huff of breath from my bed companion.

Not long after, Laurence knocks gently on the open door, one hand holding a tray with a bowl of soup and a tall glass of water. His eyes crease fondly, and he sets the tray down on my nightstand. "Eat a little before you drift off."

He bends and places a tender kiss against my brow and smooths my hair away from my face, stroking along my forehead in soft, gentle strokes. Then he pats Shakespeare's head a few times, scratching his ears. "Take good care of our girl, okay? I am trusting you."

With another chaste kiss, he whispers in my ear. "Call me if you need anything, no matter the time."

I offer him a weak smile, and sit up a little in bed, pulling the tray onto my lap. Coconut curry soup. One of my favorites.

He turns to leave, and I call to him at the last moment.

"Laurence?" He pauses, one hand on the doorframe. "Thank you."

He looks at me over his shoulder, a genuine smile lighting up his face. "Anything for you, my darling. Rest well."

He leaves the room, and not long after, I hear the front door click closed. After a few bites, I put down my tray and roll over in bed, burying my face in my pillow. I feel as if there is no emotion left to give, a void settling in me as I inhale the familiar scent. Shakespeare pushes his nose to my ear, and I scratch his ears. He rolls closer, and I fall asleep, clutching his warm body to mine.

Chapter 18

My alarm jerks me awake, a harsh entrance into the
new day. Cracking open one eyelid, I realize the world
outside my window is painted a dull gray, fog
shrouding the city in uneasy mist. I slowly sit up, and
Shakespeare heaves a great breath beside me,
stretching his legs. Wandering to my window, my
vision reaches only a block in any direction. I stare
blankly at the scenery, scoffing at how my body and
mind mimic the suffocating weight of clouds come to
earth; my entire being feels muted. I have nothing left
to give.

Shakespeare and I go for a brief run, watching as cars,
buildings, and people come and go through the veil
surrounding us. He is unnaturally subdued this
morning, keeping pace patiently beside me with little
interest in the smells and sounds of the city.

As we round the final corner to home, my phone
chimes in my pocket. A text from Ciaran. *How'd it go
yesterday, sis?*

Impassively, I clear the notification and stuff the
phone back into my pocket, finishing the run and
returning to the apartment.

I grab a dress from the closet, pull on a sweater and
some tights, and quickly coif my hair into an
updo. Knowing I'll be at the venue for most of the
day, I slip on the most comfortable pair of dress shoes
I can find, then head for the door.

Shakespeare whines a bit at me as I fill his bowl with
his breakfast, then noisily begins to eat. Grabbing the

last of my things, I leave my apartment and make my way towards the subway.

On the ride into work, I review my schedule for these final days leading up to the gala. I quickly text the dog walker, asking if she can handle a few extra routes with Shakespeare this week. Each day I'm meeting with artists, managing their installations and working with Antonio, Sanctuary's director, putting together the finishing touches for event.

Before I can get there, I have to spend an hour in my office collecting what I need and making sure Laurence's calendar is set. Now that I've been acting as Laurence's assistant on so many other projects, I know how busy he is, and how little time he will be able to devote to on-site work this week. It has felt nice, knowing how much he's depended on me, as accomplished and intelligent as he is.

When I step into the sleek glass lobby of the TMC Tower, I'm immediately rushed by Alex and Hayden, barreling through the crowds of people to reach my side. "Cam! Camry!"

I stop short, letting them finish their dash across the lobby. "Hey guys." My lips lift into an insouciant smile and Hayden's face darkens almost immediately.

"Excuse me? Don't 'hey guys' me! What's going on? Alex told me what happened yesterday, and we're worried about you!"

Immediately regretting my moment of weakness with Alex yesterday, I try and placate them. "Whoa, whoa! I'm fine. Totally fine." A dubious look settles on

Alex's features and Hayden's eyes sharpen even more, so I quickly follow up my comment. "I was having a really rough day yesterday, but I'm okay now. I promise. Everything's fine."

"Really? Because I went up looking for you yesterday morning and Mr. Mercier told me you were at your doctor's appointment." Hayden's small frame is practically vibrating with how worked up she is. Alex rests a hand on her shoulder and leans over to whisper in her ear.

"Calm down, Hays. You're making a scene. Camry doesn't need to have her business floated all over the lobby."

I'm about to be grateful but Alex turns to me quickly, cutting off that thought as he grabs our hands and drags us into a quieter corner out of earshot from most of the passersby. "That being said, what happened at the doctor's office?"

That same veil drapes over my emotions, again mimicking the heavy fog outside. I give them the easiest version of the truth; the one I can accept.

"Nothing, really. The whole experience was hard, though. It was a lot to deal with, and I was remembering all those awful appointments with my mom. It all just hit me really suddenly." My eyes earnestly seek out Alex's, begging him to understand. "I'm sorry, for all of that yesterday. I really appreciate it, though."

He stares at me for a few seconds, then slowly nods his head. "Yeah, okay. Don't worry about it, though."

A big smile spreads across his face. "I'm just that nice of a guy."

I shake my head, his slice of humor cutting through my numbed state like a flash of color in a gray sky. "Thanks, Alex."

"No problem." He places two large hands on Hayden's shoulders, squeezing a little bit. "Okay girlfriend, let's leave her be."

Hayden, who is looking thoroughly unconvinced, begins to open her mouth but Alex cuts her off. "We'll see you around, Cam." He steers her forcefully toward the elevator, and I can see her, brow furrowed, speaking in hushed tones to him. He shrugs, and they disappear behind the elevator doors.

A massive breath rolls from my lungs, grateful for the interaction's end. Straightening my back, I make my own way into a waiting elevator and join the throngs of people beginning a new day at TMC.

****

Before I know it, Friday has arrived. I'm in my office, gathering up the files for the remaining artists who need to install their work. Two this morning, two this afternoon, and then I'm leaving early for the day to rest up before the long day tomorrow. I rub at my temples, feeling the strain of these last few days. The end feels so close, and yet so far away. Tomorrow I'll be dealing with all of the vendors during the day, before dressing and getting ready in all of the glamour of the basement bathroom at Sanctuary.

Just as I'm about to leave, the painting of my mother catches my eye. The vivid colors and impression of movement stand in such rich contrast to everything I see and feel in this moment. Even the flowers in my office are wilting, a sign of neglect from all my recent time away.

My eyes turn away, closing the door on the colors. In these past few months, the painting brought me joy, gave me energy, and reminded me of my mother's spirit. Now I find I can't even look at it.

Stepping into the hallway, I'm about to throw on my coat when I hear Laurence call out to me. "Camry? Could you please come here a moment?" He sounds somewhat formal, almost stiff, and a small peel of dread curls in my stomach. I plaster on a smile, and turn towards him.

"Sure. No problem." I walk down the hall to his office and he offers me a kind smile, stepping aside as I enter and shutting the door behind me.

He turns and studies me for a moment, not saying anything, and I find myself growing irritated. "You needed to see me? I have to get down to Sanctuary; I'm meeting an artist in an hour."

Any other person might see no change in his expression, but I can see the almost imperceptible knit of his brow, the miniscule wrinkle settling between his eyes.

"Darling…" His voice is soft, almost pleading, and my patience is wearing.

"Yes, what is it?" My tone is sharp and he no longer hides his emotions; his eyebrows lift in surprise.

"Are you working yourself too hard? I am worried about you." He moves toward me, running a hand down my arm. I force myself not to step away, suppressing the shudder that threatens to escape. How can he touch me? Doesn't he realize that I'm poison? That feeling of revulsion of being in my own skin floods me once again and I swallow and close my eyes, trying to quell the rising nausea.

Laurence must think my behavior is one of relaxation because he takes me into his arms, purring into my ear. *"Ma chérie, ma colombe, mon coeur,* tell me what's bothering you. What can I do? You have been so angry, so irritable these past few days. You haven't been eating properly, and you look like you're not sleeping well. Please, darling, tell me what is wrong. Tell me how I can help you."

His soothing words and warm touch feel almost mocking, but just as I am about to voice that thought, I realize something. He cannot know what he's holding in his arms; I never told him. I never told him that I'm damaged, that my mother and I will share the same fate, that my life will always be held hostage by the way my genes decided to knit themselves together. I suck in a sharp breath at the realization, suddenly hit with the reality of it all. My god. I'm dealing with all of this and I can't even tell anyone. I can't admit it, I don't know how to deal with any of this. It's too much. It's too much!

Quickly, I push him away, feeling the weight of everything that's happened this week. The news of my disorder, the connection to my mother, lying to the ones around me, pretending nothing was wrong, even the way I'd been dismissing Shakespeare and his requests for play. Guilt, hurt, anguish; I'm overcome and I need to escape.

Blurting out an apology, I flee the office, running down the hall. I can hear him shouting behind me, calling me to come back. I fly past Miss Davis and jam my finger into the elevator button. It doesn't come, so I race for the stairs, needing some distance, some time alone.

Four flights down, I finally get into an elevator, riding in silence. I wish I still felt numb. I hate myself even more for the way I've treated people, and what's more, I can't stand that I fled just now. Why did I do that? What is wrong with me?

I glance at my phone, but embarrassment and knowing I'm on a tight deadline keep me moving forward. I hop on the subway, heading up the island to Sanctuary.

****

Antonio eyes me closely, a skeptical look on his face. "You okay?"

I finish chugging the protein shake I bought at the corner store and force a smile. "Right as rain."

Wiping my mouth with the back of my hand, I toss the container in the trash and turn to him. "I'm just tired."

He nods in understanding, smiling faintly. "You've certainly been working hard on this for a long time. It's almost here. Are you feeling ready?"

My shoulders lift, showing indifference. "I guess. I'd better be, at least. We've only got two more artists to install this afternoon and then I'm free until tomorrow."

"Good for you." He turns and peeks at my notebook. "Lucy Finch... she's the one going in the southwest corner of the main floor, yeah?"

"That's her. She'll be here in a few minutes."

Antonio studies the papers a few minutes, then turns to me. "What makes her so special?"

"Pardon?" I'm not entirely sure what he's talking about. Why does he think she's special? Or rather, how does he know that I think she is?

"Well, you've got her in a really well populated area. It's easily visible, and on a direct path to and from the entrance. You must have put her in that spot for a reason, and you're having her set up at the end, too."

I clear my throat awkwardly and begin to shake my head, but I stop. He's right. "I..." I think for a minute. "I can't describe it. You'll see when she gets here."

He shrugs, unperturbed. "Looking forward to it."

Not even five minutes later, the front doors open and a burst of bright pink comes flying into the room, shrieking loudly. "Oh my god! This is amazing! Mom, did you see that? I can't even!"

Normally I would laugh, but today I don't have it in me. "Lucy!" I shout to her as I make my way out of the back, Antonio following behind me. Her hair is dyed a vivid fuchsia, and her shirt matches it all too well. She is bright and blinding and everything I remember her to be.

"Camry!" She stops in her tracks, eyes flying wide. "Um, uh, Miss Hughes!" Her parents stand behind her and I approach them, shaking my head at her forced politeness. With a quick pat on her back, I extend my hand toward her parents.

"It's good to see you again, Sarah," I say to her mother.

Her father takes my hand, shaking it firmly. "Joe Finch. Nice to meet you."

I step to the side, gesturing to Antonio. "This is Antonio Vasquez, the director here." Greetings exchanged, Joe shoves his hands in his pockets, looking somewhat out of place. His eyes roam the event space, looking at the various art installations all around. "This is quite the operation you've got going here."

"Yes, and it's awesome!" Lucy chimes in, eager to participate. "So, where do I set up?"

"Right over here." I point to the lines I have taped off on the floor. "You can set up however you want within this space." Turning to Joe, I point towards the back of the open space. "If you pull your car around the back, there's a loading area and a freight elevator. That might help."

He smiles warmly at me, twirling keys around his middle finger. Thanking me, the three of them follow after Antonio towards the elevator space.

As I watch Lucy set up her work, Antonio steps into the space beside me. He hovers close, voice low. "I see why you wanted to put her there. Her work is incredible."

I stare at the pieces being mounted, easeled, and propped around the space, Lucy's face a firm scowl of thought as she steps back every ten seconds to observe the layout again. Her parents look on as if they've seen her at work a thousand times before, simply taking it all in with a casual gaze.

My mind begins to wander, as it has any time I've been given the chance to think. The myriad of painful emotions I've been hiding just beneath the surface worm their way through my carefully concocted layers of professionalism and I feel faint, catching a sob in my throat with a strangled sound. I quickly step away from the scene, escaping to the bathroom.

With all of the mastery I can summon, I grit my teeth and force my thoughts to the gala. I'm close. It's so close. This is almost over. And Lucy is here. I adore her, I do, and I want to be there for her now. Marcus is coming next, the featured artist, to erect his fantastic display of sculptures. Any and all breakdowns have to occur after that. I can deal with this later. But now, I've got to get it together.

I shake my head, close my eyes, and splash a little water on my face. Then with straightened shoulders and a resolve that feels it is made of shattered glass, I return to the event space.

As I step in beside him, Antonio shoots me an inquisitive glance, but I force a smile and look back to Lucy, ignoring the unspoken question in his eyes. She works diligently, critically, and after a considerable amount of time has passed, she steps back, puffing up her cheeks and bursting out a breath. She smiles, satisfied, and spins to me.

"Ta-da!" Her enthusiasm catches grins from all those around, and I offer her a small smile of approval. Her joyful expression clouds into a glower, and she twists her lips together. "What is with you today?"

Sarah and Joe wear matching looks in surprise and her mother reaches out, placing a hand on her shoulder. "Lucy!"

"It's alright." I flick my hand, waving away her comment. "She's not wrong. I'm not myself today."

Her mother's face shows evident concern, and Joe bites his lip, but eventually Lucy shrugs. "Whatever. I like you anyway."

I can't help the tight smile on my face, half grateful,
half pained, as my own self-hatred surges
within. Trying to change the subject, I focus on her
installation.

"Everything looks wonderful, Lucy. I'm really looking
forward to tomorrow night."

"Me too!" She looks unperturbed by the recent
encounter, and inwardly I'm grateful. "I guess that's it
for today, then. We'll see you tomorrow!"

"See you all then." Farewells said, Antonio walks
them out and I take solace in the silence for just a
moment.

The large space surrounding me feels so different
from the first day I walked in, and I'm pleased with
the manifestation of my vision. My gaze shifts up,
staring at the levels above me where I can see bits and
pieces of the art displays on the upper levels, their
vivid colors and engaging shapes peeking out over the
balconies. Tables and chairs litter every level,
immersing guests within the art all around, and I
close my eyes, bringing to life what I hope it will look
like tomorrow once the lighting and decor is all
present.

Antonio's voice calls me back, and I open my eyes to
see him before me, his gaze also turning round the
space.

"This place is really going to be great, tomorrow."

I agree, my eyes avoiding his. I can feel him watching
me and internally I'm begging him not to say

anything. Eventually I hear him exhale, and the shifting of papers. "Marcus Carrera, huh? The last one, then you're free."

"Yes. The last one."

I glance at the clock, seeing ten minutes until his designated arrival time, but just as I shift my eyes toward the central staging area where his sculptures will be, the doors fly open, with a great booming sound.

The February midday light behind him is so bright he is but a silhouette, an imposing figure clad in darkness making his way into the room. As he moves closer, the lighting adjusts and his features come into view.

Seeing me, his face lights up and a sonorous chuckle fills the echoing space above us. "*Querida!*" Marcus is unusually chipper today. He strides toward me and wraps me into a massive hug, enough to feel my joints popping. I slap his back, wrestling myself out of his arms.

Marcus' eyes roam around the space and he whistles in appreciation. "Look at you, *mijita*! I'm impressed."

His eyes settle on Antonio and he strides over to greet him. Antonio greets him in Spanish and Marcus laughs, responding in kind. He turns to me and slings an arm around my shoulder, pulling me close. "Thanks for working with this one. She can be quite the handful."

Mortified and dismayed at his lack of professionalism, I glare and slide from under his arm. "Marcus! I am working!"

He shrugs. "I know."

Antonio laughs. "Don't worry, Camry. You've done an excellent job and I'm honored to have worked with you on this project."

Marcus sends me a teasing grin. He opens his mouth to say something but I cut him off. "You're in an awfully good mood today. What's going on?"

"The sun is shining, I feel good, and you're doing great things. What is not to love?"

What's not to love? His words land heavily like a lead balloon dropping into the depths of my stomach. The smile vanishes from my face in an instant. I want to believe him, to see things the way he does. But I can't. There is so little to love today, and the emotional whiplash I'm feeling is wearying me quickly.

Adjusting my internal mask, I point to the center stage. "That's where you'll be. Let's get you set up."

I walk away from them towards the entrance, gesturing for him to follow, and Antonio trails behind us both.

Marcus and I approach the front door where the large truck is waiting, and he points to two men in the front. "These guys are helping me move the statues into the building. I'll take it from there." In rapid fire Spanish, he gives them their instructions and the men oblige, bringing the statues in carefully one by one, setting them near the open space. Once they're finished, he tips them and waves them away with promises to see them on Sunday for the tear down.

Marcus, Antonio, and I are standing in a sea of human forms. Antonio is visibly moved by them, walking in and out of them. "Camry, I have a thought."

I turn to him and he addresses the two of us formally. "What is the current plan on lighting for these?"

Marcus steps in, ready with his answer. "We have small lights that mount to the bottom of each statue, and I will angle them to hit the glass heart in each."

Antonio frowns, closed fist to his lips as he thinks. "I like that. Could I suggest something additional?"

Marcus' eyes flash, a look I know well, but I place a hand on his arm for a moment. "Absolutely. He'll at least listen."

Antonio nods. "Of course. No disrespect meant, and I think these are incredible. I have just one thought. If I could secure some small spotlights from the ceiling, they could shine on them from above, giving another point of contact with the glass orbs. It could scatter the light, casting fractals of gold around the space. What do you think?"

It's not my question to answer, but I love the idea. I open my mouth to add my support of the issue, but Marcus stops me short with one word. "No." He doesn't seem hostile but there's a sharpness in his eyes as he speaks. "That won't happen."

Antonio doesn't seem surprised, but I can sense a hesitation in his eyes. "Alright, just ignore that then." He gestures to the sculptures. "You obviously know best."

Marcus huffs a little but turns to me. "I'm going to set these up now." I nod quietly, removing my hand from his arm, and step to the side.

I watch him work, wishing I could help, but we've made sure to be very clear with artists that we won't be touching their artwork at all in anyway, to avoid any issues. All of them have been happy to hear this, including Marcus, and I can't help but feel a little put out. I know he trusts me, but I think back to the way I had to convince him, and how reluctant he was to go public with this. A fresh wave of guilt rolls over me, and I sigh. Maybe I was too rough with him, too pushy, but it's too late to back down now.

Antonio's phone rings and he excuses himself to answer it, stepping into the office. I focus back on Marcus and notice he's setting up the statues differently than I had expected. I cock my head, studying his arrangement, and purse my lips. What is he doing?

My instincts are telling me this is all wrong. "Marcus?"

He looks up at me briefly, grunting his acknowledgment of my question.

"What are you doing?"

He pauses, straightening up and looking at me. "What do you mean?"

"You're setting them up all wrong."

"Excuse me?"

Instantly I regret my phrasing, and I can tell that Marcus is being calm only because it's me he's dealing with, and not some random art connoisseur.

"Well, I mean... you're leaving a lot more distance between them than I thought, and you've set some up down around the edges of the platform. Is that intentional?"

He walks over to me and stands behind me, two heavy hands on my shoulders. "Look." He turns me to face one side, and walks me through them. "They'll still make the same shape eventually, but only to my eyes, and maybe yours. I want people to be able to move through them, like you and Laurence that first day."

I think again of the image he showed me at our consultation, and I can't understand this. "But what about that picture? It was so incredible to see them together."

"And you'll still see that if you're looking for it, but that isn't the point."

I'm growing irritated, feeling frustrated with myself and him. Was I so off the mark? Did I misunderstand everything? "But I thought you said the idea was -"

He cuts me off, holding up one hand, the other pressed to his forehead. "Camry. It doesn't matter what I said. Art means something different to everyone. Some people may walk away with a profound interpretation, others may just say, 'Oh, that's pretty.' But this art - I made it for me. It's for me, and I know what it means. That's all there is to it."

"That's not all there is to it!" I'm feeling panicky and I don't even know why. My brain is scrambling, trying to put coherent, rational thoughts together. "Why aren't you setting it up the way you showed in the picture?"

"Because this is immersive. I want people to be one with the art, living in it as part of the community together. If they see it only on the stage, set up as something to look at, it loses its meaning for me."

"But, you said it was about community, about having people who didn't pity you, but also supported you no matter what you were going through! You said that you had people who loved you, and that they didn't feel sorry for you, but were just there, always with you. The way they all fit together, it... I... it made so much sense! You had people who loved you no matter what, no matter what you lost, and that was important!"

I'm shouting at him and he's staring at me with a mixture of bewilderment and indignancy on his face. "What the hell is the matter with you? This is my art! Why do you care? You promised me that if I did this, you'd step aside and respect me as an artist. Did you force the other artists here today to buckle to your design? I make the rules and the choices here. What is the damn problem?"

We're standing close, his imposing figure towering over me and I feel... small. Suddenly the dam breaks and my knees crumple and I'm sobbing on the floor.

"Camry?" Marcus calls my name, but he sounds a million miles away. I look up into his eyes and I can see concern, confusion, and fear. Awkwardly navigating his prosthetics, he sits on the floor beside me, and without thinking my arms reach out to him, hugging him close. I can feel his body stiffen in surprise, but I don't care. I need him, I need this. All these days of fighting and grief and guilt and I'm exhausted and he is everything I need in this moment. Slowly, he pulls me onto his lap, cradling me gently in his arms. I feel like he's keeping me together and I let my tears fall freely, finally finding the safety and comfort I've needed. After a few minutes, I calm my breathing and I blink, shaking my head, trying to clear the gloom away. I look into his eyes, and it all becomes clear to me in that moment.

"Marcus." My voice hiccups, still unstable, and he softly shushes me, stroking along my hair.

"*Mijita*, what's wrong?"

"It all makes so much sense," I whisper. And it does. I finally understand. I've been so terrified, unsure, scared of not only myself, but of others. What if they leave me? What if they don't love me? What if they see me the way I see myself; a poisoned, damaged thing, broken and missing pieces? What if people look at me differently? What if they don't want me because I'm too much of a burden? What if I'm dealing with all of that, while struggling, fighting to stay alive? The magnitude of all my feelings spill out again and I clutch at his shirt, burying my face in his chest.

"Marcus, I'm scared."

"What are you scared of?" He slowly rocks me back and forth, soothing me, and I feel safe, tucked into his large frame.

"I don't want to die like mama."

Chapter 19

Marcus' eyes shoot open and he pulls me back slightly from his chest, staring into my eyes. "What do you mean, *mijita*? What are you talking about?"

With a slow breath that fills my lungs, I begin to speak. For over ten minutes we sit there, me cradled in his lap, him holding me gently, as I share my truth. The past pains, struggles, bizarre symptoms, to passing out and the ER trip, finally to the news of my genetic disorder and its connection to my mother. He takes it all in quietly, until finally he lets out a sigh and kisses my forehead.

"*Mijita, mi hija, mija...*" That simple phrase strikes a chord. He's called me *mijita* more times than I know throughout my life. The sobriquet started out teasing, but over the years it melted into a familiar, sentimental phrase. This is the first time he's called me *mi hija* or *mija* - my daughter - and this small step towards parental affection fills me with warmth.

I sniffle, trying to master my emotions once more. "I think I was so upset because I am afraid that I'll lose that. That no one will love me, or that I will be too much work."

He doesn't say anything, but I can feel the droop of his shoulders.

"I know it's not my place to say this, especially to you, but I feel like something's missing; like what I am is broken, what I am is wrong. I'm scared, and I feel alone, and I'm afraid no one will fill in those gaps for me."

A great sigh releases from his chest and he rests his head against mine. "I cannot speak for anyone else, but I will always be one of those people. So long as my lungs fill with air, you'll have me." He pushes me back again and places his hands firmly on my shoulders. "But listen, Camry. Don't discount the people in your life. You are worth loving. I don't believe they will leave."

I chew my lip, nodding, and he presses a kiss to the top of my head.

"You should go home."

I look at him, startled. "What? Why?"

Fingertips rough and calloused from years of hard work smooth out the lines on my forehead, massaging my temples. "Because you're exhausted. And you need to rest. You have a big day ahead of you. I can handle things here. I'll talk to Antonio. You go home. Call me tonight."

I think to protest, but it dies in my throat and I concede, slowly rising to my feet. With some effort, Marcus gets up too, and he rubs his thighs, wincing. "You're lucky I love you." He smiles at me, teasing, and I smile back. I am almost tempted to laugh at how natural it feels now. There is freedom in honesty, no matter how frightening it may be.

"I'll see you tomorrow?" I ask him.

"Without a doubt." He hugs me one last time, and I grab my things, walking out into the bright February sunshine.

****

Sleep comes quickly that night, exhaustion settling into my bones. Now that I'm thinking with clarity, I know I need to be honest, and I have plans to tell Laurence as soon as the gala is over. There's no sense worrying him now, knowing how he would hover over me all night long tomorrow. Sending a quick text to Ciaran, telling him I'll call on Sunday, I roll over and close my eyes. I'm halfway under when I'm woken with a start. A loud banging on my apartment door and Shakespeare howling simultaneously jolt me awake and I stumble half asleep to the front door. A disheveled Laurence is outside, and confused, I open the door.

He rushes inside and grabs me, pulling me into a tight embrace. Incoherent mumblings stream from his lips. His whispers are hoarse and his fingers curl over and over as he seeks to gain purchase on my skin.

He pulls back, hands on each side of my head, and kisses me with intensity. Caught off guard by this behavior so unlike him, I squirm for a bit.

His arms wind around my back, clutching me to his chest. "Camry. Please. Just let me hold you."

I don't know what to make of this, so I wrap my arms around him in return and gently rub his shoulders. "I'm fine, but what happened?"

He pulls away, a wild expression on his face, and I look at him, slack jawed. "Laurence?"

"Do not say that. You are not fine. Why did you not tell me?" His eyes are burning, his voice deep like thunder threatening a storm, and I can't tell whether he's angry or hurting or both.

"Tell you what?"

"No. No more lies, Camry. Why did you not tell me?" There is something desperate, pleading in his voice and I slump my shoulders, understanding. Seeing this he continues, pacing around the room like a lion in a cage.

"Marcus called me this afternoon. He told me he sent you home early so you could rest, since you were obviously exhausted. He spoke of your illness as if I knew everything but of course, I was in the dark. He realized I had no idea and had to tell me everything!" He lets out a cry of anguish. "*Je suis très frustrée! Tu as brisé mon coeur.* Why did you lie to me? Do you not trust me?" With every breath his agitation grows and he seems almost feral in his frustration and grief.

I'm so startled, seeing him so wound up, and I blink rapidly, shaking my head. "I... I'm sorry! I didn't, I can't..."

The words are failing me. This isn't what I wanted.

This isn't what I thought would happen! I had made up my mind, I was going to tell him. But now I'm stranded, stuck here under his icy glare and I have never felt more pitiful in my life.

"I don't know why I didn't tell you, I just didn't. I couldn't handle any of this. It was too much! I was terrified!"

Laurence shoves a hand through his hair, a rough replica of his well-known gesture of nervousness. "Terrified? When you are scared, come to me. That is why I am here. That is why you should tell me. That is why you should have come to me, to let me carry that burden with you. Why didn't you let me be there for you?"

All at once his irritation is plain to me. He wanted to be there for me, to stand with me. But as admirable as that is, he's doing this all wrong. He cares more about his own involvement in my problems than what I am going through! His words betray his perspective, and his attitude is getting under my skin. Indignation flares within me, creeping through my veins like ice. "Hold on a minute. This is not about you! I'm sorry that I didn't spend time thinking about how you would react, but I've been stuck feeling trapped and not even sure how I need to feel. Don't you dare twist this around and play the victim! This is the one nightmare I've been running from since the day they told us she was sick! This is the worst thing that could have happened to me! Don't you see that?"

"I do see that Camry, and that is why I cannot understand it. If you were so caught up in your own feelings, why did you go to Marcus? Why was he safe but I am kept in the dark, removed from your burdens like an unimportant fool?"

He crosses the room with heavy footsteps and I can feel his anger, frustration, pain, and sadness radiate from him. In that moment, I'm lost, and I back up, putting distance between us. Then as his words catch up to me, something he said grabs my attention and I try to explain.

"I only told Marcus this afternoon. In case you haven't understood, I've only just wrapped my head around all of this to the point that I can even think about it, let alone talk about it. I don't even know how to talk about this yet but I promise I was going to tell you on Sunday!"

He frowns, still agitated, and I try a hesitant step towards him. He shakes his head, pain etched into his features, putting up a hand to stop me. "*Non.*" He looks at me, and I know this is as hard on him as it is on me. "I am your boyfriend, your partner. I am the one you come to first. I am the one you call! I'm the one who is there for you, who you cry with, who you reach out for!"

I am so mad I can hardly see straight and all I'm aware of is the surging pulse I feel in my veins. "This is NOT about YOU!"

He doesn't back down. "It is, because you and I are together. You and I are a pair, a partnership, and I want to support you. I want to share with you. I want to help you!"

"Then help me by understanding the way I am processing this. Share with me by listening and saying okay. Support me by not being angry with me!"

"I am angry because I care!"

"Why?" I shout back at him, fully into this argument. "Why do you care so much? Why does it have to be you?"

"Because I love you!"

His shout echoes through the room, followed only by silence and our labored breathing. My brain is moving a million miles a minute, blood rushing and making me dizzy. What did he just say?

He speaks again, his voice defeated and somewhat unsure. "I love you."

I almost have to laugh. I feel somewhere inside that I am supposed to fawn and melt and fall under the spell of his confession- but that's far from my reaction. Instead it feels like a betrayal.

"No. No, Laurence! You don't get to say that, here, now! You don't get to say that and think everything will be better!"

Deep down inside, I've wanted to hear these words from him one day, but this is not how it should have happened. This is too convenient, too easy for him. Does he think that if he says this now, that I'll suddenly forgive his selfishness and become putty in his hands? How dare he use such precious words at a time like this! Instead of inspiring romance and requited love, his words incite anger and hurt. "I am hurting! I am lost and I am scared and you don't know anything about what I've been through these past few days! Don't you dare say that to me now! Don't you dare use that to just smooth over all of this!"

He glares at me, fuming. "I don't know anything about what you have been through, you say? That is because you could not find the time to tell me. I do not know because of you!"

I've had enough. I am exhausted, confused, hurt, and this is more than I can bear. I march to my door, throw it open and point to the hallway. "Get out."

His eyes widen and his shoulders shake. "Camry-"

"Get OUT!" I scream at him, knowing I am ten seconds away from bursting into tears.

His long legs carry him to the door and he stops just in front of me. He doesn't meet my eyes but opens his mouth as if to speak. A second of silence passes, then clamps his lips tightly together, whatever words left unspoken between us hanging heavy in the air.

With that, he strides out the door and disappears down the staircase without a backwards glance.

I slam the door and the second it clicks into place, the sobs overtake me. Shakespeare, who had been hiding during our argument, cautiously makes his way over to me, whining concern. I sink to the floor and bury my face in his fur, tears falling fast.

****

The next morning, my body feels like it's been run over by a semi-truck. Though a good cry can be therapeutic, the traumatic ones leave a body feeling stiff, sore, and out of sorts.

Every one of my joints and muscles ache and my face is still puffy from all of the crying I did last night.

My mind wanders to Laurence, wondering if he's feeling the same way. Is he upset? Is he still mad? Half of me feels awful for our fight last night; the other half refuses to back down. I'm torn and this inner turmoil hasn't faded since he walked out of my door.

I slump into my desk chair, picking up a pen. Closing my eyes I take a few quiet moments to calm myself. This isn't the day to be caught up in myself, wallowing in my own emotional ruin. Before my fight with Laurence I made the decision to be open with myself and others, and I'm going to do just that.

Collecting some small notecards from my desk drawer, I put pen to page and begin crafting my speech for tonight. In what feels like a gift from above, the words come easily, my thoughts concise and meaningful. Once finished, I read it over again, satisfied. It feels slightly risky, but I know it is what I want to say.

Once that's completed, I gather my things, taking extra care with the new dress I bought just for this occasion. I pack the necessary items for doing my hair and makeup. Deciding it safer to take a ride service than to brave the subway this morning, I arrive at Sanctuary bright and early.

Antonio is there, ready to greet me, and he has a hesitant look on his face. It's unlikely he failed to witness any of my emotional moments with Marcus yesterday, and I sheepishly approach him.

"Good morning, Antonio."

"Good morning, Camry." His eyes are warm and I let out a relieved breath, thankful for his normalcy.

"I'm sorry about yesterday. I... I've had some health issues lately and -"

He shakes his head, silencing me, and rests a hand on my shoulder. "You don't need to explain. Are you feeling better today?"

"Absolutely. I'll be fine." I nod firmly, and he grins.

"Okay! Then let's do this. Go put your stuff in the office. The lighting company should be here in fifteen minutes."

****

The hours pass quickly, vivid blues of midday giving way to warm crepuscular light. I stand in the center of Sanctuary's open space, turning in slow motion circles, eyes roving every inch. It is, to put it simply, breathtaking.

Luscious draperies of navy and gold cascade from the upper levels, reaching to the floor. Every table is set impeccably, porcelain tableware with gold edging and silver cutlery. Gorgeous flowering centerpieces seem to reach to the heavens, stems of curly willow nestled within bountiful sprays of cream colored blooms. Twinkling lights like scattered stars blanket the far away ceiling, and the darkness of the room is accentuated by striking uplighting and the various spotlights and display lights on every art installation.

I take a few moments to walk through each level, snapping photographs of displays, decor, and the layout. I know that the venue won't be repeated, as New York's list of possible sites is both bountiful and always changing, but I remember how valuable the images and notes of past galas were in my planning, and how grateful I am for this venue and the rescue it provided me those many months ago. It seems a little wistful, now, to be staring out at this. The past four months have been eventful, to say the least. Leaning against a railing, I give myself a few moments to think, to breathe, to feel the calm before the storm. Everything I've been through has led me to this moment. It's an odd feeling. I remember as a child how impatient I was, waiting for Christmas to come around, only to find myself wishing that time would stop on the morning of the twenty-fourth. The long awaited day was suddenly so close, and I always feared it would be gone before I knew it.

I feel rather like that now. This is the moment I've been working for. This is what brought me new experiences, new growth, new relationships. My stomach twists at the thought of Laurence, this man who says he loves me. When this gala is all over, and I return to my old position, what will become of us? How will things work out? I'm still tormented over the events of the night before and I can't help but tear up a little, the uncertainty driving me crazy.

With one last look around the room from my perch leaning over the highest balcony, I look down at the result of my hard work. This is it. I'm a mess of emotion, wondering what the gala will be like next year, when I'm not the one in charge. Will the new person do a better job than me? Will I be invited? Or is this my only glimpse into this world?

I can feel the unwelcome trembling of my shoulders and quivering of my chin and I look down, biting my bottom lip and squeezing my eyes shut. Slowly I count to ten, silently working my way through the fog in my mind. Almost as soon as my lips shape the word 'nine', the alarm on my phone starts to beep. Time is up. I need to get ready.

****

I take special care with my makeup tonight. Step by step, I meticulously apply every layer, line, and brushstroke. I carefully twist my hair around the back of my neck, thick waves rolling over one shoulder. A few precisely placed pins keep it in place, and with a liberal spritz of my perfume, I step back and face the mirror.

Never in my life have I looked more mature. Never in my life have I felt more beautiful. The makeup I am wearing is sultry and sophisticated and my dress is stunning. The deep midnight blue trumpet gown sits off my shoulders, subtle lace overlay on my bodice giving texture to the smooth fabric. The back is a little dramatic; a high slit up the middle covered by more of the same lace. It's just the right amount of mature sexiness, and bolder than I would have chosen before I met Laurence. I suppose that is one thing for which I must give credit where credit is due; his confidence in me has inspired my own confidence in myself.

I smile at my reflection, and decide that tonight, I'm going to enjoy this. I've worked too hard for the night to let my experience be sabotaged by negative thoughts and uncomfortable situations. Tonight is mine; I am claiming it, and I'll be damned if I let anything ruin this!

With newfound confidence, I begin to pack up my bags when there's a soft knock on the door. "Camry?" It's Antonio."

I crack open the door and see him dressed in a classic tuxedo. "Hi, Antonio. Where should I put all of this? The office again?"

I pull the door open all of the way and his eyes widen. "Camry. You look incredible."

I blush all the way up to my ears at the sincere look in his eyes and the grin that appears on his face. "Thanks," I sheepishly reply.

Without missing a beat, he adds, "The artists are arriving. I expect guests to arrive in about an hour. Are you ready to go? We can stash all that in my office."

"Sure thing. Let me just grab this last bag."

"May I escort you, my lady?" Laughing, he bows with a grand gesture, and I can't help but giggle at his movement.

"Of course." I place my arm through his and he picks up my bags, leading me away.

We move slowly up the grand staircase, his pace matching mine as I navigate the marble steps in high heels and my gown's long train. Despite my carefulness, on the last step I catch my hem on the spike of my stiletto and Antonio's grip tightens, steadying me until I can find my footing once more.

"Thanks," I mumble awkwardly, as we complete our ascent. "I'm definitely nervous."

He laughs softly, a musical sound so close to my ear that I suck in an instinctive breath at the realization that he has me clutched tightly in his arm. Though his actions are innocent, I tense, remembering the way Laurence has held me this way, and I shiver slightly.

The awkwardness doesn't last: my phone begins to ring and I slide my arm from Antonio's, grateful for the excuse to step away. I shrug apologetically, taking my bags, and slip past, stepping into the office. Truly a gentleman, Antonio doesn't follow, but closes the door behind me to give me some privacy. I mouth a thank you to him through the glass and he waves it away, unperturbed, then walks off into the event space to greet those who have arrived.

I smile at the name on the caller I.D. and when I answer, a bright voice greets me before I can say anything. "Camry!" She draws out the last syllable as she so often does when she is excited, and I giggle in spite of myself.

"Hey, Hays."

"We're here! Where are you?"

Dropping my bags off, I step out of the office and I can hear her voice both from the phone and around the corner. Rounding the corner, I sneak up behind them and tap her on the shoulder.

"Oh!" She laughs and throws her arms around me, hugging me tightly. Then she steps back and elbows Alex forcefully. "Oh my god. Doesn't she look amazing?"

Alex, dashing in his tux, grins broadly. "Absolutely." He tugs on his own lapels, proudly. "Like my rental?"

I laugh, happy to have my friends here on this night. Hayden beams widely. "You seriously look fantastic, Camry. I guess that's what having a boyfriend like 'Laurence' does for you!"

Her eyes light up with humor, and her tone is teasing. I sigh, shrugging. "Yeah, well, we had a fight, so, I don't know about that."

Their brows shoot up in perfect unison, and I scramble to lighten the mood again. "Don't worry about it!" Waving my hands in front of my face, I brush off their worried looks. "Besides, I bought this dress myself! Tonight, I get to take all the credit." I force a laugh, trying to change the subject.

Alex, always sensing my inner distress, follows along smoothly. "Well, it looks great on you. Who knew we could clean up so nicely?" He gestures to the three of us and I smile, grateful for his seamless transition.

Turning us to the event space, Alex wraps an arm around my shoulders and gives me a squeeze. "You really outdid yourself, Cam. I knew you had talent, but damn. I think it looks incredible; and I don't even do fancy." He winks at me conspiratorially, and Hayden pipes in, burrowing between us so our arms rest upon her shoulders.

"I'm very impressed, but not surprised. This girl can do anything!"

My cheeks tint rouge with all the praise and I look down, secretly thankful but embarrassed at the directness of their compliments.

Suddenly, a gruff voice calls out from before me, and I look up. "You want to quit hogging the lady of the hour?"

Marcus stands tall before us, and I almost burst out laughing at the sight of him. Never in my life have I ever seen him in formalwear; he even wore a guayabera to Ciaran's wedding, much to my mother's amusement. His posture betrays how stiff and uncomfortable he feels, and I'm touched at his willingness to go so far out of his comfort zone for this.

Hayden pipes up first, and pushes me forward a little. "Hiya, Marcus!"

He nods at her, a tight smile on his lips. "Hayden. You're looking lovely tonight."

"Marcus, you flirt, don't waste your breath on me! Camry's the belle of the ball tonight. Spoil her rotten!"

"Don't need to tell me twice. I think I'll steal her away for a little while."

Alex nods at the two of us, and steers Hayden away. "We'll go find our seats. See you later, Cam."

Marcus clears his throat awkwardly, running a hand sheepishly across the back of his neck. "You look...." There's a long pause and he grunts a little as he thinks. "All grown up."

I burst into laughter at his comment and he rolls his eyes, yanking me forward into an awkward hug. "I'm not sure where to put my hands. I don't want to ruin your dress."

"You worry too much." I sigh and breathe in his comforting scent, all but forgetting the gloom of the previous hours.

"Have you looked around yet?" I link my arms with his and we make our way through the event space, greeting the rest of the TMC Staff and artists that are arriving on site. Eventually, I see Laurence across the room, his auburn hair glinting in the sparkling light. My heart aches to see him; he looks incredible. His perfect posture, joyful smile, and obvious enthusiasm for this night are evident as he makes his way through the crowd, exchanging greetings and formalities with artists and employees alike. The sleek modern tuxedo of all black casts a marble-like tone to his skin, and it is easy to tell how much he stands out in this space. Eyes follow him wherever he goes, blushing cheeks left behind on more than one face after he walks away. A neat coil of jealousy twists inside my stomach and I grimace, wishing I was linked to his arm at this moment, instead of Marcus's. Ashamed at my own thoughts, I think to tear my eyes away from him, but just at this moment, he looks our way and our eyes connect. I look away quickly, taking in the room, before I hear Marcus whisper in my ear. "Your boyfriend is on his way over here."

Laurence winds his way over to us and greets Marcus warmly.

"Marcus, it is good to see you. Congratulations are in order! Your work is exquisite and I am truly humbled and honored to have you with us this evening."

If Marcus notices that Laurence hasn't said anything to me yet, he doesn't show it. "Thank you for that, but

I also offer my congratulations to you," he turns to me and kisses my temple, "and to this young lady right here. You have put together an impressive event. I'm proud to be here."

Laurence beams and claps him on the back. "*Merci, monsieur*. Now, if you will excuse me, I have others to greet. The guests will be here any minute, Camry, so don't let Marcus occupy you entirely. Make sure you're at the entrance in ten minutes."

I grit my teeth at the patronizing instruction but nod slightly, steel in my eyes as I glare at him. He seems utterly unbothered, and drifts away into the crowd, continuing his jovial exchanges.

Marcus looks at me for a moment and then snorts in derision. "You want to tell me what that's all about?"

I shake my head, pulling him in the opposite direction. "No, not right now. I am going to enjoy myself tonight, and I'm not going to let anything get to me."

Marcus eyes me dubiously but shrugs and lets me lead him away.

****

After getting Marcus settled by the stage and giving him a small pep talk, I make my way to the front. Laurence is nowhere to be found, but no sooner have I rolled my eyes than I hear his voice behind me.

447

"I would be lying if I said I was not proud of you."

I turn slowly, lifting an edge of my dress, and I see him standing before me, dashing as ever, holding two champagne flutes. He offers one to me and I accept it, eyes glued to his face. What is he thinking? How does he feel? I have never thought him difficult to read but at this moment his expression is inscrutable.

He clinks his glass to mine and takes a practiced sip, his gaze never leaving mine. I drink too, but find I cannot hold his stare and I look to the side, feeling oddly unveiled.

"We have many important people to greet this evening. The doors will open in a moment. Are you ready?"

His voice is steady, sure. He acts with the confidence of a man who has done this a thousand times before, ready to conquer any challenge before him. I feel only a fraction of this certainty, but I think back to what Marcus whispered into my ear just moments before as I went to meet Laurence: "If you're feeling nervous or unsure, fake it 'til you make it. Don't let them see you sweat. You've earned this, so go get it."

I square my shoulders and look Laurence dead in the eye. "I'm ready."

He smiles- a smile that instantly breaks my heart, because it's the same tender, loving one he gives me when he whispers sweet nothings in my ear, or tucks my hair away from my face, or kisses me gently. It's the smile that makes me swoon. Right now, it only reminds me of the distance between us.

Antonio arrives, eyes bright and eager. "It's time!"

A thousand butterflies take flight within me, thrums of their wings drumming up nerves and excitement. With a grand gesture, Antonio tugs open the front doors, and the cool February air rushes in. I shiver a bit in the cold and instinctively lean a little closer to Laurence. In the same moment he shifts away, and my breath catches. There is no arm to wrap around me, no sweet baritone voice to whisper into my ear, no promise of warmth. I stand alone in the cold and all of my grandiose plans for ignoring the pain in my heart dissolve in an instant. I'm shattered into a million fragments, held together only by sheer will.

Antonio turns back and beams at me over his shoulder, and I force a smile. His narrows his gaze, scrutinizing me, and then recognition settles in his eyes. "You must be cold. Laurence, why don't the two of you wait further in and mingle closer to the stage? People will surely be seeking you out and you both can move through the crowds better from in there."

Laurence nods once, and looks at me. "Shall we?"

I step in beside him and the two of us walk side by side toward the back of the room. Sure enough, within a few minutes the first guests arrive and beeline for Laurence. He introduces me, and as the professional and gentleman that he is, he does nothing to downplay my role. He states clearly that it was I who was in charge this year, selecting artists, vendors, and even this spectacular venue. But the guests all nod at me, prim smiles upon their lips, before turning to Laurence and speaking animatedly. Over the course of the next hour, I meet countless elegant people; the rich, the famous, the household names, the families that made America what it is. And with every curt hello or dismissive smile, I feel as if I'm shrinking on the spot.

Finally, the number of people waiting to see us diminishes and Laurence takes a deep breath. "That will be most of the guests. We have only a few minutes until it's time for us to speak."

"I'm going to step out for a minute." Before he can say anything, I lift my skirt high enough to avoid tripping and dash away quickly.

I race down the stairs into the lower bathroom, seeking solitude and quiet. But the room is occupied with a few of the catering staff, taking a short break. I back away, hating that the solace I desperately need feels so out of reach. Defeated, I climb the stairs again, and tuck into a small alcove, pressing a hand against my chest.

Heat pricks at the corner of my eyes but I refuse to cry. I look up to the ceiling, blinking away the threat of tears, and sniffle softly. Squeezing my eyes shut, I will myself into a calm space. No thinking about Laurence, no thinking about genetics, no thinking about my own personal chaos.

I bend one leg, pressing my heel against the wall behind me and stand there, taking a mental inventory of every muscle, bone, and fiber in my body. I convince every cell within me to master calm and claim courage. With one final grit of my teeth, I push off from the wall and enter the grand hall just as Laurence's lyrical voice rings out over the sound system.

"Assembled guests, esteemed colleagues, and all present tonight: *bienvenue* and welcome to the twenty-fourth annual 'Legacy of Health' Gala!"

Chapter 20

Applause floats high into the rafters, rushing past my ears as people take their seats. I carefully navigate the crowd until I am close to the stage, stepping in beside Marcus. From here, the whole of the assembly faces us, eyes trained on Laurence from his position at the sleek podium. Marcus' fingers slowly reach down and squeeze mine, a reassuring gesture as the nerves begin to settle within me.

"I am most humbled by all of your presence here tonight." Laurence speaks with authentic gratitude, captivating the room. "We are honored to be here at Sanctuary, a most exquisite venue. Antonio, thank you for all of your cooperation in making this night a resounding success, and for welcoming Travers-Moreau, the Metropolitan Hospital System, and all of our esteemed guests. It truly is a stunning sight to behold."

Once again the room breaks into applause and Antonio, from his space near the stage, bows slightly, gesturing his appreciation in return to Laurence.

After thanking a few of the top sponsors, hospital administration, and other vendors, Laurence's tone of voice changes. Shifting away from a professional mask, his intonation shifts to a more whimsical, personal tone. "We owe this evening to our event organizer and my right hand for this project, Miss Camry Hughes. Her vision is what we have before us, and this evening is all thanks to her. Each artist on display was hand-selected by Miss Hughes, and I know that we are all very grateful to be in the presence of such exquisite works of art this night. Please join me in welcoming to the stage Miss Camry Hughes."

Minding my posture and my dress, I step onto the platform. Laurence greets me, his hands on my arms. He leans in and presses his cheek to mine on each side of my face, exchanging the typical French *faire la bise*. For a moment I'm caught off guard, sensing his lips so close to mine, but I quickly gather my composure and smile at him. Gesturing to the podium, he steps back, giving me the space to speak.

I pull my notecard out from the hidden pocket in my dress and nervously clear my throat.

"Good evening." My voice is hoarse and shaking, and I stutter a bit at the beginning. Glares of light make it hard to see at first, and the spotlights shining down on me give a significant temperature change. I take a steady breath, and focus on searching what of the crowd I can see. I find Marcus' face, then Alex and Hayden. Even Lucy and Antonio are beaming up at me. Feeling their supportive smiles, I continue with confidence.

"Thank you all for being here tonight. And thank you, Mr. Mercier, for the kind introduction." I nod a little at him, and he smiles at me.

"Tonight, we explore The Timeless Art of Healing. Throughout history, art in its many forms has brought joy to the masses. Art can speak in a way that transcends rational thought and surpasses the abilities of language. Art moves us, changes us, and it reaches to our very core. Some soars above us, calling us to new heights, while other lays at our feet, reminding us of our humble beginnings. There is little that cannot be expressed through the stroke of a brush, the twist of a wire, the snap of a shutter. Whether the message is for one or for many is unimportant; what matters is that art is often a source of catharsis, of renewal, of growth. Art can calm a fearful heart, awaken passion, heal emotional wounds, and inspire joy. Tonight, we celebrate art as a vehicle for healing. The artists here tonight are some of the best this city has to offer. The works on display reflect a vast array of perspectives and no two interpretations are alike.

"Every artist here has been influenced or affected by a medical struggle in some way. Some of these artists have endured a difficult medical diagnosis, while others have watched as loved ones faced health trials. Mental health, physical health, and emotional health are all represented. Every creation in this room has been born of a vision, a yearning, a need to tell a story; and the hands of each artist here have masterfully crafted these works. In lieu of an evening of speeches, we ask that you visit these artists, who are exhibiting all around the building tonight. Learn their stories; listen to their words. Many of the works here today will be displayed within the Metropolitan Hospital System buildings, and some artists will be hosting symposiums for hospital patients where they can share their stories and their work.

"I have always had a passion for art, and while my mother was battling cancer this past year, she found strength, comfort, and joy in trips to museums and galleries. She would often speak of the beauty of life, even as she faced its most cruel opponent. Though in the end she lost her battle, I know that she was able to keep such a positive outlook because of the connection she felt to the world around her when viewed through an artistic lens."

I swallow and blink back tears; the words I have said are no match for the ones I am about to utter now, but I decided when I wrote this that this was the right thing to say.

"Now, as I enter my own personal health struggles, I have found connection and encouragement as I have looked upon the incredible works that are here tonight. The artists exhibiting this evening have endured their own personal challenges related to life, death, disease, and injury. This understanding and experience gives these artists the voice to speak their stories, and I am more than proud to stand here tonight, introducing them all to you."

I pause to let the clapping cease and then I look at Marcus, grinning from ear to ear. This is such a wonderful moment for him; I'm so glad he came around.

"The first artist I am honored to introduce tonight is the featured artist of the evening. Marcus Carrera is a career veteran of the United States Army, who lost his lower legs during a combat mission in Afghanistan. In 2003, Marcus returned to the States and began the long process of healing. During this time he found that the community he surrounded himself with was integral to his growth and healing, and his submission represents that. The wire sculptures you see around us are his contribution to tonight's event. These incredible works of art are crafted with copper wire and hand blown glass orbs. Please, give a warm welcome to Mr. Marcus Carrera!"

Marcus steps to the stage amongst loud cheers, strong applause, and more than a few salutes from the crowd. He salutes in return, then takes his place alongside me. One by one, I introduce each artist, highlighting their exhibits and some of their story. When the last artist is gathered on stage, I let out a shaky breath. I've done it. Laurence returns to my side, shaking my hand.

After a few additional remarks, the guests rise and the artists break for their exhibits, ready to chat with gala attendees about their work. Marcus is, of course, mobbed quite early, but I see a few of my favorite artists with their own small crowds; Lucy being no exception. Her vivid hair and cheerful voice draw eyes and ears to her from all around the venue.

A few minutes later, I'm tucked into a quiet corner enjoying a glass of water when two familiar figures approach me. "I guess you found me, huh?"

"Of course we found you! And I'm not going to ask you anything now, but you'd better believe we'll be having a conversation - and soon. Whatever health issue this is, I need to hear about it." Hayden's face is a mix of sorrow, anger, and sympathy, but it soon melds into a tender smile and she pats my arm. "You know we love you, right Cam?"

I look at Alex and Hayden's faces, warm affection apparent in their eyes, and I offer a resigned smile. "Yeah. I do."

Alex tries to ruffle my hair but I just manage to duck out of the way. His grin widens at my movement and he reaches in again before Hayden scolds him. "Don't touch her hair!" Hands on her hips, she leans forward and Alex seems to shrink in size before her. "Honestly, Alex, do you know anything about women?" A dramatic sigh, she presses the back of one hand to her forehead. Then she looks at me and groans. "What am I going to do with the two of you?"

****

As I mingle through the crowd, I hear snippets of conversation. Most are complimentary, with voices praising the artists, the venue, and the overall event presentation. The artists themselves are clearly enjoying themselves, and even Marcus, who looks somewhat awkward, maintains a steady smile on his face.

I watch him for a few minutes, loving the way he uses his hands when he explains his art. Normally so stoic and subdued, he really comes alive when it comes to his work, and I can see a glimmer of pride he so often hides. He looks up and catches my eye. His smile softens and I wink at him, flashing a thumbs up with a small giggle. His grin widens and then he is pulled away again by another admirer.

After an hour or so, many people have eaten well, and the band shifts their music, more comfortable jazz sliding into the room. A few couples take to the floor and I look around, letting my eyes take in the full site of the room. On each level, guests mingle, speaking with artists whose eyes are shining with joy and humble pride. Some sit at their tables and eat, others stand by the bar, elegantly sipping champagne. A wistful sigh escapes my lips as I scan the room. I can't believe I pulled this off. Everywhere I look, people seem happy. The faces of those around me give every appearance that they're enjoying their time, and I get a little choked up at the thought. Inhaling a slow, deep breath, I close my eyes, conjuring images of the night in my mind. I can feel the corners of my lips lift and I wonder what I must look like, standing here with my eyes closed and a grin on my face.

No sooner than does that thought hit me, a voice pulls me from my head.

"Camry?"

Sheepishly I open my eyes, and see Antonio there. "Are you alright?" he asks me in a worried tone, and I send him an easy smile.

"Yes, I'm fine. I'm just trying to take it all in."

"Ah, yes, of course. I'm sorry if I disturbed you."

"No, it's fine. Did you need something?"

He smiles casually at me, gesturing to the couples swaying in the center of the room. "I was wondering if you would care to dance."

My eyes widen at the proposal, and I stutter a bit. A dance? With Antonio? I'm caught off guard by his question, and I stare at him for a moment. Then realizing how rude I'm being I straighten my shoulders and apologize frantically.

"I'm so sorry! Yes, I would be happy to dance with you."

A bright grin comes to his face and he extends a hand. I slip my palm to his and we make our way onto the dance floor.

Antonio is nothing but gentlemanly, keeping a slight distance between us, but a firm hold around my waist. We move simply, no formal dancing required, and try as I might, I can't help but compare this to dancing with Laurence. Antonio's steps are measured, patient, sussing out my own movements, and he keeps a look of concentration on his face as he works his way through the dance. My eyes drift aimlessly, not really seeing anything, and I move along with the music.

"You should be proud of yourself. You've done an excellent job. And I'm grateful to you, for all of this."

I finally look at him, feeling a little embarrassed. I see the authenticity in his words and I blush to the tips of my ears, looking away. "Thanks. I'll admit... I was just thinking about how I couldn't believe I'd done it, when you came over just now."

"What made you think you couldn't do this?"

He seems genuinely curious, maybe even disbelieving and I puff out my breath a little, mulling over my phrasing. "I had, maybe still have, no real understanding of what it's like to live a lifestyle where you could drop two thousand dollars on a pair of tickets to a night out like this. I don't know anything about what kinds of wine and champagne to choose, I don't know what sort of beef is fancy enough, or what kind of caviar to serve." I twist my lips together, somewhat sheepish. "I guess I feel like I don't know how to pull off rich and famous."

Antonio laughs a bit, spinning me out and bringing me back in. "Ah, but as you said yourself, you certainly pulled it off. And, if you'll allow me to be so rude, you look the part. You're quite beautiful, tonight."

I shift a little in his arms, and quickly, he adds to his statement. "I apologize if that was too forward of me. I just hope you know that you have done an excellent job here, and if you ever doubt your ability to be a part of this crowd, don't. You carry yourself well and based on what I've seen, you are a very adaptable person."

"Thank you. I certainly hope so, and yes, I'll admit... I'm proud of what I've done here tonight."

"As you should be!" The song comes to a close and he dips me somewhat dramatically, bringing smiles to both of our faces. "And now, miss, it appears my time with you is up."

I follow his eyes and see Laurence standing nearby watching us intently, a tight smile on his lips. A wave of odd guilt waves over me and I scramble upright. Antonio gives me a stately kiss on the back of my hand, then bows slightly to Laurence and moves away. Laurence's gaze follows him for a moment, something I don't miss, before he looks again at me and offers me his hand.

With all the poise of a fairytale prince, his lips cover the exact same space on the back of my hand that Antonio's just touched, lingering just a little too long. He rights himself and pulls me close and I am distinctly aware of the proximity of our bodies; pressed together, leaving no room for uncertainty. The way he holds me is familiar, a declaration of tenderness laced with possession. Unlike the soft, fluid way I just danced with Antonio, Laurence's confident leadership is graceful but firm, sweeping me along with him in the dance, leaving no room for error. He does not speak, but his eyes search mine, almost desperate.

Knowing that we have yet to talk about the uneasy way we left things last night, I fidget more than I should, anxiety creeping over me. What happened between us? Does he understand me? Can he see that I need time? I sigh and look away, not willing to indulge these dark thoughts.

The entire dance, we speak not a single word, and when it is over, he leans over and plants a line of kisses along my cheek. Then he spins on his heel and disappears into the sea of people, leaving me standing alone.

****

Antonio pulls the heavy doors shut, Laurence beside him, bidding farewell to the final guest. "Alright, everyone, that's a wrap!" Antonio shouts to the remaining people, and a few let out celebratory whoops, followed by a smattering of applause. The band is tearing down their set up, artists packing up their work and collecting their items. While there's still a bit of work to be done tomorrow with vendors returning to claim their goods and loose ends to be tied up in the office over the next few weeks, the event is, in essence, at its finale.

I make my way through the venue, expressing thanks and saying farewell to the artists as they prepare to leave. Lucy is buzzing with excess energy, her parents much more subdued and feeling the exhausting night. Marcus has a long night of cleanup ahead of him, and I laugh as he runs out to a coffee stand down the street.

Once I finish my farewells, I stare into the space, a ghostly remnant of the party that has ended. Napkins, confetti, bits of food, and programs litter the floor. It is eerily quiet, save for the gentle thrum of the service elevator going up and down as artists bring their carts in and out. Occasionally a burst of laughter or rumble of wheels slice through the silence, but the high ceilings and open space now carry an odd atmosphere, a shell of what it was just moments before.

A bartender waves me over and offers me a final glass of champagne and I accept it gratefully. Wandering over to a small table closer to a corner of the room, I slump into a chair, grateful to be off my feet. I slip off my shoes and wiggle my toes, flexing and rubbing the aches away.

Hayden and Alex peek out from around the staircase and seeing me, drop into chairs on either side. We sit, taking in the quiet bustle of tired bodies, and for a moment or two, I find myself lulled into a pleasant drowsiness.

Hayden's voice calls me back, her tone insistent, but calm. "So what exactly is going on?"

I roll my eyes but give a lazy nod and take a deep breath. I know Hayden. If I don't tell her, she'll go to any length to find out and then berate me for it later. And now that I've admitted to something, she's got ammunition to grill me about it if I don't come clean. I sneak a peek at Alex out of the corner of my eye and he's carefully avoiding eye contact. He doesn't pretend that he isn't listening, but his gaze follows the work done around us, his posture relaxed and at ease. One of his hands slowly spins a spoon around on the table, a quiet methodical movement. I stare at the spoon making its rounds and let the easy repetition settle my nerves.

"So it turns out I have a malfunctioning gene, and it makes me grow tumors, and it messes with my endocrine system."

"Okay, that's not a small thing." Hayden's eyes narrow and her gaze feels like its picking me apart. "That's not why you're upset, though."

I clear my throat, shaking my head. "No, you're right." I swallow and swirl my tongue around the inside of my mouth, trying to bring back any small amount of moisture. "It looks like my mom had it too, and that's how she got her cancer."

The spoon flies an inch or two across the table as Alex's fingers twitch. He gives no other reaction but that's all it takes for me to know he understands. Hayden on the other hand wastes no time. "Oh my god. No wonder you're a mess!"

She stands from her chair, pushing her way over to me and wraps her arms around my shoulders from behind. She squeezes tightly, resting her face against mine. "Oh sweetie. I'm so sorry. That's probably so hard to hear."

Tears prick at the corners of my eyes and I rub them aggressively, dragging the palms of my hands across my face. My voice is hoarse and my throat dry but I manage to thank her, resting my hand across her arm. She sits there, taking in my tears, while Alex reaches over and rests his hand upon my knee. His fingers gently stroke back and forth occasionally, and I let the feeling of support and love from my friends overwhelm me. Marcus was right. I have my community. I know this will be hard, but I have people who love me, who want to support me.

The word 'love' brings me out of my head and I think back to the fight with Laurence last night. He said he loved me. And while I hate the way that it happened, wished he hadn't said it then, and wonder if it was genuine or simply a tactic in our argument, I still recall the look in his eyes as he shouted it so passionately. I sigh loudly, my tears easing up, and I sniffle.

"Thanks, guys." I rub my eyes again, wiping away my tears, and Hayden gives me one last embrace before letting go and sitting back in her chair. She exhales loudly, a puff of air floating a few strands of hair and I watch them fall, almost in slow motion.

She looks at me for a few minutes then frowns. "Do you need anything right now? Or do you need space?"

My heart twinges inside. "Right now I need space. But I promise to call you when I need something."

"Good."

Alex rises from his seat, stretching widely. "Okay, Hays. Time to go." He leans over, smooths out my hair, and whispers in my ear. "You did good, girlfriend. And thanks."

I look up in confusion, meeting his eyes. "For what?"

"For telling us. I'm glad that you did." He finally gets that head ruffle in, and I flash a sardonic grin. He laughs and winks before waving Hayden along.

Hayden rises and with a quick peck to my cheek, she joins Alex and the two of them walk off arm in arm.

Looking around I realize just how much time has passed. The room is mostly empty, and only a few people are left wandering around. Marcus has all of his statues moved onto the central platform and he's bent over, fussing over a joint on one particular statue. Shuffling my feet, I move over to him and he looks up, a tired smile settling onto his face when he sees me.

"Almost done?" I ask, and he straightens up, rolling his shoulder.

"Yeah. I had to move all of these to the stage here so the cleaning crew can come through tonight." He gestures to the statues now stacked together. "Ah *mija*, I'm beat."

He tilts his head from side to side, craning his neck to stretch out the stiffness. "I need to get out of these legs too."

"Do you have your chair?" I frown in sympathy and he smiles, resting a hand on my shoulder.

"It's alright, *querida*. I'll manage. I called a car. They'll be here soon." He waves his cell phone about, the warm glow of a lit up screen in his palm. "What about you? How are you getting home?"

I open my mouth to speak, but then close it, pressing lips firmly together as I realize I don't really know. I suppose, somewhere in the back of my mind, I had planned to have Laurence take me home... but now after our fight, I don't know if I'm so sure. Certain that Marcus will worry without a confident reply, I quickly point to his phone. "One of those too. Don't worry. I'll be safe."

He stares at me for a moment and I'm not sure he believes me, but eventually he pops a closed fist down gently on the top of my head. "Alright then. I'll see you tomorrow."

"Okay." He turns to leave but I slide in front of him, wrapping my arms around his torso. "Thank you," I whisper into the folds of his crisp white shirt. "I'm so glad you were here."

He hugs me back, sweat and paint and metal combining into his perfect scent. "Me too, *mija*. Me too."

Once he is gone, I head into the office. Antonio is there, his forehead perched in one open hand as he reads over some paperwork. I knock on the door, and his head snaps up to look at me.

"Oh, Camry! I'm so sorry, I didn't see you there." He moves to get up from his seat but I hold up a hand to stop him, pushing the door open.

"Don't bother, it's fine. I just came in to get my things." I eye the paperwork in his hand, trying to figure out what he's doing. "You're not going to stay much longer, are you? You look exhausted."

A wry smile comes across his features and he shakes his head. "No, I actually was just figuring out the schedule tomorrow so I knew what time I had to be in. I'll take as much sleep tonight as possible. Cleaners should be here in fifteen minutes, and then I'll head home."

"Good. You were such a big help tonight, really. I can't thank you enough for everything you've done for me, for Travers-Moreau, for this whole event. It's been a real privilege working with you."

He grins bashfully and returns the sentiment. "You as well. I'm honored to have had the opportunity to work with you, Camry. I never imagined that

Sanctuary would be the stage for an event as grand as this, but now my eyes are opened. This experience was entirely my pleasure." He turns back to his paperwork and I dig through my bag for my cell phone. Curious, I ask Antonio, "Have you seen Laurence?"

"Mister Mercier? He left a little while ago. Said he had something to take care of. He left in a terrible hurry." He pauses, looking at me. "You don't know?"

"Ah, I haven't had my phone on me so I was just going to check it now." I finally pull the device from my bag, tapping my fingers against the back.

Antonio levels his gaze upon me, a curious gleam in his eyes. "Are you and Mister Mercier dating?"

"Ah, yes." Feeling it best to admit the truth of it to him, I nod, pursing my lips. "We are."

"That explains so much!" He laughs, much too loudly for the small space we are in, then quickly settles down and assumes a more serious expression. "Well, I hope things are okay between the two of you. It seems like he really loves you."

I swallow awkwardly, feeling a sense of unease creeping up the back of my neck at his choice of words. "Yeah, I think he does," I admit noncommittally, quickly crouching and gathering up my things. "Anyway, what time do you need to be here tomorrow?"

Looking back over the papers again, he runs his hand along his chin in evident exhaustion. "First pickup is at ten, so I guess nine for me."

"Okay. I'll be here around nine then too."

He shakes his head, hand in the air as if to stop me. "No, Camry. Nine thirty or ten is just fine. Go get some rest."

He smiles, then turns back to his paperwork as if to say, "And no buts!"

I can't help but laugh a little and lifting my bags onto my arm, I step out of the office.

Finally able to turn my attention to the phone in my hand, I notice a single text from Laurence.

"Well done tonight. Take Monday and Tuesday off. You've earned it."

I scowl at the message. I puff my cheeks in indignation, frustrated with his behavior. Irritation flares in me and I type out a one word reply: "Thanks."

Deciding that my best bet is to call a car similar to Marcus, I quickly punch in the details and see that a driver is nearby and waiting. I gratefully accept the ride and before I know it I'm home, exhaustion nipping away any remaining anxieties and pulling me down into slumber.

****

Wednesday morning dawns bright and brilliant, the winter sun blinding as it reflects off the patches of snow on the street corners.

My internal mood, however, stands in stark contrast. My stomach is twisted in knots and my nervousness and confusion dominate every cell in my body. The cleanup complete, the gala wrapped up beautifully, and I remain grateful for and pleased with the entire experience. I took my two days off, trying to enjoy waking up late, long midday runs with Shakespeare, and the much appreciated downtime after such a busy few months. I even attended a new exhibit and wrote a new blog post after a few weeks off.

But through all of this, one current of unease ruins the joy that should be mine.

Laurence and I have exchanged not one word since Saturday night.

Now, as I sit on the train during my commute to work, my mind is racing through every interaction since that night. After our dance, I didn't see him again, other than across the room, or during the closing remarks. I texted him on Sunday once the last of the clean-up was finished and heard nothing. Not once did he reach out to me, and in a mix of confusion and pride, I never wrote him either.

Did I do something wrong? Does he miss me? Is he okay? I have to assume that someone would have told me if something bad had happened to him, but I can't come up with any other idea. The only thing I can guess is that he's still upset about our fight on Friday, but I know him; this behavior is odd. It is not like him to say he loves me and then let something like that argument be the end. With the way we danced on Saturday too, I don't think he's ready to let me go. But what if his confession of love was all a lie? What if he didn't mean it? I'm pushed to my breaking point, trying to master my confusion and hurt. My mind is spinning in a thousand circles attempting to make sense of something that has no explanation and I'm making myself sick with the nervousness of it all. It takes effort not to let out a sound of frustration as I spin these thoughts in my mind, and I stuff them down within, knowing I'll have an answer sometime today.

I arrive in my office and after hanging my coat and settling in with a hot cup of coffee, I open up my email. One notice stands out among the rest, its subject line catching my attention. Curious, I open the email from Human Resources. The contents are simple, asking me to come to the thirty seventh floor and visit the HR department to meet with a Ms. Cohen regarding "the future of your position at Travers-Moreau."

If I have any poise left, it disappears in that moment. "What?" I murmur out loud to no one in particular. With the time frame written only 'as soon as you are able', I quickly scoop up my purse and head for the elevator.

Stepping into the HR offices, I ask the receptionist to speak to Ms. Cohen and she calls on the intercom, assuring me that Ms. Cohen will be out in a moment.

My fingers fiddle with the side of my skirt, curling into the fabric as I wait. Am I moving back to my old position so soon? Or worse, am I fired? Did I do such a poor job with the gala? Is Laurence that sick of me?

A door squeaks open and a primly dressed woman strides down the hall. "Miss Hughes?"

"Yes?" My voice squeaks a bit and she gives me an unimpressed look before gesturing for me to follow her.

"This way." I rush behind her, trying to match her brisk pace. When we reach her office, she waves her hand at the chair set before her desk, and I take a seat. She sits, peering at me over the tips of her fingers.

"Well, Miss Hughes, this won't take long, but you're here so that I can inform you of your position change here at Travers-Moreau."

A small inward sigh escapes me. I'm not fired. Thank god!

She opens a folder on her desk, scanning it quickly before finding what she was looking for. "Effective immediately, you will now serve in the position as Executive Assistant to the Executive Director of the American Division and New York Branch Director, Mr. Laurence Mercier." She stares at me, almost sneering. "If you accept, that is."

"Wh-what?!" My eyes widen and I sit in stunned silence. This was never a possibility in my mind that would happen.

Ms. Cohen heaves a weary sigh and her thoughts are written on her face, clearly doubting the reason for my promotion.

Indignancy rises in me and I straighten up, almost glaring in determination. "I do accept! Gladly."

I'm still not sure what the future for Laurence and I entails, but I do know that I want to work with him, and I want more opportunities like the gala. That sense of accomplishment was like a drug - and I want more.

Ms. Cohen slides the folder across the desk to me. "Initial, sign, and date all of these by the end of the day today. I'll be in touch. Any questions? Email me."

I carefully take the file from her, holding it to my chest. "Thank you."

She waves me away, already moved on and mind focused elsewhere, and I realize I am dismissed. I quickly step out of her office, emotions swirling within.

As quickly as I can I get to my office, I slide into my seat and pour over the fine print, detailing every ounce of the contract. I suck in a breath at the salary and swallow, stuck on the number. I shake my head, thinking I'll digest that later, and flip through the rest of the pages, seeing information regarding security clearance, duties, and more.

Head spinning, I push up from my chair, feeling like the only way I'll make sense of all of this is to talk to Laurence. Silently praying he'll be in his office - and able to talk - I make my way down the hall and knock on the heavy oak door.

"Come in." His voice sounds cold, disinterested. I push open the door and step into his office.

Laurence is seated in his favorite arm chair, profile in view as he gazes toward the window. A stack of papers rests in the crook of his elegantly crossed legs and the trim silver frames of his glasses glint in the sunlight streaming in from the expansive windows.

He looks weary, like he's not been sleeping well and a flare of concern rises up within me.

"Laurence?"

He finally turns his head to meet my eyes and for just an instant, a flash of emotion crosses his face. Quickly mastering his expression, he turns to me with an apathetic stare. "Yes?"

I'm entirely caught off guard by his demeanor and it distracts me from the purpose of my arrival, but soon I shake myself out of my confusion and thank him.

"I just got back from HR. It looks like we'll be working together from now on, and I just wanted to say thank you. It really means a lot to me and I'm thrilled to be your assistant."

He stares at me for a minute, gaze unfeeling, almost vacant. Then his lips part and he speaks. "There is nothing to it. You are the right person for the position. We work well together, and you do impressive work. Thanks are not necessary. Please devote the rest of this week to the gala's follow ups and thank-you notes. We will go into the new position in depth on Monday."

His tone is dispassionate, and he turns his head back to his paperwork, stifling a massive yawn. He rubs his eyes, pinching between his eyebrows. I can't help myself; no matter what is between us, I'm worried about him. "Laurence, are you alright? You seem tired."

Keeping his eyes on his papers, he doesn't answer my question. Instead, when he speaks his voice is like venom, and the words that fall from his lips send me reeling, shivers of hurt and confusion hitting me like a slap across the face.

"That will be all, Miss Hughes. Please be on your way."

Chapter 21

There is no time to stifle the gasp that falls unbidden from my lips, and I stand there, dumbfounded, staring at his profile. Miss Hughes... *Miss Hughes*. No more Camry, no more *ma chérie*. Nothing in the world could make me feel as isolated and discarded in that moment than those two simple words. Feeling as if I've been struck, my body is tense and I feel sick to my stomach. What just happened?

My brain fires at a rapid pace; first shock, then confusion, then hurt... within seconds they all give way to anger. I spin on my heel, stomping out of the room, unwilling to dignify the situation with any more emotion in his presence. I fly down the hallway and when I reach my office, I slam the door shut and sink against it.

For what feels like hours, I sit there, emotions beyond name running rampant in my mind. I have no idea what to think, to feel, because in that moment, I feel everything.

The tears slow in time, more because I have nothing left to give and less because I've gathered myself together. Shakily I stand up and move over to my desk, a now cold cup of coffee the only comfort in this big empty room. What had always been a place of felicity now reeks of betrayal, feeling like everything from Laurence has been laced with deception from the start. What do I make of this? Was he only having fun with me? Was everything a lie?

I'm glad to have the opportunity to work with him; there is no doubt in my mind of that. But his behavior makes no sense. Nothing I can see from all of our time together makes me believe that he was playing with me, stringing me along. And yet... why?

That single word bounces around in my brain, and soon a headache blossoms from the constant back and forth of thought. I close my eyes and rub my temples with one hand, trying to find my way back out of the fog I'm in. After a few minutes of measured breathing, I let myself cautiously approach my thoughts again.

The conclusion that keeps returning is simple: Laurence and I are no longer a couple. His deliberate choice of words erected a wall between us, closing me off from his life. I cannot find the answers as to why; nothing seems to fit. Yet here I am, sitting alone, with the understanding that it's over, all the wonderful little details of our life together coming to an end.

The vivid colors of the painting of my mother catch my eye, and I stare at it for a few seconds, wondering what she would say in this moment. "But you're not here, are you? You're not here, so I can't ask. I'm all alone now."

My gaze leaves the colors behind, and I stare down at my desk, the crisp sheen of paper and dark ink of text reflect the contrast in my inner thoughts: black and white, all or nothing. Just weeks ago, I thought I'd been so lucky; now I've lost it all.

There is a finality to my emotions, and for what feels like the millionth time in the past week, a calming apathy settles over me, suppressing my emotions, protecting my heart. With a practiced hand, I pick up the gala lists of vendors, artists, sponsors, and more, and then put pen to page, beginning the long and arduous task of handwritten thank you notes.

****

Laurence scans the page in front of him, and eventually his eyes cease movement, finished with his reading. He hands them back to me. "Yes, that will do nicely. Well done. Submit that before the end of the day."

I thank him briefly and take the papers back, careful not to let our fingers touch. Once I have them, I leave his office, grateful that I won't be needing to do another revision. Our communication these days is entirely made up of professional discussions. He isn't cold to me any longer, but there definitely isn't the same familiar warmth I remember so well. He's just... there. Always present and yet a million miles away. The distance between us has been so carefully constructed that I'm afraid if I so much as press a finger against the barrier, the whole thing will shatter at my feet; and that's a chance I'm unwilling to take. Sighing to myself about the way things have turned out, I'm about to open my door when my phone pings in my hand and I pause, fingers on the doorknob, to check the message.

"Just arrived! Heading to your building ASAP." Ciaran's plane must have just landed, bringing him to town a few days before my upcoming surgery. I have pre-op tomorrow and the surgery the day after, and as promised he's come to town to stay with me for a week. I have to smile a bit, remembering the many conversations we've had in recent weeks. Even though the surgery is an outpatient one, both he and Marcus are determined to be present and supportive, doting on me hand and foot before and after. I'm sure some of that is due to them knowing about the falling out between Laurence and I; neither of them took it kindly, to say the least, but they've stepped up in big ways since.

Quickly typing out a reply to him, reminding of TMC Tower's address, I close my phone screen again and push open the door.

"There you are!" The voice from my couch makes me lift my head and Hayden sits there, half slumped into the cushion.

"Hey Hays! What are you doing here?"

She shrugs, looking bored. "Eh, I don't have much to do this afternoon, so I figured I'd come see you before you take off for the week."

I toss my papers on my desk and go to sit next to her, resting my head on her shoulder. "Ciaran just landed. He'll be on his way soon."

"That's good."

We sit together for a few minutes in silence, head resting on head, and I take a deep breath, relaxing. "Thanks for stopping by. It's good to see you."

"Yeah, I know." There's a hint of teasing in her voice, but she is much more subdued than normal. "How are you doing these days?"

Before I can take the breath to answer, she adds, "And I mean really. How are you really doing?"

A thoughtful sound slides across the back of my throat. After a moment, my answer comes and I realize that the words I speak are not planned, but they are the truth, more honest and raw than I'd let myself admit. "I'm not worried about the surgery any more, but I am scared. I'm scared that this will be the first in a never ending series of bits and pieces of me being taken away as more of them rebel against me. And I'm scared that one day there won't be enough of me left, and I won't recognize myself when I look in the mirror."

Hayden lets out a deep sigh, and my head rises and falls with the movement of her shoulders. "I understand what you mean. I wish I could say that you'll never have another surgery again." She lifts her head and bounces her shoulder, making me pick my own head up. Looking me in the eye, she smiles faintly. "But I do know that you'll never lose what makes you, you. I don't think there will come a day when you won't know who you are."

Her words are warm and comforting, filled with compassion and I can't help but smile. "And you'll help me, even if I do?"

"Most definitely."

"Thanks, Hays."

The tone of her voice shifts, returning more to the familiar tone I'm accustomed to. "Oh, don't you worry about that. So while we wait, how can I help?"

The corner of my lips curl upward, not missing the 'we' in her sentence. "If you're that bored, you can help me file these." I point to a giant stack of folders sitting on the shelf behind my desk.

She looks back and forth between me and the files, scrunching up her face. "I guess so."

"Hey, you asked!" I laugh and poke her side a little, then dash out of reach, moving to sit behind my desk.

"Yeah, yeah, yeah." She stretches a bit then rises and wanders over to her assignment.

The next hour passes quickly, both of us focused on our work, and before I realize it, the end of the day is drawing near. I jump when my desk phone rings and I almost drop the phone in my scrambled attempt to answer. "Hello?"

"Camry, it's Michael at the front security desk."

"Hi Michael! Is my brother here to see me?"

"Yeah, he is. Just wanted to confirm."

"Thanks a lot. You can send him up."

He says farewell and I giggle as I hear Ciaran in the background, offering a cheerful farewell. A minute or two later, I meet him in the hallway and he drops his bags, hugging me tightly.

He spots Hayden peeking out over my shoulder and he hugs her as well. "Hey you."

"Hey, little brother." I smirk at her familiar greeting, remembering the way she'd call him that when we were all kids.

He pops her gently on the head. "Little? I'm a foot taller than you."

She rolls her eyes with feigned disgust then giggles and walks back into my office. I motion towards the door. "Go on. That's my office."

Even my brother is not immune to the impressiveness of my office and he walks around, eyes alight, drinking in the details with a wide smile on his face. "Well I'll be damned."

"What?" I eye him skeptically, unsure of what he means. He turns to me, grinning from ear to ear with a devilish expression.

"Looks like my big sis is finally growing up."

I snatch a pillow off the couch and throw it at him as quickly as I can. He yelps in laughter and grabs it inches before it hits his face. Hayden rolls her lips, not bothering to hide her amusement and exasperation. "You guys haven't changed at all."

"Anyway, I have another few minutes of work to do before I can leave today. I have to make sure I've got all my bases covered before I'm gone for the week."

Ciaran settles himself in a chair, pulling out his phone, while Hayden steps out. "I'm going to go get ready to leave too, okay?"

I say farewell, our long hug saying more than any words could. For the next few minutes, I fuss about the office, tidying up, watering plants, and checking over paperwork and files. Once satisfied, I turn to Ciaran. "I have to go let Mr. Mercier know I'm leaving."

He pauses, stiffening ever so slightly, before lifting his head in forced casualness. "Sure, okay. I'll be right here." He turns his gaze back to the small screen and I head down the hall to the familiar door.

When I arrive, the door is slightly ajar. I peek my head in and I see Laurence sitting at his desk, elbows resting on the top and his face resting in his hands. His shoulders rise and fall evenly and his breathing is a quiet purr.

I suck in a breath at the sight, and his head snaps up, looking at me.

"I'm sorry!" I exclaim, ducking into the office and closing the door behind me. "I'm sorry, I didn't know you were sleeping."

His eyes narrow with hostility, his lips curling defensively over his teeth. "I was not sleeping."

I reflexively take a step back and his expression softens a bit, a weary sigh falling from his lips. "No, I apologize." He waves his hand, motioning me over.

My steps cautiously bring me closer, and I notice that he looks utterly exhausted. He has bags under his eyes, and his skin's typically bright complexion looks dull and clammy.

"What did you need?" His gaze is patient, but the intentional distance between us remains.

"I wanted to tell you I am done for the day. My brother is here to take me home."

He looks mildly perplexed, and I continue, a little unsure. "Oh, um, well since I'm leaving for the week. My surgery is in two days, so I wanted to tell you that I finished everything. And I left some details with Miss Davis for a few things you'll need help with while I'm..."

I trail off at the look on his face. His eyes are wide, and for just a second I see a hopeless, lost little boy.

"Laurence?" My voice comes out timidly, but even in the quiet I see the use of his name call him back to his senses. He stands, raking a hand through his hair, and tugging on his tie to loosen the neck.

"Of course. Yes, of course." His voice is distracted, but he seems to understand. He looks at his desk, tented fingers shifting papers beneath them.

"Thank you for telling me. We will manage without you, but we will be glad to have you back." He clears his throat and loses a little of his practiced composure. "I... I hope that your surgery is successful."

Finally he lifts his eyes to meet mine and there's something nervous in his gaze. We're frozen in place, locked in each other's gazes, and it feels like my heartbeat slows, a steady thumping in my ears. With every beat, memories I thought I had pushed below the surface come bubbling up again and I can feel my skin flush and eyes sting with the threat of oncoming tears. With nothing left to do, I look away, squeezing my eyes shut and taking a deep breath. When I look up, there is a pained expression on Laurence's face, but he quickly exchanges it for a neutral one.

"*Alors, d'accord.* Thank you for telling me. I will see you in a week."

He turns his attention back to his desk and I force a smile. "Thanks. I'll see you then."

I hold my head up high and march out of his office, lips trembling with every step.

****

The crisp February wind blows strongly and Ciaran wraps an arm around me. We stand side by side, staring down at the shiny gray slab set in the ground.

"I'm glad we came." He speaks slowly, then lays the small bouquet of flowers we bought on the grave marker. "I haven't been here at all, since the day we buried her."

I squeeze his arm a bit, leaning my head on his shoulder. "I've only been here a few times, and I haven't come in months."

"Mama," Ciaran calls to her. "Genevieve is almost one year old. She's curious, and silly, and her smile is the brightest light. I tell her all about you, and she always listens." I smile, listening to his words. "Asher is good, and I'm still hopelessly in love with him. I remember you used to say that you'd catch him staring at me, and I never believed you. But now that you're gone, I see it all the time, and I think maybe I'm paying more attention to the world I'm living in. So thank you, for teaching me that. I'm sorry it took losing you to understand. But, I love you and miss you every day. I'll always love you, mama. I'll always love you."

He falls silent, content with what he said. Feeling it appropriate that I speak up, I study the flowers, and her name just behind them. But the words that I say are almost an impulse, something unexpected, something raw. "I'm sorry, mama."

Ciaran kisses the top of my head, and I take a deep breath. "Mama, I'm going to have surgery in a few days. I think you know what this feels like, because I know you had to go through so many things in that hospital all the time." I sniffle, running my gloved hand along my face, wiping away the tears that trickle down my cheeks.

"I'm really sorry, though. I'm sorry because all those things that happened to you, all the struggles you had so many days were all because you were suffering from something we didn't know about. And now I'm going to be just like you, but this time we'll know. And I'm sorry, I'm so sorry because you didn't know." My chest is heaving, sobs choking me back. "You didn't know anything and it must have been so scary. I'm sorry you had to go through all that alone. You must have been so confused, so scared." I cling to Ciaran's coat, burying my face in his chest. "I'm sorry mama. I'm so sorry."

Ciaran holds me tightly against him, his shoulders trembling along with me. The winter wind stings against the tears on my cheeks, the only sounds distant traffic and Ciaran's heartbeat in my ear. Time slows and eventually, I've mastered my voice again enough for a whisper. "I'm going to have a lot of people who help me, and there's a lot of people who love me. I'll be okay. But I need you to send me some of your strength. I need some of whatever you had in you to get through all of that without any answers. So please, mama, please send me something. Help me get through this, and help me rely on the people who love me."

"Oh, Cam..." My brother's voice is broken, but he kisses my forehead, and whispers into my ear. "I love you. I'm here."

"I know." I smile up at him, and he brushes away my tears. "Let's go home?"

He nods, and hand in hand, we leave the cemetery behind, saying another farewell to our mother.

"This sucks." I grumble into the air, staring up at the ceiling from my place on the uncomfortable bed. My hand twitches as I fight the urge to scratch at the tape around my IV placement.

"Eloquent, this morning, aren't we?" Ciaran teases me from his place across the room but I can tell he's almost as uncomfortable as I am. We've been here for a few hours and I haven't eaten since last night.

Glaring at him, I repeat myself. "Sucks, sucks, sucks."

He snorts in laughter, then with all the harmony of a thousand cats screeching, drags his chair across the linoleum to my bedside and settles in, stroking my hair out of my eyes. "I know. I'm sorry. But you're about to get your anesthesia and then you won't even remember how pissy you are right now."

Sticking my tongue out at him, I sigh, leaning my weight into the mattress as much as possible. "When I wake up, you're taking me to The Creamery and buying me the biggest chocolate cookies and cream ice cream you can afford."

He makes a scolding noise, tapping a finger on my nose. "Not today. Tomorrow."

"Remind me again why you're here?" I pout at him, but eventually it slides into a shy smile. "I am glad, though."

"For what?"

"I'm glad you're here."

He pauses, soft laughter curling up from deep within his chest. "Ah, yes, but that won't get you ice cream today, no matter how nice you are."

"You really are no fun."

Our conversation is cut short, as two nurses enter the room. The nurse I've had since I arrived comes and stands next to me, an expression of muted enthusiasm on her face. "Alright, Camry. It's time. We're going to wheel you down into the OR now. You ready?"

"No, not at all, but I suppose that's not an option, so I'll handle it."

She laughs a little. "That's all I can ask."

Ciaran squeezes my hand with a sincere smile. "I'll be waiting!"

I return it, though a little forced, and the nurses unhook my bed, pushing me out into the hallway.

The corridors have a distinct smell that turns my stomach, like sickness being held at bay by a thin veil of magic. I close my eyes, trying to internalize my focus, playing a game with myself to see if I can follow along the maze of hallways, moving left, then right, then left again, like I'm in a real life version of Pacman. Occasionally there are jolts to my bed's frame as we open doors and cross thresholds. Finally, the pace slows, and I crack open an eye. "They're going to wheel you in there in just a minute, but the anesthesiologist is going to come out and talk with you real quick, okay?"

"Okay."

"We'll see you in a little while."

They leave, and I'm left in a small room, just off the OR. From my angle, I can see shadows of people moving around, preparing for the work. Before long, the door opens and a woman steps out, smiling brightly. She's short like Hayden and her smile reminds me of her in more ways than one, and I'm instantly more comfortable from her presence alone.

"Good morning! I'm Doctor Oelsten. I'm going to be in charge of your anesthesia today. We're going to do a general anesthetic, which will keep you out for a few hours. I know Doctor Park walked you through the procedure yesterday. Did you have any more questions?"

"I think I'm all set. Thank you though."

"Alright! I'm going to go scrub up, and then we'll be ready for you. A nurse will be bringing you in shortly."

She leaves and once again I'm alone. Given a few minutes to collect my thoughts, my mind wanders. I wonder what Ciaran is doing to keep himself busy. I picture him chatting on the phone with Asher, sharing about his visit to New York, cooing over his daughter. Hayden and Alex are probably eating their lunches; Hays chatting away happily with a crowd of friends in a busy lunch spot, Alex eating at his desk, fiddling with his phone. Marcus I picture sitting on his sofa, casually eating a bowl of his favorite mofongo, popping prawns into his mouth with practiced ease.

Before I know it, my thoughts have moved to the one person I don't want to think about. Conjuring an image of him resting in his armchair, a plate with his lunch perched on one knee. He'll be reading, or enjoying a quiet moment. I wonder if he's doing okay. I still remember the weariness on his face when I saw him two days ago. I'm worried about him. I hate that I'm still worried about him, but I can't help it. In a few short months, he became so much of my world and the loss of his presence in my life is like an empty hole. I let my mind wander a bit, coursing through memories of the two of us. I know it's unreasonable but I keep visualizing him coming through the door of my hospital room, sitting there like he promised he would before everything fell apart. I can't stop myself from wishing he'll come this afternoon or visit me at home, but I know it's only a dream. I don't understand what pushed him away, but I can feel in my heart that it's over.

Eventually the nurse comes to wheel me into the operating room. Dr. Park appears, his eyes smiling over the top of his mask. He greets me, and after a few quickly exchanged pleasantries, Dr. Oelsten attaches the sedation to my IV and the world fades to a blur. I close my eyes, willing myself to get this over with as soon as possible. The only thing in my mind now is an image of Laurence, smiling at me with warmth and affection.

****

Ciaran's bags are stacked neatly in front of the door. He tugs his coat on and waves goodbye to Hayden and Alex, then turns to me. "Bye, sis. I'll see you soon, okay?"

We embrace and he hugs me, careful of the incision on my neck. "Be good."

I roll my eyes. "Yeah, I know."

Hayden, from her perch on the back of my couch, adds her two cents to the conversation. "Don't worry, Ciaran. We'll make sure she behaves." She winks at him and now it's his turn to look exasperated.

"Ha ha, Hayden. As if you are the one to trust. You're half the reason she always got into so much trouble!" His words are strong but his tone teasing, and we share a laugh, knowing how true it is. He turns to me one last time. "Love you." Then with a quick kiss to the top of my head, he leaves the apartment and I close the door behind him.

After a few minutes, the three of us sit in my living room sipping mugs of hot chocolate. Hayden and Alex update me on work news and gossip and ask once again all about the surgery. In the five days since, I've recovered well. My voice retains only the slightest hoarseness, and aside from the slightly scratchy throat, things are in many ways normal. Even I'm amazed at how fast the recovery has gone, though doctors and nurses alike assured me that I'd be feeling better within just a few days. The only thing I hate is the calcium pills I'm taking for a week after the surgery, to ensure my calcium doesn't dip too low while my body adjusts to the loss of two of my parathyroid glands. The pills are massive and make me want to gag every time I try and get one down. I shudder just thinking of it; something Hayden's keen eyes don't miss.

"What's up? Are you okay?"

I draw my blanket in around me and shrug a little. "Just cold."

She looks sad for a moment, lips turned downward, and her fingers absentmindedly play with the strap on her shoe. "I'm really sorry he's not here for you."

"Who?" I look up, confused.

"Mr. Mercier."

My eyes shoot open, and I stutter a bit in reply. "What do you mean?"

"Well, he made you all those promises about how he'd be here for you during all this. And I still don't know what got into him, but he never actually broke up with you, did he?"

She sighs dramatically, flopping back over one arm of the sofa. "I feel like there's something else going on here. He was the perfect partner for you. I can't just believe he'd give up after such a trivial fight."

Alex shifts in his chair, interjecting himself into the conversation. "I don't know, I'd be pretty pissed if I was dating a girl and she kept something like that from me. I don't think he went about it the right way, but I can see where the guy's coming from. Maybe he just got hurt."

"Or maybe he was scared?"

Alex and Hayden trade theories for a few minutes while I sit quietly, half listening. Hayden's right, in that it doesn't make sense, and while I suppose he never straight out ended it, he did make it very clear that our relationship was restricted to a purely professional one. Eventually, their back and forth becomes too much and I pull the blanket over my head.

A few seconds later, the blanket comes off with a quick tug from Alex's hand. "Sorry, Cam. We didn't mean to unpack your love life like that."

"No, it's okay. You guys are half right. I don't even know what to think of it at all. I've just been trying not to think about it because when I do, I just want to cry."

Hayden crawls over to my side of the couch, curling around me. "Can I ask you a question?" Her voice is soft, almost cooing, and I nod a little, biting my bottom lip, certain I'm not going to like what she's going to say.

"Do you love him?"

The question gives me pause for half a second, but before long, I find myself nodding. "I think I do. Did? I don't know. But I think I fell in love with him, and I don't know if I'm done with that yet."

Hayden practically bounces off the couch, her subdued attitude gone. "Well then! I think you need to tell him that, and I think you need to tell him that now."

Alex groans, rubbing his palms over his eyes. "Hayden, what the hell are you talking about?"

She beams at us, pride shining in her eyes. "Well, it was never really over, was it? And honestly, he decided they'd be able to work together regardless of their relationship when he hired her as his assistant. So I think she'll feel better if she tells him how she feels."

We stare at her, unimpressed looks on our faces and she stomps a foot, throwing out her arms. "I'm serious! They never talked out what happened between them. They never got any closure. And for all we know, he may still be in love with her. If he's not, she'll have said her piece and she can move on. I think they need to talk about this."

"Fair points aside, why now?"

"She goes back to work tomorrow. If she doesn't talk about this now, she'll get back into work mode and never come out of this. I mean, you know her." She points at me and I can't help but shrink back into the blanket some. "Camry is the queen of avoidance! If she doesn't deal with this now, she'll never deal with it at all."

She spins and looks at me, face alight with the possibilities of her grand scheme. "You've got to go to him - now!"

"Hayden, I'm all for romance, but it is the middle of the afternoon. He's busy at work. And I'm not supposed to be there yet. If I went now, I'd be interrupting him. I'm not going to do that right now."

She folds her arms and opens her mouth to speak her rebuttal, but Alex shushes her.

"She's got a point, Hayden. Just let it go for now."

"Fine. But seriously, Camry, don't leave this unfinished. You'll either be back together or be able to move on. You deserve closure if this is really over."

****

Hayden and Alex leave once we finish an early dinner, finally finishing up the massive pot of food that Marcus had brought the night I got home. I tidy up a bit and do the dishes, but I start feeling cooped up not long after. After a week of Ciaran's constant presence and frequent visits from Marcus I am half glad that I am finally alone, and half terrified that this will be the time some morbid complication arises. Refusing to stew in my own thoughts, I take Shakespeare on a long walk, the rhythm of the city rising around me in every direction, pulsing with each of my steps. Being out in the world again seems to lift my spirits, and the thrum of the city helps me feel alive.

Tired from our adventure, we arrive home and almost immediately Shakespeare flops into his bed. Not even two minutes later, he rolls over deep in sleep, sweet puppy dream sounds rumbling in his chest.

Watching him does nothing to calm the nervous energy building up inside of me, contrary to most days. For the rest of the day I tried to avoid it, but Hayden's comments have been eating away at me all day long. Deep down inside I know she's right and I've spent the past few hours convincing myself otherwise. I stand up, pacing around the living room, trying to calm my thoughts. But the longer I stay here, the more wound up I get, and before I know it, I'm throwing on a coat and racing out the door.

I'm at the bottom of the stairs before I realize I don't know where I'm going. A quick glance at my phone tells me it's after 7:30 at night, and I start to move towards the station that will take me closer to Laurence's house. But then I picture the look in his eyes when I saw him last, the exhaustion on his face, and I know where I need to go.

The lobby is empty, save for a security guard, and I realize I've forgotten my badge. A sudden wave of panic rises within me, but the guard waves cheerfully at me. "Hello miss! It's been a long time since you've been here! Mr. Mercier said you'd be coming back to work this week."

I pause, wondering why Mr. Mercier would have said any such thing to this security guard, but I decide to use it to my advantage, flashing him a brilliant smile. "Yes, I start again tomorrow! I forgot something upstairs in my office, though. Do you think I could go up?"

He shrugs. "Sure thing. Have a great night!"

I flash him my best smile and thank him, racing into the elevator.

When the doors open, the top floor is dark and quiet, save the telltale crack of light from under Laurence's door. I practically fly down the hall, bursting into the room. "I knew you'd be here!"

Laurence drops the cup of tea he's holding and it pours all over his desk. "Camry?!" Then realizing what he's done, he leaps up from his chair, absentmindedly patting around his chest in search of a handkerchief.

"Oh my God, I'm sorry!" I rush forward and pull off my sweater, using it to sop up as much of the hot liquid that I can. I look up to find Laurence's eyes staring at me, eyes wide in confusion and surprise.

I shrink back a little, picking up my sweater and clutching it between my hands. "Ugh, that was so like me. I hope those weren't important."

He sighs, rubbing a hand along his cheek. "Only some offers. I can reprint them."

"Offers? On what?" I glance at the pages on the desk and he shifts them out of my sight.

"What are you doing here?"

"Oh." The moment all comes back to me and I remember why I'm here after eight o'clock in the first place.

"I, um... I wanted to talk to you."

"About?" His posture is stiff, and I can see the wall coming up again between us.

"Can we sit?" I point to the couches and after a few seconds, he gives a reluctant nod of his head, following me to the sofa.

Now that I'm here I'm struck by a thought. I have no idea what to say to him, or what I actually came here for. Resolution, yes, but... what else? He sits there, patiently, and I'm reminded of that first day when he listened to me explain about art and connections. So many of my memories are now laced with him, and in that moment it all becomes clear. I don't want to lose that; I don't want to lose him. And so I speak the only words that feel fitting in this moment.

"I'm sorry."

Chapter 22

He doesn't say anything. He doesn't even blink.

Feeling flustered, I continue, words tumbling out of
me in a jumbled mess. "I'm sorry I didn't give you a
chance. I'm sorry I didn't tell you. I'm sorry if I did
something that made you hate me but I never meant
to hurt you. I was just so caught up in my own mess
and feelings and I never once stopped to consider how
you felt. I... don't think I was wrong. I think I
deserved that space. But I hurt you and I'm sorry for
that."

The silence stretches between us and as my anxieties
increase, I open my mouth again, then snap it shut as
he lifts his hand to stop me.

"Don't. Please don't."

The crushing weight of his words settles on my
shoulders and all the resolve I had built up crumbles
in an instant. "Oh." The word falls from my lips,
quiet as a whisper between lovers; but lovers we
aren't, and now I understand. I thought I'd be
prepared for this, for the official end of everything,
but it feels worse than I'd ever imagined.

Squinting my eyes shut, I press my lips together,
desperately trying to master my emotions. I hear
Laurence shift in his seat, and I wait for him to stand
and walk away. Instead, a familiar warmth rests on
my hands clenched in my lap.

"Camry." His voice is warm but full of sorrow, and I
can hear the strain in it. "Camry, no, look at me."

Unsure and unwilling to cling any longer to the last remnants of hope, I shake my head quickly and try to pull my hands away.

He doesn't let me go. I can feel his breath as he sighs, and then his fingers begin to gently roll over mine. "I'm sorry too."

My body betrays me, head lifting in traitorous hope at his words. "What?"

"I'm sorry. I was hurting and I behaved horrendously."

I blink a few times and roughly pull my hand away, rubbing it across my eyes, to wipe away my tears. "I... you..." I can't formulate thought, let alone speak. He smiles a bit and I can see genuine sorrow in his eyes. He looks down, breathing deeply, and then begins to speak.

"I thought you had no trust in me. I felt humiliated when Marcus called, assuming I was aware. Even he thought I must have known! And then, though you could not find it in you to tell me, you so quickly and painlessly shared with your friends. Am I not good enough?" His voice is quiet, almost pleading and I am so completely confused and overwhelmed.

"What in the world are you talking about?"

"After the gala, I heard you telling Hayden and Alex everything. You shared it so simply, with no hesitation or concern." He looks at me finally, and whatever he sees on my face, he suddenly looks alarmed and hurries on. "I did not mean to overhear. I was coming to find you but you were talking and I did not want to interrupt. I suppose that I..."

He trails off and pushes his hands along the tops of his legs, looking up to the ceiling. "In that moment, it felt as if you could trust other people, but not me. I thought my feelings for you were misguided, unrequited. In that moment, it was all I could do to leave."

"I didn't mean it like that at all." My voice is tinged with resentment at such a situation. How could such a simple misunderstanding have robbed us of so much? "Laurence, when you came to me that day I had only hours before gotten to the point where I could even think about my health without falling apart. And with the gala coming up, I wanted to wait to tell you once it was over. I didn't want it to ruin our day. But even without the gala, I couldn't have told you before then. And if you think I could have, you're wrong. I needed that time to process and get by. I only was able to talk to them at that point *because* you knew, and because Marcus knew as well. I wanted you to be the first one I talked to, but it didn't happen that way and you can't be mad at me for that."

He rises and walks a few steps toward the window, peering out at the city at night. He stands in silence and as I watch him, I can see the set of his shoulders relax. "I don't know what to think anymore," he mutters to himself, turning to face me. "I truly am sorry. Though, I think I would still be hurt if it happened again. I wanted to be the one you could depend on, and you lied to my face about it for days. And then, when I said I loved you, you threw me out of your house!"

The look on his face breaks my heart. I can see the mask he's so carefully constructed for the past weeks begin to crack. I hate myself for asking this question, for kicking him when he's down, but I have to know.

"And now?"

"And now what?" There is an emotional catch in his voice, one that hurts us both.

"Do you still love me?"

He swears loudly, shuffling his feet. *"Poutain! Qu'est-ce que tu penses?* I can turn it off so much as I can the rain from the sky!" He thunders across the room and yanks on my arm, pulling me to my feet. "Is that what you wanted to hear? *Que je suis un connard?"*

He looks so broken in that moment that I tremble in his presence but I am certain of one thing. He is wounded and I am too, marred by the other's deeds. Without the proper words, I twist my fingers into his shirt and pull him down, hard, crashing his lips to mine.

Every muscle in his body tenses for a split second, frozen in time but then the damn breaks and he leans into me, tasting my lips, my tongue; our breathing hot and frenzied, everything between us making up for lost time.

I can't stop the moan that ripples past my lips and he pulls away, looking alarmed. He looks down, almost growling out his words. *"Ah, merde."*

I grab his chin and force him to look at me, one hand still wrapped in his clothes to keep him close. "No, please. Don't. Don't run away again. Laurence, I need you. I want you, I need you. I..." I close my eyes and take a deep breath. "I love you. Please don't run away again. I'm sorry for how I hurt you, and I forgive you for how you hurt me. Please let's just talk about these things from now on. Please." I know I'm practically begging at this point but I don't care. There is nothing left of my self-preservation. All I want is him.

I hug him tightly, pressing my face to his chest, listening to the wild beat of his heart. Then suddenly I hear him gasp and I look up at him, concerned.

"Mon dieu, I am so sorry. Are you alright?" He looks almost fearful, but the edge of it has changed. He looks worried for me.

"Of course I'm alright. What's wrong?"

One finger lifts, gently tracing along my collarbone. "I forgot all about this." His touch hesitates just above the developing scars, light as a feather as he moves around it. "Did I hurt you?"

A nervous giggle escapes my lips. "No, not at all. In fact, I feel pretty normal. But..." I look at him questioningly. "Did you hear me?"

His eyes linger for a moment on the small cuts in my neck before meeting mine. We hold each other's gaze in silence until I am too nervous to let it continue. Emotion wavers in my voice, and it comes out hoarse and timid. "Is it too late for us?"

He sighs, shaking his head back and forth. "I do not know. I could never imagine how hurt I would be by such things. I don't want to feel that again." He lifts my hands in his, curling our fingers together. "But, I suppose that is a testament to how much I fell in love with you."

I squeeze his fingers in mine, a hope bursting full of light into the darkness I've felt. "Laurence, I love you. I love you."

He only says my name before our lips meet again. This time, the kiss is slow, cautious, easing back into each other, trying to find the familiar. I feel my way around, letting the rush of it all come back to me. His hair, his skin, the taste of him each renewing the elation of him within me. We kiss again and again, and soon it is not enough for me. As my body moves closer and my lips gain momentum, I can feel him chuckle against my mouth, drawing away slightly.

"*Mon coeur*, be patient with me. I am afraid of hurting you."

I breathe back into him, keeping close enough to caress his lips with my words. "I won't break. I promise."

505

"Ah, but I cannot agree. I have been without you for so long that I must stop here or I may very well forget myself." He separates from me, and I can see how true his words are. He is trembling faintly, a sheen of sweat on his brow. Pulling me into a tender embrace, he whispers against my forehead. "This is where you belong. I wanted you here more than anything else in the world. I am so stubborn and look how we have suffered."

"It's not only your fault. I'm just as much to blame as you are, Laurence." I cuddle up a little closer, holding him tightly. "We are quite the pair, aren't we?"

"Yes, we are." He kisses me softly, a simple expression of affection, then looks me in the eye. "I love you, Camry. I love you, *ma colombe, ma chérie, mon coeur.*"

The last of my fears whisk away, escaping in a sigh. "And I love you. I'm so glad I know that now."

Framed by the silhouette of the city below, we kiss amongst the stars and glittering lights, and I make a mental promise to send Hayden a bottle of her favorite wine. The thought brings a smile to my lips, and Laurence looks at me. "What is it?"

"Everything. I'm just... I'm so happy."

He grins at me, the smile seeming to erase all of the exhaustion left on his face. *"Moi aussi, mon coeur. Moi aussi."*

We stand together, arms wrapped around each other, staring out the window. I can't stop thinking, replaying the last few minutes over and over again in my head. I laugh at the thought of the security guard's greeting to me, and Laurence taps the top of my head with his chin. "What is so funny?"

"I knew you'd be working late."

"Ah..." He gives an embarrassed chuckle and scratches at the back of his head. "It appears that old habits die hard, *n'est-ce pas?*"

I poke at his chest, feeling somewhat vindicated. "Do you need me that much to make you take care of yourself?"

"Hush, now." He kisses me gently to stop the discussion. His eyes focus on my face, roaming over my features one by one. "You look well." He takes my hand and pulls me over towards his favorite chair. Sitting, he tugs me down onto his lap, and I slide into his arms again, snuggling against his chest.

His voice resonates deeply within his chest, buzzing through my ear pressed against him. "Tell me about the surgery. How was your week?"

I share with him about Ciaran's arrival, our visit to mama's grave, the surgery and recovery time. He listens intently, asking the occasional question. We laugh how my first meal of oatmeal felt bizarre, and how I still hate those calcium pills. He frowns when I share how I missed him, and when I share Hayden's thoughts from earlier today, a guilty smile appears on his lips.

"I suppose I should thank her, for encouraging you. And I should thank you for being brave enough to come." He shakes his head solemnly, looking remorseful. "I'm so sorry that I missed everything. I'm sorry I wasn't there for you. I'm sorry I broke my promise to be with you."

I shrug a little, remembering the way I kept hoping he would walk in the door. "I'm sorry too. I really missed you."

He hugs me a little tighter, kissing my head. "I know. I know, and I will do my best to never let you down like that again."

"It might get worse, you know. I can't say what will happen, and it is likely that I'll have some issues for the rest of my life as I deal with all of this. I don't know what my life will look like and I don't know when or how I'll get sick next. There are still days when I wake up and look at myself in the mirror and hate what I see, who I am. I can only see the version of me that once was, not the one that is now. I feel contaminated, like damaged goods, waiting to break or fall apart. It's all one big waiting game, and I can't stand it. Are you sure you want to be with me through all of that?"

"Stop that. Do not hate yourself. This is still you, and it has always been you. Nothing about you has changed, not really. You have lived with this throughout your life. It is only now that you have learned about it. Every great thing you have done in your life was done as you are now. Do not hate yourself. Do not hate your body. This body has done incredible things and will do many more." He turns my face to his, eyes shining in the dimly lit room.

"Camry, as long as I am allowed to love you, I'll be there for you through all of it. I won't run anymore. I love you too much to let my pride push you away."

My emotions swell and I manage to get out the most important words. "Thank you."

"I love all of you - the broken and the beautiful. I want to be with you for the hard parts as much as the good parts. I want to be here for all of it."

I nuzzle a little closer, breathing in the familiar scent I love so much, and relishing the feel of his arms around me. The sensation is intoxicating, cozy, and a monstrous yawn erupts from my mouth. I quickly try to cover it up, but his laughter shows me I've failed.

"Let me take you home."

Too tired to argue, I let him help me up and we leave the office arm in arm.

****

Spring in New York is the most beautiful thing. Cold weather melts away into cherry blossoms and tulips, lush green grass, and rippling ponds in the parks that dot Manhattan's landscape.

I barely remember the winter's chill of the night of the gala, months ago. Today, the beautiful weather has

Laurence and me out for a picnic, a picturesque red and white checkered blanket beneath us, between us a basket full to bursting with fruits, breads, cheeses, and small thermos cups filled with wine. I giggle as we toast our cups, letting the crisp wine flow over my tongue.

"This is heaven, isn't it?" I squint into the sunlight, leaning back on my elbows. Laurence smiles at me, popping a strawberry into my mouth.

"It is wonderful."

"What is Paris like, in the spring?"

He pauses, considering. "It is beautiful in its own way. It can rain quite often, but the flowers all bloom in magnificent colors, and the city is very much alive. There are festivals and fairs, and of course the marathon. This may be my favorite month. I have always loved watching as winter bids farewell and the sunlight brings new life to the world. Paris in spring is not always warm, but it is always inviting, and there is no better city in the world when it rains." He speaks with a fondness, eyes focused on the horizon as if he could conjure the city itself with his words.

"It sounds lovely," I answer, smiling at his recollection. "I'm a little jealous that you're going there in a few weeks. I know it's for work, I do. But you made it sound so lovely." I lay back onto the blanket, staring up into the clouds. "Someday I hope I can see it."

His gaze turns to me, and he offers a lopsided smile. "Someday I hope you can too."

We finish our picnic and take a stroll, making small talk and sharing observations. As the sunlight begins to dip lower into the sky, he takes my hand in his, kissing my fingers. "What would you say to dinner together this evening?"

"I'd love that."

"*Excellent.*" He pronounces the word with a heavy accent, and I giggle at him.

The car is nearby and when we reach it he opens the door for me. I slip in, taking my seat, but realize as I'm reaching for the seatbelt that he hasn't shut the door. Looking up, I find myself caught in his gaze.

"What is it?"

"Come with me."

"Where?"

"To Paris." His expression is earnest, eyes staring deeply into mine. "Come with me to Paris."

"Can I really do that?"

He nods his head and I look at him in amazement. "Really? Really! Laurence, I would love to!" I jump from the car into his arms and he grabs hold of me, pulling me close.

"Don't worry about anything. Just come with me, help me work, and we will take a few days to explore. I cannot promise you much and it will be more work than play, but come with me."

"Of course. I'll do whatever you need." I squeeze him tighter, happiness engulfing me. "I'm so excited!"

He laughs into my ear, planting a quick kiss on my lips. "I am happy to hear that."

However, when we finally let go of each other, he looks somewhat unsure of something. "Laurence, what is it?"

"Ah, well, I suppose if you are coming with me then you will meet my mother and brother as well."

My enthusiasm is tempered and I hesitantly bite my lip. "Is that too much, too soon?"

"No!" He looks startled, and touches my face. "No, nothing like that. I was worried it might be too much for you."

"Are they that scary?"

That draws a bark of laughter out of him and he shakes his head. "*Maman* is a force to be reckoned with, but so are you. I'm sure all will be well. If you're sure about it, then it would be my honor to introduce you."

"Then let's go. Let's go to Paris!"

He kisses me once more, and we slip into the car, driving off into the city. I can't stop fidgeting, excitement overflowing. My fingers fly across my phone screen, searching and reading everything I can about the city and trips in early May. Laurence laughs, seeing what I'm doing, and shakes his head in humor.

"My love, do not worry. There is plenty of time to be excited. For now, put down the phone. Where do you want to eat tonight?"

An idea strikes me in that moment and I turn to him, enthusiastic.

"Can we go to Leo's?"

"Yes...." he trails off and an uncharacteristically sly grin steals across his features. "But we have a detour to make first."

****

"What are we doing here?" I recognize the block; we're not far from the restaurant. But instead of the cozy ivy covered walls and orange candlelight, the facade before me is grand and bustling, people streaming in and out of revolving doors under a large burgundy awning.

A valet pulls open my door, extending a hand to me. "Welcome to the Grand Manhattan, miss."

The sound of surprise that tumbles from my lips is anything but eloquent and I quickly clap a hand over my mouth in embarrassment. I can see Laurence off to the side, standing behind the valet with a hand to his mouth in an attempt to cover his laughter but his eyes squint and shoulders shake and I shoot him a glare before softening my expression and giving my hand to the valet.

He deftly helps me upright and then with calculated quickness, Laurence steps in to take his place, amusement still sparkling in his eyes. We move across the busy sidewalk and enter a lobby grander than I can imagine.

"Whoa."

Laurence snorts in laughter at my pronouncement, watching me as I look in every direction, taking in my surroundings. A soaring ceiling and majestic staircase fight for my attention, but I gasp at the immense chandelier of crystal dazzling from above. I'm so caught up that I barely notice Laurence slipping away to speak to someone at the large counter. I wander, enjoying the incredible space. Velvet sofas and glass tables provide comfortable spaces for tourists and business people, and hanging on the opposite wall is a gorgeous modern painting the size of a wall in my apartment. I stare at it, soaking in the way the shadows play across the canvas.

Eventually I tear my eyes away, curious to see what Laurence is up to, and see him accept a key card from the clerk before turning my way. He holds out his arm, gesturing to the wide marble staircase.

"If you would be so kind, *ma chérie*?"

I tuck my fingers into the crook of his elbow and we ascend the steps. I feel almost like royalty as I glide alongside Laurence. Even in casual clothes he looks every bit the part and his graceful steps suggest nothing but comfort in his own skin. At the top of the stairs, he steers me off to the right, and we tuck into a little alcove of elevators. We wait with a crowd of other people and eventually, the doors open before us.

I lift my foot, ready to move into it, but a gentle pressure on my hand keeps me in place, as Laurence encourages others to go in ahead. He is a pristine gentleman, sacrificing our space in the lift with a winning smile, and when everyone is settled, they look back at him, expectant.

"Thank you, but we will catch the next one. Enjoy your day."

The doors slip closed and almost instantly another elevator opens. With carefully measured steps, Laurence leads me through the doors.

A light laugh falls from my lips, and I stare up at his shoulders as he presses the button for a floor very close to the top. "You are such a gentleman, you know that. You're so kind."

When he turns to face me, the expression on his face is an unexpected one; guilt and a little embarrassment. His fingers reach for his cufflinks, and then he pulls back in momentary surprise when he finds none; his light sweater is no office attire.

I cock my head at him, curious. "What are you nervous about?"

"Nervous?"

For a few seconds I study him and confirm my suspicions. Knowing that this is a rare find, I can't help myself wanting to tease him.

I move a little closer, hyper aware of the way I let my hips fall in fluid motions with each step. When I reach him, I walk my fingers up his chest. "Oh, you're not, are you?"

My lashes flutter and lips pout, trying to be sultry, sexy, but before long I've burst out laughing, pressing my forehead to his chest. "God, I can't!" I descend into a fit of giggles before he snakes an arm around my waist, pulling me flush to his side.

"Oh, but you can." His fingers grab my chin and pull it up, and before I can take a breath his lips are on mine. We kiss feverishly, hands roaming. At one point I slide my fingers down and rub against him and the groan that rumbles in his chest is deep and fierce.

Without warning, the elevator doors open and we fly apart, pressing into the corners. Two poshly dressed elderly women with striking white hair step into the space with us, eyeing each other knowingly.

"I, um- hello." I say awkwardly, barely managing eye contact, and I can hear Laurence flustered with the effort to resume his typical countenance.

"Oh, goodness! What have we interrupted?"

One of them winks at me and if I wasn't already blushing to the tips of my ears, I'm certain I would flame crimson at the smug look in her eyes.

Suddenly Laurence grabs my hand and pulls, sending me flying past them and out the elevator doors. "Bye!" I squeak, as the doors slide closed.

We race down the hall, barely stopping for Laurence to push open the door to the staircase. "We're only one floor down," he explains, and takes to the stairs, two at a time. I scramble to keep up with him, breathless and giddy. When we burst onto our floor, I take his hand again and he leads me along the hallway, muttering room numbers under his breath.

His frustration seems to be mounting the longer he searches but eventually he slips the key card into the lock and the second it lights up, he pushes open the door, tugging me inside.

With the lust filled eyes of a boy half his age, Laurence slams the door and me against it, hands sliding down my thighs to lift me into the air, held up by strong forearms and the cold metal at my back. His fingers stroke my sensitive skin while his lips sear white hot kisses along my jawline and neck, dipping every so often to meet the swell of my breasts.

"Laurence, what-"

My sentence is cut off by another kiss and I let myself go, fingers weaving into soft strands of auburn hair. With a grunt of effort, he pulls us away from the door and I wrap my legs around him more tightly. We move to the bed and he sets me down, scrambling to loosen the buckle on his belt. "Your purse. Where's your purse?"

I point to its place where I dropped it by the door and he grabs it, sifting through it with fast fingers. Finally he pulls a condom loose and smirks at me, dropping the bag to the ground at his feet.

Before he can do anything else, I grab his collar and pull him back down to me, sweeping my tongue into his mouth. I can hear him curse under his breath, a whisper ghosting across my skin, and I pluck the condom out of his hands, pulling up the flowing folds of my skirt at the same time. Using my teeth, I tear open the little package and he just barely has time to get himself free of his clothing when I slide it over him, gripping a little more firmly than necessary, my own look of smug satisfaction on my face.

He tenses at the pressure then in one swift movement his hands tug my underwear down and he's on top of me, pushing himself inside.

I gasp and my eyes fly open, fingers gripping into his shoulders to pull him closer. He tries, readjusting his position, and stumbles from his pants still clinging to his thighs. I try to steady him, but the motion is too much, and we tumble to the floor, a mess of limbs.

I can't help but burst out laughing and stroke his hair, aware that his fingers are laced behind my head to cradle me from the fall.

"I would ask if you are alright, but might I assume that your laughter gives me an answer?"

I purr against him, peppering kisses along his cheeks. "You may."

He shudders a heaving sigh, nipping gently at my neck. "I'm sorry, my love."

I sit up a little, propping myself up on my elbows. "For what?"

"I was so impatient with you. I could not help myself. I acted - !"

I press my fingers against his lips and with a sneaky smile, squeeze myself around him. His pupils flare, and he sucks in a breath. I can feel him throbbing inside of me and I kiss him.

"I don't mind."

He eyes me warily but when I pull him back to me, lips hungry, searching, he gives in. We find ourselves again, safe within treasured touches and whispered desires. We take time now, savoring each other, and when I reach the peak of pleasure I can feel the way my nails rake down his back, igniting trails of fire. He groans against me, quivering, and I urge him along until he joins me in release.

We lay there, sweat slick bodies on the floor, breathing shallow and raspy. Laurence's lips press countless kisses against my skin, taking a deep breath as if to inhale our scent.

He settles in again beside me, curling his arms around me to keep me close.

The silence is comfortable, sweet, and I cuddle a little closer, content and blissful.

"Camry?" His voice is soft, slightly hoarse, and I can feel it deep within his chest.

"Yeah?"

He opens his mouth to speak but a loud gurgle of hunger rumbles from my stomach and I freeze up. He laughs, loud and free, and pulls himself upright.

"How about that dinner I promised you?"

I giggle, dipping my head in embarrassment, but let him pull me up. We take our time getting dressed, sweet kisses exchanged at every turn, caresses lingering on skin to remind ourselves of the love we share. We step into the hall and Laurence pockets the key card, shutting the door behind us. "Just in case," he murmurs, winking at me.

****

The little French bistro is just as I remember it. Ivy crawling along the walls, warm orange lighting on brick and brass creating an ephemeral glow. Once again we greet the Valet, and a familiar face waves from inside the restaurant. "Look, it's Andrew!"

"*Oui, chérie.* When I called, I asked for him to serve us this evening."

We are barely in the door when a large white frame object comes barreling towards us, turning heads with his booming voice. "Laurence *et* Camry! Ah, *les amoureux* have arrived!"

He bends, catching my hand in his and kissing my fingers. "*Enchantez, ma chère.* I knew this one would succumb to your charms, eh?" He laughs proudly, slapping Laurence on the shoulder.

"*Bonsoir, mon ami.*" Laurence tries but fails to suppress a grin and I laugh at the two of them.

"*Alors, mon pote,* I shall hear the story later. Follow me!" He turns and strides off through the tiny restaurant, charming customers with greetings and smiles as he goes.

Once again, we pass through the kitchen and the energy in it is boisterous, chefs shouting from one to another, the air filled with the sounds of knives chopping, liquids boiling, and the rush of flame as a man pours a splash of wine into a pan full of scallops.

We meet Andrew at the back door and he smiles at us. "Welcome back! It's nice to see you again."

"You too!" He and Laurence shake hands and Leo pushes open the door, bowing with a grand gesture.

The small patio out back is empty, save a small table for two. Candlelight and twinkling lights glimmer all around, and it takes my breath away as I absorb the scene before me. "Oh my god. This is beautiful!"

"A special gift for a special couple," Leo says, grinning from ear to ear. "Andrew, take the finest care of them tonight!"

"Of course sir." He bows his head, and Leo laughs.

"You're in good hands, *mes amis*. I'll be back soon!" Leo disappears through the door as quick as he came and I laugh. Something catches my fingers, and see that Laurence has taken my hand, leading me over to the table. We sit, and Andrew brings two flutes of champagne to the table, then disappears into the kitchen, leaving us alone.

Laurence lifts his glass, twirling the stem between his long fingers. "A toast, *mon coeur*?"

"Of course. To what?"

"To the future." Our glasses touch, the crisp sound echoing through the garden. I smile, thinking of the past, our present, and what is still to come.

"To the future."

The End.

Thank You and Acknowledgments

This book was a delight to write, but even when the words almost write themselves, there's a lot of work that goes into every book. Research abounds, and there are people who help you see the forest through the trees. One person's eyes are not enough.

I have nothing but unending thanks and gratitude toward so many people in my life who have been a large part of bringing this book to life.

First, this was a book born from NaNoWriMo, so to that organization I give my thanks - but mostly to the NaNoRDU group. This amazing group of people breathed life into the experience and I will never be able to express my gratitude for the support I received even in my short time with them. Thank you for keeping things fun, and for providing motivation and community.

To the multiple 'tweeps' who have guided me along this process, both encouraging me and supporting me through so much - your antics and lifts continue to be one of my favorite things about being a writer. CS, KC, TT, Sandy, Laura, Kaitlyn, HF, Jason, LT, Chris, and so many more of you - I wish I could mention you all but alas, space is limited. Thank you to all of you; I am so glad we 'met' and I can't wait to make that writers retreat happen!

To my family and friends who have asked how it was going, encouraged me with kind words, and offered hugs and high fives - thank you!

To Angela K, who patiently walked me through a world to which I'd never known, I thank you.

To Angela F, whose art inspires me- may you know and love Lucy as I do!

To Jessica - your insight helped make Marcus come to life. I am so grateful for you sharing your knowledge with me.

To Jason and Beth - I couldn't have asked for better support than you two! What a way to jump into something bigger than you imagined, but Laurence and Leo will forever be their best because of you. Many thanks to you both.

To Leonid Afremov - while you were living, your paintings set into motion this story. Your work was brilliant - and "Dance of Passion" is eternal in my heart - and now, in this novel.

To Sarah, who made me laugh, who encouraged me, and who helped me with the things no writer likes to do – thank you!

To Denise - thank you for the time you gave to me, and for your inexhaustible encouragement. You kept me going when not much else could.

To Jenn, whose enthusiasm kept me going through the final stages when weariness was paramount and frustrations were high. Thank you for the biggest and best compliment I have received to date, and for being a cheerleader loud and proud. I'm so glad you're my friend, and I'm so glad God brought us together!

To Honor, whom I could never have written this book without - the number of frantic phone calls, the long talks, the time you spent giving when I didn't have any to give in return - I love you, I love you, I love you. I'm sorry for the timing on some of it - but I'm so glad you were there.

To Marcia- When I was stuck or wavering, you always had the right words. You've been with me since the start and I never could have done this so well or so quickly without you. From the bottom of my heart: I love you and thank you. (Also, keep reading.)

To Marcia, Rebecca, Katy, Amy, and Lisa - where would I be without you? This book is here because of you and it is its best because of you. There are no words to express the depth of my gratitude to the five of you. Thank you for the time, the chats, the continued promotion and skill and encouragement. Thank you for having my back. Thank you for walking alongside of me and pulling me back when I wandered away. Thanks for fixing things, and for strengthening things, and for seeing what I couldn't. You all are my angels, and I can't imagine my life without you in it.

To my parents who put up with weekends, family gatherings, holidays, and more where I spent my time with my nose to my computer screen or with a stack of papers on my knee. Thank you for the never ending support I get from you both and for encouraging a creative spark in me from a young age.

To my girls, Paisley and Isla - you are so young, yet you open my eyes to view the world with curiosity and imagination. In your own little ways, you gave me what I needed to keep going. Knowing this was important, you'd offer kisses and hugs, and ask if I was having fun. My little ladybugs, you are so much more a part of this than you will ever understand. I love you!

To James - my lover, my friend, my partner. In all of this you simply said "yes." Yes to NaNo, yes to afternoons away to write, yes to late nights and early mornings, yes to my dreams and yes to me. I know what you have given up and I know what you have gained and I love that you want this for me as much as I do. Thank you for picking up where I struggle. Thank you for searching for solutions and reading fine print and for navigating the 'other side' of this. I'm so grateful you have my back. I'm glad you are my partner in life and love. The day we married I never saw this coming, but I'm so glad I have you as the one beside me through this all.

And lastly - to the God who celebrates with me in the sunshine and holds my hand in the dark... I thank you.

About the Author

Emmie Brown currently lives in North Carolina with her spouse, children, and pets. Aside from writing, she is an avid cook, whipping up meals for friends and family on a daily basis. Her love affair with coffee is intense, reflected in all of her stories. This is her debut novel.

You can find Emmie on twitter @cornerwriting or on facebook: www.facebook.com/authoremmiebrown.

Credits

Cover design: Lance Ramsey

Cover image: Photo by Chris Barbalis on Unsplash

Book ISBN: 978-1-7342484-1-8

Made in the USA
Columbia, SC
04 February 2020